Praise for

# Fierce Blessings

Book Two of *The Star-Seer's Prophecy*

"*Fierce Blessings* is a wonderfully compelling read. A page-turner of the highest order. But more than that, it is a powerful spiritual teaching. A step-by-step guide on how to keep our hearts open in the face of unimaginable suffering, how to forgive the unforgivable, and what it means to allow the sweet mercy and compassion of the Divine Feminine to be an ongoing healing presence in our lives." —Chris Zydel, Author, *Conversations with the Brush; Love Letters from the Creative Heart*

"*Fierce Blessings* brilliantly explores archetypal themes of life, which have coalesced in the heart and soul of the heroic yet tormented protagonist, Kyr. His awakening and struggle to become the hallowed vessel of the Goddess are poignant and heart-wrenching, yet readers of his story will be well-rewarded as his transcendent and redemptive spiritual path unfolds. This is a profound and inspiring work that grapples with the universal themes of brutality and forgiveness, trauma and recovery, and the liberating power of compassion." —Merideth Bowen Shamszad, Psychotherapist; Author, *The Story of Little Feather*

Praise for

# Dark Innocence

Book One of *The Star-Seer's Prophecy*

"…[T]his novel can take its place amongst Tolkien and the best of science fiction writers such as Ursula LeGuin. It is a well-sustained, exciting and suspenseful narrative written in a lucid and powerful style." —Harris Smart, Author, *Passion Play; Tom Bass: Totem Maker;* and *Sixteen Steps and Other Journeys in SUBUD*

"I had the pleasure of reading *Dark Innocence* several years ago as a manuscript. At the time I was reading many manuscripts, writing book reviews and working as an editor. *Dark Innocence* stood out almost at once. The story is compelling, gripping even. The journey is intense, rich and rewarding. I highly recommend *Dark Innocence*. This is a book that is at once action-packed and deeply provocative. *Dark Innocence* will resonate with you for years to come." —Stephanie Rose Bird, Author, *No Barren Life* (a Young Adult fantasy), and five non-fiction books

"*Dark Innocence* is a beautifully written and richly woven tale of the archetypal themes of wounding and redemption. The author looks fearlessly into the darkest aspects of human experience and explores the true nature of healing. Her wisdom as a psychotherapist permeates the story, but this is no dry textbook…it is a gripping and inspiring page-turner! The story has stayed with me and continues to amaze. Highly recommended. (For adults only!)" —Merideth Bowen Shamszad, Author, *The Story of Little Feather*

"Rahima Warren has written a daring, taboo-breaking, visceral, intensely felt and moving novel. It's impossible not to get wrapped up in the characters and their passions, only to be surprised again and again. …You won't be able to let go of this book, any more than it will let go of you. Highly recommended!" —Jodie Forrest, Author, *The Ascendant*, and *The Rhymer and the Ravens*

"A must-read for everyone. ...I could not stop reading this book. Not only was the story fantastic, but you could see each little step of self-healing, discovery, acceptance.... It's beautiful and sad and hopeful and inspiring." —Tiffany H., from her Five-Star Review on GoodReads and her blog, "A TiffyFit's Reading Corner"

"In the beginning, the author Rahima Warren...makes it clear that there is more to Dark Innocence than just a fantasy fiction tale, and that her purpose is to provide a deep, meaningful, healing and spiritual fantasy story. "Wow, fascinating concept," I thought, "a therapeutic story written in Tolkien style—MUST READ!" (From an interview with a reader: See p.206)

"The book is engrossing, entertaining, and inspiring. The Star-Seer's Prophecy describes the torturous journey taken by two humans seeking love and redemption. The gift they bring back to their community is of great importance—human love." —George Taylor, *MFT*, Author, *Talking with Our Brothers*

"Kyr?"

At the sound of Jolanya's gentle voice, Kyr could neither move nor breathe, could neither go forward nor turn back. With all his heart, he longed to rush into his beloved's arms, to grow great wings and fly them both to his secret childhood haven under the ice where no danger or vileness could touch them. But she was the Kailithana, forbidden to him. And his true Atonement, his inevitable and well-deserved fate, awaited him.

She stood at an inner entrance to the sanctum, green velvet curtains falling shut behind her, wearing her indigo robes, her silken black hair escaping its usually tidy braid. She gazed at him steadily, her storm-grey eyes grave with foreboding. "What is it?"

Quietly, he said, "It's Gauday, come to take me."

She made a little sound of protest, but he held up his hand. "It's my Atonement. I must go." His tone forbade any argument.

Wiping away her tears, Jolanya came and wrapped her arms around him. He felt her trembling and held her close. Their frightened hearts beat roughly against each other. Her lips brushed his ear and he shivered.

"I love you, only you," she whispered, giving him a priceless gift: the truth of her heart.

Scarlet lightning flashed through him, body, heart and soul. He stepped back and stared at her, unsure if he had heard her correctly. She gave him the slightest of nods, and his heart absurdly leapt for joy.

Then the Kailithana grasped his hands in hers. Kyr gasped as a powerful Flow of kailitha rushed into him. At first it was silvery, then crimson, then a coppery gold: a flood of steadfastness and courage and faith.

The Flow abated and the kailitha contracted into a glowing golden ball in his core. The Kailithana released his hands and stepped back, her eyes deep with divine compassion and vast respect.

"Most valiant one, keep the Goddess in your heart, as She keeps you in Hers. Remember the Truth of Her Love and Forgiveness."

He drank in the sight of his beloved Jolanya, the last sunshine in a world about to go forever dark. After an infinite, fleeting moment, he tore his gaze away from her, and left the Temple, shedding his dark Temple robe as he fled toward his fate.

# Fierce Blessings

## ALSO BY RAHIMA WARREN

**Dark Innocence**
Book One of *The Star-Seer's Prophecy*
Rose Press, 2012


## ALSO PUBLISHED BY ROSE PRESS

**Healing Civilization**
*Bringing Personal Transformation into the Societal Realm* (2009)
Claudio Naranjo, M.D.

**Starting Your Book**
*A Guide to Navigating the Blank Page*
*by Attending to What's Inside You* (2011)
Naomi Rose

**MotherWealth**
*The Feminine Path to Money* (2012)
Naomi Rose

**A New Life**
*Poems* (2014)
Ralph Dranow


**All are available from www.rosepress.com**

# The Star-Seer's Prophecy

## Book Two:
# Fierce Blessings

## Rahima Warren

**Rose Press**
Oakland, California

*The Star-Seer's Prophecy. Book Two: Fierce Blessings.*

Cover illustration: Brenda Murphy
Interior Book Design: Joe Tantillo
Cover Design and Formatting: Anastasia Creatives
Editor and Book Developer: Naomi Rose
Proofreader: Gabriel Steinfeld

Rose Press
www.rosepress.com
rosepressbooks@yahoo.com

First edition published 2015
Printed in the United States of America.

ISBN#: 978-0-9816278-7-8

# The Star-Seer's Prophecy

When the Wanderers
form the Dire Cross
under the Firebird's wings,
sorcery and murder
must give him life.
He must be abandoned.
May we be forgiven.

Star-cursed, twin-souled,
knowing only evil, pain and ice,
the dark innocent
is our salvation.
He must be forsaken.
May we be forgiven.

Through three hells,
through blissful heaven
and its loss,
he surrenders all
yet never yields.
He must be betrayed.
May we be forgiven.

Hollowed by suffering and evil,
Hallowed by expiation and submission,
the Vessel of the Goddess is created.
We must ensure his Fate.
May we be forgiven!

# Author's Note:
# Writing from Darkness

"Often the most powerful and successful translucent art deals with the darkest and most difficult aspects of our humanity, but in a way that reveals inherent sacredness."
—Arjuna Ardagh, *The Translucent Revolution*

"Writing about trauma is more than simply documenting experience—it's about illuminating life on earth. It's about transforming tragedy into art, and hoping that somehow that piece of art may help someone else who's gone through something unbearable and doesn't see yet that there truly is a light at the end of the dark tunnel."
—Tracy Strauss "A Topic Too Risky," *Poets & Writers Magazine* (Sept./Oct., 2013)

"Art is high alchemy. As writers, as artists, we take the most devastating of our human experiences and we turn them into something of healing and service to the world. We drag the ugliness out of the shadows while it's kicking and screaming and we bear witness to the nature of the unspeakable and formless fears of our collective psyche. We reveal it to the world for what it is. We transform it, like magicians, and invite the world to gaze upon itself, to watch itself shape shift and contort before finally giving up and letting go, dissolving the barriers of shadow and light...."
—Alison Nappi, Author, *Lies You Were Told About Grief*

These powerful quotes reflect my experience of writing the trilogy, *The Star-Seer's Prophecy*. When I first began receiving and writing this visionary story of wounding and healing, evil and redemption, suffering and forgiveness, I had no plan or purpose to write any such thing. But the story came through me in a dark, wild, creative rush, and I did not resist.[1] It was a process of writing from darkness... from the unknown... from the fertile void.

Even after *Dark Innocence* (Book One of the trilogy) was published in 2012, I had no idea why this story had come through me. And so, in a deep meditation, I asked about its purpose. I received that the mission of this story is "to end the inner and outer culture of hatred, revenge, and punishment, and to evoke an inner and outer culture of compassion, forgiveness, and healing."

To do this, the story takes the reader on a transformational journey on the hard path through the underworld of the soul and psyche, and into the dark heart of forgiveness. Forgiveness is not for the faint-of-heart. It requires the spiritual courage to confront our own trauma and shame, anger and vengefulness, and to reach for the light of greater kindness, compassion and forgiveness—both for ourselves and for those who have oppressed or harmed us.

The process of writing this trilogy has been, as Alison Nappi says, one of bearing "witness to the nature of the unspeakable and formless fears of our collective psyche." Although I personally have not suffered the kind of abuse I write about, still it exists in me, as it clearly is part of the collective human psyche—whether horribly acted out in life (as in the childhood experiences of some of my psychotherapy clients), or portrayed in many forms of art, including film and television.

Through my own inner work, I learned to allow inner darkness and ugliness to be safely expressed through art and writing. Finding myself compelled to write and edit this dark yet redemptive story was (and is) an intense and challenging, yet soul-satisfying, task. I have wrestled to see beyond my judgments of good and evil; to see with the Goddess Zhovanya's eyes, as the hero, Kyr, does in *Fierce Blessings*.

*The Star-Seer's Prophecy* confronts the evil and cruelty that we humans suffer and inflict in our dark innocence, and holds forth a vision of the healing, compassion, and forgiveness so needed in our world. Awed by the mission of the trilogy, I feel a great responsibility to do my best by this story, and to send it into the world to fulfill its purpose.

I hope that this book may help a reader see "a light at the end of the dark tunnel," in a way that "reveals inherent sacredness" even in the darkest of experiences.

A warning: If you seek a fun escape story, this book is not for you.

---

1 More about that at: http://www.starseersprophecy.com/2012/06/

However, if you seek a deep, rich story that explores the fierce gift that is life as a human being… takes you on a transformational journey… and portrays the kind of courage needed to endure and transcend the worst of experiences, read on.

Many Blessings for your journey on the hard path. May this book help to light the way.

*Rahima Warren*

December, 2014

Book Two:

# Fierce Blessings

*"She is so bright and glorious that you cannot look at her face*
*or her garments for the splendor with which she shines.*
*For she is terrible with the terror of the avenging lightning,*
*and gentle with the goodness of the bright sun;*
*and both her terror and her gentleness are*
*incomprehensible to humans....*
*But she is with everyone and in everyone,*
*and so beautiful is her secret that no person can know*
*the sweetness with which she sustains people,*
*and spares them in inscrutable mercy."*

—Hildegard of Bingen

# Table of Contents

# Part One ~ Turns on the Spiral

*"We don't receive wisdom;*
*we must discover it for ourselves*
*after a journey that no one can take for us,*
*or spare us."*

—Marcel Proust

Chapter One

# The Demands of Love

G*ods, I will miss this place,* Kyr thought to himself, as he waited for
Rajani and Luciya on the wide porch of the dining hall. He had
found the peace and order of the Sanctuary disturbing when he first
arrived, but had come to love this place where he'd gone through such
tremendous healing and transformation. He looked around with sad
fondness at the tidy brick courtyard, with its fountain bubbling quietly at
the center, and its large pots of flowering plants, now looking a bit dusty
and withered in the late summer heat. On either side of the courtyard
stood rows of white-washed, slate-roofed rooms, one of which was his
own. But what he would miss the most was Zhovanya's graceful Temple.
A heavy sigh gusted out of him. *I must leave and begin my Atonement, but
I know next to nothing of the world outside the Sanctuary. How in all the
hells am I going to find my Slave-brothers?*

His thoughts were interrupted as Rajani and Luciya joined him for
breakfast. Kyr looked up at his friends, noticing how similar they were in
spirit, yet so different in appearance. Strong and stern, Rajani's hair was
coal-dark and his eyes a shadowed blue. He was every inch the Warrior
Mage in his dark leathers. In contrast, Luciya was slight and moody, as
mutable as fire with her ember-red hair and warm brown eyes. But she
had the same inner determination and strength as her companion.

Over a breakfast of porridge and bacon, Luciya chatted about all the
changes going on in the City and all over the land of Khailaz since the
demise of Kyr's old Master, Dauthaz, known as the Soul-Drinker. Eyes
sparkling, she waved her spoon in the air as she described the cleansing
of the Soul-Drinker's labyrinth.

"We're scrubbing every inch, repairing or re-plastering every surface.
We've torn down those ugly brick walls of the old Hall, and let in the air,

sunlight and the sounds of the ocean. Soon Zhovanya's Temple will be restored to its true function as a place of worship, music and dance. It's so wonderful!" She glanced at Kyr, and frowned slightly at his preoccupied expression.

"What has happened to the other Slaves?" Kyr asked.

"Oh, them," she said with a curl of her lip. "Well, of course, those who were strongly mind-bonded to the Soul-Drinker died when you killed him, including all the Watchers. Some went mad. Others died at the hands of angry mobs. In any case, the Slave-run bureaucracy collapsed into chaos."

"And good riddance to those arrogant parasites!" Rajani added.

"I see." Kyr's shoulders sagged. *More blood and suffering on my hands, Goddess forgive me.*

He put that thought aside, and asked, "What has been done with the Slaves who survived?"

"Unfortunately," said Luciya, "many of them disappeared with Gauday. Other than that, the hopelessly mad have been sent to a place where they can be tended, and can do no harm. Those few who can be of any use have been set to work helping the rest of us cleanse the City of the Soul-Drinker's desecration, and to rebuild what was destroyed in the riots. I can't wait to show you all the changes!" she added, glowing with excitement again.

Rajani smiled at her enthusiasm. "We'll get to the City someday. But first, we'll go to Ravenvale, our home. We have much to do there. On the way we can show you what you have made possible by destroying the cursed Soul-Drinker. Even now, freedom, hope and joy are spreading like wildfire throughout Khailaz, and it's all because of what you did, Kyr."

"Perhaps you were right in what you said to me back at the cabin: whatever harm I did as a Slave may be outweighed by the benefits brought about by the death of the Master." Kyr frowned. "But I still don't understand how or why I was able to kill him—or even if it was me...."

Rajani broke in quickly. "I *was* right!" he declared. Then he jumped to his feet and threw his arms wide, embracing the sunny, breezy morning, the pellucid sky, and the green-clad earth. "Look at this glorious day! Come, let's stretch our legs with a good hike up that mountain beyond the Temple."

"You two go on," said Luciya. "I had enough hiking getting here."

Kyr eyed Rajani, and stretched like an indolent cat. "Perhaps I'll stay here with Luciya."

"Lazyboots," Rajani retorted. "Up, up! Let's go!"

Reluctantly, Kyr set his mug down and got to his feet. Then, with a yell, he leaped down the stairs, leaving a startled Warrior Mage gaping.

"Trickster!" he yelled, and started after Kyr.

Hot and sweaty, Rajani and Kyr reached the wide ledge where Kyr had seen the Firebird and made his vow to Zhovanya. They quenched their thirst and splashed their faces with the icy water of the burbling spring, then found places to rest in the shade of the big pine. Kyr leaned against its trunk. Rajani lounged against a shaded boulder. For a while, they sat catching their breath, taking in the ranks of mountains receding into the hazy distance, the billowing white clouds drifting in the blue depths above, the dusty scent of sun on stone.

Rajani glanced at Kyr, who had transformed so greatly in such a short while. Instead of a dour, bewildered Slave, he was now a strong, clear, courageous young man. "Is your Atonement complete?" Rajani inquired. "Are you ready to leave the Sanctuary?"

"I am ready to leave, but I haven't started my Atonement yet." Kyr searched Rajani's eyes, wondering how he would react. "I will be looking for Gauday and my Slave brothers, to offer them the kind of help I have been so generously given."

"'Brothers?'" Rajani snapped, sitting bolt upright. "How can you *call* them that? They are not your brothers! They want to hunt you down and make you pay for killing their infernal Master. They are your *enemies*, Kyr!" The Warrior Mage looked ready to jump up and do battle that instant.

Kyr recoiled, but then firmed his jaw. "We Slaves are all sons of the same evil 'father.' If I can be redeemed from the Soul-Drinker's corruption and viciousness, why not them?"

Rajani blew out a breath and leaned back against the boulder behind him. "Well, you are beyond me! I can see you have learned much here. I could not be so compassionate toward my enemies."

"They are *not* my enemies, not even Gauday! They are my Slave-brothers, and my chosen Atonement is to try to help them find the forgiveness and love of the Goddess, just as I have."

"But that's not your job, Kyr!" Rajani looked more disturbed than Kyr had imagined possible.

"It's what I have chosen to do," Kyr said flatly.

Rajani gave him a startled look, and conceded, "Well, if any of them actually ask for redemption, you can send them here."

Kyr frowned, recalling his failure to help Larag. "One of them did come here."

"Hmmm?" The Warrior Mage sounded distracted. Indeed, he was staring at the steep cliff across the secret valley of the Sanctuary. "Have you seen large rock falls, over there?" He pointed at a large cloud of dust on the hidden trail that led down to the Sanctuary."

"No. Why?"

"I don't like the look of that." Rajani got to his feet. "Come on." They started down the mountain.

"What's wrong?"

"Could be nothing, but a band of horsemen would stir up dust like that. Who was it that showed up here?"

"His name was Larag, but he didn't stay."

"Didn't stay?"

"No. I was supposed to help him get settled his first night here. I didn't do a very good job. He was gone in the morning."

"Gods and demons!" Rajani cried. "This Larag could have been a spy for Gauday." The Warrior Mage gestured at the dust cloud. "And *that* could be Gauday and his gang."

"Goddess forfend!" Kyr was horrified at the thought of the havoc Gauday would wreak on the sacred peace of the Sanctuary.

"Indeed," Rajani agreed grimly. "I hope I'm wrong."

They broke into a run. The steep, rocky trail back to the Sanctuary required all their attention and breath.

When they reached the Sanctuary's courtyard, Rajani demanded of Kyr, "Where's Maray? I've got to warn him. Gods, I hope they have some defenses here that I haven't seen."

Kyr quickly led Rajani to Maray's room in the main hall, but he didn't go in, saying, "I'm going to the Temple to pray for Zhovanya's help."

"Go ahead. We'll need all the help we can get."

Kyr raced up to the Temple, heart drumming in his chest. By the time the silent priestess had blessed him with the sacred smoke, his heart had slowed and he was fit to enter the inner sanctum. He paused to look at this cherished place, perhaps for the last time.

Tall columns of gold-streaked green marble, shaped in the likeness of trees, circled the round chamber, topped by a dome of silver-flecked blue stone. Daylight shone through the eight narrow windows beneath the dome. Large sitting pillows were scattered across the carpeted floor, before a raised dais, where Zhovanya sometimes danced.

As he bowed toward the empty dais, a terrible image of what Gauday's men would do to the priestesses—to his beloved Jolanya—filled his mind. He fell to his knees and stretched out his arms, pleading, "Zhovanya! Keep Jolanya safe! Please, please, show us how to keep this Sanctuary and everyone in it safe."

He strove for the quietness to hear Her guidance, and then the cruel truth stabbed home. *Merciless gods! I am the one who brought this danger to the Sanctuary. Gauday is after me.* Tears filled his eyes. "O Goddess, forgive me!"

A vast, listening silence filled the Temple—a silence that received his tears as precious jewels, absorbed his fears, and filled him with resolute calmness. And he knew what he must do.

He swayed a little, as if hitting flinty ground after a year-long illusion of softness, then bowed his head. "Guide me, Zhovanya. How can I survive?" One word he received, only one word.

*"SOFTEN."*

Grateful for this gift of counsel, he whispered, "Thank You," and turned to leave the Temple.

"Kyr?"

At the sound of Jolanya's gentle voice, Kyr could neither move nor breathe, could neither go forward nor turn back. With all his heart, he longed to rush into his beloved's arms, to grow great wings and fly them both to his secret childhood haven under the ice where no danger or vileness could touch them. But she was the Kailithana, forbidden to him. And his true Atonement, his inevitable and well-deserved fate, awaited him.

She stood at an inner entrance to the sanctum, green velvet curtains falling shut behind her, wearing her indigo robes, her silken black hair

7

escaping its usually tidy braid. She gazed at him steadily, her storm-grey eyes grave with foreboding. "What is it?"

Quietly, he said, "It's Gauday, come to take me."

She made a little sound of protest, but he held up his hand. "It's my Atonement. I must go." His tone forbade any argument.

Wiping away her tears, Jolanya came and wrapped her arms around him. He felt her trembling and held her close. Their frightened hearts beat roughly against each other. Her lips brushed his ear and he shivered.

"I love you, only you," she whispered, giving him a priceless gift: the truth of her heart.

Scarlet lightning flashed through him, body, heart and soul. He stepped back and stared at her, unsure if he had heard her correctly. She gave him the slightest of nods, and his heart absurdly leapt for joy.

Then the Kailithana grasped his hands in hers, and opened to the Flow. Kyr gasped as a powerful Flow of kailitha rushed into him. At first it was silvery, then sanguine, then a coppery gold, a flood of steadfastness and courage and faith.

The Flow abated and the kailitha contracted into a glowing golden ball in his core. The Kailithana released his hands and stepped back, her eyes deep with divine compassion and vast respect.

"Most valiant one, keep the Goddess in your heart, as She keeps you in Hers. Remember the Truth of Her Love and Forgiveness."

He drank in the sight of his beloved Jolanya, the last sunshine in a world about to go forever dark. After an infinite, fleeting moment, he tore his gaze away from her, and left the Temple, shedding his dark Temple robe as he fled toward his fate.

As he ran down the hill toward the central courtyard, his face hardened into the mask of cold iron he had worn for most of his life. When he arrived, Luciya, Maray, and Naran were there, and more people were arriving every moment as the news of the intruders spread. Rajani was at the gate, looking out through the spy hole.

The sound of thunder rumbled, but the sky was clear. The rumbling grew louder and louder, then subsided into a cacophony of shouts and jeers. Rajani spoke to someone on the other side of the gate, asking, "What do you want?" He listened for a moment, then shut the spy hole and turned to Kyr.

"As we feared, it's Gauday. He's demanding that we give you up to him or they will attack the Sanctuary. I could hold them off for a while, but...." He looked at Maray. "You're sure you don't have any other means of defense?"

"Our only protection was our secrecy."

Naran put a protective arm around Kyr's shoulders. "Rajani, how many men does Gauday have?"

"Too many. He must have a hundred well-armed men out there. I could take on a dozen or two, but not that many. Are there any other trained fighters here?" A handful of men stepped forward briskly.

"NO!" Kyr waved them back. "No fighting. I want no more blood on my hands." The warmth of Naran's arm seemed, for once, an annoyance, and he stepped away. "They must not attack the Sanctuary!"

He started toward the gate, his fate a heavy shroud cutting him off from all that he had learned to love. A dark voice inside gloated, *You can never escape the Master's last curse.*

"No, Kyr! What are you doing?" Luciya blocked his path.

Naran grabbed his arm. "You can't! Don't go out there!"

"Naran-ji, this is my Atonement: to go to my Slave brothers and try to help them as you have helped me. The greatest lesson I have learned here is that *all* are children of the Goddess, even me, even them." He freed himself from Naran's grip. "They can do no worse to me than the Soul-Drinker has already done. I'll survive."

"How can you say that? They'll kill you!" Naran's voice was tight with anguish and fear.

"No. They will obey the Soul-Drinker. His last command was never to grant me the mercy of death." He couldn't block the next thought: *I'm sure I'll end up wishing they would.*

The Warrior Mage shuddered. He understood what Kyr had left unsaid. His mind raced, considering spells and enchantments, trying to find a way out of this trap. He snapped his fingers and started for his room to fetch his bow and arrows. All he had to do was take out Gauday. A headless snake is no danger.

Then he sucked in a breath, as if gut-stabbed. The oath-bind struck him with such force that all his muscles froze; he couldn't take a single step. "Gods curse it!" he groaned, "This is the second hell!" The Star-Seer's Prophecy demanded that the star-cursed one face three hells, and the oath-bind was making it clear that Kyr now faced the second. As much as he hated it, Rajani knew that neither he nor anyone else must keep Kyr from his prophesied fate.

"What is it?" Luciya demanded. "What's wrong?"

"Never mind. Won't work," Rajani choked out. His muscles finally relaxed, and he began pacing up and down like a caged panther. "We can't fight, and we can't run. Gauday's gang has horses and would easily catch up to us." He glared in the direction of the gate. "Unfortunately, that madman Gauday only wants revenge on Kyr so there's no way to bargain with him."

Grim-faced, the Warrior-Mage made himself look straight at Kyr. "You're right. It's a choice between them taking you and the Sanctuary, or just you." He stopped and looked around. "Unless anyone has thought of something I can't see?"

"What's to stop them from looting the Sanctuary even if we turn Kyr over to them?" asked Maray, his brown face ashen.

Kyr wished they would just let him get on with it. "You'll be safe," he assured Maray. "Once I am in Gauday's hands, he'll be blind to anything else. He's been obsessed with tormenting me since we were rivals for the Soul-Drinker's favor, and has craved vengeance ever since Dauthaz chose me as his Favorite instead of him." He took a deep breath. "I have to go."

He reached out and embraced Naran, his Aithané and friend. "You have given me so much, Naran-ji. I will keep to your teachings, and they will give me strength. As I promised, I will try to pass on the blessings I have received here."

His face as gray as his robe, Naran reluctantly let go of him. "Goddess guard your soul."

Luciya took Kyr's hands in hers. "We'll come for you, I promise! Never forget. We will come." She stepped back to stand beside Rajani.

Kyr turned abruptly to Maray. "Promise me you will find ways to protect the Sanctuary from this kind of threat, build up your defenses somehow."

"On my life, I swear it," Maray said, "as one Guardian to another. Goddess guide you."

Kyr smiled, grateful for this reminder that he was yielding not to Gauday's madness but to Zhovanya's will. "I am in Her hands."

As Rajani watched Kyr head toward the gate, his lips thinned defiantly, and he hurried to Kyr's side, unbuckling his sword belt.

"I'll go with you!" he declared. "It will give them someone else to torment, take some of their attention off you."

Luciya, Naran and Jolanya all looked at Rajani. Then they stepped forward to join him.

"*NO!*" Kyr rounded on them with sudden ferocity. "Are you all mad? They won't kill *me*, but there is nothing to stop them from torturing, raping and killing all of *you*, just to make me watch. I want no more blood on my hands—not yours, not theirs, no one's!" He added more quietly, "Besides, I need you to find a way to free me and put a stop to their predations, once and for all. We must keep the Sanctuary and Khailaz safe."

"I am so sorry!" Rajani's scowl hid bitter shame.

"I need *you* free most of all, Rajani. I'm counting on you to rescue me, again." A slight smile touched his lips. "But let's not make a habit of this."

The Warrior Mage snorted at Kyr's attempt at humor, and shrugged as if settling a heavy pack on his back. "I will come for you as soon as I can raise the troops I'll need to overcome Gauday's band." The two men clasped forearms as warriors do. Rajani met Kyr's gaze and said, "Remember the eagle."

"Zhovanya nara lo," Kyr answered. Then he turned to go out to his crazed and vicious brothers.

# Chapter 2

# Recurring Nightmares

Kyr opened the spy hole in the Sanctuary's gate and looked out. There were nearly a hundred mounted men, all armed with swords or battle axes. About sixty were soldier-slaves, distinguished by their short hair and shabby uniforms of brown leather. They sat in stolid silence, keeping their mounts still, except for an occasional swish of a tail at the buzzing flies. The rest were former Slaves of the Master, his Slave brothers, distinguished by their long hair, motley finery, and arrogant bearing. Restless as their riders, their horses snorted and sidled, stirring up the late-summer dust from the dried grasses of the small meadow outside the Sanctuary gate.

One man rode an eerie-looking horse, black except for a completely white face with dark, staring eyes. The man dismounted and stalked toward the gate. *Is that Gauday?* Kyr wondered. His old nemesis had worn his long, brown hair sleeked back in a neat braid and had carried himself with a proud swagger. This man slouched along with a sly, predatory air. His hair was loose and tangled, with bangs covering his forehead.

Whoever he was, he peered at Kyr through the spy hole, and said, "So here you are, my boy. I was wondering where you'd hidden yourself after you killed our Master and betrayed us all. Luckily, Larag found you for me."

That patronizing tone was unmistakable. It was Gauday, staring at him with rapacious hunger. Kyr shivered. *Merciless gods, he can't wait to get his claws into me.* Lurid colors squirmed in the depths of Gauday's dark eyes, reminding Kyr of something. He looked deeper, trying to see what it was. *It's like the Master's Crown, the way those colors move.*

"Do come and join us, cur. We all must obey the Master's last command, especially you." Gauday's eyes turned a glowing red, and fiery pain lanced through Kyr's head.

Though the pain was intense, Kyr fought to show no reaction, as he had learned to do so well in the Soul-Drinker's hell. He called on the Kailithana's gift, the kailitha in his core, glowing silver-white now, filling him with steadfast courage. He met Gauday's burning gaze straight on. It was Gauday who blinked, his eyes returning to their normal pale blue. The pain vanished as if it had never happened, and Kyr took a deep breath. Still keeping his eyes on Gauday's, he demanded, "Swear on your Master's soul to leave the Sanctuary and all the people here unharmed if I turn myself over to you."

"Gone soft, have you? All the better." Gauday raised his hand and struck a solemn pose. "Yes, my dear, I swear on *our* Master's immortal soul, I and my men shall leave the Sanctuary and its people untouched, but only as long as you are my prisoner— my *living* prisoner."

"What do you mean?"

"If you manage to escape, or die, we'll return and have our fun with this sweet little Sanctuary of yours."

*He'll keep his oath only as long as he has me to torment.* Dread settled over Kyr like a net of iron, but he bowed his head, accepting this heavy penance. *After all that I learned here at the Sanctuary, what I'm grateful for is that my Trainer taught me so well. I can endure whatever Gauday does to me.* He straightened, smiling grimly.

"Alright. I understand."

Gauday frowned, then affected a nonchalant stance. "Dear boy, there's one more thing you must do for me if I am to protect this precious Sanctuary of yours from my men."

"Yes?"

"Tell me what you did with the Rod. It shouldn't be left lying about, you know."

"It was destroyed."

"What kind of fool do you take me for? Tell me where it is!" Gauday's eyes turned dangerously red.

Instantly, Kyr's brain was on fire again. Through gritted teeth, he said, "Ask the Warrior Mage, if you don't believe me." He stepped aside and waved Rajani over. The moment he broke eye-contact with Gauday,

14

the strange pain that had burned in his head was snuffed out. Kyr rubbed his head, wondering, *Where did he get that power? Is he a sorcerer now?*

Rajani took Kyr's place at the spy hole, and smiled coldly at Gauday. "I destroyed the cursed thing myself, to prevent scum such as yourself from ever laying hands on it." Rajani's matter-of-fact tone left no doubt that he spoke the truth.

"NO!" Gauday slammed his fists into the gate, howling, "Gods curse you and all your progeny!"

Rajani gave a harsh bark that could not be called laughter. "You'll have to do better than that. I have no children, and the gods have done their worst to me already." Kyr frowned, wondering what Rajani meant, but this was no time to ask. He traded places with Rajani at the spyhole.

"A pox on you!" Gauday stomped away, rubbing sore knuckles. Kyr watched Gauday's men eyeing their leader uneasily. Noticing this, Gauday stopped and tugged at his tunic. With a casual shrug, he turned back to the gate.

"Ah, well, what's done is done. We'll just have to make do with you, dear cur, er, Kyr. Do come and join us." Gauday's voiced dripped with honeyed venom.

Kyr felt ill and shaky. *Kill him!* he wanted to beg Rajani. *Kill him with your Warrior Magic.* He kept silent, knowing that Gauday's obsession with him was the Sanctuary's only protection. He squared his shoulders.

"I'll come out as soon as you all get far enough away that you can't rush the gate. Get back across the meadow. Wait for me by that stand of oak trees."

"Fine, my boy, fine. It will be so good to have you back with us, where you belong."

As he watched Gauday's band back away, Kyr's heart thudded unevenly in his chest and he had to lock his knees to keep them from shaking. Too soon, all of Gauday's band had crossed to the far side of the meadow, and were waiting for him in the shade of the oak trees.

Without looking back, Kyr stepped through the gate of the Sanctuary, and shoved it closed behind him. The solid thunk of the gate's inner bar falling into place struck him like a blow to the stomach. He could barely breathe, but he clenched his fists and forced himself to move forward. With every step, he felt the Sanctuary fading away like a pleasant dream as he woke to familiar nightmare, the harsh reality he had known most of his life as a Slave of the Master.

"Zhovanya nara lo, Zhovanya nara lo, Zhovanya nara lo." From behind the walls of the Sanctuary came the sound of the Kailithana chanting, sending him her love and support. Naran's velvet bass joined her warm alto, then Luciya's clear soprano and Rajani's husky baritone . The chorus gained strength as more and more of the people of the Sanctuary joined in, a rich harmony of many voices singing—for him.

His courage nearly did fail him then. He stopped, heart-pierced with longing for all he was losing this day. His feet would not move, though all he loved would be destroyed if he fled his fated penance.

"Goddess, help me!"

His whispered prayer was answered by a high, harsh cry. A tawny eagle soared just overhead in the pale summer sky. Heartened by this sign that Zhovanya was with him, he went on. *These are my brothers, lost in the Master's madness.* Kyr knew the kind of life Gauday and all the Slaves had lived, understood better than they the deep pain that burdened their souls and distorted their minds. *I must try. It may be my only chance—and theirs.*

Kyr's boots crunched through the dead grasses as he left the Sanctuary behind and crossed the meadow toward his Slave brothers. Large insects with long antennae and big hind legs jumped away, wings whirring. Listless breezes did nothing to alleviate the late-summer heat, but only wafted the odors of sweaty horses and their smelly deposits toward him.

Squawking in alarm, a dozen crows swirled above the grove of oak trees where Gauday and his men waited. As Kyr approached, he could see Gauday astride his white-faced black stallion. Next to Gauday stood scar-faced, black-haired Larag, holding the reins of a raw-boned reddish horse. Next to Larag stood a tall, lanky redhead with a golden-brown horse, which nudged his shoulder. The redhead shoved its head away, whispering, "Not now, Comrade." Gauday shot an annoyed glance at the soldier.

"Look at 'im come crawling back!" yelled a Slave from amidst his cronies. Another chimed in, sneering "Thought ya could get away with killing our Master, didja? We'll show you!"

Kyr ignored them, but Gauday glared at his men and they fell silent. Apparently, this was to be solely Gauday's moment of victory. No one else was allowed to participate.

16

Kyr stopped a short distance away. Gauday grinned, triumphant at having Kyr at his mercy. "Welcome, dear boy!" he drawled. "Here you are at last. We'll have some fun together, won't we? It'll be just like old times." Gauday paused as if expecting Kyr to cringe or beg for mercy.

Instead, Kyr shouted, "Brothers! Free yourselves from the evil life the Master forced on us all. If you throw down your weapons and humbly seek admittance to the Sanctuary, you will be blessed with kindness, healing, forgiveness and love by the true sovereign of Khailaz, our Goddess, Zhovanya, and Her helpers here at the Sanctuary. Take this chance to save your own souls!"

A few Slaves laughed uncertainly, but others were looking curiously at the Sanctuary. Gauday glared at Kyr with glowing red eyes, but Kyr called on the kailitha glowing at his core and stared back, unaffected by Gauday's strange power.

Gauday gritted his teeth, smoothed his face, then laughed as if highly amused. "Why, my dear, how presumptuous! *I* am the Master here. You speak when I allow it. Well, we'll knock that arrogance right out of you. Larag, why don't you give our guest an appropriate welcome?"

"My pleasure." Larag dropped his reins and stalked toward Kyr, uncoiling his whip. Kyr retreated a few paces, and Gauday sniggered. "Afraid, are you? Good, good. We'll teach you a little respect. Then we'll be on our way."

But Kyr showed no fear, and raised his voice again. "I accept whatever you do to me as part of my Atonement for the terrible things I did as a Slave. And I forgive you all."

"Shut your mouth, cur!" Larag lashed the side of Kyr's head with his heavy whip handle, knocking him to the ground. "You thought you were safe here in this bitch-goddess's nest of rebels, but *I* found you, didn't I?"

He stood over Kyr, gloating. Kyr rolled into a crouch, head to knees, hands clasped behind his neck. Blood trickled from his scalp and dripped into the sun-heated dust and withered grasses of the meadow.

"You murdered our Master! You'll pay for that for the rest of your despicable life!" With a scar-twisted smile, Larag sent his bullwhip snaking out.

The bitter sting of the lash made Kyr gasp. He sought the ice but it was gone, melted away by love and kindness, leaving him no sanctuary from the pain.

"Lost your old silence, have you? Excellent!" Larag cracked his whip over Kyr's head, but he was prepared this time and didn't flinch. The ice was gone but he still had the iron discipline drilled into him by the Soul-Drinker's cruel Trainer.

Disappointed, Larag snarled, "Because of you, we've been hounded out of our City and into the blasted wilderness. I'll make you pay for that, too."

Again, the whip hissed and stung, but Kyr bit his lip and kept silent. The Slaves clapped and jeered. Rage bade him leap up and fight back, but he forced himself to remain still, to accept his fate, to endure, as he had learned to do as a Slave. It was his only choice if he wanted to safeguard the Sanctuary and survive his crazed brothers' wrath.

"Zhovanya nara lo, Zhovanya nara lo." From behind the walls of the Sanctuary, the people continued chanting, their voices full of love and sorrow, reminding him of their love, of the Love that had transformed his life, and of his Goddess and Her gift of counsel, the one word she had given him. *Soften, soften, soften,* he chanted to himself.

As Larag coiled up his whip for another strike, Kyr took a quick look at Gauday's men. Many of them were staring at him or the Sanctuary with puzzled frowns. Some had even covered their ears against the disturbing chant, resonant with a kind of power they had never experienced before, the power of love and forgiveness. He uncurled, got to his knees and shouted, "Zhovanya loves and forgives us all!"

"Shut up, traitor!" yelled Larag, lashing Kyr's unprotected chest. He gasped and quickly returned to his defensive crouch.

As the people of the Sanctuary continued chanting, the Slaves' clapping and jeering tapered off into an uneasy silence. This was punctuated by another snap of Larag's whip, and Kyr's gasp of pain.

Gauday glowered at his silent, disturbed men, and abruptly said, "Alright, Larag, that's a good start. Let's get this traitor back to our fort, where we can begin his proper punishment."

Larag gave Kyr, still crouched on the ground, a kick in the ribs, and stalked away. Dazed and aching, Kyr stretched out and pressed himself into the unharmful earth, wishing he could sink into its stony embrace.

The redheaded soldier knelt beside Kyr. "Have you ever ridden a horse?"

"No," Kyr whispered.

"Here." The tall redhead offered a hand up, but Kyr ignored it. Though he could not fight back, he needed to be as strong as he could before this mob of feral, violent men. Gathering the remnants of his strength, he struggled to his feet, his bruised ribs aching, his back stinging. He wavered on his feet, white-faced and shivering despite the heat.

The lanky soldier went over to his horse, took his cloak from his saddlebag, and draped it gently over Kyr's shoulders. "Name's Craith. I'll want it back when we get to the fort." Kyr gave the redhead a slight nod of thanks, and pulled the cloak closed.

Craith turned to Gauday. "Sir, he can't ride."

"It'll be my pleasure to take him on Skull." Gauday leered at Kyr. "Please join me, my boy."

Kyr examined the horse. Gauday sat astride a thick wool pad, strapped to the horse with leather bands. Gauday's feet were thrust into metal hoops attached to a pair of additional leather bands. Kyr wondered how the hells he was supposed to sit up there, let alone get up on the horse. He shrugged and stepped toward Skull. The horse laid back his ears and snaked his head at Kyr, snapping at him with huge teeth. Kyr flinched back, and Gauday laughed, but reined Skull's head away.

"Hurry up, sergeant. Get him up here."

"Aye, sir." Craith knelt and cupped his hands. "Put your foot here." Kyr obeyed and Craith boosted him up in front of Gauday. Kyr struggled to get his legs astride the horse. Skull was making it even harder by taking little hops and shaking his head in annoyance.

Gauday chuckled gleefully at Kyr's difficulty, but then grabbed him and helped him get settled. "So you've never been on a horse before, my dear? I've come to quite enjoy riding over this past year, but it *is* quite difficult at first. This will be your next punishment."

Kyr ignored this, focusing instead on praying that Gauday would keep his promise to leave the Sanctuary unharmed.

"Alright, men, let's go!" Gauday yelled. Led by Craith, the soldiers obediently turned away from the Sanctuary, and headed back across the oak-studded valley, muddying the stream that wandered through the valley as they splashed through it, making for the steep cliff trail they had come down. A few cast curious glances back at the Sanctuary but quickly looked away, to avoid Gauday's ire.

Meanwhile, the Slaves sat on their horses, looking disgruntled. A short, blond man with eyes the color of old ice yelled, "You gonna leave all that untouched? What about the treasure? The wimmin?"

19

"Shut up, Viro!" Larag snapped his whip over the blond's head. Viro ducked but stayed put. "We came all this way for nothin'?" he demanded loudly. Some of the other Slaves chimed in, saying "Yeah!" or "What about the treasure?" Others looked away, and started to follow the soldiers, though with sullen looks on their faces.

"Do as you are told!" Gauday glared at the smaller man, his eyes glowing red. Viro grabbed his head, howling in pain. Viro's supporters cast fearful glances at Gauday, turned away, and slunk after the other Slaves and soldiers.

Gauday snickered at Viro, and his eyes stopped glowing red. Viro subsided into short gasps. "Go!" Gauday commanded, and Viro turned and trailed after the rest of the band, coughing from the dust kicked up by the horses as they crossed the summer-burnt floor of the valley.

Gauday kicked his horse into a trot. Skull's jarring gait sent stabs of pain through Kyr's battered body, but he gritted his teeth and clung to Skull's mane.

As they all rode off, leaving the Sanctuary untouched, Kyr breathed a sigh of relief that was almost a sob.

Gauday chuckled. "You see? Your precious Sanctuary is unharmed. I always keep my promises. For example, I promised the Master I'd carry out his last command, and now I shall." Gauday breathed that last word down Kyr's neck. Kyr shivered at the malice in Gauday's voice.

Gauday and Larag kicked their mounts into a canter, and raced to the head of the line. Kyr hung on as best he could, sure he would fall off the horse and be trampled. Part of him hoped that he would. But Gauday wrapped one arm around his waist. "No, my boy, you can't get away from me that easily. I won't let you fall."

As the horses began to climb up the steep path out of the secret valley, Kyr looked back across the valley at the Sanctuary, his throat aching with unshed tears for all that he was losing that day: love and kindness; beauty and grace; understanding and forgiveness. He nearly sobbed aloud, but he looked away and stifled all signs of his distress, knowing that he must not show any sign of such vulnerability to his captors. Resolutely, he told himself, *I must keep all these gifts in my heart, and try to share them with my brothers.* The glowing ball of kailitha in his core flared up, giving him strength and courage.

As if sensing Kyr's determination, Gauday pressed Kyr's throbbing back tight against the roughness of his tunic, and laughed at Kyr's hiss of pain. "So good to have you back where you belong, my dear." Gauday slowly licked up the blood trickling down Kyr's neck from his scalp wound. Kyr shivered with disgust. Then Gauday began crooning in his ear. "You're mine now, my boy. Mine forever."

After the sacredness of his time with the Kailithana, Kyr already felt degraded and ashamed, though he knew he was doing what was necessary. He closed his eyes and sought the solace of the forgiveness chant. *Zhovanya nara lo. Zhovanya nara lo.* As the chant filled his mind, the ugly dissonance of Gauday's crooning receded, becoming nothing more than the droning of insects.

They had been travelling for half the day through wide, sunny meadows, and occasional stands of blessedly shady trees. Kyr's legs and buttocks were protesting loudly against the new torment of riding a horse. The welts on his back throbbed, and his head ached. Thirst added to his misery, and he was dizzy from Larag's vicious blow to his head. The sun beat down on him as they rode through yet another meadow. Skull's white head bobbed in front of his dazed eyes, disappearing into grayness, returning, disappearing. He lost hold of the chant, of where he was. A strange sound filled his head.

A cloud of carrion flies descended on them, buzzing and darting at the blood oozing from Kyr's cut scalp. "Disgusting piece of offal," Gauday snarled as if Kyr were bleeding just to annoy him. He let go of Kyr to bat at the flies. Kyr slumped forward, the world spinning into darkness.

Cold water shocked him awake. He was on the ground, surrounded by a forest of legs, human and equine. He struggled to his knees, but his screaming legs refused to function. He knelt there, bracing himself with his hands on his thighs, head down, staring at the thick grasses of a meadow, trying to regain his wits.

"Can't even stay on a horse." Larag gave Kyr a kick in his buttocks, making his cronies laugh. Kyr clenched his fists and looked up, fighting not to lash out at Larag.

"Let's leave him for the vultures." Viro gestured toward a flock of the carrion birds tearing at a carcass on the far side of the meadow.

"I'm already surrounded by vultures," Kyr retorted. Then he bit his lip. *Ah, Goddess, forgive me for forgetting your gift of counsel so quickly.*

"Vultures, are we? Well then, you have nothing to fear from us." Gauday laughed. "You're not dead meat yet." He turned to his restive men. "You know what the Master said. We must keep the traitor alive. Where's that healer we, ah, recruited on the way here?" He looked around. "Ah. Viro, do bring our guest over here."

Viro dragged a gray-haired man forward. Small but solid and compact, the healer shrugged off Viro's hand and glared at Gauday. "Are you in charge of this rabble? Why have you abducted me? I demand that you release me at once!"

"Welcome to our little band, my dear healer. Just the man for the job, I'm sure. I'm Gauday." He bowed with a florid flourish of one hand. "And what, pray tell, is your name?"

"Medari. I'm the healer of Stonewell Village. You must let me return there. The people need me."

"Quiet!" Gauday's eyes flashed red.

Medari gasped as pain lanced through his head, then glared at Gauday. "What did you do to me?"

"Oh, old man, that was nothing compared to what I'll do if you don't keep quiet and listen." Gauday smiled at Medari's stricken look. "That's better. I am putting this traitor's life in your hands. You are to keep him alive, not comfortable, just alive. I don't want you protecting him from his punishment."

Medari glared at him. "You expect me to keep this man alive so you can torment him? That goes against my Healer's Oath, against everything I stand for."

"You will break your damnable oath and be quiet about it. That is, if you want to spare your dear family particularly unpleasant deaths." Gauday smirked to see the gray-haired man go rigid and pale.

"Gods and demons! You have my family? What have you done with them? Have you hurt them?"

"They're quite, ah, secure." Gauday pretended to cough, suppressing a chuckle. "They will remain so, as long as you do your job. If the traitor dies, however…. You do understand, don't you, my dear man? Now, do what you can for our prisoner."

Eyes speaking his fear, fury and contempt, Medari snapped, "I'll need my satchel."

"Viro, fetch the healer's bag, won't you?"

22

As Gauday remounted Skull, Viro glowered at Gauday's back, then grabbed the satchel off the healer's white mare and shoved it into Medari's hands.

"That's the last time I do any fetchin' for you, old man." He stomped off to join Larag and his cronies.

Medari knelt beside Kyr on the grass of the meadow, and helped him shed Craith's cloak and his own tunic. With gentle precision, he cleansed the cut on Kyr's head with an astringent and applied a salve to the welts on his back, and to the large purple bruise on his ribs, where Larag had kicked him.

When no one was looking their way, he held a small flask to Kyr's lips. "Quickly, before they see!"

For an instant, Kyr looked into the healer's brown eyes. Seeing only urgent concern, he drank as much as the older man allowed. Soon he felt a blessed numbness spreading though his body. He gave Medari a grateful nod, got to his feet, donned his tunic, and wrapped himself in Craith's cloak.

Gauday sauntered over and draped an arm around Medari's shoulders.

"Got the traitor on his feet, I see. Good job, old man." He turned both of them to face his men.

"Now, boys, listen to me. I give this old man here the authority to keep the Master's murderer alive for our pleasure, our revenge. If he says the traitor is in danger of dying, you will stop whatever it is you are doing to him. Otherwise, when we get back, feel free to enjoy yourselves!" This was greeted by a ragged cheer. Gauday held up his hand and the cheers died off. "One more thing. No whips, no knives."

Larag and Viro groaned in protest. Gauday glared at them with red eyes, and they bowed their heads.

"Craith, tie this fly-bait on a horse. I've had my fun with him, for the moment." He mounted and jerked on the reins, causing Skull to rear and neigh. "Alright, men, let's go!"

Craith tied Kyr to the saddle of a black mare and took her reins. Kyr clung to the mare's mane and closed his eyes, relieved to be free of Gauday's lewd, sadistic grasp for the time being. With the help of the healer's numbing elixir, he was able to stay on the horse and keep his mind on the forgiveness chant. Soon the chant fit the rhythm of the smooth-gaited mare's steady plodding. *Zhovanya nara lo, Zhovanya nara lo.* After a time, velvet wings enfolded him in gentle darkness, and he left misery and dread behind.

# Chapter 3

# Oath-bound

Watching Gauday and his band ride off with Kyr, Rajani longed to race after them, to slay Gauday and bring Kyr back to the Sanctuary. Every muscle clenched, the Warrior Mage strained against the oath-bind. Sweat beaded his forehead. He couldn't breathe. The oath-bind was too strong. As always, it kept him to the path dictated by the Star-Seer's Prophecy, no matter how much he hated it.

"Zhovanya nara lo." The chanting died away, and the people of the Sanctuary turned to each other sadly, speaking almost in whispers, with an air of shock and disbelief, awe at Kyr's sacrifice, and relief that the gang of Slaves and soldiers was truly leaving the Sanctuary untouched.

Rajani turned away from the spy-hole, muttering, "Gods curse it!" For a moment, he closed his eyes, gathering up the rags of his composure.

"This is horrible!" Luciya quivered with outrage. "We've got to rescue him, Jani. Let's get going!"

"Calm down, Ciya. Think! We can't go racing off unprepared. We have to get back to the City to get a troop together, as I said."

"I know, but...." Luciya fell silent, seeing the anguish in his eyes. But, inwardly, she raged against the Prophecy that ruled all their lives. And her heart ached for Kyr. To suffer so much, and to become such a good man, only to be sent back into hell!

"How long will that take?" asked Maray, who had his arms around a sobbing Gaela.

"Well, with no horses, it will take us a half-moon to get back to the City. Then I will have to get a troop of our best fighters together. Unfortunately, they scattered once the riots after the Soul-Drinker's death ended and the new City Guard had established order. So it will take a month or more, depending on where Gauday takes Kyr; how long it takes me to find the fighters and locate Gauday; and the weather and road conditions. Longer, if the rains come and the roads become impassable."

Gaela wiped her tears on her apron, and objected, "A month or more before you even begin to search for Kyr? That Gauday will torment him. You could hear it in his voice. Can't you do it any faster, Warrior Mage?" Many people turned to listen to Rajani's answer.

"Nothing I would like more." Rajani took a deep breath, seeking patience. "But we must face the realities. I ask you, no, I beg you, to pray for him every moment of every day."

"We will." Gaela gulped down a sob. "Goddess bless and guide you." She nodded, and joined the stream of people already heading for the Temple.

Rajani turned back to Luciya. "Come on, let's get packed up." She put a hand on his arm to keep him still.

After looking around to make sure no one could overhear, she demanded in a fierce whisper, "Is this ordained by the Prophecy? Is that why you let that vulture Gauday take Kyr?"

"Why else?" He glared at her. "You think I'd let this happen if the oath-bind hadn't kept me from doing anything to stop it?"

"No, no," she faltered. "I'm sorry. Of course you wouldn't."

"Sorry, Luciya," Rajani softened his tone. "Remember, the Star-Seer's Prophecy says Kyr must face three hells? This is the second one."

"Why does this have to be so difficult for him? For you? For all of us?" she cried.

"Ask the Star-Seer. I have no idea," he said with a sardonic twist to his lips. "But if we want to return Zhovanya to Her rightful place, we must follow the Prophecy. Come on. Let's get packed."

Her shoulders sagged as she hurried after Rajani. The Star-Seer was long dead, but they were all still imprisoned by her Prophecy, Kyr most of all.

After an exhausting half-moon march, Rajani and Luciya reached the outskirts of the City. The sun was setting over the ocean, casting a crimson glow over buildings near and far. "Home," Luciya sighed, loving the sounds of the distant waves crashing onshore, and the wind rustling through the palm trees scattered along the roadside. But her nose missed something. She sniffed, trying to figure out what was different.

"Look, Jani, it's amazing! No garbage heaps along the road. No stink! No flies!"

"No potholes, either," Rajani added with a smile.

And indeed, there was little trash anywhere, and the road was in good repair. Even the small homes of the poorer residents showed signs of improvement: new thatch on the roofs; bright red brick showing where walls had been repaired. As the two returnees trudged along, their hearts were lifted by all the positive changes they saw.

They looked up toward the City on its bluff overlooking the ocean, the skyline black against the crimson sky. Only a few jagged shapes of burnt-out ruins stood among the many buildings of the City, stark reminders of the chaos that had followed the end of the Soul-Drinker's five-hundred-year reign of horror.

"By all the little gods!" Rajani laughed. "It's incredible what progress they've made since we left two moons ago! The Council is doing well."

"Oh!" Luciya gasped. "The Temple is so beautiful in this light." They stopped to gaze at the Temple sitting on the highest point of the cliff above the City. Now freed from the Soul-Drinker's imprisoning walls, the open-sided Temple was bathed in the rosy light of the setting sun, which almost obscured the scaffolding used by the workers still repairing the columns and roof.

As they continued onward, they were startled to see a large sea-blue banner floating between two tall palm trees growing on either side of the road. "Welcome to Kardhiya, the Heart of Khailaz," it proclaimed in golden letters.

"I see the Council has finally agreed on a name for the City," Rajani said.

"Took them long enough." Luciya chuckled, then stopped short. "Oh! Guards, way out here!"

By each palm tree stood a member of the City Guard, wearing knee-length, dark blue tunics and sandals, and armed with pikes. A muscular, dour-faced female Guard stepped forward. "What is your business in Kardhiya?"

With a smile, Rajani asked, "Ah, Lunya, have you forgotten us already?"

"Commander!" A bright grin transformed her stern face. "We didn't expect you back so soon."

"Something's come up. We'll need to have a meeting with the Council and the Guard in the morning. Will you pass the word?"

"Yes, sir."

"We'll be in our quarters."

"But *first* we'll be in the *baths*," Luciya proclaimed.

The next morning, Luciya lay abed, luxuriating in feeling clean and refreshed by a bath and a good night's sleep on a soft bed, soothed by the sound of the waves coming through her open window. It was wonderful to be home in her own room in Government House, where all those engaged in building up the new structures of government and administration now lived. She loved having this small room to herself, with its white-washed walls, woven mats of golden rushes on the floor, and blackwood storage chests.

Remembering Kyr's captivity, she sighed, relinquishing once again her small moment of pleasure. Sitting up, she looked for her pack. It was sitting beside her bed where she had dropped it the night before. She dug into it for her one clean tunic, which she had carefully saved throughout their trek back to the City. Something hard met her hands.

"Oh, Goddess," she whispered, and cringed. It had been so dangerous for so long to say such a thing, even in a whisper. The Soul-Drinker and his mind-bonded Watchers heard every word, every thought. Dauthaz punished the slightest mention of any power but himself, or any objection to his rule, with his evil sorcerous powers. With an impatient growl, she shook off dark memories.

Unrolling her relatively clean but wrinkled tunic, she found the small clay figure Kyr had given her at his special dinner at the Sanctuary. She sat holding it gently, stroking the bent back of the grieving woman, tears welling in her own eyes. Recalling her promise to Kyr, she set the figure on the chest beside her bed, and knelt down before it.

She couldn't keep back her tears, but was unsure if she was weeping for Kyr; for the woman Kyr's figure represented, who had been one of his victims when he had been the obedient Slave of the Soul-Drinker; or for her own losses to the viciousness of the Soul-Drinker, including her mother, her beloved Lanir, and most of her own life. After a few moments, she deliberately took some deep, soothing breaths, wiped away her tears, and sat still until she was calm. Then she raised up the little statue with both her hands.

"O, Great Goddess of Life and Death! O, Zhovanya! Please bless the soul of this woman, this victim of the Soul-Drinker's unholy cruelty by Kyr's hand. Soothe her soul-pain, and let her feel your unfailing Love. Let her dwell in your heart until she is ready to return her kailitha, her life force, to the web of life, to strengthen her soul-kin. For this I pray."

She set the statuette down, and clasped her hands before her heart. "Dear Zhovanya, be with Kyr in his captivity. Star-cursed he may be, but he is now a good man, doing Your will. Please, please protect his heart and soul from the spite and evil of his captors. Give him strength and patience. And I beg you to help us find and rescue him as quickly as possible." Her voice trembled and tears splashed down her cheeks. But she again calmed herself, and said, "For this I pray."

# Part Two ~ Into the Fire

*"Our word 'sacrifice' comes from the same root as sacred,
and sacrifice has to do with making something holy....
the (Bhagavad) Gita ...says,
'others offer, as a sacrifice, their own soul in the fire of God.'"*

—Ram Dass, *Paths to God: Living the Bhagavad Gita*

## Chapter 4

# Enemies and Allies

As the sun set, Gauday called a halt in a vale well-hidden by a thick wall of tall evergreens, with a creek chuckling to itself nearby. Craith examined the prisoner slumped over the black mare's neck. Shaking his head, the redheaded sergeant untied Kyr, hauled him down and sat him next to a pine tree, tied him to it by the waist and chest, and bound him hand and foot. Turning away, he gave quiet orders to his soldiers. Some got a fire going and started cooking the evening meal, while others began setting up a large tent for the Slaves, who had spent most of their lives cooped up in the Master's labyrinth. They couldn't bear to sleep without walls around them. They even kept a candle lantern lit in their tent all night. As they worked, the soldiers quietly joked among themselves about the dainty ways of the Slaves. Hardened to a soldier's rough life, they preferred their bedrolls under the stars.

Meanwhile, the former Slaves of the Master, used to being waited upon by the drudges in the Soul-Drinker's labyrinth, were lounging around the fire, drinking and harassing each other with jibes and jabs. They'd have preferred to be badgering the soldiers, but Craith had insisted that his men be left alone.

When Gauday had objected, Craith simply pointed out that if his men stopped working, the Slaves would have no food to eat, no tent to sleep in. Gauday had glared at him with his red eyes, but Craith said through the pain, "You can't do this to all of us at once." And his men set down their tools, and stood unmoving. Gauday had quickly relented, before their rebellion and the limits of his power became obvious, and laughed as if they had been joking around. Later, he had commanded his Slaves to leave the soldiers alone to do their work.

Now the two bands of men existed in an uneasy truce. Craith sighed, wondering once again what he and his men were doing with Gauday and his cronies. But he had found no other master to follow. The General had died with the Master, and Gauday did have the Master's Crown, though he hadn't worn it lately. Without a commander to obey, what were mere soldiers to do? Loyalty and obedience were all they knew.

Kyr's back and legs ached and burned from the new torment of riding a horse. His mouth was dry as old glue, and despite the cloak Craith had given him, the pine's rough bark grated against the welts on his back. *Gods, I wish this tree was the Heart of the Forest with its healing powers.* He sighed, knowing he had to put all such wishes out of his mind. They would only make his captivity seem worse.

Arm in arm as if they were good friends, Gauday escorted Medari to Kyr's side. "Take good care of our prisoner."

"This man needs food and water. We both do."

"Oh, he can have water, alright. Viro?"

Larag laughed. "Yeah, Viro, give him some water!"

"My pleasure!" The ice-eyed blond grabbed his waterskin off his pack.

The Slaves gathered around, laughing and jeering as Viro made a game of pouring water down Kyr's throat. Soon Kyr was choking and soaking wet. The stone-faced healer stood to the side with his arms crossed on his chest, watching the Slaves' antics. Every line of his body expressed his contempt.

Smiling indulgently, Gauday took a swig from the flask that was passing from hand to hand among the Slaves. After a few moments, he clapped his hands sharply.

"Alright, boys, enough! Let's not drown him before we get him home. Come on. The food is ready." The men left off, grumbling away to their supper.

Kyr sagged against his bonds, gasping for breath. A cool evening breeze set him shivering and brought the enticing odor of rabbit stew, making his stomach growl. He snorted to himself. *At least I'm not thirsty anymore.*

The healer went over to the fire and spoke to Craith. They returned with a ragged towel, a rough woolen blanket, some trail-biscuits, and a

34

large bowl of stew. Craith untied him and took back his bloody, wet cloak. Medari knelt beside Kyr and dried him off with the towel, then wrapped him in the blanket. Craith bound him to the tree, and retied his hands and feet. Kyr clenched his jaw and kept silent, though his abused body protested every movement, every touch. Craith took his cloak and went off to eat with his men.

Since Kyr's hands were tied, Medari fed him chunks of biscuit soaked in gravy and bits of rabbit, and ate his own share, too. The numbing elixir had worn off. Exhausted and aching, all Kyr wanted was oblivion, but he forced himself to eat. *If I am to survive until Rajani finds me, I'll have to eat every crumb they give me.*

When the food was gone, Medari tucked the blanket around him. It reeked of horse sweat but it was dry and warm. Between it and the warm food, his shivering abated.

"Thanks," he whispered, and dropped into a black pit of sodden sleep.

Two days later, they left behind the meadows and trees of the highlands, and then spent the third day making their way out of scrubby foothills. Now they were riding through a desert, populated only by scattered clumps of gray-bush, thorn-vine, and the occasional small creature scuttling from one shade patch to the next. Vultures soared overhead, patiently awaiting their due. Kyr suspected that they were keeping an eye on him as the creature most likely to die soon.

The only blessings were that he was less dizzy, and that the cloud of buzzing flies that had tormented him earlier—being sensible creatures—had not accompanied them into the desert.

The next few days crawled by in a blur, the withering sun beating down on man, horse, and sand. Kyr rode in a haze of thirst and exhaustion, the chant often slipping from his grasp. Throughout the early, cooler part of the day, Kyr clung to the chant that protected his soul: *Zhovanya nara lo. Zhovanya nara lo.* Craith's ropes cut into him painfully, but were all that kept him from tumbling into the dusty sand of the desert. Worse than the aching welts from Larag's whip were the saddle sores and screaming muscles, caused by long days of riding the black mare. *Goddess help me*, Kyr thought wryly, *I don't know which of my tormenters I need to forgive more: Gauday, or my horse.* It was his last conscious thought as exhaustion took him into darkness.

A quarter-moon had passed since Gauday had taken Kyr away. As she had every day since then, Jolanya was praying for Kyr in Jeyal's chapel. But this day, exhausted by worry and grief, she could not keep her mind from going back to that horrible moment when she had watched Kyr, bruised and bloody, disappear into the cloud of dust kicked up by Gauday's band as they rode off, taking Kyr back into the kind of hell he had worked so hard to escape.

Then, as now, unshed sobs blocked her throat. She remembered how she had no longer been able to sing the chant for Kyr, and, around her, the chant had faded away as the others too ceased singing.

*Rajani, Luciya and Maray descended to the courtyard of the Sanctuary, but Jolanya remained standing on the sentry's platform. Her tight grip on the wooden railing was all that kept her from crumpling to her knees. Silently, she wailed,* Oh, Kyr! After all you have gone through, to sacrifice yourself to that madman's obsession! How can the Goddess ask this of you?

*But she was the Kailithana. It was important not to show how much she was affected by the abduction of her former kailithos, her forbidden beloved. As always, she must stand apart from normal human love in order to carry out her sacred duties as the one and only Priestess-Healer.*

*Yet behind her frozen mask of calm dignity, a storm raged. Grief for the loss of Kyr, the only man she had ever loved, warred with rage at Jeyal, the God she served.* How can You send him away! He's the one You promised me, I know it! My heart would not be torn into pieces like this if he were not. Bring him back now! *She clenched her jaw until it ached, keeping back the wails that threatened to break forth.*

*Only silence answered her demands.*

*Angrily, she thought,* If Jeyal won't help, I must do something! I don't care what others may think! *Whirling around, she flew down the rough wooden stairs to the*

36

courtyard. Grabbing the first person she saw, she demanded, "Where is that so-called Warrior Mage?"

The gray-robed woman, her eyes wide with shock at the surprisingly harsh tone from the ever-serene Kailithana, pointed toward the dining hall. Jolanya nodded her thanks and ran to the hall, where she found Rajani standing alone on the wide porch, staring ferociously in the direction Gauday had taken Kyr. Jolanya slowed her pace, puzzled by the odd tension emanating from the Warrior Mage. It was as if he was straining to move, to act, but could not.

With a deep sigh, she sought to compose herself, and approached Rajani. "Please, can't you do something for Kyr? You are the Warrior Mage." Despite her effort to appear calm, her voice was high and pleading, and tears pooled in her eyes.

He seemed to struggle to speak. "I can't explain," he choked out.

She frowned and studied his kailitha. In her inner vision, dark bands surrounded his throat, shoulders, arms and legs. "You are under some kind of spell, aren't you?" He seemed frozen, his dark blue eyes full of anguish.

"It prevents you from taking action to help Kyr?"

He closed his eyes, his face flushing in shame.

"Perhaps I could unbind you. I will try, if you wish, if you will help Kyr."

"No! It is forbidden!" he squawked in a harsh voice, and jerked away from her as if pulled by strings.

She bit her lip and stood silently, fighting a turmoil of disappointment, anger, and fear for Kyr. Clearly, the Warrior Mage was oath-bound not to interfere in Kyr's fate. Rajani stood a few paces away, looking at the wooden plank floor, his fists clenched. It was also clear to Jolanya that he hated being unable to act. As he fought the oath-bind, his kailitha flared raggedly, like a sputtering fire. But if he would not allow her to, she could not help him. Her shoulders sagged in defeat.

*Sadly, she said, "I am sorry…" spreading her hands out in a helpless gesture. Her sorrow was not only for Kyr. It was also for Rajani, for herself, and for all the people still caught in the broken strands of the dreadful web woven by the Soul-Drinker.* It's a miracle that Kyr managed to kill that horrible sorcerer, after so many others failed. And I'm glad he did But we aren't free of the Soul-Drinker's vicious legacy yet. Oh, Jeyal! How long must we wait until Kyr and I can fulfill the destiny you have foretold?

*Determined to demand answers, she left the hall and sped up the path toward the Temple. As she arrived, she heard many people chanting within. "Zhovanya dagantalo, Zhovanya dagantalo, Zhovanya dagantalo." They were praying for the Goddess to protect Kyr. She was glad of this, but she slipped around to the side entrance and entered the priestesses' quarters. Grateful that no one was about, she hurried deeper into the maze of corridors and chambers and halted before an unassuming wooden door. In a strong voice, she said, "Kaa'a-tay!" The door swung silently inward, and she entered the chapel of the Moon Lord, Jeyal.*

*The door closed behind her, and she stood still for a moment, letting her eyes adjust to the dimness. A basin beside the door was carved into the rock wall. Into this trickled a tiny rivulet of water, adding its slight, gentle sound to the otherwise silent chamber. Cupping her hands, she caught some water and cleansed her face and hands. Then, smoothing her black hair and indigo gown, she pressed her hands together before her heart, and bowed to the center of the room. Only then did she approach the still, dark pool in the center of the chamber.*

*She knelt upon the carpeted floor in the West, Direction of Obstacles and Transformation, and began to chant. "Jeyal sumarali." (Jeyal, I call You.) At first, her voice was shaky and tight, but slowly the familiar magic of the chapel and the chant steadied her, and her voice grew stronger, almost demanding. "Jeyal sumarali. Jeyal sumarali."*

*A silvery-blue mist arose from the middle of the pool, and begin to shine. Her heart lifted but she continued to chant as the light grew brighter and took the shape of the Crescent Moon. Still she chanted, her voice more insistent. The light shifted and transformed into the ghostly shape of a man, shining silvery-blue.*

*He spoke, and words formed in Jolanya's inner hearing.*

"BELOVED, WHY DO YOU CALL ME?"

*Jolanya did not hesitate.* "Tell me why you have allowed Kyr to be taken by his enemy, back into pain and degradation, after all the healing and transformation he was able to gain here!"

"HIS FATE WAS CAST GENERATIONS AGO BY THOSE WHO WISHED TO DESTROY DAUTHAZ AND RENEW THE SACRED BALANCE."

"He is the one You promised me. I know it in my heart! How can I fulfill my role in the Great Renewal without him?"

"ALL IS AS IT NEEDS TO BE. HAVE FAITH."

"But I love him! How can he be taken away just when we have found each other?" *She leaned forward over the shining pool, reaching both arms toward Jeyal. Her tears splashed into the sacred waters.*

"THE TIME IS NOT YET, BUT WHEN YOU ARE CALLED, YOU MUST GO TO HIM."

"What about my vows as Kailithana?"

"THAT IS FOR YOU TO DECIDE, BELOVED."

*The silvery light began to wane.*

"No! Wait! Can't you help Kyr somehow? Protect him? Please!"

"I WILL BE WITH HIM AS I AM WITH ALL BELOVEDS."

*The silvery-blue flame faded as it shrank into a round moon ... a crescent ... darkness.*

Jolanya came back to herself, feeling bereft and betrayed. Jeyal had not answered her pleas since that first time she had come into the chapel to beg for protection and mercy for Kyr. As she had then, once again the Kailithana bowed her head and wept. But after a few moments, she raised her head and vowed, "We will find you, Kyr. I don't know how, but we will!"

Why had they stopped? It was only mid-morning, too early to camp for the night. With an effort, Kyr raised his head and stared blearily at the wall of trees—no, upright logs—that blocked their way. He blinked to clear his eyes, and saw a wide wooden gate in the log wall, and a square tower to one side of the gate.

Gauday grabbed the reins of Kyr's mare from Craith. The gate creaked open, and Gauday led the way inside the wall. "Welcome to Fort Kedos, dear boy." He made a sweeping gesture, as if his hide-out were a grand palace. Kyr didn't care if it were a dungeon or mansion, as long as he could get off the horse and never get back on.

Inside the tall walls, one-story wooden buildings surrounded a courtyard of hard-packed dirt. The buildings shared walls, and were connected by a roofed boardwalk that ran around most of the courtyard, except for the main gate, and a gate at the back of the courtyard. Wherever plank doors provided entry into the buildings, two stair-steps led from the dirt of the courtyard up onto the walkway.

Bright, raw planks and roof shingles stood out from gray, weathered wood, testifying to recent repairs on long-abandoned buildings. Scattered piles of old boards, broken barrels, and other debris, and the odors of hot dust and rotting garbage mirrored the squalid minds of the current occupants.

Nothing green grew in the courtyard, but, through the open gate at the back of the compound, Kyr saw a green meadow, a scraggly garden, and various wooden out-buildings, one quite large. Two soldiers guarded this gate, watching the goings-on with curiosity.

Two whip-wielding Slaves harried forth a ragged group of sullen boys. As the travelers dismounted, the boys led the horses out through the gap, across the meadow, and into the large building. *A building for animals?* Kyr wondered blearily.

Dozens of men, all Slaves as reflected by their motley finery and long hair, came pouring out of the buildings into the dusty courtyard.

Facing them, Gauday raised his voice in victory. "Success! We have the traitor. He's all ours now." He leapt off Skull, untied Kyr, and dragged him down off the mare. Kyr fought to stay on his feet but his trembling legs gave out and he fell to his knees.

Cheering, the Slaves crowded around to congratulate Gauday. His eyes glowing with mad glee, he laughed and bowed. Flasks of liquor exchanged hands as the Slaves began to celebrate. Larag grabbed one flask, took a swig, and handed it to Gauday. Triumphantly, he took a long drink, then pulled Kyr's head up by his hair and forced the flask between his lips.

"Can't leave you out of our celebration, can we, my boy?" He laughed as Kyr choked and coughed.

The harsh liquor hit Kyr's empty stomach and sent fire racing through his veins, burning away some of his muzzy exhaustion. Summoning his remaining pride and strength, he struggled to his feet.

Medari thrust his way through the crowd and confronted Gauday. "He must rest *now.*"

"Only until the feast is ready," Gauday allowed. "Tonight we are having a gala to celebrate. It simply won't do to have the guest of honor absent.

"Where can I take him?"

"Follow me. We have an infirmary set up just for you, old man."

"Rest up, cur!" Viro yelled "You'll need it!" He and his cronies jeered at Kyr, as he stumbled and nearly fell while trying to climb the two steps onto the boardwalk. Medari put his arm around Kyr and helped him up. Gauday threw open a door and bowed them inside with another grand gesture.

The infirmary, however, proved to be merely a large room, holding a scarred table and a couple of stools. Dusty shelves on the right-hand wall held a jumble of oil lamps, basins, ewers, bowls, cups, plates, and utensils.

"This is your workroom, healer. Through that door is your sleeping room." Gauday gestured toward a door on the left wall. Further along this wall, there was a stone hearth with a blackened kettle on a hook, a stack of firewood, and a flint striker. "You'll see that I have provided all you need."

Medari snorted. "Most gracious of you."

"Yes, indeed." Gauday glanced at the healer, a red flame in his eyes. Medari looked down. Gauday smiled archly and turned his attention to Kyr.

"Now," he told him, "I've had particular accommodations made for you, my dear." At the back of the infirmary, a small alcove was separated off by a wall of iron bars, creating a prison cell barely wider and no longer than the straw-filled pallet on the floor. The back wall held a small, barred window, through which a tree branch and a bit of sky could be seen.

Gauday swung open the cell's door. "In you go, my boy. This cell will be yours whenever Medari declares you are in need of rest and healing, which he had best do only when it is truly necessary." Gauday glared at the healer, who gave a grudging nod.

All Kyr saw was the pallet on the floor. With Medari's help, he lowered himself painfully onto it and curled up on his side.

"Have a good rest, my boy. The festivities begin at sundown, and we must have you at your best."

Kyr was already asleep.

"Not a word, my boy? How ungrateful!" Gauday chuckled, and handed Medari a large, rusty key. "You're to keep him locked in here. If he escapes, you and your family will pay."

"This place is filthy," the healer protested. "It must be thoroughly scoured."

"I'll set some of the village boys to do your bidding, but tomorrow is soon enough." Gauday hurried out, eager to join in the revelry in the courtyard.

Medari stared down grimly at his patient. A rough woolen blanket was folded on the end of the pallet. He pulled it over the sleeping man, stepped outside the cell, locked the door, and pocketed the key. Then he stood looking around the barren workroom.

"By the Lights, how am I to keep this poor wretch alive with the few herbs and potions in my travel-bag? Do they think I am a Healer Mage? Gods curse these villains to the blackest hell!" He slammed his fist down on the table. It wavered but stood its ground. He sank onto a stool, leaned his elbows on the table and grasped his head with clawed fingers, fighting helpless rage.

"Excuse me, healer. Here are your things."

Medari raised his head. Craith set three heavily loaded satchels on the table and said, "We often have need of a healer, here."

"I'm sure you do," Medari said in a bitter tone.

"If you need anything, let me know."

42

"Why? So you can go raid some poor sod and steal what I ask for?"

The redhead's fair skin turned red. "Sorry, sir. I just follow orders."

"That's the problem, isn't it?" the healer snapped. He opened one of the satchels, then glared at Craith. "Ah, I see. You not only abducted me and my family. You stole my own things."

"Better than stealing from some other poor sod." The sergeant stalked out the door.

In the satchels, Medari found jars of his medicaments and potions, and baskets of dried herbs, cushioned by wads of his own clothing or cloth bandages. Taking one of the cloths, he began to wipe the dust off the shelves with furious precision. When the shelves were clean, he set out the jars in orderly rows. He got a fire going, fetched water from the well in the courtyard, and set a potion brewing in the kettle.

Then he entered the room assigned to him. On the right, a narrow cot and straw-filled mattress filled most of the space, topped by a jumble of blankets. On the left, a small window gave a view of the barren courtyard. Under the window, a wide bare shelf ran the length of the room. He set his satchels, now containing only his clothing, on the shelf and peered out the dusty, cobwebbed window. Tight-lipped, he watched the drunken horseplay of the Slaves for a moment, then snatched the ragged curtains shut, and made up the bed with military neatness.

"No, no," Kyr mumbled, brushing at the hand on his shoulder. "Let me sleep, Naran-ji."

"Wake up, son. Let me do what I can, before they come for you."

It was not Naran's voice.

"Merciless gods," Kyr groaned as he recalled where he was.

"Currently, I'd have to agree with that assessment. Here." Medari handed him a warm mug. "Drink up. It's a strengthening potion."

"Thanks." Aching muscles protested every move as Kyr propped himself on one elbow and drained the mug. The potion was sour but refreshing.

"Now please lie on your stomach."

Gingerly, he turned face down, suppressing a groan.

The healer cleansed his saddle sores, applied a soothing salve to them, and to his welts and bruises, and then began massaging the salve into his aching back and sore legs.

"Why does Gauday hate you so?"

"We were rivals for the Soul-Drinker's favor from the start," Kyr explained wearily, "but Dauthaz chose me as his Favorite. I was given the Collar, which we both thought we wanted more than anything." Suppressing a shiver at the thought of the terrible craving for the pleasure of the Master's Rod, which only the Collared Favorite could endure without going mad, he added, "Gauday was furious."

"Is that why he calls you 'traitor'?"

"No. He calls me that because we Slaves were all trained to be utterly loyal to Dauthaz, but I killed our Master. Gauday and his cronies hate me for their loss of status and privilege as Slaves of the Master."

"So *you're* the one who liberated Khailaz from that monster!" Medari exclaimed. "I'm certainly glad the so-called immortal Master turned out to be mortal, after all. Gods bless you!"

"The Goddess *has*." Kyr smiled to himself. "Don't know about the gods, but I hope they hurry up. Mmmph!" he winced suddenly.

"Sorry. That's quite a cramp you have there. Just breathe and relax." Medari continued to massage Kyr's knotted muscles with skillful fingers. Kyr tried not to tense up; but being touched with kindness reminded him of the Kailithana's slow and gentle work to help him learn to endure, and even enjoy, human touch. Remembering Jolanya was more agonizing than any physical pain. He clenched his jaw and swallowed hard, glad for the distraction of Medari's next question.

"What Goddess are you talking about?"

"Zhovanya was our Goddess before the Soul-Drinker usurped her place with his sorcerous powers and his army of red-eyed Watchers. She was a beneficent Goddess, who loved and cared for all of Khailaz."

"Never heard of Her."

"No, most have not. Dauthaz killed anyone who mentioned Her, and took over or destroyed most of her Temples. Only a few hidden places have maintained a connection with Her. The Sanctuary is one of them." Kyr fell silent, fighting a surge of rage and tears.

Sensing his tension, Medari changed the subject. "What is this 'last command' Gauday goes on about?"

"Ah, gods. That's why you are trapped in this hellhole with me. As Dauthaz was dying, he sent out a last command: to make me suffer, but never allow me the mercy of death."

"So *that's* why Gauday left the Sanctuary untouched. He wants revenge on *you*, and has this last command to justify whatever he does to you."

"And he's been twisted by the Soul-Drinker's tortures, as all us Slaves were."

"Doesn't seem to have twisted *you* all that much."

"Only because I was guided to the Sanctuary, where I was healed and received great blessings from Zhovanya."

"Ah, I see." Medari wiped his hands on a rag. "Well, that's the best I can do. Feel better?"

Kyr moved experimentally. "Unfortunately, I think I might live." He propped himself up on one elbow. "Sorry you got caught up in this. If I hadn't killed Dauthaz...."

"Even if the worst happens, I'll still be glad you freed us all from the Soul-Drinker." Medari handed him the small flask. "Finish it. You'll need it."

"Thanks for this, and everything you've done for me." Kyr drained the flask and handed it back, then sagged down onto his pallet, exhausted but more relaxed than he'd been in days.

"Spare me your thanks. I'm not doing this for you."

Medari did not mention that, if not for Kyr, he and his family would still be together, safe at home. But it hung between them like a mourning veil. The healer moved to sit on a stool by the work table, and buried his head in his hands.

Seeing his despair, Kyr thought for a moment about telling him that Rajani would be coming to rescue them; but he decided against it. If Medari slipped and told Gauday, their captor would take them to an even more remote location, making it difficult, if not impossible, for Rajani to find them.

For now, he had to fight off the dogs of dread snapping at his heels. The ice was now gone. How could he protect himself?

He still had the tremendous self-control that he'd learned from his vicious Trainer. And he also had Zhovanya's love, the forgiveness chant, and Her gift of counsel: "Soften." He had Jolanya's secret love, and the golden ball of kailitha in his core. He locked these treasures deep in his heart, now, and girded himself with iron and the knowledge that whatever was done to him stemmed from the terrible lostness of his tormentors' souls. It was all he could do to prepare for the ordeal to come. Then he noticed one more gift: the elixir Medari had given him was now spreading a kindly numbness throughout his body, until he felt he was floating just above it, detached from whatever his body might experience.

In their separate worlds of woe, the two captives awaited the coming darkness.

Luciya jerked awake at the rapping on her door. "What? Who is it?" Rajani opened the door a crack and poked his head in. "The Council will be meeting after breakfast. Better get dressed." He withdrew and closed the door.

"By the Lights!" Luciya grumbled, pulling the covers over her head. "Couldn't they wait 'til afternoon? I could sleep in this lovely bed for a week!" But after a moment, she threw the covers back and got dressed. Stepping out the door, she muttered, "Rajani could have mentioned *where* breakfast is being served."

After a few wrong turns, she found the refectory, a spacious room full of tables and people chatting as they ate. She stood on the wide steps leading down to the main floor, taking in the friendly scene. Large arched windows with their heavy wooden shutters thrown open gave a view of the sun shining on the ocean called the Blue Desert, which sent back sparkles dancing over the newly white-washed ceiling with its dark beams.

"Ah, here you are," said Rajani, coming to stand beside her.

"Oh!" Luciya sighed. "It's so good to be here! The mountains are beautiful, but I love seeing the ocean after all those years cooped up in the Soul Drinker's hellhole. Everything feels so fresh, so open!" She glowed with delight at the ocean's beauty.

Rajani smiled, enjoying a different view. Luciya's dark auburn hair had grown out of the short drudge's cut she'd had to wear as a spy. Now it fell to her shoulders in graceful waves.

As others caught sight of them, many people stood and bowed to them, honoring them for their leadership and sacrifices in the Circle's long effort to rid Khailaz of the Soul-Drinker. "Smile and wave," Rajani said. Luciya complied, her mood darkening as she thought of all they had gone through, and still had to do. She hurried down the steps to the counter, and served herself some porridge, bacon, and tea. Rajani followed suit and they ate quickly.

The Council Hall was one floor above, with arched doors leading onto a terrace built on the roof of the refectory. Most of the twenty-one councilors were already in their seats, chatting with one another and looking ready to begin. But seeing that some were not yet present, Luciya went out onto the terrace. The view of the ocean was magnificent, and she spread her arms, glorying in the airy spaciousness and crisp, briny breeze.

"Let's get started." Rajani's firm, no-nonsense voice carried over the chatter. From the terrace, Luciya sighed, let her arms drop, and dutifully went back inside, taking a seat next to the Warrior Mage in the circle. Each of the twenty-one councilors represented one of the guilds: farmers, merchants, craftspeople, artists, maintainers, parents, the newly restored priestesses, and more. All were wearing their varied traditional garb.

In his black leathers and sleek, dark hair, Rajani struck a somber note in that colorful array. Luciya thought he looked very much like Raven, his soul-kin, as he rose with sober dignity to speak.

"Thank you all for coming to this Council meeting on such short notice. I've called you here because our Liberator, Kyr, has been taken captive by his enemies, that band of former Slaves led by Gauday." Gasps of dismay swept around the circle. Rajani held up his hand. "Kyr is still alive. He turned himself over to his enemies in order to protect Zhovanya's Sanctuary and all the people there from Gauday's band of marauders. Once again, he is valiantly helping his people! And that is why I have called this meeting. I need a band of fighters to rescue our Liberator."

"*You're* the Warrior Mage. Why couldn't *you* protect Kyr and the Sanctuary?" demanded a stout, red-faced merchant.

Rajani frowned at this rudeness, but kept his voice even. "Gauday has over a hundred men. More than half are soldiers from the Soul-Drinker's army. I could not fight so many at once, and the Sanctuary had no protection other than their secrecy."

A lean, austere woman in the dark blue tunic of the Guardians spoke next. "He's probably already dead, isn't he?"

"No, Captain Shayla. Kyr told us that Gauday will obey the Soul-Drinker's last command: to punish Kyr and never grant him the mercy of death."

"Ah. Then we certainly must rescue him." Many others nodded their agreement.

"As I indicated, that's why I'm here. I need a troop of fighters and some good scouts to help me find and rescue him."

The head of the Council, an older woman with silver hair and sharp blue eyes, held the staff of her office. It was blackwood, inlaid with silver stars and the phases of the Moon, topped by a golden sunburst. She nodded to Rajani and asked, "How many fighters do you need?"

"Good to see you, Demalya." Rajani smiled at his old friend. "To be sure of victory, we need twice what Gauday has."

"Two hundred? I'm sorry, but we can only spare a few of the Guard. Most of them are needed to keep order here and in the rest of Khailaz. There is still much disarray, crime, and confusion as we get the new laws and procedures established."

"I see." Rajani paused. "What of the militia that helped overthrow the Soul-Drinker?"

"I regret to tell you this, my friend, but those who did not join the Guard scattered to find their long-lost families."

Luciya jumped up. "But we *can't* leave our Liberator to suffer at the hands of those vicious Slaves!" Shayla and a dozen others called out their agreement.

Demalya banged the floor with her staff of office. "Quiet! We will discuss this matter with the respect and dignity it deserves." She waited until everyone had subsided, then continued. "I understand that something needs to be done for Kyr, but my responsibility—*our* responsibility—is to *all* the people, not just one man, no matter how important he is. We can't have the chaos and violence that followed the Soul-Drinker's demise break out again."

Rajani and Luciya shared a glance of dismay. Used to giving orders, Rajani was unsure how to proceed in this new circle of equals. Luciya reined in her temper and spoke in a conciliatory tone. "How may we proceed to find the fighters we need?"

"That is what we must discuss," said Demalya. And they did—endlessly. Or so it seemed to Luciya.

# Chapter 5

# Savage Carnival

The Moon was dark that night. Jeyal had turned his face away. The Slaves were in a frenzy: drinking; boasting about what they would do to Kyr; shoving and pushing each other or the servants. Tables had been set up in a square around the whipping post at the center of the courtyard. Village youth hurried to set out a lavish feast, stolen from their villages, just as they themselves had been. Sweating boys turned whole geese or haunches of mutton over hissing beds of red-hot coals. Others lit tall torches as the sun disappeared behind the trees. Red-eyed girls set out baskets of bread and bowls of stewed fruit. The odors of roasting meat, resinous torches, and unwashed bodies created a sickening miasma, which wafted around the courtyard on the evening breezes. At every entrance, stolid soldiers stood guard.

When all was in readiness, Gauday paraded across the courtyard and into the infirmary. "Ah, my dear healer, I've come to escort you and our special guest to the celebration."

"I won't be joining you in this depraved carnival," the healer grumbled.

"Oh, yes, you will." Gauday bent his flaming gaze full-force on Medari, who fell to his knees, moaning. Gauday laughed and relented. "Don't forget. I have your precious family. Now bring him out." White-faced and shaking, Medari went and unlocked the cell.

Grateful for the numbing effect of the elixir Medari had given him, Kyr got to his feet, showing no reaction, his eyes distant, his mind on the Zhovanaya chant. "Strip," Gauday commanded. Kyr obeyed impassively. He placed his neatly folded clothing on the table, and set his boots under the table.

Trailed by Medari, Gauday escorted Kyr out onto the porch and exhibited his prize to the crowd. "The traitor is ours!" he crowed loudly. "We shall carry out our Master's last command, beginning tonight, and for the rest of his miserable life! Just remember, he must be kept alive; no choking; no whips, no knives. Otherwise, enjoy yourselves!"

The crowd of Slaves erupted in raucous cheers. Kyr was chained to the whipping post in the center of the yard, so that he could only crouch on his hands and knees. Viro made a flamboyant show of pissing on him. Others threw food at him or took turns punching or kicking him. Yet as wild as they all were, they seemed to be holding back, as if waiting for something.

Gauday watched, laughing gleefully at Kyr's gasps and groans. Tossing back a last cup of wine, he rose and strolled over to the whipping post. Larag came with him, carrying a small pot.

Gauday looked down at him, his eyes avid. Kyr knew that look, and couldn't suppress a slight moan of protest.

"Larag, you're right. He's lost that old silence of his. This will be even more fun than I thought. Alright, men, who wants to be first?"

The Slaves shouted, "Gauday, Gauday, Gauday!"

Gauday bowed. "As you wish, girls. Let a man show you how it's done. Grease him up, Larag."

As the watching Slaves passed around skins of harsh liquor, cheering savagely, Gauday raped him there in the dirt yard of the squalid fort. Larag followed Gauday's example, and then other Slaves did, one by one. Kyr found it all so familiar: the usual nightmare of his life, save for the past year.

Yet everything was different now. Knowing the reality of friendship, kindness, and love, and without the inner ice that had been his protection, he keenly felt the viciousness and degradation of what the Slaves were doing to him. Though Medari's elixir gave him some distance from what was happening to his body, rage rose up in him, making him desperate to fight back in any way he could.

But he could not afford such indulgence, if he wished to protect the Sanctuary and Jolanya. Instead, he clung to Zhovanya's gift of counsel: *"Soften."* As long as he followed Her command, his tormenters' hatred washed through him into the earth; and he could feel the Kailithana's gift, the golden warmth of the kailitha hidden deep in his core, where nothing could touch or harm it. This was his only salvation now.

When it was over, he crouched in his chains, forcing himself to remain still. While the Slaves cheered and clapped, he fought to slow his breathing, to regain control. Slowly, he raised his head and met their gloating stares, ending with Gauday. The cheers died away.

"Zhovanya nara lo" Kyr said to him. "The Goddess forgives you, as do I."

In the edgy silence, Gauday gave a strident hoot of laughter. "Well, lads, I hope you've all enjoyed tonight's entertainment, but I'm afraid our guest has had enough. Don't fret. He's ours now. He'll have lots of time for your attentions." He waved his hands expansively. "Enjoy yourselves!" With a ragged cheer, the Slaves returned to their drinking, and began groping the young villagers.

Medari started to go to Kyr, but Gauday beckoned him over. "Our guest is not enjoying our attentions fully. What, pray tell, did you give him, old man?"

"What I wish I had for myself. Shanawa elixir."

"My dear healer, didn't I tell you not to protect the traitor from his punishment? Yes, I know I did."

Gauday's eyes flared red. Medari clasped his head and groaned in pain. After a moment, Gauday's eyes darkened. Medari fell silent, and rubbed his aching head.

"Defy me once more, and you will watch your family beg for mercy before I finally let them die. There are other healers in the world."

"I was following *your* damned orders!" the healer protested. "I gave him the elixir to help him survive this—this gods-cursed brutality. Don't worry. I have no more, and I cannot make it myself. He will suffer as much as you like."

"Good, good!" Gauday laughed, in a sudden squall of ghastly gaiety. "Glad to hear it. Now I must get back to the party. Craith, take care of our guest." He sauntered back toward the head table, chuckling.

Medari glared at his back, then hurried toward the infirmary. Craith, who, along with his men, had taken no part in tormenting the captive, unlocked Kyr's chains. "Can you walk?" he asked.

Kyr tried to stand, but his abused body refused to obey. Craith gestured to two of his soldiers. "You two, take him to the infirmary." The two men grabbed Kyr's ankles and started to drag him across the yard.

"No, you louts!" Craith growled. "Pick him up. Don't forget. We are not Slaves. We are *soldiers*."

51

"Yes sir." A bit shame-faced, the two men carried Kyr back to the infirmary.

Kyr collapsed on his pallet, shuddering, and retching into the basin Medari swiftly fetched. Afterwards, Medari knelt by his side, wiped his face, raised his head, and placed a cup to his lips. "Drink this. It will help."

Kyr gulped the bitter potion down, and his stomach quickly calmed. The healer sponged him clean, then tended to his bruises and cuts. As the potion took effect, Kyr stopped shaking, his aches and pains receded, and he began to feel drowsy.

"Thanks, Medari."

Shame-faced yet still courageous, like a soldier facing a dishonorable death, Medari met his gaze. "I should at least know your name. I'm sure it is not 'cur,' as they have been calling you."

"I'm *Kyr*." It felt good to assert his existence as a person in this small way.

"I'm sorry I have to be part of this." Choking back a storm of rage, shame, and grief, the healer stumbled to his room and closed the door.

Bone-weary, Kyr turned on his stomach and buried his face in the crook of his arm, wondering how he could endure without the ice. Even his victims had been granted the mercy of death, sooner or later. He was not so lucky. Thankfully, Medari's potion brought sleep down on him like a hammer blow.

Medari, on the other hand, got little sleep.

Long into the night, Gauday's men drank and shouted, forcing themselves on weeping girls and stone-faced boys, fighting amongst themselves, trying to convince themselves they were happy with their great "victory" over one unarmed man.

Late the next morning, Kyr woke to find Gauday sitting on a stool just outside the cell.

"Ah. Did you sleep well, my dear? I am so sorry for the crude welcome you had last night. The men are very angry with you for killing our Master, you know. You were a very bad boy, and they must have their revenge." He shrugged in a mimicry of helplessness, as if both he and Kyr were at the mercy of the angry band of Slaves.

"I've got this healer here to take care of you. We'll do what we can to protect you. We can keep you here one more day before the men will insist on continuing your punishment. It's the best I can do, dear boy." Gauday leaned forward, reached through the bars, and caressed Kyr's cheek. Smiling at Kyr's involuntary shudder, he rose and departed.

Covered with bruises and cuts, Kyr ached in every muscle and joint. That was bad enough. Worse was the feeling that he was drowning in a pool of sewage. *Last night—without the ice.... Gods, now I know how my victims felt.* He cringed, imagining his victims suffering as he debased and tortured them. *I always had the ice before, but they didn't. This time, I must suffer as they did.* Something did not quite ring true, but he shook his head. *It* is *part of my Atonement, or Zhovanya wouldn't have sent me here.* With this astringent consolation, he felt more prepared to endure his situation.

The next day, he was again chained naked to the whipping post. That first day in the yard of the fort was the worst. Led by Larag and Viro, the Slaves took turns venting their hollow hatred on Kyr with fists and feet, delighted to have a target for the painful emptiness of their souls. Drinking ale, and egging each other on, they made games out of throwing small stones or offal at him, pissed on him, and derided him with meaningless insults. Gauday took no part, merely watching from the porch of his quarters, sitting on a stool, sipping from a goblet.

A few off-duty soldiers watched and jeered at Kyr, but when they tried to take part in Kyr's torment, Larag snarled, "Hands off! The traitorous cur is *our* meat."

"Yeah, dog meat, you're ours, forever!" Viro spat in Kyr's face.

Kyr wiped his face and took a deep breath. "No, I belong to Zhovanya, our true Goddess, and so do you, my brother. She loves and forgives us all."

"Shut up, whoreson!" Viro slugged Kyr in the face and began kicking him. Kyr crouched down low, trying to protect his belly.

At a signal from Gauday, Larag grabbed the enraged Viro and pulled him away from Kyr. "That's enough," Larag said. "Gotta keep him alive to enjoy our attentions. Wouldn't be much fun if you killed him before we barely got started. Besides, it's almost sunset."

"Awright, awright. Lemme go!" Viro stalked off a few paces, muttering to himself.

"Come on, men," Gauday said. "I've been saving a bottle of good brandy to celebrate our successful hunt for this cursed traitor." Larag planted one booted foot on Kyr's back and shoved him face-down into the dirt. The gang of Slaves cheered and followed Larag toward Gauday's quarters. Still fuming, Viro went with them.

Kyr resumed the crouch that was all his chains allowed him, and dabbed at the blood dripping from his split lip. Reminding himself that he had been just like them, he made himself relax and breathe slowly. *They are my brothers. I can't start hating them if I want to reach them with Zhovanya's message of forgiveness.*

As darkness fell, he leaned against the post, aching, exhausted, and filthy. Lamp light glowed from windows in the surrounding buildings. Raucous laughter erupted from Gauday's quarters, on the opposite side of the yard from the infirmary. Good-natured cursing and the rattle of dice sounded from the soldiers' barracks near the back gate. Erratic breezes rattled loose shingles and set an unlatched shutter banging sporadically. Kyr had never felt so alone, so helpless.

He smiled. *You're clever at breaking a man's spirit, Gauday, but it won't work. I have gifts you can't imagine: gifts from Zhovanya; gifts from my beloved; gifts from my friends. They will sustain me until Rajani arrives.* He settled into meditation. *Zhovanya nara lo, Zhovanya nara lo, Zhovanya nara lo.*

Later that night, Gauday showed up, trailed by a frightened young village lad carrying a bundle, a tray, and a torch. Kyr forced himself to his knees, determined not to huddle at his immaculate captor's feet.

"I'm so sorry, my boy. As I said, my hands are tied. I've forbidden the men to bother you after sundown. It's the best I can do for now. Here, boy, hold that torch where I can see the poor man." He examined Kyr carefully. "Just a few bruises and scratches. No need to bother Medari tonight. Let me make you a bit more comfortable." He loosened the chains so that Kyr would be able to lie down.

"That's better, isn't it? And I've brought your supper and a nice, warm blanket." He snapped his fingers. The village boy set small jug of water and a bowl of stew by Kyr's knees and draped a ragged blanket over his shoulders. "Enjoy." Gauday sounded as if he were hosting a dinner party.

Kyr eyed his captor, wondering what game his old nemesis was playing. He decided that the only way to handle Gauday's strangely solicitous behavior was with unfailing neutral politeness. "Thank you, sir."

"Why, you're quite welcome, my boy." Gauday sounded pleased. "Have a pleasant evening." He headed for his quarters, dragging the reluctant village boy by the hand.

"Poor lad," Kyr whispered. "Goddess, please let Rajani come soon, for the sake of the villagers and Medari, as well as for my sake." He looked at the stew. Gauday had, of course, failed to give him a spoon or fork. He picked up the jug and drank most of the water, then wet a corner of his blanket to clean his filthy hands. He managed to eat half the stew before collapsing from exhaustion.

As he drifted toward sleep, a dark shadow slunk across the yard toward him. It was too small to be a man. *Gods, what now?* He raised himself up onto one elbow.

# Chapter 6

# Small Blessings

One of the fort's skinny dogs sidled closer, whining hopefully. In the fitful light from the torches set at intervals about the fort's inner perimeter, the bitch looked almost as wretched and abused as Kyr felt. He tensed, ready to fend her off, but the Goddess's word came into his mind.

"Alright, dog, I'm too tired to eat it anyway." He lay down and curled up in his blanket.

Listening to her slurp down the remainder of the stew, he fell into an exhausted sleep. Late in the night, he woke. Though the rest of him was cold, his back was warm. In too much pain to puzzle about it, he moved a little to give a different bruise the chance to complain about the hard ground. There was a sleepy protest. The dog adjusted to Kyr's new position, making a contented clucking sound with her tongue as she settled down again. Kyr felt obscurely comforted. At least *one* creature here did not hate him.

Sleep, having driven off the worst of his exhaustion, retired from the field. Anger, hatred, and despair danced seductively at the edges of his mind, but he reminded himself of his purpose: to shield the Sanctuary, his friends, and his beloved Jolanya from Gauday and his minions. He called up his last sight of the Kailithana, remembered holding her hands as the kailitha poured into him, hearing her whisper her secret to him, seeing the love in her eyes for him, only for him. The golden warmth of the kailitha flared up, and his heart was joyous for a few blessed moments.

Then a chill breeze cut through his meager blanket, bringing him back to harsh reality. He choked back a cry of loss and anguish at the cruelty of finding and losing Jolanya's love in almost the same moment;

of entering a world of friendship, kindness, and forgiveness, only to return to Gauday's world of hateful depravity. Looking up at the stars where he had once danced with the Goddess, he whispered, "*Zhovanya, forgive me. This one punishment, I must refuse.*"

In order to survive in this new hell, where any reminder of beauty, kindness, or love was intolerably painful, he had to refuse. Methodically, he buried the memories of his friends, of the Sanctuary, and of his beloved Jolanya, locking her love deep in his heart. Though he could not let himself think of it, still, like an ember under ashes, her love was there, warming and strengthening his soul.

If he kept his attention only on Zhovanya, he could endure his Atonement. Otherwise, he knew he would be lost. As the stars wheeled overhead, he filled his mind with the chant. *Zhovanya nara lo. Zhovanya nara lo. Zhovanya nara lo.*

Misery assumed a routine. The days began at sunrise, with Craith taking him to the latrine. The redhead left Kyr's chains loose enough that he could sit and lean against the whipping post. Then Medari brought him gray porridge and strengthening potions disguised as hot tea, cleaned him up, and tended to his cuts and bruises. The fort was tranquil, as the Slaves were still abed. Under Craith's command, soldiers and captive villagers went about their daily tasks in an orderly fashion. Kyr took advantage of this peaceful time to meditate, focusing on the forgiveness chant. After a few days, Craith and a few other soldiers were to be found sitting nearby, quietly repairing clothing or horse tack.

In the afternoons, he suffered the crude and vicious attentions of the drunken Slaves, lost in their witless nightmare of brutality and revenge. But using the same iron discipline that the Soul Drinker's Trainer had drilled into him, he kept his mind focused on the forgiveness chant, even while the Slaves were tormenting him. When he forgot and glared at them in helpless rage, they laughed and redoubled their cruel attentions. Yet when he could soften and endure without reaction, they lost interest and left off sooner.

Only after sunset was he safe from them. After a long day exposed to their scorn, to the heat of the Sun, to the dust and flies of the yard, he longed for the soft blues and grays of twilight that heralded his safe time. After another trip to the latrine, Medari brought him supper: gray stew, stale bread, and more tea, this one with a potion to help him sleep. Sometimes Gauday brought the food, exclaiming in apparent pity over Kyr's bruises or filthiness.

After that first night, Kyr made himself eat most of what he was given, though he saved a bit for the bitch who had adopted him. She turned out to be a blessing, fending off other night prowlers who sought to steal his food. Growling low and fierce, she attacked any dog or rat that came too near. At first light, she abandoned him to hide from the bored and vicious Slaves. Yet every night, she slunk back to share Kyr's supper and curl up with him. He found her warmth and companionship a comfort. It was more than he had had in the Master's compound, and he was grateful.

Late one night, after an artful beating by Viro, he and the dog were curled up together. Aching and miserable, he couldn't keep his mind on the chant. Unbidden memories breached his defenses, bringing back Naran's patient, obdurate kindness; Gaela teaching him how to sculpt; Jolanya's gentle touch. Fighting back tears, he clutched the dog tight. She made no protest, only licked his face gently. At this unexpected sympathy, his tears broke loose and he buried his face against her warm, rank body, sobbing silently.

When this storm had passed, he felt calmer. He gave the dog a grateful squeeze. "Dog, you are my only friend here. Can't keep calling you 'dog.' What is your name?" She said nothing. "Well, I'll call you what you are to me—Friend. How about that?" Friend sighed gustily and tucked her nose under her tail.

Through the long nights when painful bruises kept sleep away, Kyr studied the steady march of the stars, and the silvery, shifting face of the Moon. When Jeyal's face was full and bright, he remembered the night that the Moon Lord had shown him what his Atonement should be. He started trying to share with his Slave brothers the message of Zhovanya's redemption and forgiveness. They could not listen, but jeered or raged at him, and prolonged their abuse. For many nights, he prayed to Jeyal for guidance in how to reach them, but the Moon Lord remained cool and distant, dwindling each night, finally turning His face away altogether. Dark of the Moon

Discouraged, Kyr retreated into silence. He could not see how he was to carry out his chosen Atonement. He was sustained by the golden flame of the kailitha in his core, though sometimes despair nearly snuffed out that flame. To keep it burning, he buried his head on his knees, blocking out the walls of hate that surrounded him, remembering Zhovanya's Grace, and silently singing the forgiveness chant.

Twice, Medari insisted that Kyr be allowed two days' respite in the infirmary. The healer didn't dare do more, for fear of losing his credibility with Gauday. And so, between Medari's care, Friend's companionship, and these few days of rest, Kyr survived the first month of his captivity.

As the Moon began to wax again, most of the Slaves grew bored with Kyr's silent, yielding endurance. Left alone, he surreptitiously tugged and pulled on his chains, not to break loose but as exercise, to keep his strength up as best he could. Otherwise, he had little to do but observe his surroundings. When he tired of the dusty squalor of the yard, he kept his eyes on the treetops swaying and nodding beyond the walls of the fort. Small brown or gray birds flitted back and forth among the branches. Purplish birds with pointed wings swooped through the air. Large black birds cawed and croaked, fighting over scraps from the trash heaps outside the walls. Sometimes, they simply soared overhead, circling and diving as if dancing with the wind. Once, when an eagle chanced to soar high above in the pristine blue, Kyr dropped his eyes to the ground, his heart aching with envy.

Late one afternoon, Viro and Larag staggered toward him. As they leaned over him, leering and laughing, he choked on their fume-laden breath, his skin crawling with disgust. Viro glanced over his shoulder toward Gauday's quarters, then pulled something from his tunic.

"Gotta li'l present for ya, cur." He held a flail of knotted leather strips before Kyr's face. Kyr clenched his teeth and kept his face blank.

Larag grinned, his scarred face turning into a demonic mask. "He been gettin' off too easy, right, Viro?"

"Righ', righ'. Time 'e got some real punshi – punishent - ment." They both giggled. Viro took a long swig from a flask and handed it to Larag.

Kyr wished they'd just get on with it. He slid the blanket off his shoulders. No use getting it ripped to shreds. Then he went into his defensive crouch, offering them his back as target.

"Look, Viro. He's all ready for ya. Jus' what he been waitin' for."

60

Viro brought the flail down on Kyr's back, but it hardly stung at all. Viro stumbled and nearly fell on top of Kyr. He grabbed the whipping post and dropped the flail.

"Yer too drunk." Larag lunged for the flail. "Lemme do it."

This time the flail whistled as it came down, and stung sharply. Kyr flinched but kept silent.

Larag raised his arm for another blow. With a gasp, he dropped the flail and fell to his knees, holding his head.

"Ow, ow, ow!" Viro fell to the ground, wailing and writhing.

A demon with glowing red eyes strode toward them. "I TOLD you. No whips, no knives." Gauday kicked his groveling cronies, then bellowed, "CRAITH! GET YOUR MEN OUT HERE!" As he waited for the soldiers, the fire went out of his eyes, and the two Slaves' howls subsided to whimpers. Gauday rubbed his forehead as if it hurt him greatly, revealing a red scar that banded his forehead.

Kyr's hand went to his throat, where a similar scar circled his own neck. *Gods! Gauday must have been wearing the Crown when Rajani's ritual destroyed the Rod and Collar. It must have destroyed the Crown too.* Remembering the foul miasma that had clamped itself over his face when the Collar burned into smoke, he looked at Gauday with sad compassion. *With that foulness inside him, how will he ever hear the truth of Zhovanya's love and forgiveness?*

"What're you looking at, cur?" Red flame flared anew in Gauday's eyes. Kyr clenched his jaw against an assault of sickening pain, but it was only a pale shadow of the agony Gauday had inflicted before. After a blessedly brief moment, Gauday grunted and the pain ceased. As Kyr breathed a silent sigh of relief, Craith and three of his soldiers arrived. Gauday gestured at Viro and Larag, who were cowering at his feet.

"These two idiots defied my orders," he told the soldiers. "Strip them and chain them in the traitor's place until tomorrow evening." He tossed Viro's flail to Craith. "Lock this up with the rest of the weapons."

"Very good, sir." Craith nodded at Kyr. "What do I do with him?"

"Ah." Gauday smiled down at his captive. "Well, my dear, I'll grant you a rest in the infirmary. Enjoy!" He dug a key out of his pocket and handed it to Craith, then glared down at the sullen Slaves. "As for you two, don't dare to interrupt me with such foolery again." He started back to his quarters, muttering, "Gods, I need a drink."

61

Craith unlocked the chains and helped Kyr to his feet while the soldiers stripped the subdued Viro and Larag of their ragtag finery. Kyr choked back laughter at their drunken confusion and rage. For the price of one lash, he now got an entire day of rest, while they took his place.

Medari examined Kyr's back. "Didn't break the skin. Just needs a little numbing salve. Let's get you cleaned up first."

After a thorough wash, Kyr felt half-human again. He wrapped the clean blanket Medari had given him around his waist and sat on his pallet in his cell, combing his wet hair with his fingers. He tried braiding it, but the smooth, wavy strands came loose in an instant. He pushed it back from his face. His hair and beard were longer than they'd ever been and made him feel like some shaggy stranger. He smiled ruefully. *At least I'm a* clean *stranger.*

"Here." Medari reached through the bars, offering a leather tie.

"Thanks."

Medari turned back to his work with mortar and pestle. Kyr sighed, wishing the older man would talk with him. He pulled his hair back at the nape of his neck, and captured it with the tie before it could escape. Glad for the safety and semi-privacy of his cell, he settled down to meditate, but his mind was chewing over what had just happened.

Thinking of Viro and Larag chained to the post made him smile, but then he sighed. *Now they'll hate me even more, and be even less likely to hear Zhovanya's message.* His head ached with a remnant of that sickening pain Gauday had inflicted. *No wonder the men all fear him. Feels as if your brains are being twisted inside out.*

*And how* did *Gauday gain this power to inflict such pain? Ah, yes. The smoke from when the Crown burned,* that's *what gave him this power. Thank the gods it hurts him to use it. Keeps him from using it more often. Gods know what else that evil smoke is doing to him.*

He slumped against the wall, ignoring the sting from the lash mark on his back. *I've yet to reach Gauday or any of my brother Slaves with the message of Zhovanya's forgiveness.* Weighed down by the misery of his captivity and the impossibility of his mission to help his Slave brothers, he couldn't reach the peace he needed for meditation. The comfort of his pallet and the refuge of sleep proved irresistible.

Craith returned Kyr to the whipping post the next evening. Larag and Viro hurried off to their quarters, shame-faced and furious. Kyr could hear their fellow Slaves taunting them unmercifully. For a few days, the two cronies made themselves scarce. While he enjoyed their absence, he worried what their revenge would be.

On the night of the Full Moon, Gauday strolled up, dressed in an elegant wine-red jacket, pristine white tunic, and fine black leggings and boots. His current houseboy set down a large basket, and placed a wooden chair in front of Kyr.

Gauday seated himself and declared genially, "I've brought you a treat, my boy." He waved a hand. The boy reached into the basket and carefully handed Kyr a plate of sliced roast venison with carrots and onions sautéed in butter, then retrieved a bottle of wine and two pewter goblets from the basket.

The delicious aromas nearly had Kyr drooling, but he looked at the plate in dismay. How was he to eat such fine food with his bare, filthy hands? He knew his tormenter was trying to humiliate him. The problem was that it was working. Gauday's condescending smile was the final insult. Rage snapped its leash and Kyr snarled, "Thank you but I'm not hungry."

"Why, I'm sure that's not true. What's the problem, old friend?" Gauday examined Kyr, a suppressed smile twitching his lips. "Ah. Feeling fastidious, are you? You *are* rather filthy. Here, let me help." Gauday snapped his fingers and the boy set a fork and knife on Kyr's plate.

"There you are, my dear."

He eyed the knife, his heart racing, his muscles automatically tensing for the kill. How many times had he cut a sacrifice's throat for the Master? One strong slash across the jugular, and he'd never have to play these odious games with Gauday again.

"Now, now. You wouldn't want to harm me, would you, my boy? After all, if you did kill me, who would keep my men from sacking your precious Sanctuary or killing Medari's family? Who would protect *you* from them?"

Kyr looked down, grinding his teeth. *He's right. Only their fear of him keeps them in check. They'd take their whips and knives to me the moment Gauday was dead, then head straight for the Sanctuary. Oh gods, I suppose I should be grateful to him.* The thought made him choke.

"Ah. Need something to drink?" Gauday filled the two goblets and handed one to Kyr.

There was nothing to be gained by fighting Gauday. In fact, that would only please his captor. He took a deep breath, exhaling his rage, calling on his Goddess-given word of counsel once again. As he softened, he smiled, realizing it would be a victory to enjoy this small pleasure despite Gauday's attempt to demean him. He set aside the goblet of wine, picked up the knife and fork, and began to eat. Chewing slowly, he savored the richness of the gravy-covered meat, the sweetness of the carrots and onions.

"It's been two months since we brought you back where you belong. I thought we should celebrate." Gauday raised his goblet. Having nothing to celebrate, Kyr ignored his.

"Drink up, my dear," Gauday growled, his eyes flaring an ominous red.

Kyr took a miserly sip of the harsh wine, but his tormenter leaned forward and forced him to drain his goblet.

"Ah, that's better." Gauday drained his own goblet and refilled it.

In moments, Kyr's face was hot, and he was slightly giddy. As Kyr continued eating, Gauday helped himself to more wine, and chatted about the weather, the latest fight between two Slaves, how many village girls had Slave babies in their bellies. Then he refilled their goblets, crossed his legs, and leaned back in a nonchalant manner.

"It seems that most of my men have tired of punishing you. You have endured it all quite well. How *do* you manage, my dear?"

Kyr heard the frustration in Gauday's voice, and smiled into his empty plate. Though fuzzy-headed from the wine, he tried to think how best to answer. He had to take this chance to reach Gauday.

"Zhovanya's love gives me strength. She forgives us all, Gauday, even you. All you have to do is ask."

"Traitor!" Gauday slapped Kyr in the face. "Don't speak to me of that bitch-goddess. Our glorious Master dethroned her ages ago." He stood and straightened his jacket. "I see you have learned nothing, my dear. I will have to devise a stricter regimen for you. Don't you worry. You are mine, now and forever. I am your Master, and you will learn to obey and love me, just as we did Dauthaz." He strode off, carrying the bottle and his goblet. His young servant lagged behind, gave Kyr a curious glance, then followed his master, carrying Gauday's chair and Kyr's plate, goblet, and utensils.

Kyr sagged against the post, rubbing his stinging face. *Gods and demons, what am I doing, trying to reach these madmen? A few words from me can never overcome a lifetime of brutality under the Soul-Drinker's inhuman rule. Look at all it took for me to recover something of my humanity, all the help I had.* He gazed up at the cold, bright face in the heavens. Jeyal seemed to look down upon him with sad reproach for his failure to reach even one of his Slave brothers with Zhovanya's message of love and forgiveness.

*Jeyal, what You asked seems impossible. Did I misunderstand your message?* A thin cloud veiled the Moon's face, giving it a more sinister cast. He shivered with an inner chill. *Or are You laughing at me?* He curled up under his blanket, despair nibbling at his dwindling hoard of faith. After the last window went dark, Friend came and licked his face, but there was no food for her. She sighed and settled down with him anyway. He hugged her close, feeling a little less bleak.

The next morning, he watched as soldiers bullied a gang of villagers with shovels and buckets into an unused storage room. From the amount of dirt being carried out, it was clear they were digging a deep hole inside. He frowned. It might have nothing to do with him, but if it did, there was nothing he could do about it. He shrugged and returned to his silent chanting.

For a quarter-moon, the work in the storage room continued. Kyr couldn't help wondering what Gauday was up to. Surely it would be nothing good. After digging out barrows-full of dirt, the workers carried old boards and tools into the storage room. Then Kyr heard unfamiliar rasping and pounding sounds coming from within the storage room. He was puzzling over these noises when Gauday sauntered up.

"Curious, are you, my boy?" Gauday chuckled. "You will soon find out what they are doing. It's all for you, my dear." He patted Kyr on the head, and walked away, still chuckling. Hot with humiliation and rage, Kyr bit his lip against useless curses, but couldn't help whispering to the indifferent earth, "Merciless gods, I *hate* him!" He clenched his fists and silently pulled against his chains as hard as he could, until he was sweaty and exhausted.

# Part Three ~ Shades of Hell

*"Be soft. Do not let the world make you hard.*
*Do not let pain make you hate.*
*Do not let bitterness steal your sweetness."*

—Kurt Vonnegut

# Chapter 7

# Blessed Solitude

Raucous chaos filled the courtyard. Slaves cursed at scurrying village boys, who were packing saddlebags and saddling horses. The boys tugged on cinches and cursed the horses. The horses huffed and stomped, and shook their heads. The dissonant ring of clashing swords added to the clamor as some soldiers practiced their swordplay, adding the odor of their sweat to the odors of horse piss and manure filling the warm air. Other soldiers sat on the porches, honing their weapons and bantering. Slaves and soldiers alike were obviously glad to be doing something besides sit around the fort.

Kyr leaned against the whipping post, utterly ignored and glad of it. He was almost enjoying watching all the activity, but the dust stirred up by feet and hooves made him cough. He buried his face in his blanket. A few moments later, there was a sudden quiet, and Kyr looked up, and tensed. *Merciless gods, what now?*

Gauday was stalking across the courtyard toward him, eyes fixed on him like a hawk spying a mouse. Boys, men, and horses quickly shifted out of his way. He stopped by the post and looked down at Kyr, shoving his tangled brown hair back with an impatient hand. "Well, my boy, we're off to gather supplies and new servants. Can't leave you out here all alone, can we?"

As he unlocked Kyr's chains, Gauday added with a gleeful smirk, "I've had a special place prepared just for you. I'm sure you'll like it." He grabbed Kyr by one arm and hauled him to his feet. "Come along, my pet. I know you've been curious about what I've been building over here."

Clutching his blanket around his waist for a scrap of dignity, Kyr stumbled after his tormenter on legs unused to walking. Gauday led him into the storage room, where there had been so much excavation and construction going on over the past half-moon.

The Slave Viro had his blond hair back in a braid so tight it gave his face a skeletal look. He was playing cards with one of the soldiers, a balding, burly man with the muscled arms of a woodcutter. They slouched on benches on either side of a rough-hewn table, their swords near to hand.

"Viro, Wareg, here's your new houseguest." The two men rose and gave Kyr mocking bows. Viro fingered the flail hanging from his belt, while Wareg bent down and opened a trap door in the floor, revealing crude wooden stairs leading down into darkness. Gauday lit one of the oil lamps on the table and waved it toward the stairs. "After you, my dear."

Ignoring the smirking guards, Kyr skirted the table and started down. At the bottom, there was a small space just big enough for two people to stand, and a heavy wooden door, which stood ajar, revealing only darkness.

Gauday opened the door wide and held up the lamp, revealing a windowless prison that was a mere three paces in either direction. "Here's your new home. Quite snug, isn't it?"

Kyr stood staring at the black hole that awaited him, ready to engulf his soul. A sudden blow to the back of his head knocked him against the wooden door, and he grabbed the edge of the door to keep from falling.

"Answer me when I speak to you!" Gauday snapped.

Stunned, Kyr took a deep breath and righted himself. "Yes, sir. Very snug."

"Sorry, dear boy. I quite forgot my manners." Gauday fluttered his hands. "I was so sure you would appreciate your little retreat here after your time in the courtyard."

"Thank you, sir." Sudden violence in the midst of ludicrous courtesy had Kyr nearly hysterical with laughter. He bit his lip hard.

"In you go, my boy."

Eager to get away from Gauday before he burst out laughing, Kyr stepped inside and turned around. Gauday peered at him with an odd blend of apprehension and avidity.

*Why is he looking at me like that? Does he want me to beg him not to leave me in here? Well, he shall not have what he wants this time.* Kyr smiled. "This is a nice change. Thank you."

Gauday's face fell, as if a long-awaited gift had been snatched away from him. "We'll be gone for a half-moon or more," he snarled. "I do hope I remember to let you out when we return." He slammed the door and locked it, leaving Kyr in utter darkness.

Wareg and Viro looked up from their card game as Gauday stomped up the stairs towards them, emerging from the trap door like a red-eyed demon from the lower depths. Gesturing at their swords, he ordered, "Wareg, get those damn things out of here. And that cursed flail too," he added, glaring at Viro.

"But what if…." Viro's protest ended in a grunt of pain. "Sorry, sir." Eyes icy with resentment, he handed his flail to Wareg.

"If you two can't handle that half-starved cur without weapons, you can come visit my special room. I might get some use out of you, there." Gauday's eyes returned to their usual dark brown. He tugged at his tunic, smoothed his hair, and went out, calling for his horse.

Wareg left to take their weapons to the armory. Alone, Viro muttered, "Filthy cur! Keeping me from going on the raid! I'll make him pay somehow."

Meanwhile, Kyr leaned his head against the door and laughed until tears rolled down his face. *Oh, Gauday's face! He was so surprised and frustrated! He was sure I'd beg and plead not to be shut in here. He should try being chained out in the yard for a couple of months. This is a black hole, but it's* private. *Gods, what a relief!*

Still shaky from Gauday's punch, he took some deep breaths to calm himself, and began to stretch muscles cramped from crouching in his chains for so long. Then he felt his way around the small space. The walls were lined with rough wooden planks, the floor and low ceiling felt like hard-packed clay. A fetid odor announced the purpose of the bucket by the door. A straw pallet was the only other furnishing.

He sat on the pallet and wrapped up in his blanket. The cool darkness was welcome after being so long in the summer sun. His heart lifted at the thought of an entire half-moon free from the attentions of his polite tormenter, and the cruder persecutions of the Slaves. Just to be alone, unobserved and undisturbed, was a peerless blessing.

The darkness of this black pit reminded Kyr of a different darkness, the shimmering blackness of Zhovanya's heart, where his soul had been healed. In the privacy of his new prison, Kyr allowed himself to remember this most sacred time, when he had first met the Goddess in the Temple at the Sanctuary, and She had danced for him:

*A golden Goddess danced in a vast starry void, glorious and majestic, fierce and serene. As She danced, She changed. She aged and withered into a silver-haired crone, eyes deep with awareness and wisdom. She died and rotted away. Her white bones danced in the black void. She was reborn as a chubby infant, grew into a golden young girl dancing in happy innocence, then a maiden dancing in sensuous abandon with Her lover. The Goddess died young, torn apart by childbirth. She was raped and killed. She was a mad-eyed killer, dripping with blood. She was holy and hideous. She was terrible and beautiful. For eternity, She danced through endless permutations of life and death, holiness and defilement.*

*Zhovanya's lambent glance called him into Her heart. He was gently held, his aching heart, his wounded soul immersed in Her love and peace. Long he rested there in the shimmering blackness, in the intimacy of Her vast heart.*

*After a sacred eternity, Kyr became aware again of Her magnificent golden form, still dancing, now in a dance of celebration. He watched in awe, knowing that every action, every soul, every creature is a part of Her Dance. The Goddess knows all the joys and horrors of life, and keeps dancing.*

Now Kyr felt again Her great love and forgiveness. Gratitude and reverence filled his soul. In a quiet, rusty voice, he began to chant. "Zhovanya nara lo, Zhovanya nara lo, Zhovanya nara lo."

As he chanted, he prayed for his own release, prayed that Rajani and his men would come soon to free him, Medari, and the villagers. As his heart warmed with his love for the Goddess, his prayers expanded. *Zhovanya, show me how to help my brothers. Bless me with the words to reach their hearts. By Your grace, may they be liberated from their prisons of hate and rage.* After a time, the darkness expanded into a starry void, and

Zhovanya's love  embraced him. Still chanting, his voice began to soar in joyous worship.

"QUIT YOUR YOWLING, you filthy cur!"

The angry shout shocked Kyr into silence. Viro kicked the prison's door a couple of times before stomping back up the stairs, and slamming the trap door shut with a thunderous bang.

Resting his head on his knees, Kyr tried to regain contact with the Goddess, but all that came was a plea from his tired heart, *Let it end. Let this end.* He curled up under his thin blanket on the straw pallet, missing Friend's warmth against his back. His mind began scratching at every corner in a vain search for escape from his dilemma. With severe focus, he made himself silently repeat the chant, instead. Eventually, he fell into a fitful sleep, despite the cold and damp.

It had been three or four days now since Gauday had locked him in this black hole. In the darkness, Kyr wasn't sure how long it had been. No one had come, not even to bring him water to drink. With hunger and thirst clawing at him, he was finding it more and more difficult to keep his mind on the chant. Worse, he was losing his grip on himself. Had he ever been anything but the slave and plaything of the Soul-Drinker, and now Gauday? Were Zhovanya, the Sanctuary, Naran, and Jolanya merely wraiths of his imagination, delusions caused by thirst, hunger and darkness? Lying in a daze on his pallet under his thin blanket, shivering, he begged sleep or death to come for him, but they too ignored him.

The thump of the trap door being flung open startled Kyr from his daze. Someone came down the stairs and the key rattled in the lock. Kyr prayed for water if nothing else. The door of his prison opened and a dark figure loomed against the light filtering down the stairs behind him. For Kyr, even that dim light was too bright and he squeezed his eyes shut.

"Wareg, take that slop bucket up and empty it. Bring it back clean." Medari spoke with such cold contempt that Wareg obeyed without argument.

"Medari?" Kyr spoke in a cracked whisper, all that his dry throat would allow. "Is that you? I can't see...."

"Yes, it's me, Kyr," the healer said in a far gentler tone. "Don't worry. Your eyes will get used to the light in a few moments. Here's some water." He helped Kyr sit up and placed a cup in his hands. "Slowly, now. You don't want it coming back up."

Thirst was clawing at Kyr's throat but he made himself take measured sips of the water. It was the gods' nectar, and his body its desperate worshipper. His hands began to shake. "Here, take it." He handed the cup back to the healer, not wanting to spill a drop of the precious liquid. Then he hunched over and wrapped his arms around his middle, fighting the sobs rising up now that relief had arrived.

"Gods, I'm sorry," Medari apologized. "Those damnable guards wouldn't let me down here until now."

Kyr swallowed hard and straightened up, then tried opening his eyes. They greedily gulped in the faint light coming through the half-open door. *Gods, it's good to be able to see something—anything!*

Medari handed him a large bowl of soup. "Now eat this as slowly as you can, the broth first."

"Thank you."

"I deserve no thanks." The healer avoided Kyr's eyes.

Kyr shrugged and sipped at the broth. It was difficult not to gulp it down, ravenous as he was; but he took it slowly, savoring each sip, then each lump of unidentifiable meat and vegetable. Even so, the bowl was soon empty. He handed it back to the healer. "How long have I been down here?"

"Nearly four days." Medari said. "Sorry, they won't let me linger. I'll be back as often as I can." Medari returned to the world of light above, leaving behind a jug of water, a loaf of bread, and a thick wool blanket, ragged but clean.

Wrapping up in his old and new blankets, Kyr sat for a while. As his body absorbed the water and food, he began to feel more like himself. The healer's brief visit had only deepened the loneliness of his lightless prison, but he was grateful for the water, food, and especially the extra blanket.

When he felt some energy returning, he got up and did some slow stretches and Flowing Poses. Soon tired, he sat and wrapped himself in the blankets again. Repeating the chant in his mind, he opened his heart to Zhovanya.

The enforced fast had left him feeling as empty as a desert. The water and food had quieted the cravings of his body but had not touched this emptiness. He went deeper into meditation than ever before, all concerns and thoughts lost in a deep inner stillness. Into this void came the Presence of the Goddess, engulfing him in Her vast silence. His wearied soul absorbed Her compassion as his body had the food and water.

Opening his heart to Zhovanya's love allowed his hidden memories to flood forth. He remembered when he had first learned what love may be at the cabin; Naran's relentless loving kindness at the Sanctuary; and inevitably, his time with Jolanya, a sacred time of deep healing and transformation. As the Kailithana, she channeled the kailitha to heal his body so that he could endure and even enjoy human touch for the first time in his life. He remembered sharing small pleasures with her—brushing her lustrous black hair, sharing a meal, learning to dance with her; and her greatest gift: showing him that sex did not have to be rape, but could be a wondrous sharing of love, respect, and pleasure. Wrapped in these pleasant memories, Kyr drifted into a restful sleep.

When he woke, the chill darkness of his prison seemed even more onerous than before. Longing for the life he had for that brief time between being a Slave of the Soul-Drinker and now being Gauday's plaything was too bitter to bear. He sighed, and once again methodically banished his precious memories from his awareness.

Time passed, unmarked by Sun or Moon, but only by Medari's regular visits. No longer tormented by hunger for water or food, Kyr soon found a new hunger clawing at his mind—hunger for light, for colors, for shapes, for space and distance; for some sound other than his own breath. Knowing that everything he craved was just on the other side of his prison door made him want to slam his body against it until it, or he, shattered into pieces. The unrelenting darkness gave birth to twin offspring: madness and despair. They lurked in the corners, stalking his mind.

To fight them, he began practicing the Flowing Poses that Naran had taught him at the Sanctuary. After a few bruises from bumping into the walls and knocking himself to the floor, his body knew the limits of the space and he could move freely through a limited set of Poses. When he tired, he sat in meditation, repeating the chant quietly. But even his disciplined regimen betrayed him.

With his returning strength, his confinement became less and less tolerable. He found it difficult to meditate, and even the escape of sleep began to elude him. After many days, rage and desperation joined the dark twins, and he started pacing back and forth, bumping hard into the walls of his prison. Soon he was jumping up and down, punching the air. Then he slammed his fists into the wall, and a roar burst forth from his gut: "LET ME OUT! LET ME OUT!"

Chairs scraped on the floor above, and footsteps sounded. He waited, bloody fists clenched, taut as a drawn bowstring, desperate for light. When there was no other response, despair and madness pounced.

Screaming wordlessly, he slammed his body against the door and the walls, over and over, until he fell and couldn't get up again, couldn't make another sound. He was exhausted, bruised, and shaky; but the frantic energy dwindled, and his mind began to clear.

As he sprawled on the cold floor, panting, he heard men laughing in derision. From the sound of it, there were half a dozen or more. A gleam of light under his prison's door told him that they were standing at the top of the stairs with the trap door open.

"Well, Wareg, you were right," said Viro. "None of us thought he'd last this long. Here's the pot." There was a jingling sound of coins clinking together.

"Thanks, boys. Maybe next time, you'll listen to old Wareg. Well, I better get the healer down there to make sure he hasn't damaged himself too much."

"Who cares?" Viro said. "If he dies, we get to raid the Sanctuary."

"Don't be an idiot," growled Wareg. "If he dies, you and I will be the first ones Gauday punishes."

The trap door slammed shut, cutting off the sliver of light.

Alone in the darkness again, Kyr rolled onto his pallet, aching all over. Warmth trickled down his forehead. He wiped at it and put his finger to his lips. It was blood. Probably just a scalp cut. It would stop bleeding eventually. He managed to pull his blankets over him before falling into a deep sleep. He barely roused when Medari came to tend to his bruises and cuts.

When he woke, he knew he had to regain his balance, and fight off the despair and madness that still threatened to engulf him. But he had no will to resume his regimen.

"Ah, Zhovanya, help me," he whispered. "Please help me. I know I promised to serve You, to be tempered by the fires of suffering, but, dear Goddess, I'm going mad down here! I need Your help!"

He fought back sobs of desperation, and began to silently repeat the chant for guidance and protection. *"Zhovanya dagantalo, Zhovanya ganaralo. Zhovanya dagantalo, Zhovanya ganaralo."*

Then a memory filled his mind.

*It was one of his worst times at the Sanctuary. He had finally told Naran—after resisting for days, and even trying to kill himself—of a young girl named Dahana. Mindlessly obeying the Soul Drinker's orders as always, Kyr had tortured, raped, and killed her. Telling her story was his last and most painful confession of his crimes as a Slave.*

*Naran had only said, "Here is a practice to ask for forgiveness. I want you to do it at least twice a day, once for each of your victims." Chanting "Zhovanya nara li (Zhovanya forgive me)," Naran bowed from the waist, knelt, then prostrated himself full length on the floor. Then he came to a crouch, forehead on the ground, then rose to kneeling, spreading his arms wide, offering his heart to the Goddess. He continued this series of movements, chanting all the while. When Kyr joined in, he found that the movement and chanting brought him more true peace than had the inner ice, his only protection while a Slave of the Soul-Drinker.*

In his dark prison, Kyr got to his feet with an involuntary groan. He ached all over, but he began doing the prostrations Naran had shown him, whispering "Zhovanya nara li," praying for forgiveness for himself and each of his Slave brothers. Slowly, humbleness and peace filled his soul, and the dark twins retreated to their corner. After that, he did this practice any time he felt them encroaching on his mind, and was able to keep them at bay.

A thunder of hooves that shook the ground above Kyr's head told him that Gauday and his band had returned at last. Kyr hoped and prayed that this would mean a return to the world of light, even if it meant being chained to the whipping post again. Anything would be better than this unending darkness.

B ack in the City, the debate about rescuing Kyr was still dragging on, as it had been for a quarter-moon now, vexing Rajani and Luciya to the edge of fury. Rajani grew grim and silent, while Luciya flared up at the least frustration. To remain polite and politic in the Council meetings was more than she could bear, and she took refuge in long hikes down to and along the beach. Rajani did not appreciate being left to deal with the Council on his own, and soon they were barely speaking to each other.

As the Moon reached its fullness, the Council finally came to a decision. They would allow Rajani to select only three of the Guard. Accordingly, he asked for Lorya, an excellent spy and scout; Jakar, a capable lieutenant and fine swordsman, to be his second-in-command; and Berano, a reliable sergeant.

As most of the well-trained fighters had joined the Guard and were not available, Rajani would be forced to rely for the rest on volunteers. That would mean going from village to village to recruit ex-militia members who had gained some fighting experience in the battle to take over the Soul-Drinker's labyrinth. The Council gave him a fine sorrel stallion to speed up his recruitment efforts, perhaps out of guilt or embarrassment.

"Three? Three?" Luciya shouted when Rajani came to her room to tell her the news. "Is that all? Gods curse their livers! Kyr is our Liberator. There would *be* no Council, if it weren't for him." Strong and tough as she was after many years as the Circle's spy on the Soul-Drinker, she surprised both of them by bursting into tears. "Oh, poor Kyr! I know what those Slaves do to each other, what they are doing to him."

All Rajani's irritation at her melted with her tears. He reached out, and for once she let him hold her. "I know, I know," he murmured. "I'll work as fast as I can, Ciya. We will rescue him, I promise."

Soon Luciya stifled her tears and stepped back, wiping her eyes on the back of her hand. "I know you will, Rajani. But I think I must stay here to keep this Council from getting too officious and puffed-up. They need one of us from the original Circle to remind them what Kyr has done for Khailaz, and to make sure they don't replace the Soul-Drinker with a *bureaucratic* soul-sucking tyranny."

"I agree. That is vital. But, Ciya, they *are* trying to do what's best for Khailaz. And you can't get so emotional with them. They will just try harder to defend themselves and their ideas."

"You're right." She stood tall, and said gravely, "I will keep a tight rein on my impatience and distress, as I did while I spied on the Soul-Drinker."

Rajani had never seen her look so regal and beautiful. He longed to hold her again, tell her how much he loved her. But she turned away. "Thank you, Jani. I hope you won't mind, but I want to go to the baths—alone. I, uh, need to clear my head."

"Of course," he said stiffly. "I have to make preparations for my recruiting trip. Jakar will be going with me."

The Warrior Mage traveled ceaselessly, making inspiring speeches about Kyr's role in liberating Khailaz from the Soul-Drinker's vicious reign and his noble sacrifice to protect the Sanctuary. Many young people wanted to join the rescue party, but Rajani had to sort through them to find those who had some experience with battle, or at least, with weapons and horsemanship. After a month, he had recruited a band of nearly two hundred volunteers, and returned to the City.

On his first evening back, he and Luciya were sitting on the terrace outside the Council Hall. It was a pleasantly cool evening and the sun was sinking into the Blue Desert in a royal splendor of scarlet and purple, accompanied by the sounds of waves crashing on the cliff far below, and the faint cries of seabirds. Rajani was silent, and sat slumped in his chair with his eyes closed. Luciya kept quiet, realizing that her companion was exhausted. But after a while, impatient to hear his news, she poured a little more wine into their goblets and inquired, "How did your recruiting go?"

Rajani sighed and straightened up a little. "I have enough men and women now. Most of them came with me. They are at an old army camp on the edge of the City. About a dozen more had loose ends to tie up, and are on their way." He scratched his dark beard in frustration. "But we will have to organize and train them into a cohesive fighting unit."

"What? Gods and demons, this is taking too damned long!" Luciya drained her goblet and snarled, "I'll never understand why Kyr has to suffer so much." Rajani was too tired even to indulge in his usual anger at the Prophecy.

"Well, there's one good thing," he said. "These recruits are enthusiastic about rescuing Kyr. They have named themselves the 'Companions of the Liberator.'" He chuckled. "At least they didn't name themselves Champions. They have some humility."

Luciya smiled. "I'm glad they care." But she could not keep herself from asking, "How long will this training take? When can you leave to find Kyr?"

"Gods, Ciya, give me a day or two to figure that all out, will you?"

"Sorry, Jani. I know you're tired. I'm just so worried about Kyr."

"I know." Rajani took another sip of his wine. "I will put Berano in charge of the training. He's an excellent sergeant. I'll know more after he and I put the recruits through a few drills. Perhaps it will only take a half-moon." He glanced at the clouds that had swallowed the sun and were glowing with inner fires. "Gods, I hope we can be ready before the rains arrive."

"Isn't there anything we can do now? Can you send out some scouts to look for Gauday's hideout before these Companions are ready?"

"Good idea, Ciya. I'll ask the Council tomorrow." He frowned. "By the Lights, I hate having to ask their permission. I'm so used to giving orders. But I don't want to end up being another tyrant."

Luciya smiled at him. "Oh, you're too honorable for that, Jani."

"I have no choice," he said with a bitter laugh. Luciya turned away, hiding a hurt frown.

But the enthusiastic Companions had much to learn. Uniforms had to be made, and horses and weapons found for each one. After a month, it was clear they would not be ready before the rains turned the roads into quagmires. And the scouts had found no hint of Gauday's trail.

## Chapter 8

# In Durance

But nothing changed. Kyr remained buried alive in the black hole. He couldn't keep himself from pacing the three steps his prison allowed, back and forth, back and forth, driven to escape into the light. Broken hope allowed madness and despair to creep closer, chuckling as they closed in on their prey. Still he fought back, pacing and chanting, "Zhovanya nara lo, Zhovanya nara lo." Only the chant kept his screams and mad laughter at bay. "Zhovanya nara lo, Zhovanya nara lo."

Over his head, he heard someone stomping across the room to the trap door, slamming it open with a heavy thunk. "Be quiet, traitor!" Viro screeched, sounding frantic, almost terrified. "Stop that damned noise!"

Kyr could not hear, could not stop. "Zhovanya nara lo, Zhovanya nara lo."

Above, in the guard room, Wareg rolled his eyes at Viro. "Why does that yapping bother you so much? Just ignore it. Can't hurt you."

Red-faced and furious, Viro yelled, "I'll stop his cursed yowling if it's the last thing I do!" He stomped to the back of the room, and returned with the flail he had hidden there despite Gauday's orders.

"Hey, better not do that," Wareg warned. "You know what the new Master said."

"Get outta my way!"

"It's on your head." Wareg shrugged and headed out the door.

Viro grabbed the key from its hook, stormed down the stairs, unlocked the prison's door, and shoved it open. Kyr turned his back on the sudden light but kept chanting. Infuriated, Viro raised the flail and slashed Kyr's back full force. Without thought, Kyr whirled, grabbed the whip, and yanked Viro off his feet. They went down together, Kyr on top.

As they hit the floor, Kyr realized that this attack gave him a chance to escape the darkness. Backing off, he dropped the flail, and crouched down, covering his head with his arms.

Viro lunged for his flail and rained blow after blow down on Kyr's undefended back, yelling "Gods-cursed traitor! Shut up! Shut up! There *is* no cursed Goddess! I'll show you! I'll show you!"

The light from the stairs dimmed. Suddenly, Viro gave a strangled yelp. Kyr peered through his long, tangled hair, and saw that Craith had Viro in a headlock and was dragging him up the stairs, leaving the door open.

Kyr stared at the open door, fighting a fierce desire to bolt for the light above. Instead, he flopped face down on his pallet and made himself go limp as if he'd fainted, keeping his face half-hidden in the crook of his arm. Blood trickled down his sides into the straw beneath him. His back ached and throbbed. *A small price to pay if it gets me into the light.*

From above came the sounds of Viro cursing and struggling, and Craith giving orders. "You, and you, shackle this idiot to the whipping post. I'll deal with him later. Wareg, get the healer over here, then inform Gauday."

Golden light preceded the sergeant as he came back downstairs carrying an oil lamp. Kyr longed to stare at the light, but it was too bright, too bright. He squeezed his eyes closed.

Craith knelt to examine Kyr's back, which was crisscrossed with bloody welts and red stripes. "Gods damn that Viro!" he muttered. "I should never have assigned him to guard duty. Some of these Slaves are crazy-mad and he's one of the worst. I thought Wareg would control him. I'm sorry."

Startled and touched by this unexpected apology, Kyr bit his lip and kept still. All that mattered was getting out of the darkness.

Someone trod half-way down the stairs. "I can't see to do anything in that dark hole," said Medari. "Bring him to the infirmary."

Kyr clenched his fists in victory. His ruse had worked. *Thank the gods! Bless Medari—and that madman, Viro!*

In the infirmary, Kyr sat on a stool, leaning forward with his arms on the table as Medari cleansed and salved his back. The whip cuts stung madly but were not deep. Only a few stitches were required.

Kyr hardly noticed the healer's ministrations, absorbed as he was in staring out the open door toward the yard, drinking in sunshine, colors, and shapes with hungry, dazzled eyes. The light caressed the worn wood to silver gray, turned the dusty yard to a subtle gold, painted shadows inky black, sparked off sword hilts and buttons, haloed man and beast in glory. Even this mean, ugly place was wondrous with light and life. In awe, he whispered, "It's so beautiful!"

"What?"

He glanced up, but Medari's bitter face did not invite such revelations. "Uh, the light. It's wonderful!"

"Gods curse Gauday for leaving you in that black hole for so long!"

"Thanks for getting me out of there." Kyr continued to stare out the door, but the radiant glory of life had hidden itself from his eyes again. He sighed, and asked, "What happened with Viro?"

"Ha, Gauday was furious at being disobeyed, and punished him with those red eyes of his, then banished him. Viro left the fort, sputtering curses and threatening revenge. Good riddance!"

"Ah," Kyr said, thinking, *Another one gone, another Slave brother I couldn't reach.* Sagging under the futility of his attempt at Atonement, the brunt of Viro's wrath, and the dread of being returned to his lightless prison, he dropped his head into his hands.

"I don't know if I can take any more, Medari," Kyr confided. "Can't sleep or meditate or even exercise. All I want to do is throw myself at the door until it breaks, or I do." He looked up at the healer with desperate eyes. "Please don't let him put me back down there!"

"Sit up and let me listen to your lungs." Medari took an odd wide-mouthed tube from his satchel and placed the wide end on Kyr's chest, the narrow end to his own ear. "Take some deep breaths." After repeating this procedure a few times, he put his instrument away and sat down beside Kyr. "Yes, I do think you may be getting lung rot. You've been coughing, haven't you?"

Kyr looked at the healer for a moment, then produced a convincing cough. They smiled at each other.

The next morning, he woke as dawn-light filtered in through the small, high window of his cell in the infirmary. He sat up and fixed his eyes on the growing light. Faintly, he could hear a few birds singing the sun up in the scraggly forest around the fort. For a time, he meditated in peaceful silence, but then the rats of worry and fear began to gnaw at his mind. What if Gauday sent him back into the black hole? All he could do was pray that he would not.

"Ah, my dear, you look much better."

Kyr winced inwardly and turned to face his visitor. Gauday stood outside the cell, looking haggard despite his impeccable tunic of gold velvet, black leggings and tall boots. He pulled up a stool and sat.

"I have to thank that cretin Viro for reminding me of your existence. I'd quite forgotten I'd left you in your snug hole before we left. I've banished him, by the way. He won't be attacking you again."

"Thanks." Kyr remembered to cough.

"Has your nice, dark hole been agreeing with you?"

Medari emerged from his room, wearing only his nightclothes, and came toward them. "It's too damp down there. He's getting lung rot. He'll die if you put him back down there."

Kyr coughed again, praying this ruse too would work.

"I see. Hmmm. Well, a few days in the yard should dry out his lungs just fine."

"It's too dusty out there, and his back needs tending. If you want him to live, let him stay here."

Gauday frowned and red flame flickered in his eyes, but then he rubbed his scarred forehead and closed his eyes. "Alright, a quarter moon in here. Then we'll see."

"Do you have a headache?" the healer asked with counterfeit concern. "I could brew you a potion."

"HA!" Gauday jumped up, knocking over the stool. "Don't you think I know what you're up to, old man? I'll brew my own potions, thank you." He shook his finger at them. "And just to be clear, if I die, my men will make you watch as they slaughter your family. Then they'll take their time killing you." He glared at Kyr. "The same for you. They'll make you watch as they sack that precious Sanctuary of yours and torture your friends to death, before doing the same to you." He stomped out.

Kyr and Medari looked at each other in dismay, each thinking of their threatened loved ones. Gauday had them in an inescapable trap, and despair snuffed out the brief spark of triumph at their successful ploy.

After his respite in the infirmary, Kyr was again chained to the post in the yard, but the Slaves ignored him. Bored with their own unimaginative torments and baffled by his impassive demeanor, they preferred fresh victims from the villages.

As the days shrank and the nights lengthened, Kyr came to be just an uninteresting part of the daily scene, a gray lump in the middle of the yard huddled under the new, thick blanket Medari had given him. This allowed him the freedom to meditate or do his surreptitious exercises. He feigned more weakness than he felt, keeping his strength a secret from everyone. Otherwise, he watched the life of the fort going on around him. At night, he enjoyed Friend's companionship and warmth, always saving her a small portion of his stew.

He rarely saw Gauday, who remained in his quarters most of the time. Occasionally, the despot showed up, playing out his continuing charade of condescending pity and kindness. However, Gauday seemed half-mad, quite forgetful and erratic, and he had dark crescents under his oddly glittering eyes.

*What's wrong with him?* Kyr wondered. *What is he doing in there?* But then he shrugged. *The gods may care. I'm just glad I don't have to put up with him very often.*

With Gauday preoccupied, there was little to hold the Slaves together. By twos and fives, they slipped away, returning to the City. Those who remained clung to the idea that Gauday was the new Master and would restore their glory as privileged Slaves, or were too cowardly to start new lives on their own. Even when Larag disappeared, Gauday showed no interest.

Craith became Gauday's lieutenant by default, keeping order, settling disputes, assigning tasks or punishments, competent in all he did, and unexpectedly fair. Kyr wished Gauday had never found such a capable assistant. *If it weren't for Craith, this place would fall apart in days.*

Though the redhead kept good discipline with his soldiers, the dwindling band of ex-Slaves was a fractious and miserable lot, often fighting among themselves. To keep them from killing each other, Craith had most of the weapons locked up in the armory when the Slaves were not out pillaging.

One odd thing happened. Wareg had disappeared for a half-moon. Kyr had assumed he'd left the fort, but one night, he staggered out of

Gauday's quarters, blank-eyed, mute, and helpless. He stood in the middle of the yard, doing nothing.

Kyr yelled, "Medari, come out here. Wareg needs help."

The healer hurried down the porch steps and over to the stocky Slave. "Alright, Wareg. Come into the infirmary where I can see what's wrong." Wareg didn't respond or move.

"Good gods, what's going on?" Medari muttered. In a gentle voice, he coaxed, "Come along now. Let's go into the light so I can help you. Come on now." The healer took Wareg by the hand and tugged him step by slow step into the infirmary.

Later that night, Medari came out and sat on the ground beside Kyr, rubbing his head wearily.

"What's wrong with Wareg?" Kyr asked. "Is he sick?"

"No. He just has small burns and cuts all over his body. But they do not account for his mental state. He is completely unresponsive. It's like he's been scared out of his wits. Perhaps he'll recover himself with some rest and care."

Kyr's skin crawled with an ominous chill. "I wonder what kind of games Gauday has been playing with him."

"Games? This goes beyond any game!" Medari growled. "Gods curse that vicious madman!"

But Wareg never did come back to himself. The stocky Slave could not even care for himself. A grim-faced Craith ordered him kept in a locked room and tended by a village girl.

A cool, fitful wind played with twigs, leaves, and dust in the empty yard. White billows drifted across the azure sky. Kyr spent the day wondering at the shapes the clouds made. His heart lifted when he beheld a misty white eagle floating high above, and he sent his soul soaring with it, pristine and free, until the cloud eagle dissipated, abandoning him to his chains. He shivered and wrapped his meager blanket tighter.

After four months as Gauday's captive, Kyr was having a hard time remembering his purpose, even his name. The Slaves called him "cur" or worse. Gauday continued demeaning him, calling him "my boy" or "my dear." In the increasing chill of the lengthening nights, despair whispered that Rajani would never come, that everyone had forgotten him, that he would remain Gauday's prisoner and plaything until the Dark Lady—Death—freed him.

Only the Zhovanaya chant helped Kyr keep any sense of connection with the Goddess, his friends, and with the man he had become at the Sanctuary. Most days, the chant was enough. Most days, he trusted that the Warrior Mage would come for him soon. Closing his eyes, he gave thanks for a peaceful day, and began to chant silently. After a time, even the chant disappeared into spacious stillness.

"CAW!" The harsh sound was loud and close. Mildly curious, Kyr opened his eyes to find a crow perched just above his head on the whipping post, preening. It ruffled its feathers into place and peered down at him, tilting its head side to side with comical curiosity. Kyr chuckled, and the crow flew off in a rush of dark wings, joining its fellows, soaring and bathing in a glorious sunset of saffron and crimson fire. Listening to their joyous racket and watching their aerial antics, Kyr was reminded of another sunset, when he and the Warrior Mage were on their trek to the Sanctuary. Rajani had demanded that he set aside his misery long enough to appreciate the wild beauty of a glorious mountain sunset. Kyr sighed. It seemed like that had happened a lifetime ago, in another, kinder world. But it was a good reminder. He set himself to enjoy this sunset, despite his current miserable circumstances.

Medari arrived as the Sun reached the horizon, bringing water, bread and yesterday's stew.

"Isn't it beautiful?" Kyr waved his manacled arm at the sky, his chains clanking.

"How can you care about that when we're trapped in this hell-hole?"

"I had a good teacher. He taught me not to let misery blind me to beauty. Will you stay?"

Medari shook his head in disbelief, but a slight smile lightened his usually grim face. He retrieved his own supper and sat beside Kyr to watch the glowing pageant in the sky. They said nothing further, but the common humanity of sharing a meal was balm to Kyr's abraded soul. As the flames died in the West, Medari returned to the infirmary, leaving Kyr to the peaceful darkness.

The evening seemed full of haunting magic. The Full Moon freed itself from the scrawny pines, and sailed upwards in silver majesty. Dark clouds drifted by, outlined in luminous brightness. Then the wind died, leaving a quiet expectancy, and the clouds bloomed and multiplied. Soon they covered the sky, allowing only an occasional glimpse of Jeyal's bright face.

The first shower seemed like a blessing to Kyr after days in the dusty yard. He shed his blanket and turned his face up, letting the rain wash him clean. But then came a steady rain, turning the brief blessing into a curse. Barely protected by his ragged blanket, he wrapped his arms around his shins, and buried his head on his knees. *Rajani was supposed to get here before the rains did. Why hasn't he? Has he forgotten about me? I've given them enough time to strengthen the Sanctuary's defenses. It should be safe by now. Perhaps they have no further use for me.*

Friend came and stood by him, whining. He looked up at her, and she started toward the barn. After a few steps, she stopped and looked over her shoulder, clearly waiting for him to follow her to drier quarters. When he did not, she returned to lick his face as if in apology, then plodded off, head drooping, tail down. A sharp feeling of abandonment stabbed through his core.

He glanced around the yard. Surely someone was coming to take him to his cell in the infirmary, or even the black hole. The yard was empty, but light gleamed from Gauday's open door. He was leaning against the door frame, holding a goblet of wine and staring in Kyr's direction.

Kyr stared back. *Why doesn't he send someone? He wouldn't go against the Master's last command and leave me out here to die, would he? What is he waiting for?*

"Is there something you want, dear boy?" Gauday took a sip of his wine. "You might try asking nicely."

*Gods and demons, he wants me to beg.* A fierce refusal stormed through his soul. *Never! Not even to save my own life. I'll never beg him for anything!*

"*Soften,*" Zhovanya reminded him from within. But Her gentle word of counsel was drowned out by his sudden flare of anger and pride.

Gauday raised his goblet. "Have a pleasant evening, my boy." Smiling, he went inside to his warm fire.

Rage flared high, warming Kyr to the bone. *I'll never forgive him for this! Even dogs have someplace dry to sleep. How can he leave me out here?* Like coal burning underground, buried resentment added to the fire. *And how can You leave me here so long, Zhovanya? The rains are here but Rajani is not. Has he abandoned me? Have You?*

Aghast at his faithless thoughts, he shook his head. *Forgive me! It's my own fault for being a prideful fool. A few words and Gauday would have relented. So what if I had to grovel?* He forced himself to repeat the forgiveness chant that was his lifeline to the Goddess; but this night, forgiveness seemed absurd, impossible. And the words held no magic against the bitter rain. He was soon chilled to the marrow and shivering uncontrollably. Unable to keep two words together, he lost hold of the chant, lost track of the gifts he had received from Zhovanya and the Kailithana. Under the inexorable drumming of the storm, his sojourn at the Sanctuary faded into a meaningless child's story from long ago.

Despair, victorious at last, reared up and crushed him into the cold mud, whispering: *Zhovanya has turned Her back on you. Your friends have abandoned you. You are condemned to suffer forever as the Master ordained.* Kyr's heart shattered. He felt certain that death would be the only mercy he could hope for, and even that would be fraught with guilt and sorrow for giving over the Sanctuary and Medari's family to the viciousness of Gauday and his Slaves.

In the depths of that cold, blustery night, his shivering stopped and his mind went numb. Nothing made sense any longer. There was only one reality. He was bereft and forsaken in the dark, empty yard, at the mercy of his worst enemy.

## Chapter 9

# Dark Lady Dancing

Late in the night, Medari groaned. His head was throbbing, his mouth tasted vile, and his bladder demanded relief. He groped on the floor beside his bed and found the flask he sought, but it was empty.

Where had the flask appeared from? Oh, yes. Gauday had sent it over. Though Medari hadn't been able to fathom Gauday's sudden generosity, still he'd taken full advantage of the escape the whiskey offered from the fretful monotony of his life as a hostage, from the grinding millstones of rage at his captor and his fear for his family.

"Gods, what'n idiot," he mumbled. "Shoulda saved some for 'nother night." He dragged himself out of bed, pulled on his boots, and stumbled out the door. Returning from the latrine, he barely glanced at the whipping post, sure that Gauday had sent Kyr to the hole because of the rain. Then he saw the huddled figure lying in the mud, only an occasional shiver denying lifelessness.

"Cursed fool!" he accused himself. "Drank myself into a stupor, and now he could die—my wife and children with him!"

Medari charged across the yard and started pounding on Gauday's door. After what seemed an eternity, a half-dressed Gauday opened the door a crack.

"Gods and demons! How *dare* you bother me at this hour?"

"How dare *you* leave Kyr out in the rain? Are you mad? No, of course you are!"

"And don't you forget it." Gauday's eyes glowed red but he only laughed—a feral, demented sound.

"Kyr's chilled to the very marrow. If I don't get him inside immediately, he will die of rain chill."

"Put him in the hole until the rains stop. I don't want to hear another word about him."

"No. That damned hole is too cold and damp. He'd die of lung rot for sure. You must let me bring him to the infirmary."

"Alright, alright," Gauday snarled, and grabbed something off a peg inside the door. "Here's the key to his chains. Bring it back in the morning." And he slammed the door.

Medari hurried across the yard, and shook Kyr gently by the shoulder.

Kyr looked up through bleary eyes at the figure of a man, a dark shadow against the cruel storm clouds. Hope flared brighter than lightning.

"G-go's, Jani, yur 'ere!"

The man unlocked his shackles and helped him to his feet. "Come on now."

"Yeah, le's g-go 'fore he s-see us." He started stumbling toward the gate.

"Whoa, whoa. This way. Got to get you dried off and warmed up."

"Oh, yeah. 'm v-very c-c-col'."

They went up the steps, into the infirmary, and over to the hearth.

"Give me that." Medari held out his hand for Kyr's sodden, muddy blanket.

"N-no, m-mine." Dazedly, Kyr clung to his only possession.

"I'll give you nice, warm blankets after I dry you off. Drop that wet thing on the floor and have a seat on this stool."

"Aw righ'. Th-then we g-go?" He slumped onto the stool. The warmth from the banked coals felt like a benediction from the gods. His eyelids felt so heavy, he let them close, only vaguely aware of being toweled off and wrapped up in dry blankets. He clutched the blankets gratefully, soaking up the heat from the now-blazing fire. Paradoxically, he began to shiver again. His bones were made of ice.

"M-m-mersless g-go's. N-n'ver b-bin s-so c-col'."

"Here, drink this. It will help."

Desperate for warmth, Kyr took the mug and drank down the foul-tasting potion. Soon, his shivering began to diminish.

"Now drink this."

He cradled the hot mug in clumsy hands and sipped. It was tea with lots of honey this time. Though he was still shivering now and again, he managed to drink it without spilling any. He frowned in confusion. *Why does Rajani have gray hair?*

"Alright, let's get you bedded down. Come on." The gray-haired man helped him lie down on a pallet by the fire, and placed warm compresses on his neck, chest, and groin. Kyr's shivering got worse.

"You can rest for a little while now, but I have to keep you awake until I'm sure you'll be all right." The man covered him with the blankets. Heated from within and without, Kyr's shivering slowly waned. All he wanted was oblivion, but the gray-haired Rajani kept fussing at him: changing the compresses when they cooled; insisting he drink more hot potions or sweet tea; helping him use the pisspot.

At last, gray light crept through the window, and Medari relented. "Looks like you'll make it. You can get some sleep now."

"Then we'll get outta here, righ'?" Kyr mumbled as he curled up and pulled the blankets up over his ears.

As Kyr slept, Medari stayed nearby, keeping the fire going.

Something warm and heavy weighed him down, but his bones ached with cold. The heaviness was inside him too. Now he was too hot. He struggled with the pile of blankets.

"Ah, you're awake. Let me help."

A gray-haired man knelt by his side and helped him sit up. Everything was blurry, and it was hard to get a breath.

"Rajani?"

"What? No, I'm Medari. Don't you remember me?"

"*You* brought me inside last night?"

"Yes, who else?"

"Merciless gods." That meant Rajani hadn't come. Now he knew what that inner weight was: stone, where the golden kailitha had burned; silence, where the forgiveness chant had lived; despair, where the mirage of hope had shimmered.

"I feared you'd die of rain chill, but it looks like you'll survive."

"Regrettable," Kyr mumbled.

"Can't say I blame you, but I haven't heard such bitterness from you before."

"I was a fool before."

A frown creased Medari's face. "But you can't give up! You must live to protect the ones we love. I promise I won't let him leave you out in the rain again."

93

"Doesn't matter." He turned his back on the healer.

"Kyr?" Medari sounded upset. After a moment, he sighed. "Well, I'll let you rest. Perhaps you'll feel better tomorrow." The healer returned to his endless grinding of herbs for salves and potions.

Buried under his blankets, Kyr lay brooding. *Zhovanya cut open my heart and soul, then abandoned me in the cold mud. Her only gift has been to melt the ice, leaving me with no defense against Gauday's madness and cruelty. I thought she was different, but I was right: Lady Death is the only merciful god.* He filled his mind with a new chant. *Lady Death, only You are truly compassionate. I offer myself to You. Please take me now.*

He slept most of the day. By evening, it was clear that their earlier ruse had come true. To his morbid satisfaction, he was feverish and coughing with lung rot. A quiet inner voice urged him to remember Tenaiya, Svahar, Naran, Jolanya, Zhovanya and Her Sanctuary, but he drowned it out with his new litany: *Lady Death, please take me. I am Yours.*

"Please, Kyr, please drink this," Medari begged for the hundredth time, holding out a cup of sweetened herbal tea. This time, Kyr deigned to look at him.

"Will you give me the Final Grace?"

"Final Grace? Oh, gods." Looking guilt-stricken, the healer sagged onto a stool, but he shook his head. "Sorry. I can't. My family...."

"Then leave me alone. I want nothing else from you."

"If you won't take this, I'll have to force it down you."

"Yes, you will."

Shame-faced, Medari called in two soldiers and force-fed Kyr broth and healing potions. Kyr fought with what feeble strength he had, but only succeeded in exhausting himself. Afterwards, he stared at the healer in stony, reproachful silence. This went on for two days. Despite, or more likely because of these exhausting battles, he continued to slip towards death.

On the third morning, Medari roused Gauday from his den.

Unkempt and haggard, Gauday glared out the door. "By the Master's black soul what now, old man? It better be important."

"Kyr is refusing to eat or take any of my potions. I've force-fed him but it isn't working. He's willing himself to die. He'll succeed within a quarter-moon if we don't do something."

"Trying to escape, is he? Amazing. The rain did in one night what my Slaves couldn't do in four months. Well, every man has his breaking point."

"You whoreson!"

Gauday laughed. "Probably. The gods know what bitch bred me. Come along. Let's pay the dear boy a visit."

"So, my dear, you want out of our little arrangement, eh?" Gauday shook his head. "Perhaps you've forgotten. The Sanctuary is safe from attack only as long as you are my prisoner. If you die, so does our bargain." When Kyr made no response, Gauday shrugged. "Oh, well. A raid on the Sanctuary might be just the thing to settle the boys down before winter sets in for good."

Kyr said nothing, believing he no longer cared.

"Yes," Gauday purred, "a raid might be just the thing. Plenty of supplies to take, and Larag tells me they have some whore there who really knows how to please a man. Calls herself the Kaili – something." Gauday half-closed his eyes. "Mmmm. Can't wait to try her out. If she's really good, I'll keep her for myself."

*JOLANYA! Gods and demons, NO!* A primal, protective fury flooded Kyr, urging him to beat Gauday's head to bloody mush, but he knew that showing the slightest reaction would tell his tormenter how important Jolanya was to him, and heighten the danger to her. Using all the discipline he had ever acquired, he kept silent, kept his eyes closed, kept his breathing steady, and didn't move a muscle. It was the hardest thing he had ever done.

"Well, my dear, I'll give you a day or so to think about it. Let me know if you change your mind." Gauday sauntered out.

Kyr buried his face in his blankets, muffling a growl of impotent rage. *I can't face this misery any longer, but I must protect Jolanya! Merciless gods, what can I do?*

His mind zigzagged like a rabbit fleeing a hawk. *How long have I been here? More than four months. Surely I have bought Maray enough time to build up the Sanctuary's defenses. Jolanya will be safe there.* Bone-weary, feverish, and soul-sick, he surrendered to the comfort of that thought.

But the buried ember of Jolanya's love had re-ignited, lighting a small flame in his heart. Unseen, it burned steadily, though he returned to his silent courtship of Lady Death.

At his wits' end, Medari was sitting at the table in the main room with his head in his hands. Over in his iron-barred cell, Kyr slept fitfully. As wind slapped rain at the windows, a silence of hopelessness filled the infirmary, broken only by the snapping of the fire and Kyr's heavy bouts of coughing.

A sudden gust of cold wind made the fire dance wildly as Gauday dashed into the infirmary. He doffed his wet cloak, shook it, and hung it on a hook by the door. "How's our patient doing?" he asked.

"How dare you act as if you care?" Medari sprang to his feet, eyes blazing. "You are the *cause* of his illness!"

"Now, now," Gauday chuckled. "I've come to see how I can help. What do you suggest?"

"He simply can't face the miserable existence you've inflicted on him. You've got to promise him something else, something more bearable."

Gauday grinned like a fox about to pounce. "Alright, I have an idea." He pulled up a stool just outside the iron bars of Kyr's cell. Sitting with his legs crossed, he fiddled with the ornate hilt of the dagger at his waist. "Wake up, dear boy. We need to have a little chat."

Kyr opened one eye. "Go away." He closed his eye and pulled the blankets up around his ears.

"You've got to listen to him," Medari pleaded.

"Gods and demons!" Kyr glared at them from his nest of blankets. "What is it?"

"Well, my boy, I see that our little game has palled on us all. My men have even lost interest in punishing you. But I have thought of a new game we can play."

"Not interested."

"Ah, but they're such fun!" Gauday chuckled. "Now, do listen to my offer, dear boy. If you choose to live, thereby keeping your precious Sanctuary safe and… What else? Oh, yes, saving Medari's family from a nasty death. I'll make you my personal servant. You'll live in my quarters, eat as well as I, stay dry and warm. No more confinement in your dark prison; no more being chained in the yard, no more beatings by my men. I promise. You will just have to take good care of me and do as I ask."

"Ha." Kyr snorted in derision, setting off a coughing fit. He knew what kind of demands Gauday would make; yet the thought of being well-fed, warm, and dry evoked a desperate animal demand from his treacherous body. A smug smile crossed Gauday's face, as if he sensed his prey faltering.

"I'll even find you some decent clothes. Think about it. I believe it will be more amusing for both of us."

"I'd rather sleep with rats in a dung heap." With a faint hope that his insult would goad Gauday to slay him on the spot, Kyr closed his eyes.

"Kyr, please!" Medari begged. "It will be better for you now, don't you see? Don't let them kill my wife, my children!" The older man broke down in tears, sobbing like a young boy.

The healer's terror and grief slashed through Kyr's thin armor of apathy, reminding him that he wanted no more blood on his hands, no more tears of grief and loss on his soul. The thought of being Gauday's personal servant was nauseating. On the other hand, his captor had often been solicitous in his own peculiar way. *Perhaps it wouldn't be so bad?*

He opened his eyes and studied Gauday, trying to gauge his true intentions. His Slave brother, his life-long rival, looked up and their eyes met.

For an instant, before his usual arrogant mask slipped into place, Gauday's gaze was sad, hollow, almost pleading. It reminded Kyr of the face of the Full Moon the night he had discovered his true Atonement. Then he remembered his own question to Rajani. *"If I can be redeemed from the Master's corruption and viciousness, why not my Slave brothers?"* He cringed, wishing he hadn't looked at Gauday, but it was too late.

*Oh, gods. That's right.* That *is my Atonement: not just to suffer as my victims did, but to try to help my Slave brothers awaken from the Soul-drinker's nightmare. I can't let Gauday kill Medari's family, nor allow him to touch Jolanya with his maggoty hands. And I did promise her and Naran that I would pass on the blessings I received at the Sanctuary.* He almost laughed as he realized, *Doesn't make any difference if Zhovanya is as merciless as all the other gods. I didn't make that promise to Her, but to them.*

Defeated by compassion, he let his dream of Lady Death's peace and surcease fade away. "Alright, Medari, you win."

"Thank you. Thank you." Medari sagged onto a stool by the table.

"Excellent, my dear," Gauday said with a rapacious smile. "I'm sure we'll have a lot of fun. Do get well soon." He rose and left.

"Merciless gods," Kyr groaned. Now, even the Dark Lady seemed pitiless, ignoring his fervent plea long enough for him to be beguiled into living.

"I'm very sorry, Kyr. If it were just myself...."

He gave the healer a bleak glance. "I know."

"Can you sit up a bit? You need to drink this now." Medari held out a mug. Kyr propped himself up against his pillow and drank the bitter potion down, and the mug of rich broth that followed.

"I hope life will be more bearable for you now, son. At least you will be within doors, warm and dry."

"Yes, but.... Well, never mind." He curled up under his blankets, too ill and disheartened to voice his fears.

"Rest well." Medari banked the fire and went into his room. Candle-light glowing from the crack under the door and restless footsteps soon told Kyr that the older man was far from sleep.

The healer's herbal concoction soothed his cough and made him drowsy. As he drifted in this twilight state of mind, an image of the Soul-Drinker loomed up, sinister and potent, cursing him to eternal torment. *He was my Master, and I killed him. Why did I ever think I could escape his curse?* It seemed clear that the interlude of healing and kindness after the Master's death was meant only to intensify his appreciation of Gauday's cruelty.

In a fog of dreary acquiescence, he resigned himself to his fate.

Kyr's recovery was slow. In addition, Medari kept him in the infirmary as long as possible, aiding him in feigning weakness to avoid his new role as Gauday's servant. After a half-moon, Kyr was dismayed to find his vitality returning. No longer could he drowse the entire day away.

That evening, the Full Moon flooded through the window, its austere white light competing with the warm yellow light of the oil lanterns in the main room of the infirmary. *Gods, I've been here four months now. I guess Rajani won't be rescuing me anytime soon, if ever. Why the hell did I agree to live? Gauday's games will be loathsome, at best.*

To distract himself, he began watching Medari through the bars of his cell. The healer was at work again. The pestle scraped and thumped rhythmically in the mortar, releasing a pungent odor.

"Would you tell me about your family?" Kyr asked suddenly. "They're one of the reasons I am still here."

The healer's shoulders tightened, but he continued working. In a choked voice, he said, "I can't talk about them."

"Oh. Sorry." Wistfully, Kyr added, "I never had a real family."

The thumping ceased and Medari looked at him in surprise. "You never knew your family?"

"All I remember is being trained to be a Slave since I was about four."

"Four? Ah, gods, that must have been dreadful." Medari set his pestle down, and made them both some tea. "Let's see. Where to start?" He began to speak, haltingly at first, but soon his stories came pouring forth: how he and his wife fell in love and got married; the births of their three children, two girls and a boy; the scrapes and adventures of his children; the round of family holidays and celebrations.

To Kyr, it was like a guided tour of a foreign land, exotic and mysterious. Thinking of all that he and Medari were enduring for their loved ones, he saw how perilous it was to allow love entry into one's heart. And he realized anew how distorted and cruel his life had been, his and the lives of all the Slaves, and all their victims. The suffering the Soul-Drinker had inflicted and its continuing legacy of pain and degradation was so immense, he had to ask: *If Zhovanya is our true Goddess, why does She permit it?*

He almost laughed aloud at the remnant of faith his question revealed, and reminded himself not to expect human mercy from Her. *She showed me all Her faces that first time I saw Her in the Temple. She embraces suffering and vileness as fiercely as joy and kindness.*

The following morning, Medari unlocked the cell door and brought in porridge and tea. Rather than retreating to the far side of the table for his own breakfast as usual, he brought a stool and sat in the doorway to Kyr's cell.

"I thought I'd join you, for a change."

Pleasantly startled, Kyr smiled. "Welcome."

When they had finished eating, the healer said, "Well, I've told you about my life. Now it's your turn."

"Gods, no." Kyr shook his head, afraid to stir up the memories he'd so carefully buried.

"I too thought it would be painful, but it was actually a relief to talk about my loved ones. And I'd like to get to know you."

Kyr looked down, touched by this unexpected display of humanity. Someone here actually wanted to know him as a person.

"Are you sure? It's not so kindly a tale as yours."

"It's my duty as a healer to know my patient, a duty I've shamefully neglected. I'm sorry, son. It's just been easier to keep my distance."

"I understand."

"But now, well—we're not quite allies, but we have the same enemy. And I need a friend here in this hellhole, before I end up as mad as Gauday."

Kyr returned the healer's rueful smile. "Alright. I'll try to keep this brief." He rearranged his pillow and propped himself up on his side. Moving made his half-healed welts ache and sting.

"I was born and raised to be a Slave. Through torture and indoctrination, my Trainer taught me to endure and inflict great pain without making a sound; to rape, torture, and kill with no remorse, no emotion at all."

"Gods and demons, I had no idea what that cursed Soul-Drinker put you through."

Over the next few days, Kyr shared his story in small pieces. It was too painful to speak of all at once. He told of killing the Soul-Drinker; his rescue by Rajani and the Circle; painfully learning about kindness, friendship, and love; being cured of the craving by Svahar and the Great Tree; and being driven to the Sanctuary by deep remorse.

However, bitterness kept him from speaking of his difficult healing and transformation with Naran, or of receiving the forgiveness and love of Zhovanya. And he kept his time with Jolanya secret and sacred in his own heart. He merely said, "At the Sanctuary, I received much help in becoming a man instead of a Slave of the Soul-Drinker. They were very kind to me."

"But," Medari protested, "for you to end up here after being at that Sanctuary... how *can* the gods be so cruel?"

"Ask them," Kyr said bleakly. "I don't know."

Their eyes met in shared anger and despair at their cruel fates, and from that moment, though unspoken, their friendship grew and was a solace to them both.

The heavy tread of boots told Kyr his visitor was not Medari, nor mincing Gauday. But his curiosity wasn't strong enough to make him open his eyes.

"Ah, healer, how is he?" It was Craith's voice.

"Ask him yourself."

"Isn't he asleep?"

"What do you care?" Medari stalked back to his mortar and pestle, leaving the big soldier standing by Kyr's cell.

Craith stared at the figure huddled under the blankets for a moment, then cleared his throat. "You there. Gauday wants to know how you're doing."

Kyr opened his eyes and saw not one of his tormenters but a fellow human being.

"You weren't a Slave, were you?"

"Uh, no, no. Just a soldier." Craith shifted a little, looking flustered.

"Why do you serve Gauday? He doesn't hold you in thrall as the Master did."

"Well, um, the General died when you... when the Master did. There was no one to give orders. None of us soldiers knew what to do. Then Gauday showed up wearing the Crown, so we did as he said."

"You are not chained. Others have left. What keeps you here?"

Craith paled, his cinnamon freckles standing out starkly. "I'm a good soldier. That's all you need to know. Now, how soon will you be well enough to serve our new master?"

Kyr's somber stare drove Craith back. He didn't know which was worse, dealing with his vicious commander or this unnerving prisoner. Uneasy with the thought of sending anyone into Gauday's clutches, he reported that Kyr was still ill and would need more time to rest.

At the dark of the Moon, Gauday sent over a set of clothing, and demanded that Kyr make himself presentable. After a bath, Medari cut Kyr's hair to shoulder-length, and shaved off Kyr's beard, as Gauday had ordered.

Kyr rubbed his bare chin, feeling like a stranger to himself, then pulled on a gray tunic and leggings and slipped his feet into leather sandals. He stood still for a moment, amazed by how much better he felt simply being dressed. The leg-irons that Craith locked onto his ankles, however, were a cold reminder of his situation.

# Part Four ~ Vicious Intimacy

*"Letting go gives us freedom,
and freedom is the only condition for happiness.
If, in our heart, we still cling to anything
—anger, anxiety, or possessions—
we cannot be free."*

—Thích Nhất Hạnh, *The Heart of the Buddha's Teaching:
Transforming Suffering into Peace, Joy, and Liberation*

# Chapter 10

# Insidious Affection

Gray clouds churned across a cold blue sky, their bellies burning with sullen fire from the sinking sun. Outside the log palisade, tall pines tossed their tousled heads, protesting the swirling wind. Rain had stayed away for a half-moon, and the muddy yard had dried into hard ruts with a scattering of dirty puddles.

Kyr shuffled across the yard, hobbled by the leg-irons. His stomach was clenched tight, and his limbs felt icy. *Gods, I wish I had let myself die. How in all the hells and I going to put up with Gauday's games?* Trying to avoid a muddy hole, he stumbled over a rut. Craith caught his elbow to steady him.

"Thanks."

The redhead looked at him, his eyes troubled.

"What is it, Craith?"

"Nothing. Just…." He glanced at Gauday's door. "Gods protect you."

"Ha! Never have." Dread had dried Kyr's throat, and he started coughing. Craith turned to face him, putting his back to Gauday's window. He furtively slipped a flask out of his shabby leather jacket, and offered it to Kyr. Kyr gulped down a big slug. His eyes widened and he sputtered, "That's not water!" Craith put a finger to his lips, took the flask back and hid it in his jacket again. "Thanks," Kyr whispered, already feeling the liquor's warm haze spreading through his mind and body.

Craith turned away and they crossed the yard to Gauday's quarters. Hobbled as he was, Kyr stopped at the foot of the stairs leading up to the porch. The redhead held Kyr by an elbow to steady him, and helped him up the two steps, then hurried off as Gauday threw open the door.

"Ah! Here you are, my boy! Come in, come in!"

Kyr shuffled inside. The thud of the closing door sent a shiver down his spine, despite the heat from a smoky fire flaring in the stone hearth on the far wall.

"Welcome to my home!" Gauday gestured grandly, as if his modest quarters were a palace. A dark red rug hid most of the rough plank floor. A tall-backed padded chair hunched by the fire, with a small table crouching by its side.

"Let's take those ugly chains off for tonight." Gauday unlocked the leg irons and tossed them aside. They landed on the stone hearth with a jarring jangle. "If you're a very good boy, we may be able to dispense with them permanently."

Gauday inspected him with a voracious gaze. "Well, my dear, you're a bit too lean, but we shall remedy that. Let's get started, shall we?" He gestured toward a long, plank table surrounded by a clutter of mismatched chairs and stools. The flames of the two oil lamps reflected off of a glass decanter of ruby wine like a pair of glowing red eyes, and evoked dull gleams from pewter plates and goblets. Steam rose from covered dishes on a dark wood sideboard. Kyr dragged out the chair at the head of the table, and stood waiting.

"No, no, it's just us tonight, my dear. No need to wait on me this time. We'll serve ourselves."

They filled their plates and took their seats. The aroma of roast venison in gravy, fresh-baked bread, and herbed carrots reminded Kyr of the good food, safety. and kindness of the Sanctuary. He swallowed a painful lump in his throat, grateful for the mild haze Craith's liquor had brought him.

Gauday filled their goblets and raised his. "To old friendship renewed!"

Kyr winced inside, remembering when he had first learned of this custom. It was at the special dinner at the Sanctuary with all his friends—Naran, Rajani, Luciya, Gaela, and his beloved Jolanya. He had given each of them one of his small sculptures as a gift to honor all the ways they had helped him become a human man instead of an obediently vicious Slave. It had been a feast of warmth, friendship and love; a heart-full evening he would always treasure.

And now here he was, engaging in this travesty of friendship with his mad tormenter. The contrast was nearly intolerable. With a shaky hand, he raised his goblet. "To friendship. May you, ah, we know its true meaning." He sipped the wine and nearly choked. It was harsh and raw, but Gauday swilled it down unheeding.

"Go ahead, my boy, eat, eat."

Kyr set his goblet aside and took a bite of the gravy-covered venison. He closed his eyes as its savory richness filled his mouth. *Gods, this is good! Might almost make it worthwhile putting up with Gauday's games.*

"Delicious, isn't it?" Gauday dabbed his lips with a frayed napkin and swilled down more wine. "Terrible weather we're having. Sadly, you'd know that better than I, wouldn't you, my dear?"

His malicious laughter turned the food tasteless in Kyr's mouth. Trapped in his tormenter's bizarre pretense of civility, he wished he was back in the black hole, cold, hungry, and alone. Nevertheless, he made himself finish his plate. *If I'm going to survive Gauday's games, I've got to gain whatever strength I can.*

"Drink up, my boy. One doesn't like to drink alone."

Reluctantly, Kyr drained his goblet. Already affected by the swig of Craith's liquor, he felt the harsh, strong wine flood through him in a dizzying rush.

"Ah. Quite satisfying." Gauday pushed his empty plate away. "Now for dessert." He rose, his eyes glittering. "This way, this way." He led them into the next room.

Kyr's heart lurched. Another windowless chamber from which he could not escape. A large bed piled with pillows and furs took up the center of the room. Beside it, a nightstand held a glowing oil lamp. A wash stand and tall wardrobe were crowded against the right wall. On the left, the back of the main room's hearth exuded heat, making the small room warm and stuffy. Used to the cold and flushed from the liquor, Kyr broke into a sweat and took an involuntary step back.

"Ah, you don't like my humble abode? I do apologize. The furnishings are the best I could—ah—find in this miserable backwater. Even the richest merchant in the biggest village lacks style, though he does clean my rooms rather well, don't you think?" Gauday opened the wardrobe and pulled off his black wool tunic, hanging it on a hook, fussing until it was just so, then turned and licked his lips, eyes half-closed.

"Come in and close the door. That's a good boy." Gauday chuckled. "Though having an audience was rather fun, I fear our reunion when you first arrived was less than ideal, as you may recall. I hope to remedy that tonight."

Kyr froze, red lightning exploding through him. *I knew it! Merciless gods! All I've been through isn't enough. Now I'm to be Gauday's whore. Why didn't I just let myself die?*

"Ah! I see you remember. Why, I'm getting aroused just thinking about our little escapade. Do take off your clothes, my boy."

Longing to flee, craving to kill, Kyr stood with clenched fists, frozen in place by dreary duty.

"Now, now, don't be naughty. You wouldn't want to break our new agreement on our first night, would you? I'd hate to have to put you back outside."

Still, Kyr made no move and spoke no word. *I'd die out there. It's my only chance to escape this hell.* In the silence, wind slapped a scatter of hail against the roof. He shivered, his bones aching with remembered cold. *Curse me for a coward, I can't face being out there again.* His shoulders slumped in defeat. *Ah gods, what does it matter? I can't escape the Master's curse. And what other kind of hell did I expect? I know Gauday's idea of fun all too well.* He kicked his sandals into a corner.

"Ah, good, good. Let me help." With sensuous, intrusive hands, Gauday pushed him down onto the bed and undressed him. "Don't worry. You're my boy now. I take good care of my boys." His captor smiled and stroked his face. "You're my boy, now. You're my boy," Gauday crooned, caressing and licking.

Confused by his tormenter's unexpected gentleness, muddled with wine and despair, Kyr yielded to Gauday's parody of love-making.

Afterwards, he had never felt more devastated. Even his own body had betrayed him.

Gauday smiled down at him, lurid colors writhing in his dark eyes. "See? I take good care of my boys. Much better than being chained to that old post, isn't it?"

Deluged by memories of making pure, sweet love with Jolanya, Kyr shoved his captor away in utter revulsion. But Gauday only laughed and patted Kyr's cheek. In that moment, Kyr realized that it was the subtler rape of the soul that his tormenter enjoyed most. He gritted his teeth, knowing that he would have to be always on guard against Gauday's devious assaults, as well as enduring cruder forms of abuse.

Gauday pulled the covers over them both. "We'll have such fun. Sleep well, my boy."

Longing for darkness and oblivion, Kyr leaned over to blow out the lamp on the nightstand.

"NO! Leave it be."

He gave Gauday a startled glance. Catching a gleam of fear in his tormenter's eyes, he looked away.

"As you wish," he said in a carefully neutral tone. Long experience in the Master's hell had taught him that it was dangerous to notice a bully's fear. He lay down near the edge of the bed, but Gauday pulled him close again. In moments, he was snoring.

Used to the cold after months outdoors or in the black hole, Kyr lay sweating under the heavy furs, his skin crawling with disgust and loathing. Snared in his tormenter's web, sick from wine and rich food, he feared he'd never find the haven of sleep. Yet exhaustion and inebriation soon trumped all.

One morning, Gauday sat at the table in the dining room, while Kyr set a plate of eggs and toast before him, and filled his mug with tea.

"Thank you, my dear." Gauday grabbed Kyr behind his neck and pulled his head down for a long, lascivious kiss. Kyr endured this without response. Gauday let him go, chuckling. As Kyr turned away, wiping off his mouth with his sleeve, Gauday patted him on the behind, and asked cheerfully, "What shall we do today, my boy? What would be fun?"

"Whatever you wish—sir."

"What would you like us to do? Don't you have any ideas?"

"No—sir."

Gauday set his mug down hard, sloshing tea onto the dark wood of the table. "Stop calling me that!"

Hiding a smirk, Kyr mopped up the tea with a napkin. "Calling you what—sir?"

"Sir! Stop calling me that."

"What shall I call you—sir?"

"We're so close now; I want you to call me by my bed-name, 'Day."

Kyr stood silent for a moment, wringing the tea-soaked napkin with both hands, wishing it were Gauday's neck. Through clenched teeth, he spat, "As you wish—Day."

"Very good, my pet."

"*My* name is *Kyr!*"

"Ah, yes. Cur. So it is. Thank you for reminding me, my dear. I had quite forgotten. Now fetch me some hot tea."

A different anger flared up—bitter anger at his own stupidity for giving Gauday such an opening. He turned away to fetch the teapot from the hearth, feeling as if a large spider had wrapped another sticky strand around his soul. Trapped and unable to free himself, or even *be* himself, he felt despair snuff out his anger, leaving only ashes. This was all his life offered now: this hopeless duel of insult and innuendo between him and his tormenter, this unending service to the mad whims of his soul-lost Slave brother. *I wish I was still a Slave of the Master. At least then, I knew nothing better.* Kyr's shoulders slumped. Gauday, watching him every moment like an evil hawk, smiled.

One night a half-moon later, Gauday had finished with him and fallen asleep. Lying there trapped in Gauday's arms, Kyr didn't know whom he hated more, his tormenter or himself. He waited until Gauday was snoring before stealthily disentangling himself from his captor's arms. Curling up on the far side of the bed, he eventually sank into a miasma of sleep and nightmares, but even this was no escape.

*"Kyr? Kyr?" Jolanya was searching for him, calling for him. "Kyr, I love you. Where are you?" He tried to call out to her, but his voice was locked in ice. He longed to go to her but heavy chains held him down. All he could do was listen in silent anguish as her voice faded away.*

He woke flooded by memories of the Kailithana's kind strength and gentle wisdom, her generous body, her healing touch, the love in her eyes. The contrast with Gauday's odious affections broke his iron control. Overwhelmed by severe longing for Jolanya, for the love they had shared, for all that he had lost, Kyr couldn't keep hot tears from running down his cheeks.

Like brandy poured on embers, his tears ignited fury at his cruel fate, at himself for believing in illusions of kindness and love, at his patronizing tormenter. *Goddess, how cruel you are to show me your blessings, to teach me kindness and love, and then send me back into hell!* Trembling, he fought to keep from leaping out of that soft, abhorrent bed to run screaming into the icy storm raging outside.

Next to him in that bed, Gauday moaned, lost in his own nightmare, then stirred restlessly and groped for Kyr. Overwhelmed with disgust, Kyr jerked away, waking his captor.

"What's the matter, dear boy? Bad dreams? There, there. Let me make it better." Gauday began to caress him.

"DON'T TOUCH ME!" Kyr grabbed his tormenter by the throat, determined to choke the life out of him, but months of imprisonment had weakened him. Gauday easily broke his hold and pinned him face-down on the bed.

"How exciting, my boy! A little rough play in the middle of the night!"

Kyr wrenched and twisted, desperate to get away. Further enflamed by this futile resistance, Gauday forced himself on Kyr, grunting and groaning to a triumphant climax. Kyr's humiliation was complete when he became aroused and reached climax soon after. His captor's laughter rang with malevolent exultation.

"What a delightful surprise! Just the thing to spice up our love life."

Sick with loathing, Kyr buried his face in the bedclothes. Gauday got up, rummaged in his wardrobe and emerged with a manacle.

"This was rather fun, but you've been a very bad boy. My throat is a bit bruised." Despite his easy victory, he chained Kyr by one wrist to the iron bedstead, and returned to bed. He ran his tongue up Kyr's back, then leaned over as if to whisper lover's endearments into his ear.

"A little reminder. If you kill me, it will bring about the same consequences as if you die or escape. My men will sack your precious Sanctuary and kill everyone there, not to mention your friend Medari and his sweet little family. I'm afraid my men won't be very nice about it, either. Without me to protect you, you'll be at their mercy again, as well. I'm sure you prefer my attentions." He slid down and pulled the covers over both of them. "Now don't seduce me again tonight, my dear. A man needs some sleep." He was soon snoring, one arm thrown over Kyr's back.

Pinned under the too-warm furs, cold iron biting his wrist, Kyr ached with hatred and despair. *Gods be my witness, I can't take any more of this.* For a long, dark time, he hunted for a way to kill his tormenter or himself, while somehow keeping the Sanctuary safe, but he could see no way out of the wicked web Gauday had spun. From the depths of his soul arose a forlorn plea to the frail memory of a loving Goddess.

*Zhovanya, if you are real, if you ever loved me, please help me now.*

It was his last try before succumbing to Gauday's downward spiral of hatred, depravity and self-loathing.

# Chapter 11

# Turnaround

In the silent depths of the night—in that warm room, stuffy with the scents of the burning oil lamp, sweat and sex—a soft hush of vast wings brought the cool clarity of a starry winter sky. Kyr awoke with Dekani's last words to him resounding in his mind: *"Call me if you need me. I will awaken."*

At first, Kyr felt his old defiant anger at Dekani for abandoning him twice: once, when Kyr had been made a Slave, and again when he had been about to enter the Sanctuary. But this anger now seemed stale and useless. Worse, it was blocking him from his only source of help in this nightmare. Desperately needed help.

Taking a deep breath, Kyr focused on releasing his old anger as he breathed out, long and slow. After three such breaths, he could see how his defiant anger had helped him survive earlier on, but was foolish now. *Zhovanya, nara lo*, he said in the depths of his heart, *I forgive Dekani, and myself.*

Then he called, *"Dekani, I need you. Wake up! Please, wake up!"*

For a long while, nothing happened. Kyr had no more strength to plead or beg. He sagged in defeat, feeling his soul sliding toward the slime pit of Gauday's madness.

And then Kyr found himself crouching on a dusty plain barren of all but a few twisted tree skeletons. A chaos of storm clouds swirled above. Kyr was shocked to find that he appeared to be a crippled wretch, hair and beard wild and filthy, skin covered with oozing sores. Shivering, he called one last time, *"Dekani, Teacher, please wake up! I need help!"*

In a swirl of brilliant white, Dekani appeared, holding a staff. *"Gods above and below! Is that you, Kyr?"* He frowned in concern, his changeable robes darkening from white to smoky gray. *"What's happened to you?"*

Kyr couldn't bear to look above his teacher's sandal-clad feet. *"I – I'm sorry to wake you, Teacher. I... I... uh...."*

Before Kyr could find words, Dekani said kindly, *"Never mind now. Come, let's go home."*

Atop Dekani's staff, a crystal glowed brightly, lighting the way across the desolate plain. With each step, the landscape reshaped itself. Soon they were walking through the familiar forest-edged meadow. A few more steps and they reached the Teacher's cozy cottage. Dekani went in, but Kyr stood by the door, uncertain of his worthiness to enter.

*"Come in, son. You're always welcome here. You look chilled. Go sit by the fire while I fetch you a shawl."*

Kyr crept in and crouched on the edge of his usual chair by the small hearth, stunned to be in this familiar place of safety after so long. Still unable to look his teacher in the eye, he sat hunched over, staring at the fire. The flames cowered in the hearth, seeming to radiate shadows and sadness. Since he had last seen his teacher at the Heart of the Forest, he had been healed, forgiven, transformed, and sent back into hell to be degraded and corrupted again.

*"Here, this should help."* Dekani handed him a woolen shawl of an indeterminate brown-gray, a bit ragged but warm and soft.

*"Thank you."* He clutched the shawl around his shoulders. At this touch of kindness, tears threatened to flood the cottage. He clenched his jaw and swallowed them down.

*"Ah, son, I am saddened to see you in such a state. If you will allow it, I can alleviate some of your distress. I am a Healer Mage, after all."*

Kyr nodded, unable to speak for the tightness of his throat.

Dekani suddenly seemed taller, brighter, vibrant with unleashed power. This strange and majestic version of his inner teacher moved to stand behind him. Singing a deep, soft tone, Dekani held both hands just above Kyr's shoulders. Kyr sensed something being gently drawn out of him, something the color of ashes. After a time, his anguish and despair diminished to a bearable level. He heaved a deep sigh and straightened up. Dekani raised the tone he was singing to a high, clear tone, and Kyr sensed a golden-green flow of love and compassion filling his heart.

Dekani smiled to see that no longer did Kyr appear to be a woeful cripple but a strong young man, though gaunt and tense, with shadowed, weary eyes. The Healer Mage resumed his usual more humble appearance and took his seat before the fire, which glowed warm and bright in the hearth. *"Feeling better?"*

*"Gods, yes! Thank you."*

*"Are you ready to tell me what's going on?"*

An empty calmness allowed Kyr to describe his situation. He ended by saying, *"If I die or escape, Gauday and his men will destroy the Sanctuary...torture, rape, and kill Jolanya and many others...and kill Medari and his family. I don't want to let any of that happen, but I'm losing hold. I tried to kill Gauday tonight, even though his death would unleash the same consequences."*

*"Goddess help us! I had no idea it would be so bad!"*

Kyr frowned in puzzlement. *"What do you mean 'you had no idea'?"*

Dekani ignored his question, but met Kyr's gaze. *"Know that you are no longer alone in this. Together, we will endure until Rajani arrives."*

*"Ah, gods."* Kyr bit his lip, fighting back tears of relief and gratitude. *"Thanks."*

Dekani seemed to debate something with himself, then nodded. *"Alright, I am going to give you some gifts. All you have to do is accept them. You can relax, even sleep. Just let yourself go heavy, relax into the chair. Close your eyes. Good."* Dekani stood and held one hand over Kyr's chest, the other over his head.

As Kyr drifted into a relaxed, dream-like state, he felt something strange happening: new understandings awakening in his mind; a new strength flooding into him. He rediscovered the kailitha still glowing deep in his core, that golden warmth of love and faith he had received from Jolanya. A slight smile touched his lips as he slipped into a restful sleep.

At first light, Kyr woke with a new sense of composure and solidity. Gauday slept on, his arm still pinning Kyr to the bed.

*"Dekani?"* Kyr waited but his teacher did not appear. His heart sank. *"Teacher? Are you here? Or did I just dream of you?"*

*"Don't worry. I'm no dream."* Dekani looked gray and haggard.

*"Thank the gods! You're really here!"* Noticing Dekani's appearance, Kyr frowned. *"Are you all right?"*

"I'm just feeling a bit drained. I'll be better after I rest a while."

"That's good. I don't know what you did for me but I feel a lot stronger and calmer. Thank you!"

"I will help you survive. Call on me whenever you need me."

"Gods, it's so good to hear that! But I'm afraid I may need you all the time. This situation is—very difficult."

"Don't worry about me, son."

"I can't express how grateful I am, Teacher."

Dekani brushed this aside with a wave of his hand. "Why did you wait so long to wake me?"

Kyr's face grew hot. "I was being a dolt. I was mad at you for abandoning me before I reached the Sanctuary, and earlier, when I was accepted as a Slave of the Master."

"Ah. I'm sorry, but it was...."

"Necessary. You were right. Earlier, you had to hide from the Soul-Drinker's mental powers. He would have torn my mind apart to find you. And later, at the Sanctuary, I needed to go through the healing there on my own."

Dekani smiled kindly. "Well, son, don't wait so long next time."

"I won't." Kyr's heart ached with unaccustomed warmth.

"Now, while I rest, you need to consider how to survive until Rajani gets here. Will you be all right for a while?"

"Yes, thank you, Teacher." Hands together before his heart, he bowed deeply to Dekani, tremendously grateful not to have to face his imprisonment alone any longer. His teacher smiled and returned the bow before fading away.

Gauday was soundly asleep. Kyr slid out from under his captor's arm, settled himself more comfortably on the bed and considered his situation in the light of Dekani's presence and help. *Ah, now I see. Rajani hasn't had enough time to gather and supply the force needed to conquer Gauday's armed band. He'll be arriving when the roads are dry enough for horses.* Hope, given new fuel, re-ignited from the ashes of his heart.

*Gods, how could I make myself forget my friends, my beloved, my Goddess? I thought I had to forget in order to survive in Gauday's mad hell. But I was wrong. My experiences with my friends and at the Sanctuary are not a weakness, but the source of my one true advantage over Gauday. From them, I have learned that there is a way other than the Soul-Drinker's vicious path of rage and cruelty. I know that kindness, friendship, and love are real. I have received the blessings of the Goddess: forgiveness and healing. These memories, this knowing, are my true, shield against Gauday's madness, not the false protection of anger and hatred.*

And at once, all his memories returned: memories of his friends and healers: Rajani and Luciya, Tenaiya and Svahar, Naran and Jolanya; memories of the beauty of waterfalls, mountain sunsets, and the magnificence of the Great Tree. Most treasured of all were his memories of dancing with Zhovanya in Her Temple; and of dancing with Jolanya in the sacred chamber, the Kailithama, crucible of his healing. These memories did not bring the devastating pain of loss and grief he had expected, but instead were blessings bringing him a quiet joy and calm strength.

But then he remembered that terrible night when Gauday had left him out in the rain. *Why did I lose hold and give up, that night? Gods, I got so cold! And I felt so forsaken that I abandoned the hard path.* With a rueful sigh, he realized that, despite his previous certainty, Zhovanya had not deserted him. On that cold night of mud and despair, it was *he* who had turned his back on *Her.* And now he recalled Zhovanya's gift of counsel. *Soften, soften, soften*, he coaxed his desiccated heart. As he repeated Her gift of counsel, a hard shell of blame melted away, and his soul opened like a new flower to Zhovanya's sunshine.

*"O, Goddess, I beg Your forgiveness for abandoning You. Thank You for reminding me to call on my Teacher. With his help and Yours, I will return to the hard path."*

The subtle velvet cloak of Her Presence settled upon him, reawakening compassion and softness, filling him again with an understanding of Her love for all Her children as aspects of Her very Self. In the silence of his melting soul, he sang, *Zhovanya nara lo, Zhovanya nara lo, Zhovanya nara lo.*

Much later that morning, Kyr woke, bruised and aching. The cold iron of the shackle on his wrist reminded him of last night's assault. He frowned in puzzlement, finding no anger or despair weighing down his heart. But then he breathed a quiet sigh of relief. He was no longer alone in the battle with Gauday's madness.

Gratitude for that new calmness and strength that Dekani's healing had brought him filled his heart. And he realized that, more importantly, he had forgiven Dekani and Zhovanya for seeming to forsake him. He had even forgiven himself for turning his back on them, and for abandoning the hard path. No wonder his heart felt lighter!

Instead of brooding over the terrible trap Gauday had him in, Kyr thought now of all the blessings he had been granted: the forgiveness and love of the Goddess; friends who cared for him; the golden ball of kailitha the Kailithana had given him; and a secret treasure in his heart: Jolanya's love for him.

Kyr looked at his sleeping captor, and asked himself, *What gifts has Gauday been given?* Only the torment all Slaves had suffered as children while being tortured into being mindlessly obedient Slaves of the Soul-Drinker. Only the agony and pleasure their Master had inflicted on them all. Only the smoke that Gauday had breathed in: the vile sorcerous remnant of the Master's Crown, which was continuing to twist and distort his mind and heart. *Gauday, too, is a child of the Goddess, a lost child,* Kyr thought. *Perhaps I can help him somehow.*

Still pinned down by Gauday's arm, and trapped by the shackle on his wrist, Kyr relaxed into a peaceful doze.

"Alright, lazy cur, time to wake up." Leaning on one elbow, Gauday bent over Kyr, licked his ear, and murmured, "You are mine, now, my boy. You belong to me now and forever." There was a triumphant gleam in his eye.

Kyr shivered at Gauday's lewd possessiveness, but thinking of all that Gauday had suffered, he said, "I'm so sorry, Day."

"What?" Gauday recoiled. Shaking his head, he gave an unsteady laugh. "No need to apologize, my boy. If you like it rough, I'm sure I can oblige you."

"That's not what I meant." Kyr regarded his captor steadily. *It will take a long time to help Gauday free himself from the Master's evil taint, if it's even possible. Perhaps kindness will win him over eventually, as it did me. I have to try. It's my chosen Atonement.* His face went hot with shame at having forgotten this for so long. Gently, he asked, "What may I do for you, Day?"

Gauday glared at him in consternation. "Bring me my tea and draw me a bath," he snapped. "I certainly need one after our little wrestling match."

Kyr held up his manacled wrist. Gauday grabbed the keys off his bedside table and unlocked the shackle.

"Hurry up," he snarled, grabbing Kyr by the arm and yanking him out of bed.

In the following days, Kyr treated his captor kindly, took initiative in housekeeping chores instead of awaiting orders, even showed a mild affection in their sex life. Vexed by Kyr's calm patience, Gauday began to strike out with less subtlety. He often kept Kyr nude and chained at his feet, especially when his cronies came for meetings or meals. Using Kyr as a chip in some obscure game with them, he began giving him to one and then another of these men for sex.

"Don't damage my favorite boy," he'd say as he handed Kyr over to the chosen one.

One night, after Te'ordo, a stout, red-faced Slave, stumbled off to his own quarters, Kyr lay abed, waiting for Gauday, who was still drinking and gambling with his cronies. In these few moments of blessed solitude, Kyr's attempt to meditate was blocked by a nagging sense of distress. *Why does it bother me to be handed around to Gauday's men? I knew what I was in for when I walked out of the Sanctuary's gate. It isn't as if being used for sex is anything new.* He sighed and turned onto his other side. *At least now, the cruder forms of brutality are not allowed, so why do I feel so badly?* He followed the thread of hurt into his heart, where he discovered that a part of him actually wanted to believe that deep down, Gauday did care for him somehow.

*Gods, how could I let myself believe that for a moment? Well, I even tried to believe that the Master loved me, didn't I? I guess the heart needs love so much, it will try to find it in the least likely places. I should know by now where the true Source of love is.* He turned his heart toward the Goddess, praying for strength and patience. A gentleness of soft wings enfolded him.

119

# Chapter 12

# Painful Kindness

A few nights later, Gauday and two of his cronies, Craith and Lorno, a Slave with a penchant for cruelty, were sitting up late by the fire, drinking wine and brandy, and playing at dice. Kyr was the prize. He knelt by Gauday's chair, nude and in chains. One side of his body was hot from the fire, the other chilled.

"Come on, pretties! Give me the victory!" Lorno rolled the dice, leering at Kyr. "Blast!" He drained his glass and slammed it down in disgust. "You win, Craith."

"Ah, Craith, my dear," Gauday said. "This is your first time, isn't it? Be good to my favorite boy now. Kyr is yours for the rest of the night."

"Ah, thanks, thanks. I won't damage him—too much."

The others laughed at this and went back to their dicing. This time the stakes were a choice of the village girls they had enslaved. Craith poured himself another glass of brandy and watched the game.

Despite his remark, the redhead was slow to take advantage of his win. Kyr glanced at him, briefly curious, but was distracted by something else. The way Gauday had said "favorite boy" reminded him of the day he had become the Master's Favorite. This felt important somehow, but Kyr couldn't quite put his finger on what was bothering him. As he knelt near Gauday's chair, waiting for Craith, he closed his eyes and retreated into memory. Since Dekani had gifted him with strength and serenity, he found solace in recalling the kindness of his friends and Jolanya's love.

"Wake up, lazy cur. Time to play."

Craith's voice brought Kyr back to his current misery. With a sigh, he focused his mind on the Goddess's gift of counsel and followed Craith down the hall past Gauday's bedroom and into the next room.

Craith draped himself over Kyr's shoulders like an overly friendly drunkard, but his whispered words undercut that picture.

"I'm only here because Gauday expects it. He is probably watching us through spy-holes. Just do me and I'll leave you be."

Kyr froze for a moment, startled by such thoughtfulness, then gave a slight nod.

"Awright, li'l cur," slurred the redhead loudly, "y' know what I wancha ta do." Craith stumbled over and fell onto the bed, yanking his trousers open. Kyr knelt between his legs and carried out the task. Afterwards, Craith dragged him up onto the bed and fumbled at him for a few moments, then subsided with his leg and arm pinning Kyr to the bed, and began to snore in a fine imitation of drink-sodden sleep.

Kyr was just about asleep himself, when Craith's sham snoring ceased. He buried his face in Kyr's hair. "I'm sure he's gone off to find something more entertaining than my snoring by now." Despite this assurance, he was still whispering.

"Thank you," said Kyr softly.

"For what? Not hurting you?"

"Well, yes. Kindness is not common here."

Craith snorted. "I am not one for the pleasures of the Master's court."

"Yes, I see that. Why are you still here?"

"I don't know what else to do."

"You do not seem pleased to be under Gauday's command."

"True. But here, I have a place, a job to do. I wouldn't know where else to go." He shrugged. "I'm just a soldier."

"How long have you been a soldier?"

"Since I was ten, and the Master's Gatherers took me." Craith's voice was steady, but his eyes betrayed a deep sorrow. Kyr looked away.

"I think you would be happier under my friend's command. Rajani, the Warrior Mage, is a man you could respect." Kyr tried to imagine what would happen to Gauday's band if Craith defected. *Gods, they'd be at each other's throats in no time. Might be good for me, or it might make things even worse.*

"No, no." The redhead was quivering with tension and his eyes were fearful. "I can't risk it. What Gauday would do to me if he caught me trying to desert—I can't face that again."

Kyr subsided, wondering what Gauday had done to make Craith so fearful. He shivered, hoping he would never find out.

After a few moments of silence, Craith shifted onto an elbow so he could look Kyr in the face. "This may be my only chance to tell you. I never saw a braver act than when you stepped through that Sanctuary gate."

"Oh, gods," Kyr whispered, overcome with grief for all he had lost by that act.

"I'm sorry. I didn't mean to upset you."

Wanting any distraction—pain or pleasure—as long as it kept him from knowing his heart's sorrow, Kyr leaned up and kissed Craith hard on the mouth. Craith pushed him away.

"No, you don't have to...."

"I want to." Using all he had learned from Jolanya, Kyr aroused the redhead again. Their love-making—for so it was, despite everything—bloomed into an incandescent fusion of passion, grief, guilt, pain, and tenderness.

Afterwards, Kyr and Craith rested in each other's arms. They knew without speaking that they must never let anyone see their new-born affinity. The slightest flicker of acknowledgment between them would set Gauday tearing at them like a jackal, until the living flesh of the love his famished soul hungered for was nothing but offal. It was all Gauday knew to do with love and kindness.

The thought of leaving the haven of Craith's arms was so odious that Kyr suddenly felt sick. "Gods, I never want to leave, but if I don't, Gauday will come looking for me." He groaned softly and buried his face on the redhead's chest.

"Shhhh, shhhh. Just a little while longer." Craith stroked his hair gently, and Kyr shivered with the pain of tenderness after so much cruelty.

"If he found us like this, he'd be furious. He'd find ways to torment you as well as me. I have to get up. Merciless gods, I have to."

"I've gone and made it harder for you. I'm sorry."

"No, no." Kyr looked up and met Craith's green eyes. "Thank you. You've reminded me that there is more to life than Gauday's madness."

"Yes, me too." Craith caressed Kyr's cheek sadly, rose, and tugged his clothes into place. "Don't know what good it does either of us." Avoiding Kyr's eyes, he left for his bunk in the barracks.

Kyr dragged himself off the bed and started up the hall toward Gauday's room. With each step, he became more nauseated. Gasping, he hurried outside onto the porch and heaved his dinner into the mud. Afterwards, desperate to feel clean, he held his hands out to the downpour. With handfuls of rain, he rinsed his mouth out and splashed his face, over and over. At last, his frenzy subsided and he stood watching the storm rage in the empty yard.

The sentry tower by the gate was dark, but dim light crept from the crack around a nearby door. In all likelihood, the sentries were inside, playing at dice. He stared at the unguarded gate, shivering, but shook his head. Escape would only mean a slow, cold death in the mud and rain. Besides, nothing had changed. He was still trapped by love and duty.

He turned to go in, but could not force himself through the door. Heart-wounds reopened by Craith's kindness ached so fiercely that he still couldn't face returning to his captor's bed.

*"Teacher? Please, I need help."*

*"Yes, son. I know. Sing with me."* Dekani spoke without appearing, and began the chant. Its resonance slowly calmed Kyr's heart. With a deep sigh, he joined in, silently repeating, *"Zhovanya nara lo. Zhovanya nara lo. Zhovanya nara lo. Zhovanya nara lo."*

After a time, he found the strength to go inside. Gauday was sprawled on the bed, fully clothed but snoring heavily. Chilled and exhausted, Kyr wrapped himself in one of the fur coverlets and lay down as far from his sleeping tormenter as he could.

Stale, wine-laden breath choked Kyr into wakefulness. "Didja have a good time with wha'shizname, that redhead?" Gauday planted a drunken kiss on Kyr's neck.

Kyr fought not to show any sign of his utter repugnance. "It's late, Day. Let's just get some sleep."

"Don'cha defy ME!" Gauday lunged at him, trying to pin him down. Disgusted, Kyr tried to evade his captor's drunken embrace. In their struggle, an elbow or knee bumped the nightstand. The low-burning night lamp went out, plunging the room into darkness. Gauday sprawled on top of Kyr, clutching him in an iron grip.

"Nonononono!" Gauday's voice was high and panicky, like a young boy frightened beyond endurance. Shocked and perplexed, Kyr stopped struggling to get free.

"What is it? What's wrong?"

"It's dark, dark, oh, nonono, please, no!"

"I can't get the lamp lit unless you get off me."

Gauday gripped Kyr even tighter, whimpering "Nonononono."

"Come on, Day. You have to let go of me."

It did no good. Kyr realized that Gauday was lost in a childhood nightmare. He took a breath and adopted a soothing, reassuring tone.

"Calm down now, Day. It's all right. Let me up so I can light the lamp. Come now. It's all right. I promise I'll get the light."

"You'll get the light? You're getting the light now?"

"Yes, Day, let go and I'll get the light. Let me up now."

Gauday released his death grip and rolled over, muttering, "He's getting the light, he's getting the light now."

Kyr felt about on the bedside table for the flint striker, and, after a few tries, relit the lamp. Gauday sat hunched up on the bed, staring at the low light of the night lamp as if it were the only thing in the world.

Seeing his tormenter frightened and vulnerable, Kyr realized more clearly than ever that Gauday was a deranged child, crippled and twisted first by the Soul-Drinker's torments, and now by the sorcerous smoke from the Crown. He placed a comforting arm around his captor's shoulders. Gauday leaned into Kyr for a moment.

Then he stiffened and shrugged Kyr's arm off. "How dare you?" he snarled in a low, furious voice. "You put that light out, after I forbade it." His eyes flared red.

Kyr grabbed his head. A burning vise gripped his brain, tightening with each breath. "S-sorry," he panted. "Ac-ci-dent."

"Liar! You did that on purpose!"

Gauday got up and jerked his garments into place, his eyes returning to normal. Kyr slumped in relief as the scorching pain ceased.

"You shall pay for this, boy. You shall pay." Gauday stalked from the room.

Kyr was left wondering what his crime had been. *Ah, yes. I saw through his facade, saw his fear. He'll never forgive me for that.* The calm patience he had felt ever since Dekani had awakened was drowned by dread.

That afternoon, Gauday was sitting in his padded armchair by the fire, relaxing with a glass of red wine. A pottery cup was sitting on the low table by Gauday's elbow, steaming slightly.

As usual, Kyr knelt at Gauday's feet, shivering a little despite the fire. His captor had denied him clothing ever since the night the lamp had gone out. He was glad in a way, because it reminded him of his true status here, despite Gauday's constant endearments.

"Are you cold, my boy?" Gauday picked up the pottery cup. "Here, I have a special treat for you. Drink this down now. It will warm you up." Seeing Kyr's guarded look, Gauday took a good swallow, then handed him the cup. "See, it's safe enough."

The cup was full of a dark, oily liquid with a sinister reek. Kyr's heart sank. He glanced up to find his captor watching him avidly.

"Go on now. Drink it all."

Kyr sighed. *No matter what it is, it will do me no good to refuse. He'd delight in having his men force it down my throat.* He bowed his head for a moment, seeking once again to release his fear, to soften his heart. *Zhovanya, give me strength.* He drank the venomous potion down.

"There's a good boy," Gauday said with a predatory smile. "You'll feel ever so much better soon."

At first, Kyr felt no effects from Gauday's venom. It certainly wasn't warming him, though the fire seemed brighter. No, the cold was still biting him. In fact, it seemed colder. A sharp clink made him jump, but it was merely Gauday setting the pottery cup down.

"Come with me, my dear." Kyr winced at the painful loudness of his captor's voice. Gauday unchained him and pulled him to his feet. As they walked toward the bedroom, Gauday draped one arm across Kyr's shoulders. He gasped at the intensely sensuous touch of Gauday's soft velvet jacket on his bare skin. Gauday chuckled. "Ah, yes. Good, good. The potion is working. I'm sure you will enjoy the new games I have planned for you." Kyr's stomach heaved, and he stumbled. He knew what kind of games Gauday meant.

Bypassing the bedroom, Gauday led him down the corridor to an unfamiliar room, and threw open the door. "Welcome to my special room!"

Kyr stopped in the doorway, and shook his head, trying to clear out the buzzing of potion-intensified sensations. The light from the hallway fell on a long table cluttered with bottles of dried plants and oily liquids, mixing bowls, and a mortar and pestle. Windowless, the room was dimly lit by three red glass oil lamps sitting on the table. An unholy altar loomed further back. As Kyr's eyes adapted to the dimness, he saw that it was a wide bed, its four posters festooned with leather straps and chains. Beside the bed, red embers smoldered in an iron brazier, and a small table offered scraps of silk and fur, knives, small metal rods, clamps, and needles.

"Oh, gods!" Kyr whispered. Hopeless, he still had to try. "Listen to me, Day. Don't drag us back into the Master's hell. This will only deepen the quagmire your soul is trapped in."

"Oh, pah! What's this nonsense about souls? I have so much to teach you, my boy. Such intensity, such passion! You'll love it. I promise."

"There's so much more to life, Day. Please, let me show you. Let *me* teach *you* the beauty and wonder of real love, real love-making."

"Shut up and get in there!" Gauday's eyes blazed red.

Kyr's knees buckled under the assault of scorching pain. With brutal strength, Gauday shoved him into the ill-omened room. The heavy door closed with terrifying finality.

# Chapter 13

# Fierce Gifts

Impatiently, Rajani wiped at the sweat that was threatening to drip off his face and onto the map he was studying yet again. "Gods and demons!" he muttered. "Where could they have gone?" Though the rains were tapering off, and they had been scouring the land for a month, they were no closer to finding Kyr than when they began this search.

Now they were pursuing a rumor about some kind of trouble on or near the Thumb, a stubby arm of the Sand Sea, which cut into the eastern quadrant of Khailaz. Blessedly, the Sun was nearing the horizon, bringing some relief from the desert heat. "Gods curse it!" Rajani let the map roll up into its tight scroll, slid it back into its leather tube, and stepped out of the stuffy tent.

A slight evening breeze cooled his face and ruffled the knee-length linen tunic he was wearing. With only sandals on his feet and without his black riding leathers and boots, he felt oddly light. But his heart was weighed down with guilt and concern for what Kyr must be enduring. Rajani trudged up to the top of a nearby sand dune, and stood watching the Sun sink toward the violet haze on the horizon.

Below him, the camp of the self-named Companions of the Liberator spread out, with bedrolls laid out in circles around ten campfires. People were playing card games, or practicing swordplay or hand-to-hand combat. Rajani frowned, knowing they were getting edgy and bored with the lack of action. "By the Lights," he growled. "How am I supposed to rescue Kyr so he can fulfill the Prophecy if I can't find him?"

He'd sent out his scouts, followed every hint, but had not found a trace of Gauday and his band. At his wits' end, he knelt on the hot, gritty sand, and held his arms out toward the Sun. "Zhovanya, Kyr has suffered enough! If he is to have the strength to fulfill the Prophecy, he must be found. Help us find him!"

A rosy beam of light broke through the darkening haze, bathing his weary soul with gentle warmth, and bringing with it the ethereal weight of the Goddess's Presence.

*"Zhovanya!"* he whispered, surprised that this time, She was answering him. *"Dear Goddess, please!"* he more demanded than implored. *"Help us find Kyr! If he is to restore You to Your rightful place, You must help us!"*

*"AH, STRONG ONE, CAN YOU NOT TRUST THAT ALL IS AS IT NEEDS TO BE?"*

*"Trust?"* Rajani was suddenly furious. *"Trust? I trust that Kyr is suffering unholy torments, while I wander in the desert trying to find him!"*

*"THE RHYME AND REASON OF DESTINY ARE NOT THE SAME AS YOUR HUMAN WISHES."*

*"My whole life, my brother's life, Kyr's life are evidence of that,"* Rajani snarled. *"You ask too much!"*

*"I AM SORRY,"* Zhovanya said, her tone soft yet heavy with a staggering weight of grief.

*This astonishing divine apology shocked through Rajani like lightning and cracked open his stony heart. He buried his face in his hands, and his shoulders heaved with silent sobs. Long-suppressed tears leaked through his fingers.*

*When his tears ebbed, Zhovanya's Presence was gone. Feeling cleansed of much of his anger and guilt, the Warrior Mage got to his feet and bowed to the fiery crescent of the Sun as She disappeared into darkness. Quietly, he stood watching the evening stars begin to shine.*

"Ah, sir?"

Rajani whirled around. "Gods, Lorya, don't sneak up on me like that!"

"Isn't that why you asked for me?" She gave him a sly smile. "Sneaking is what I'm good at."

"Hah! You're right." Rajani had to laugh. "Any news?"

"Maybe. There's a man who says he can show us where Gauday is hiding out—for a price." Her tone revealed her disgust with this mercenary offer.

"We've had other such offers. Upon questioning, they have proved worthless. But bring him to my tent.

"Sorry, sir," Lorya broke in. "He insists on meeting us out in the open, over by that little oasis where we're keeping the horses."

"Hmmph. Well, I don't see why not." The sudden chill of the desert night made Rajani shiver. "Find Jakar while I change."

A short time later, the Warrior Mage was feeling more like himself in his black leathers, with his blackwood wand, sword, and knives on his person where they belonged. He joined Jakar and Lorya on the path toward the oasis. "Tell us about this man as we walk, Lorya. How did you find him?"

"I was in a camp of some nomads to the south of us. They are taking their goats across the Thumb to their springtime pastures. This man was there asking where he could find 'those idiots who are hunting for Gauday.' The nomads were telling him nothing, and he was yelling at them, all arrogant and nasty." She rolled her eyes. "As if that would get them to co-operate."

"Sounds like a pleasant character," snorted Jakar.

They reached the oasis, and were greeted by the nickering and wuffling of the Companions' horses. They were tethered to ropes strung between the scattering of palm trees that surrounded the pond of slightly brackish but drinkable water.

"There he is." Lorya pointed to a figure pacing back and forth by the far edge of the pool.

Rajani headed toward the man. "Well, let's see if he's got anything useful to tell us."

Perhaps a half-moon had passed. It was impossible to tell in that windowless room. Kyr was exhausted, and his endurance was eroding. He trembled with terror and desire every time Gauday came near. As he watched his tormentor mixing another batch of the venomous potion, he thought, *After all, we were both Slaves of the Master. We* are *alike.* Gauday proceeded as usual, but this time, his crooning incantation changed. "You're my favorite boy and I am the Master now. I am the Master. You will always do as I say. I am the Master now."

Afterwards, Kyr lay alone, dazed and drugged. He was helpless and at the mercy of his tormentor, just as he had always been. *It is true. Gauday is the Master now. As usual, all I can do is obey.*

"*KYR!*" Dekani's cry was a thunderclap, jolting Kyr out of his daze. "*Wake up! He's getting to you. Don't give in to him!*" In an instant, they were in their usual chairs by the fire in Dekani's cottage. The Healer Mage held his hands up and sent a Flow of cool, crystalline kailitha that washed away the effects of Gauday's venom.

Kyr stared at Dekani in dismay. "*Gods and demons! I almost lost hold. What is Gauday doing to my mind?*"

Dekani sighed heavily. "*I guess it's time I told you. He's using spellchants and his noxious potions, trying to mind-bond you like the Soul-Drinker did with his Watchers.*"

"*WHAT? NO!*" Kyr leaped to his feet, arms up as if to defend from a blow. "*Merciless gods! Not that! Not that!*"

"*Calm down, son.*"

Kyr dropped his arms and stared at Dekani in disbelief. "*Calm down? Don't you know what that means? I'd spend the rest of my life enslaved to Gauday's vicious whims, torturing and killing people in whatever mad ways he demanded. No will of my own, just like the cursed Watchers! I'd rather die, and damn the consequences. You can't let that happen to me!*"

"*I'll protect you. Try to calm down.*"

"*By all the hells, why didn't you warn me?*"

"*I didn't want to add to your fear. I've been protecting you the best I can, helping you resist his enchantment. Luckily, he isn't a trained sorcerer, and doesn't know much about what he is doing, only what little he can decipher from the Soul-Drinker's grimoire—his manual of black magic—and some understanding from the smoke he inhaled when the Crown burned.*"

Kyr stalked to the open door, staring out at the peaceful meadow and taking deliberate breaths. After a few moments, his heart slowed and he could think again. He turned to face his teacher. "*How can I defend myself?*"

"*You need a counter-chant. Anything you can repeat and hold onto will help block Gauday's spell. The forgiveness chant works especially well, as it helps dissolve hatred. You've been using it on your own, but now you need some help. I will reinforce it, chant it with you.*"

"Alright. But I can't go on unless you promise me that you won't let him mind-bond me—even if that means granting me the Final Grace."

Dekani was silent, frowning down at his clenched hands, obviously struggling with this demand. Then, for many moments, he stared into the fire as if looking into some distant place or time. Finally, his shoulders slumped and he whispered, "Zhovanya nara li." With a sigh, he straightened and faced Kyr. "Alright. I promise, and damn the consequences." His eyes were haunted and dark with anguish. "If Gauday is about to succeed in mind-bonding you, I will end your life, even though it means ending mine. But only if there is no other choice."

The tension drained out of Kyr, and he returned to his chair. "I'm sorry, Teacher. I know this might mean your death also, is that not true? You exist within my mind, don't you?"

"Yes, but that does not matter. Let's set all that aside for now. We must focus all our efforts on preventing Gauday from succeeding."

Reassured by Dekani's promise, Kyr slumped back in his chair. "Gods, I'm tired."

"Sleep now, son." Dekani held up a hand, and Kyr was carried away by a wave of kindly darkness, from which not even Gauday's attempted torments could awaken him for the rest of that day and half the next.

One night, instead of leaving to drink with his cronies, Gauday remained with Kyr in that ghastly bed. Kyr shuddered at his touch, but Gauday clung close, whispering the spellchant in Kyr's ear. "You are mine, my boy, mine forever. I am your Master. You will always do as I wish. You are mine." At last, snoring replaced the insidious whispering.

Though his body begged for sleep, Kyr lay wakeful, his skin crawling. *What is this? He's clinging to me like I am his beloved.* A shock ran through Kyr's body. *Gods! All those years as rivals for the Master's attention—no one is closer to him than I am. Thanks to the Soul-Drinker, this horror is all Gauday knows of closeness. Merciless gods! Does he actually think he loves me? Oh gods, oh gods!*

Tears, laughter, and screams all bubbled in his throat. He buried his face in the covers and fought to be still, but ended up choking on hysterical giggles. Gauday slept beside him undisturbed. Chained and helpless, Kyr was desperate to flee far, far from his tormentor's twisted, deadly idea of love. He tried to return to his soul-saving chant, but his heart was thundering, and his breath came in rapid gasps.

*"Teacher, help me! Help me!"*

*"Alright, I'm with you. I'm with you. Listen now."*

Dekani began to sing the song that had saved Kyr's soul during his horrendous Training to become the Soul-Drinker's Slave.

> *"High above the ice, he flies,*
> *alone and disregarded,*
> *lordling of the skies."*

*The song had not lost any of its power. Soon Kyr was again in the pristine haven of his childhood, soaring over the white plains of ice as a great bird. For a time, he knew only the fierce serenity of the eagle's flight. Then, Kyr's pain and despair returned, and the eagle screamed out his anguish in harsh cries, shattering the sterile tranquility of the icy world.*

"WHY? O GODDESS, WHY?"

*The white ice broke apart and Kyr was flung into a dark void. Swirling winds threatened to tear his soul apart, and he was glad for an end, any kind of end.*

*But then huge claws enclosed him and fiery wings raised him higher and higher into the blackness of the star-strewn sky, until all of Khailaz lay spread out beneath him. Looking down, he could see with preternatural distinctness the dusty, desolate fort below him; the northern forest and mountains, which hid the Sanctuary; the Sand Sea to the east; the City to the south by the ocean called the Blue Desert.*

*As he stared in awe, the land began to glimmer with a multitude of shining, vibrant threads, loosely interwoven in the sparsely settled lands; drawn into dense, tight tapestries in villages, towns and, largest of all, the City. All the threads were alive and slowly growing in accordance with an incomprehensible pattern. As some threads winked out, others came into being. Beginning as glorious, golden bursts of light, they slowly elongated into shimmering, silver threads, some shining brightly, some tarnished and dim.*

"Ah, Goddess!" *he breathed, as understanding filled his mind.* "Those silver threads, they are our lives—our entire lives from birth to death. This is how You see our land, how You see us!"

*For a time, he was lost in rapt contemplation of the ethereal splendor of Zhovanya's vision. He saw how the dimmer threads helped create the pattern as much as did the brighter ones. Eliminating either would destroy the wondrous beauty of the tapestry of life.*

*Then, with an eagle's dispassionate clarity, he began to contemplate his own life.* At the Sanctuary, I thought I had escaped the merciless gods of my childhood. Now I know that Zhovanya is as merciless as they. Why is it that the Goddess gives us these lives, these bodies that can suffer so?

*He remembered the first time he had seen Zhovanya, dancing in the Temple. She danced through every aspect of life, dark and light, savage and beautiful.* Does She want us to undergo all aspects of life as She does?

Perhaps *that* is my atonement: to experience everything in its purest form: agony, abasement, terror, hatred—*and* pleasure, ecstasy, exaltation, love. *His heart ached with banished tears as he remembered Jolanya's luminous smile.* No, I mustn't think of her. Forget the past. There is only now. Only now—and Gauday.

*He turned his eagle eye on his present predicament. From a distance, he sensed his degradation and helplessness, his terror and despair. Yet, in this detached state of mind, he saw something almost unthinkable. The pain and pleasure that Gauday imposed on him was so pure and so intense, it was almost holy—a sacred, cleansing fire. Even Gauday's hatred, unmarred by conscience or guilt or shame, had its own purity. It was, in truth, a dark and twisted search for love, driven by the deepest longing of a lost soul for what he needed but never knew—and which he deserved, as all souls do.*

*Determined to understand why it was that Zhovanya had cast him into a life of such suffering, Kyr sought for the thread that was his own life, hoping to trace out its meaning and purpose. A silver cord led from his heart to a particular thread in the pattern. Almost, he could see the beginning of his thread; but unlike all the other threads, there was no burst of golden light, only an obscuring smokiness. Striving to see through the smoke, he dove toward his filament. As he got closer, he saw that when his thread emerged from the initial smokiness, it was nearly as dark as the smoke, but slowly grew brighter.* And look, my thread seems to be a double strand. That's odd. And what is that brilliant glow further on down? *It was brighter than anything else he could see. He dove closer to that enticing radiance.*

*Small figures appeared in the glowing light. A woman with lustrous black hair was big with child. At her feet knelt a man, his arms wrapped around her, looking up at her with a radiant smile. It was himself. She looked down at him and tenderly caressed his cheek, wiping away a smudge of dust.*

Jolanya! *Kyr's heart exploded with love and joy, and he strove to get closer. But something was tugging on him, pulling him away.* No! Let me see her! Jolanya! *He struggled to return to the tapestry, but was inexorably drawn down the silver cord and back into his physical body.*

"LIVE." *Zhovanya's command echoed through Kyr's being like rolling thunder, carrying the weight of a curse and a caress. With it came a wave of strength and courage. He bowed his head in acquiescence, condemned once again to life.*

He woke lying on the bed next to his tormenter, quivering with the need to scream or laugh or sing praises to the Goddess. But he kept himself still to avoid waking Gauday. Calling on his iron self-discipline, he forced himself to watch his breath until he could relax into the moment. Then, stunned and humbled, he contemplated the transcendent vision Zhovanya had granted him. Though his mind mumbled over the peculiarities of his thread, there was, hidden deep in his soul, a new, sustaining peace, a tranquility of acceptance. Now he knew that his life was a part of the great tapestry that Zhovanya was weaving. And, in a time yet to come, he would somehow be reunited with his beloved.

He called to mind the lambent beauty of the Fire-Bird and the promises he had made to Her on the mountain,: to serve Her and to endure whatever She required of him. *I am Yours, Zhovanya. I am keeping my promises.* He had made another promise, then: to become Her Vessel. *I don't know what this means. Guide me, Zhovanya, and I will fulfill this promise too.* As he drifted into easeful sleep, he whispered, "Such a fierce gift, such a difficult blessing, this life You have given me."

But countless days passed, and there was no respite, no rescue.

He'd lost all track of time. There was only Gauday or his absence, one as bad as the other. When Gauday was there, Kyr begged the Goddess to send his captor away. When his tormentor was absent, he suffered agonies wondering when Gauday would return. His endurance was near an end. All he felt now was a heavy downward pull toward surrender, a longing to give up resistance, to stop fighting, to let go.

Kyr lay supine, chained to the bed. At this moment, Gauday was absent. The small cuts and burns his tormentor had inflicted on him were misery enough, but the mental torture was much worse. His mind reeled and lurched under the impact of Gauday's spellchants and venoms. He could barely recall who he was, and he felt his soul slipping from his grasp. In the stifling silence of that vile chamber, dark voices whispered seductively.

*No one's coming to rescue you,* a leaden voice whispered. *You'll never get free of him. Dekani will never let you die, for it would mean his own death. There's no escape from the Master's curse. You will suffer forever, one way or another.*

More enticing was the fiery tempter who argued, *He's your worst enemy, your torturer. Why do you keep trying to forgive him? Stop being such a milksop. Hatred will make you stronger. You can fight him harder if you let yourself hate him.*

Another voice murmured soothingly, *Why are you fighting so hard? If you let go, you won't really be yourself any longer. If you let him mind-bond you, you'll be no one, just a tool that Gauday uses. You'll never have to struggle or suffer again. Just give in to him. It'll be so much easier.*

"*Kyr!*" Dekani broke in. "*Don't listen! Your soul would be enslaved, not destroyed. Deep inside, you would know what Gauday was using you for—to torture and kill, just like the Soul-Drinker did. For your own soul's sake and for all those Gauday would use you to harm, you must not give up!*"

"*Dekani, please, let me die. Surely Maray has strengthened the Sanctuary's defenses by now. There's no reason for me to keep fighting. Gods curse it! I can't. I can't!*"

Dekani frowned with grim concern. "*Come with me. I'll help you.*"

"*You will? Oh gods, thank you!*"

"*This way.*" Dekani waved his hand and suddenly there appeared a path leading to a glowing, golden Temple.

Kyr followed Dekani, believing that his teacher was about to end his suffering, end his life. They entered the Temple and knelt before the emptiness of the dark dais.

"*Remember!*" Dekani commanded in a penetrating voice.

Before Kyr could object, buried memories blazed up and took over his mind.

> *Zhovanya appeared once again, dancing her dance of fierce serenity, as She had the first time he had seen Her.*
>
> "Goddess, take me home," *he begged.* "Please take me home."
>
> *Radiant with grace and majesty, She paused and stood before him.* "YOU ARE MY BELOVED."
>
> *Anger mixed with simple wonder made Kyr ask,* "If I am Your beloved, what do You do to those You hate?"
>
> "ALL ARE BELOVED. IT IS THOSE WHO TURN AWAY FROM LOVE WHO INFLICT SUFFERING. TO SAVE YOUR SOUL, DO NOT TURN AWAY FROM LOVE."
>
> *The truth of Her words rang through him and he writhed with shame.* "Forgive me, Zhovanya! I have tried, but I can't endure any more. Help me!"
>
> *Unfurling Her great, dark wings, She took him in Her vast arms. He rested in Her embrace as She soared through the endless star-strewn void that was Her Home. As they flew, She absorbed all his pain and fear, love and worship. For a blissful time, all he knew was peace.*

He came to himself in the grassy meadow near Dekani. He felt more strongly than ever that desire for submission, that downward drive to kneel and yield himself up. He knelt and bowed his head.

*"Accept my submission to You, Zhovanya. Accept my submission."*

*"BELOVED."*

From Her vast Heart spilled forth a cascade of shimmering golden light, filling his desiccated heart with sweet nectar. After a time, he sighed and looked around. The sweet scent of wildflowers floated on a quiet breeze, and the stately trees of the forest swayed toward him as if bowing their heads. His teacher knelt by his side, tears trickling down his wrinkled cheeks.

*"Oh, my son, you are the bravest soul ever born in Khailaz!"*

*"I would be lost without you. You fight for my soul even when I have given up."*

Dekani buried his face in his hands, and Kyr was silent, resting in the love they shared and the peace of his surrender to the Goddess.

When Kyr awoke, he was still strapped to the bed in the chamber that had almost been the tomb of his soul. Remembering his teacher's devotion, and the love and peace of his communion with the Goddess, he renewed his determination to fight Gauday's sorcery. Noting the pain of his burns and cuts, the chafing of his bound wrists and ankles, his parched throat, he narrowed his attention to the exact sensation of his breath moving in his body.

As his concentration deepened, he was able to follow his out-breath deep down inside. There was such stillness there at the bottom of the breath, such peace: doing nothing, wanting nothing, resisting nothing, forgiving everything. Kyr's lips curved in a slight smile. If he was to live, the in-breath would come. If not, he was free. It was not up to him.

The breath flowed in and with it came a delicate joy. Though he had no earthly reason for joy, joy it was nevertheless—a subtle, causeless joy that was deeper and more true than anything he had ever known. He rested in this joyous peacefulness, feeling his whole body breathe in, breathe out, until it seemed that the air was a sourceless wave flowing in from everywhere to a point that, in another reality, was his heart; then flowing outward in all directions, unbound. As he drifted into a healing sleep, he was once again blessed with a gift of counsel.

*"LOOK AT HIM THROUGH MY EYES."* Zhovanya's smile was kind, yet Her eyes were stern with implacable wisdom.

The sound of the key turning in the lock brought Kyr awake. Gauday stepped in the door.

Following Zhovanya's counsel, Kyr gazed at his tormenter, and was shocked by what he saw. *Gauday is so sad, so frightened. Ah, Goddess! How does he live? His soul is writhing in shame and horror, and he is so terribly lonely.* It was unbearable, what compassion revealed. Now he understood a little better Zhovanya's sad smile.

Gauday stood just inside the door, frowning. "Why, what have you been up to, my boy?" He waved his hand before his face as if brushing away cobwebs. "No matter. Today, I believe we shall succeed. You will be mine and then.... Ah! We'll have such fun!"

Rubbing his hands together, he started forward, but veered aside, going to his work bench instead. He stood there, fidgeting with various bottles and canisters to no purpose. Still seeing with Zhovanya's eyes, and radiating compassion, Kyr watched his tormenter. Gauday was growing more unsettled by the moment. He tried for his usual condescending poise, but only sounded nervous and petty.

"So sorry, my boy. I think we will have to stop for today. I need to, uh, get some supplies. You can look forward to our session tomorrow. I'll, uh, think of something especially delicious for you." Unable to bear Kyr's compassionate, golden gaze, he hastily retreated from the room.

Kyr almost laughed. Could it be that easy to deter Gauday? Giving thanks to Dekani and to Zhovanya for once again protecting his soul from the trap of bitterness, he slipped into a peaceful dream of working in the garden at the Sanctuary alongside Naran.

Much later, Kyr was deep in meditation, silently chanting *Zhovanya nara lo, Zhovanya nara lo, Zhovanya nara lo.*

A rattling of several keys being tried in the lock and muffled cursing announced Gauday's return. Finally, he yanked the door open and stumbled to the workbench, where he pumped a small bellows to fire up the coals in the brazier, and thrust rods and knives in to heat. Then he loomed over Kyr, reeking of harsh wine, and snarled, "Tonight, you will be mine—or die."

Underneath Gauday's harsh tone, Kyr heard a bewildered lostness and soul-deep weariness. He saw a soul in a torment of hatred, envy, vengefulness, and hidden despair. Looking deeper, he saw the fearful need for closeness and love that was buried under Gauday's games of domination and cruel intimacy. *Those games are all he knows, all he has ever known. O Zhovanya, it's so sad!* Tears filled his eyes.

"What's this? Tears?" Gauday pounced like a cat on a bird. "Why, perhaps we can end this unpleasantness now." He leaned forward, smiling with triumphant glee. "Tell me what's in your heart, my boy."

"As you wish, Day," Kyr said softly. "It makes me sad to see your soul in so much pain."

Panic flashed white across Gauday's face, followed by red fury. In a frenzy, he punched Kyr again and again, then whirled and stalked out.

# Part Five ~ Ordeal of Deliverance

*"Hate is a dead thing.*
*Who of you would be a tomb?"*

—Kahlil Gibran

# Chapter 14

# Downfall

Clopping and jingling, a dusty army of two hundred mounted men and women rode across a plain of tall green grasses with a scattering of red flowers the size of a baby's fist, and low shrubs dotted with tiny yellow flowers. The Warrior Mage in his black leathers, astride his chestnut stallion, rode at the forefront. Next to him, riding a burly bay gelding. was Jakar, Rajani's second-in-command, a brawny man with olive skin and black hair. He had a quiet, no-nonsense air about him, with a sparkle of wit and intelligence in his brown eyes. Behind them rode the self-named Companions of the Liberator, on their way to rescue Kyr.

They were approaching a line of hills studded with sparse trees like ragged bristles of an old brush. "Scrawniest forest I ever saw," Rajani said.

"True enough." Jakar wiped his sweaty forehead with a bare forearm. "But even sparse shade will be welcome."

"How much further to Gauday's hide-out?"

Jakar jerked a thumb over his shoulder toward a short, blond man riding a short distance behind them. "According to our guest, it's over the next ridge."

"Any sign of patrols or scouts?"

"Nah." Jakar's tone expressed his disdain for such negligence.

"How about water?"

"Lorya says there's a decent creek this side of the ridge."

"Good. Let's make camp there."

"According to Lorya, they got themselves one whole sentry," Jakar drawled. "Better be a cold camp. He might see our smoke—if he isn't dozing."

Rajani laughed. "Well, this might be easier than I feared. Get the men started making scaling ladders soon as camp is set up." Rajani raised his arm and signaled to the troops, and they nudged their horses into a trot. Their tired horses did not protest, but pricked their ears toward welcome shade and water.

Soon, a tidy camp sprang up, sentries were posted, and the forest rang with the blows of ax and hammer. In the command tent, Rajani was sitting on a three-legged canvas stool at his camp table. The only other furnishings were his bedroll and two more stools. A lean young woman sidled in and came to a halt before him. With her bland face, mouse-nest hair, and shapeless gray dress, she looked dull and commonplace.

"Ah, Lorya, good."

"Sir." She straightened up, revealing sharp blue eyes. She was their best spy, clever and elusive.

"Scout out the fort, find out what's going on there, especially what's happening with Kyr, and determine the best time to attack." She nodded and slipped out of the tent. Next, the short blond man entered the tent, followed by Rajani's burley sergeant, Berano.

Rajani pushed a small, heavy bag across the table toward the smaller man. "Viro, you have our thanks. Here is the agreed-upon sum."

Viro took the bag, opened it and counted the coins carefully. Satisfied, he tucked the bag into his pocket. "Alright, when is the attack?"

"Our business is concluded. You are free to go."

"You can't send me off, just like that! You'd never have found this place without me. Wasting all that time searching the desert. Pah! I'm going with you. I have unfinished business at the fort."

Rajani eyed him coldly. "Leyr, find an appropriate escort for this man. Make sure he gets back safely to the City."

Viro glanced up at the impassive boulder of a man looming over him, then glared at Rajani, and sputtered, "You'll regret this!" He gave a mocking bow, turned, and left, with the burly Companion at his heels.

Late that night, Lorya slipped into Rajani's tent. "Couldn't get inside the fort, but I contacted a village boy when he came out to dump the slop pails. He says Gauday disappears every afternoon into a locked room and allows no interruptions. He's in there for several hours. That's the best time to attack." She looked away, unusual for her.

"What else? Tell me everything you heard."

"I'm sorry, sir. That room is where he's keeping Kyr, these days. Gauday's taken others in there before. Some died, others survived, but...."

"Go on."

She firmed her stance and looked at him. "One survivor is mindless, helpless as a babe. Others have come out vicious and twisted."

Rajani nodded, hiding his dismay. "Thank you, Lorya. Good job. This gives us time to get in position. We will attack tomorrow afternoon. Inform Jakar."

Alone, he sank down onto his bedroll and dropped his head into his hands. "Gods and demons!" he whispered. "I hope we're not too late."

"Y ou're mine, you're my boy. I am your Master now and forever." Gauday's spellchant seemed like the only thread Kyr could hold onto in the crazy whirl of fierce pain, intense pleasure, and venom-induced confusion that engulfed him. Exhausted beyond measure, he had lost hold of the forgiveness chant some time ago.

*"Kyr, don't give up! Fight him! Fight him!"* Dekani's voice was far away, a meaningless drone, nearly drowned out by Gauday's spellchant.

"I am your Master now. Submit to me. I am your...."

Insistent pounding broke through the hateful spellchant. Kyr sagged with relief as Gauday stepped back and turned toward the door.

"Gods curse it! Whoever that is will be sorry!" Scowling, Gauday threw his slender knife at the rough plank wall, where it lodged, quivering. He pulled on his blood-spattered robe, stomped to the door, and opened it a hand-width. "Ah, Craith. I'm sure you realize it's forbidden to interrupt me. You must want to join in the fun. *Do* come in."

Kyr shook his head, trying to clear his mind. *Craith? Isn't he a friend? Oh gods, did he come to help me?* Clinging to this faint hope, Kyr kept his eyes on the young man, and ignored what the two men were chattering about.

"We're surrounded, sir! There's an army all around the fort."

"What madness! None of these villagers would dare to defy me."

"They're not villagers, sir. There are about two hundred well-armed soldiers out there."

"What the hell do they want?"

"Him." Craith cast an involuntary glance past Gauday's shoulder. Kyr met Craith's horrified eyes, and mouthed, "Help me!"

The redhead blanched and jerked his attention back to Gauday. "They demand that you turn him over to them."

"They can't have him. He's mine! Go arm the men."

"Sir, we only have fifty fighting men left. They have two hundred. We can't win."

"You dare to defy me?" Gauday glared at him with red eyes.

"Aaaagh!" Craith fell to his knees, grasping his head.

"Do as I command."

Watching Craith leave, Kyr's meager hope for help died. Gauday returned and stared down at him.

"Very unfortunate that this is happening just when we're about to succeed, isn't it, my dear?" He caressed Kyr's cheek tenderly, but his eyes were mad with frustration. "I'll just have to dress and go send this rabble away. We shall continue shortly. Soon you will be mine forever." As he left, he slammed the door shut; but in his hurry, he failed to lock it.

At this rare chance for escape, Kyr struggled to break free, but it was no use. He hadn't the strength to break his leather bonds. Helpless, he lay where Gauday had abandoned him, his soul teetering at the edge of an unholy abyss.

*"You have a chance now, Kyr. Remember the chant. Remember who you are.*

*"Leave me alone,"* Kyr begged the intrusive voice. *"No more, no more."*

*"Your name is Kyr. You belong to Zhovanya. Your name is Kyr."*

The name reminded him of who he was, of his unbearable existence, of the peril of his very soul. Silently he screamed, *No, I'm not Kyr. I'm not!*

*"Your name is Kyr. You belong to Zhovanya. Your name is Kyr. You belong to Zhovanya."*

"No, no, no, no," he moaned, seeking darkness, madness, any escape from unbearable reality. But Dekani's painful litany hammered the scattered pieces of his mind and memory back together.

*"Stop it, Dekani! Let me alone!"*

*"Remember now. Remember who you are. Hold onto the chant. Zhovanya nara lo."*

*"I can't fight him anymore. He'll take me over soon as he comes back. You must keep your promise!"*

*"Don't worry. I won't let him enslave your soul."*

*"Please, Dekani! I've given Maray enough time to build up the Sanctuary's defenses. There's no need for me to keep on living. Keep your promise now!"*

*"What about Medari's family? We can't give up yet. Hold on to the chant. I'll sing it for you. Zhovanya nara lo, Zhovanya nara lo, Zhovanya nara lo."*

The chant was as meaningless to Kyr as a cricket's creaking. He had no more strength to resist hatred. He hated not only Gauday, but also Dekani and Medari for refusing to help him reach the sanctuary of death. Ignoring his teacher, he took up his old prayer.

*Dark Lady, have mercy. Take me home now. Don't let him devour my soul! Take me home, take me home, take me home.*

Heading toward the armory, Craith muttered under his breath, "Crazy demon! He'll get us all killed. And I've got to help Kyr somehow. Should've done something long before now, gods curse me for a coward. What if I…?" He paled and shook his head. "Gods, no. He'd take me back into that hellhole, do to me what he's done to Kyr." His steps slowed. "But not if…." He shuddered as he shook off his ingrained habit of unquestioning obedience. Changing direction, he hurried to the barracks instead.

A short time later, he had his soldiers assembled in the yard. In addition, all the ex-Slaves had emerged from their dens, eager for any excitement. Like a flock of molting peacocks, they clustered together in their shabby finery, passing a flask around and squawking useless questions at each other.

Craith strode to the gate and opened the spy-hole. "Gauday refuses to surrender the man you want."

Outside the fort, orders were shouted, and the walls shook with a series of heavy thumps.

"Scaling ladders!" screamed the sentry from his tower by the gate. Craith's soldiers looked at him nervously, but he gave no orders.

Gauday strode out of his quarters, dressed in tall black boots, tan leggings, and maroon tunic cinched to his narrow waist by a black sword belt, with scabbarded sword. He stomped up to Craith and hit him. "I told you to arm the men!"

149

With the back of his hand, Craith wiped at the blood trickling from his split lip, and smiled. "Sir, you have the only key to the armory."

"Gods curse you!" Gauday howled, but there was no more time for recriminations. Led by Rajani, the Companions were swarming over the walls and scrambling down ropes to the ground. A few mad-eyed Slaves flung themselves at the invaders with knives or whips, but Craith knelt and gestured for his soldiers to do the same, and many Slaves followed suit.

Gauday charged at Craith, sword raised, screaming, "TRAITOR! I'll KILL YOU!"

With menacing grace, Rajani raised his sword. In a move of blinding swiftness, he had Gauday disarmed and nursing a throbbing hand. "You'll kill no-one today, or ever again." The Warrior Mage bent Gauday's sword, and murmured, "Kaa'a ta lak!" The sword, made of the best steel, snapped in two like a dried-out twig. The Companions cheered, while the Slaves and soldiers gasped.

Trembling with thwarted rage, Gauday glanced around. His men were all now kneeling in the dust at sword point, a few Slaves bleeding from minor cuts. He glared at them with contempt, smoothed his face, and bowed to Rajani. "I am pleased to turn this rabble over to you." He made a sweeping gesture with one arm. "The fort is yours. I ask only that I be allowed to leave with my personal body servant. He is, ah, very ill. I need to take him away for, ah, for special treatment."

Rajani shook his head in amazement. "You are incredibly arrogant and quite deluded. Let me explain. You are now my prisoner, and in no position to make demands. Furthermore, I wouldn't place a diseased weasel in your care."

He turned to the red-headed soldier who had prevented a senseless slaughter. "You seem relatively sane. What's your name?"

The soldier looked up and Rajani was surprised to see not hatred or fear in his eyes, but deep relief. "Craith, sir."

"Where can I lock up this madman?"

"There's a cell down the stairs inside that room behind you."

"NO!" Gauday screamed, his eyes flaring red. Rajani grunted as burning pain assaulted his brain. He became very still and held up one hand before his own face, then snapped his palm outward and shouted, "Kiiiyaaa, KA!"

This time, it was Gauday who cried out and grabbed his head.

Jakar laughed. "Don't try your tricks on a Warrior Mage. You'll get a dose of your own poison."

"Hold him," Rajani commanded.

Leyr took hold of the whimpering would-be sorcerer, and pinned his arms to his sides. Rajani tore off Gauday's lace-edged neckerchief, blindfolded him with it, and stepped back, wiping his hands on his leather leggings. "Alright, he won't be able to use his sorcery now. Lock him up."

"NO! No, no, no!" cried Gauday in a high, childish voice, trying vainly to tear off his blindfold. Jakar nodded at Leyr, and the blacksmith dragged the writhing, screaming prisoner away.

"The key is on a peg outside the cell door," Craith called to Leyr.

Rajani turned to his lieutenant. "Jakar, confine these men to their barracks and keep them under guard. If they cause any trouble, tie them to their bunks."

"Do as he says," Craith told his soldiers. "He is your commander now." The soldiers nodded, but the Slaves set up howls of protest.

"SILENCE!" Rajani roared. "Any of you who do not obey our orders will be tied and gagged." The Companions stepped closer and raised their swords. A sullen silence replaced the Slaves' clamor.

"My thanks," Rajani said to Craith. "Where is Kyr?"

"I'll show you." Craith jumped to his feet. "He was alive when you got here, but…. Well, we'd better bring the healer." He beckoned to Medari, standing on the porch of his infirmary, already holding his healer's kit. "Come on!" They raced toward Gauday's quarters.

"In here, sir." Craith gestured to a heavy wooden door and stepped back, clearly unwilling to go in.

Rajani steeled himself and opened the door. His stomach churned as a nauseating miasma swept out. Sickly sweet incense overlaid harsh odors of venomous potions, sweat, urine, blood, and burned flesh. Red glass lanterns provided murky light, revealing a bizarre altar with sinister banners of chains and straps dangling above it. Below, a dark form lay spread-eagled.

Pale as linen, Craith remained outside the door. Medari shouldered past him and hurried to the dark altar. Shamed, Rajani made himself step forward into that hellish room. The "altar" was a crude four-poster bed, and it was Kyr who lay there, bound hand and foot to the posts. He was in a terrible state: gaunt, pale, covered with small cuts and burns: some scabbed over, some bloody or blistering. Pared to the bone by suffering, he seemed nearly insubstantial.

"Oh, gods," Medari whispered. "I'll never forgive myself for this!"

"What do you mean?" Rajani demanded. "What have you done?"

"I've forsworn my oath to heal and do no harm. To save the lives of my wife and children, I kept him alive through all these months of torment and degradation, curse my...."

"Later for that," the Warrior Mage snapped. "What has Gauday been doing in here?"

"Sorry. Kyr told me that Gauday has been using venomous potions and spellchants, trying to turn him into something like a Watcher. Perhaps you know what that means better than I."

"Gods and demons! This is worse than anything I imagined." Rajani's voice rose. "Gods curse that madman's soul!"

# Chapter 15

# Bizarre Reversal

Loud cursing startled Kyr from his daze of despair. *"Oh, gods! He's back. Teacher! Don't let him mind-bond me! Keep your promise now!"* There was no answer. Panic set his heart racing. *"Please, Dekani! You promised!"*

The door, always closed before, was now open, letting in fresh cold air. Kyr shivered as two dark figures came toward him. Neither was Gauday. He stared at them in confusion.

"It's over, son," said a familiar voice. "You're safe now."

"M-Medari?" Screaming had reduced his voice to a cracked whisper.

"Yes, son. And here is your friend...."

"Medari, Final Grace, quick! Before he comes back!"

"Oh, gods!" the healer said in a stricken voice. "You've never wanted the Final Grace before, even when I offered it. And now I can't.... Things have changed, son. Your friend...."

Kyr turned his head away and ceased listening. His last hope erased, he felt as if he were sinking down a long dark hole into unending hell. Even his allies had turned against him. Soon, he would have no choice but to do exactly as Gauday said, forever. In his utter exhaustion, the dark peace of capitulation was a relief. He could stop fighting now. Gauday had won.

The other man spoke from the shadows by Gauday's workbench. "Medari, what's going on with him?" The voice was oddly familiar. Kyr turned his head back, trying to see who it was.

"He's confused by Gauday's venoms and spells."

"I have something that will help." The man pulled a small flask from the pocket of his black leather vest and handed it to Medari. "Here, it's Shanawa elixir."

153

"Gods be praised! Just what he needs." Medari gently lifted Kyr's head and held the flask to Kyr's lips. "Here, son, this will make you feel better. Just two sips now."

Having no more will to resist, he gulped down the oddly sweet potion, then lay back and waited for swirling chaos to engulf him again. Instead, a pleasant numbness began to spread through his body. *Perhaps this is my reward for giving up. Well, nothing matters now. Gods, I'm tired.* His eyes sagged shut. A short while later, the pain of his cuts and burns diminished. His tiredness and the whirling confusion in his mind began to subside. Wondering why Gauday was allowing this reprieve, he opened his eyes.

"Ah, good," Medari said. "Listen, son, I have wonderful news. Your friends have taken the fort. It's over. No one is going to hurt you anymore. You're safe now."

Kyr gave a faint huff, a ghost of a disbelieving laugh. *He's gone mad before I did. How unfair! Well, he's right about one thing: it's over. Gauday has won.*

"It's true, Kyr. You're safe now." The other man removed a red glass chimney from a lamp. Soft light, clean and yellow, revealed an almost forgotten face, someone he'd known in another lifetime. *Who is that? Oh, gods. It's Rajani. Cruel Goddess to send such a dream!*

"I'm here. I'm finally here." The solid touch of Rajani's strong, warm hand clasping his cold, trembling one told Kyr that it was no dream. He peered at the Warrior Mage sadly.

"Gods, Jani, how'd he get you?"

"Kyr, listen to me. It's the other way around. *I've* taken the fort and captured Gauday."

It made no sense. Gauday was all-powerful. No one could resist him. *Oh, gods! Rajani, Medari, Craith—they're all part of Gauday's game!* A sudden storm of rage at such betrayal rose up, driving him to the brink of madness. *Oh, gods! Oh, gods! They're all in on it, all these so-called friends. Gods curse....*

"*Calm down, Kyr.*" A haggard-looking Dekani appeared and raised his hands, sending a blue wave of calmness and reassurance pouring into Kyr's soul, drowning his rage, driving him back once more to the shores of sanity. "*Listen to Rajani, son. Believe him. He wouldn't lie about this.*"

Kyr trembled with the effort to keep from thrashing madly against his bonds, to slow his breathing. Even with Dekani's help, it was a few moments before he could speak. "Rajani? What's happening?"

"We've taken over the fort from that madman, Gauday, and locked him up. You're safe now." Rajani's voice broke. "I'm very sorry it took me so long to get here." He released Kyr's hand and drew his knife. "Let me free you."

"Oh gods, please!" At last someone would grant him the mercy of death. No more pain and degradation. No more whirling chaos. No need to fight anymore.

But Rajani only sliced the leather straps binding him to the bedposts. Bitterly disappointed, Kyr fought back tears. Air stung the raw wounds circling his wrists and ankles. Rajani gently helped him lower his arms from the spread-eagled position they'd been in for so long, causing frozen muscles to scream in protest.

But this pain was not Gauday's venom-enhanced agony and madness. It was just pain, ordinary pain. Sharp and clean, it cleared his mind further.

"You're really here? It's—over?"

"Yes."

"Ah, Goddess!" He could barely comprehend this bizarre reversal. Absurd laughter welled up, emerging as a ghastly, broken chuckle. *I was so close to the brink—and* now *Rajani shows up? Now? When Gauday has fouled my soul? What game is Zhovanya playing with me?*

Medari and Rajani were looking at him in grave concern, which made him laugh even more. But that hurt and started him coughing.

"Here's some water, son." Medari held a different flask to his lips and he gulped down precious elixir, untainted water. The cool liquid spread like a balm throughout his body. This sudden ending to the long nightmare, this implausible freedom from hell, seemed like a preposterous dream. His mood of fey amusement grew stronger.

"You've rescued me from hell *again*, Rajani. I'm very grateful—but let's not make a habit of this."

Their startled laughter filled that macabre chamber, breaking the spell of horror that had filled it for so long.

Rajani sobered. "I promise. Never again will you suffer such torment."

Kyr glanced up at Rajani, so strong and straight, so clean in his neat black leathers. Feeling filthy and corrupted, he looked away. "As Zhovanya wills," he muttered.

"Yes," Rajani sounded uncomfortable. "Well, let's get you out of here."

"Wait. Where is he?"

"Who?"

"He means Gauday," said Medari. "Son, they locked him in that black hole he kept you in."

"My cell? No, no. Too dark for Day, too dark."

"What are you saying?" Rajani demanded.

"He needs light. Get him some light in there."

"You want me to give the monster who did this to you some light? Why? Let him rot in darkness the rest of his very short life!"

"Can't explain. Too tired. Please...."

"Alright," Rajani sighed. "Makes no sense to me, but I can see it's important to you."

"How did you find...?"

"Enough for now, Kyr." said Medari. "We'll talk later, after we get you to the infirmary, and you get some rest."

A short while later, Medari rose from beside Kyr's pallet in the infirmary. "Well, I've done what I can for now. Wish I had some kanna for him."

"Ah, that I have," said Rajani. "Jakar, get someone to fetch my saddlebags."

"I'll get 'em." Jakar left, and Rajani turned to the healer. "You have no better place for Kyr than this cage?" He jerked a thumb at the barred cell.

"Damn sight better than being chained to the whipping post day and night, or being kept in that dark hole you've got Gauday in."

"That's how he's treated Kyr?"

"As you have just seen, worse, much worse."

"Gods damn Gauday's soul!" Rajani took a deep breath and blew it out. "I'll find a better place for Kyr in the morning."

"Not so soon. This 'cage' has been his only haven this whole time. He'll feel safer here until he's himself again."

"Alright. Let me know when he's ready."

Later that night, Kyr was sleeping the sound sleep brought by kanna smoke, which Rajani was glad to have provided. The prisoners and villagers were finally settled down for the night. The Warrior Mage walked the perimeter of the fort, nodding to his sentries.

All was quiet, even that madman in his dark hole. As soon as they'd placed a lantern in his cell, as Kyr had asked, Gauday had gone from frantic raving to quiet mumbling. Rajani shook his head, disturbed by Kyr's concern for his torturer. "What the hell was that gods-cursed Slave doing to Kyr? Gods and demons, I have to find out." He finished his rounds and headed for what had been Gauday's quarters.

Carrying a bright oil lamp, he opened the door of Gauday's torture chamber and stalked over to the bench. He began to examine the jumble of vials, scrolls and vicious implements, growing paler by the moment. Most of the scrolls were in languages or codes he could not decipher, and by their stained and crumpled condition, neither could Gauday. The ones Rajani could read brought a ferocious scowl to his face. "He *was* trying to mind-bond Kyr, but in the crudest, most barbarous way. He is no sorcerer!"

He set the scrolls to one side and methodically sniffed each vial and bottle to check its contents. Some were maleficent, but none was sorcerous. Under a pile of silk rags, he discovered a small wooden casket, and lifted its lid. "Gods, no!" He slammed the lid shut and stood there for a moment. "Maybe it's not...," he whispered. "I have to be sure."

Steeling himself, he re-opened the casket and lifted out a small box of blackwood. The lid was inlaid with a silver figure of an entwined couple. With shaking fingers, he opened the box, took out a silver flask, and removed its stopper. A heavy floral aroma wafted forth, tinged with odors of rotting fruit and sour wine. Instantly, he shoved the stopper back in place.

"Oil of Tramantha! He's been using *this* on Kyr? Blood of the gods!" He raised his arm, about to throw the flask against the wall; but then he jerked to a stop, unable to complete the motion. "Damn oath-bind!" Replacing the silver flask in the ornamented box, he reluctantly slipped the box into his pocket.

Kyr felt as brittle as the early winter ice that had laced the ponds at the Sanctuary. One touch and he would shatter. But he didn't hurt. Oh, there were aches and pains, but they were muffled. His wrists and ankles were bound as usual, but the binding was softer. He moved tentatively. No chains. No straps. Just cloth bandages.

*What happened?* Confused images tumbled through his mind. He remembered giving up at long last, consigning his soul to eternal hell as

Gauday's mind-bonded slave. Yet he also recalled Medari telling him that Rajani had arrived and locked Gauday up. *Oh gods, is it really over? Or—Goddess forfend!—am I Day's slave now?* He had to know.

*"Dekani? Teacher? Please answer!"*

There was a dreadful silence.

*"Nononono,"* he whispered, sure that Gauday had taken over his mind and destroyed Dekani.

*"Sorry, son. I was asleep."* Dekani waved a hand. Instantly, they were in his cottage. He dropped into his chair by the hearth. Kyr stood over him, desperate for the truth.

*"Tell me what happened. Did Rajani really come, or...?"*

*"Yes, Rajani came, took the fort, locked Gauday up. It's over."*

*"Oh, gods!"* Kyr's knees went watery and he sank down into the other chair. *"It's really over?"*

Dekani said gently, *"Yes, it's over. I am very proud of you, son. You did not yield."*

*"I wanted to give in so many times! You wouldn't let me—and I hated you for that."* With a rueful glance, Kyr added, *"But I wouldn't have survived without you."*

*"We did it together."* Dekani's smile was as warm as ever, but now Kyr noticed that his teacher's hair was dull, his face was lined, and he had dark half-moons under his blue eyes.

*"What's wrong? You look awful."*

*"I'm worn out, is all. That was a long, hard battle."* Dekani raised a shaky hand and rubbed his forehead. *"We both need to rest and recover. I'll be asleep, but you may call if you need me."* With that, Dekani and the cottage faded from Kyr's awareness.

Instead of red-lit murk, Kyr opened his eyes to the clean, gentle light of dawn spreading like a benediction from the small window above him. Instead of deathly silence or mind-bending spellchants, a solitary bird sang outside, its sweet song unearthly to his ear.

He sighed, already missing Dekani's protective presence. In his mind he could still hear Gauday's hateful spellchant: *"You are mine forever. I am your Master now."* He shuddered with ingrained fear, and tried to reassure himself. *NO! You're NOT my Master! Rajani locked you up in that black hole. You will never come back, never take over my mind and will. It's over, and I won.*

Instead of relief or triumph, all he felt was a sad and weary pity for them both. He had seen the agony of Gauday's soul, knew the dark, voracious need for love that drove him, knew that the smoke of the Crown, the last remnant of the Soul-Drinker's sorcery, had driven his Slave brother's mind deeper into the Master's madness.

Great grief filled his heart for the intimate torment they had endured together—here at the fort, and earlier: as boys being tortured into becoming obedient Slaves, and as rivals for the Soul-Drinker's favor. His sorrow spilled over, and he grieved for Medari's agony of fear for his family; for the suffering of all his Slave brothers and their victims, and all the victims of the Soul Drinker; for the endless suffering of the tormented and the tormentors of the world. Almost—almost—he understood the depths of sorrow and mercy in Zhovanya's fierce, loving heart.

He turned onto his stomach and buried his face in the crook of one arm. Outside, the solitary bird still sang full-throated, each crystalline note a diamond dagger piercing his heart, drawing forth salt tears from this deep well of sadness.

# Chapter 16

# Struggle to Recover

Terror jolted him out of dark dreams. *No! No more!* His heart pounding, he braced against more pain, more cuts and burns, more invasion and degradation.

"Easy, son. It's Rajani."

He let go of the breath he was holding, and took two more slow breaths, trying to slow his heart. "Sorry. I...."

"Natural reaction, after what you've been through. It will wear off after a while. You've slept all day. Water?"

"Gods, yes." He gulped down some water from the flask Rajani held for him.

"Here's a dose of Medari's pain-killer."

Kyr drank that too, and lay back. Tired from even this small effort, his eyes drifted shut. But after a moment, he murmured, "Sanctuary safe? Everyone safe?"

"Yes. I sent some of my best men to help Maray. Remember Seranu and Gorth? They and twenty others are there, helping to build stronger fortifications. Maray didn't want any guards, but.... Well, my men know what else they're there for."

"Good." Jolanya was safe. Jolanya, Naran, Gaela, everyone. The Temple, the beautiful gardens, the statue he had created as a gift for the Sanctuary, in honor of Love. All safe. Somewhere deep inside Kyr, an iron grip relaxed. "I can—rest now?"

"Yes. As long as you need to." Rajani's voice was choked. "I'll see you tomorrow."

The potion was starting to take effect. For a time, he drifted in a peaceful haze of relief. *You're mine, boy. Mine forever.* Suddenly, he was sweating with fear, his heart racing. Angry at this disruption of his fragile peace, he dredged up a scrap of determination and resorted to what Dekani had taught him: focusing only on each breath, and repeating the forgiveness chant.

The evil whispers were soon banished. His heart calmed, and for the rest of the day he kept his attention on the chant, or small, immediate things: the blessing of diminished pain, the comfort of clean blankets, the simple, delicious tastes of chicken-and-carrot soup and freshly baked bread.

*The hands touched and touched, bringing terror, intense pain, depraved desire, pleasure. Crushed by dread, he couldn't move, couldn't think, couldn't breathe. His name, where he was, who it was that the all-powerful hands belonged to—all were lost in a nightmarish haze. There was no escape. "You are mine! Mine forever!"*

"Wake up, son. You're safe now."

Kyr remembered this voice. It came when the dreadful hands went away. Gathering memory and courage, he opened his eyes. "M-Medari? Where? What?"

"You're in the infirmary. Your friend Rajani came, remember? It's our second day of freedom from that madman."

"That really happened?"

Medari nodded, and Kyr sagged with relief. He rubbed his face with both hands, trying to erase the nightmares. "Gods and demons, I was back in that room with him whispering his cursed spellchants."

"I'm sure that monster's evil potions have affected your mind a bit. Don't worry, they'll wear off. You'll be all right."

"NO! I'll NEVER be all right after what he's done to me!" Shocked by his own bitter words, he took some deep breaths, trying to calm down, to soften, as he had so painfully learned to do. "Sorry, it's been—difficult."

"To say the least. It will take some time, but you *will* recover. You have my word on that." Medari held out a cup. "Here, time for another dose. Three good swallows, alright?"

He grimaced. "Day kept forcing his venomous potions down me."

"I know. But right now you need to get your strength back so we can get out of this place."

The thought of ever moving again seemed unbearable; the idea of being strong again, unimaginable. He took the cup and stared at it.

"Drink up, son."

He obeyed and handed the cup back to Medari, who seemed tired and sad. Kyr frowned. *Why is he still here?* "Your family, go find them now."

Medari looked at him somberly. "Not until you're on your feet, son."

"No, go now."

"After what I've done to you...."

"Not your fault. Gauday...."

"No. I chose to help that monster keep tormenting you all this time. I'd never be able to live with myself if I didn't undo at least some of the harm you have suffered. I must stay until you are well."

"As you say." Kyr wanted to argue further but his tiny hoard of strength was used up.

"I have to tend to your cuts and burns now. It will be painful for you. I'm sorry."

Indeed, the healer's ministrations seemed nearly as vexatious as Gauday's mortifications. Kyr bit his lip to keep from snarling, *Stop it! Stop touching me! Can't you leave me alone?*

Medari finished and put away his salves and bandages. "Alright, now let's try getting some food in you. I have soup and porridge keeping warm on the hearth. Which do you want?"

Kyr frowned. *Gods! I just want to rest.* But his stomach cramped sharply. He had no idea how many days it had been since Gauday had bothered to feed him anything but maleficent potions and noxious sweets. "Porridge," he said, not really caring as long as it was plain, solid food. While Medari stepped into the main room, he struggled to prop himself up with his pillows, despite the pain of his burns and cuts. He was pale and shaking when Medari returned with a bowl on a tray.

"Take it easy, son. Don't do too much too soon." The healer sat beside his bed on the stool and spooned up some porridge.

"I'll feed myself, thanks," Kyr snapped. With a startled look, Medari handed him the tray and spoon.

He focused all his will on keeping his arm steady as he ate, exhausting himself in the process. But it was better than being meddled with. All he wanted was to be left alone, unmolested. He stared out his small window at the unsullied, undemanding sky until his eyes refused to stay open any longer.

One evening a few days later, Rajani brought a supper of chicken soup, bread and a delicious honeyed custard. After they'd eaten, Kyr felt a little stronger.

"Thanks for coming to my rescue again." It was odd to see the tough Warrior Mage flush in shame.

"I can't tell you how sorry I am it took me so long to find you."

"Never mind," Kyr sighed. *Too cursed late*, he thought, but was too exhausted to indulge in anger and recriminations. After a moment, he asked, "How did you find this place?"

"A nasty little man named Viro guided us here."

"What?" Kyr burst into startled laughter. "Ow!" Laughing made the cuts and burns on his torso flare up in protest. He took a couple of deep breaths.

"I take it you know him?" Rajani said dryly. "He said he had unfinished business here. With you?"

"He attacked me without permission and got banished for it. Probably blames me. Where is he?"

"Sent him back to the City under guard. He won't be bothering you anymore. None of them will."

"It wasn't the soldiers, just my Slave brothers. Craith's a good man."

"I know. He disobeyed Gauday and surrendered the fort to us. A sensible young man, quite helpful in keeping his soldiers in order." Rajani got to his feet. "Well, I know you're worn out. I'll let you rest."

"Thanks, Rajani." Kyr slid down under his blankets, and closed his eyes. *Craith did help me, after all, bless him!* His heart warmed at the thought. He turned on his side, vainly trying to find a comfortable position. *Gods, I wish he'd found his courage sooner.*

The next afternoon, Rajani pulled up a stool. "Feeling any better?"

"Some," Kyr muttered, still too exhausted to enjoy conversation.

"I did as you asked. Had a small window cut into the door of that black hole. Why did you want Gauday to have some light in there?"

"It's so dark," he whispered, remembering. "The dark terrifies him. He always needs some light."

"How can you care, after what he did to you?"

"Couldn't let myself hate him. I'd have lost myself, lost my one advantage." He glanced at Rajani. "Never mind." In the face of Rajani's scowling skepticism, he was unwilling to explain the terrible intimacy he had shared with his captor, the agony he had seen in Gauday's soul, the difficult lesson of seeing his tormenter through Zhovanya's eyes.

"Medari told me Gauday was trying to mind-bond you?"

"Yes," he said with bone-chilling bleakness.

"That's horrible!" Rajani's dark eyes looked haunted. "I'm terribly sorry we couldn't get here sooner."

Abrupt anger urged Kyr to shout, *What good does that do? Stop saying that!* But Rajani's guilt-stricken expression reminded him to soften and forgive. He tried to keep his tone mild. "Well, you got here in time."

"In time?"

"One more day and I would have been his mind-slave, or dead." Kyr shuddered, and stared at the Warrior Mage with haunted eyes. "Merciless gods, it was so close! I would have had to obey his every mad, vicious whim forever."

Rajani went white, and choked out, "I'm so sorry...."

"Stop it! Stop apologizing!" Kyr snapped. "What the hells *did* take you so long?"

"Ah, gods." Shamefaced, Rajani looked down, and said quietly, "This isn't much excuse but.... It took me half a month to get back to the City, and another couple of months to recruit and train the Companions. After the rains subsided, we hunted for you, but couldn't locate you until Viro showed up."

"Companions?"

"The fighters who volunteered to help rescue you. They named themselves the Companions of the Liberator."

"Liberator?" he repeated, feeling dim-witted, which inflamed his anger.

"That's you, Kyr. You liberated all of Khailaz from Dauthaz and his reign of horror."

"Curse it! I TOLD you it wasn't something I did. Some god or demon forced me to."

"As I told you, that doesn't matter. You are the one who freed us. And now you have sacrificed more than anyone can know, protecting the Sanctuary of the Goddess. You are a hero to almost everyone, like it or not."

"A hero?" Kyr laughed bitterly. "There's nothing I feel farther from!" He turned his back to Rajani, angry, confused by his anger, and exhausted. "Leave me alone!"

"I'm sorry to have upset you."

Kyr said nothing, and closed his eyes.

"Kyr? Talk to me. Please!"

Kyr ignored him, and Rajani finally left. Alone, Kyr slowly calmed down. *Why did I get so mad at Rajani? It didn't feel quite right, somehow.* But he was too tired to puzzle it out. He stared through the bars of the cell that had been his only refuge here at the fort, watching the flames dancing in the hearth in the main room of the infirmary.

In the flames, he saw Jolanya dancing before the mosaics of the Goddess and Her Consort in the sacred chamber called the Kailithama. He groaned softly, remembering the bliss of holding Jolanya close there amongst the scattered pillows and coverlets; recalling the precious words she whispered just before he stepped through the gate of the Sanctuary and entered Gauday's hell.

*She is the Kailithana*, he thought wearily. *I mustn't think of her.* But his aching heart demanded, *Then why did she say that she loves me?*

One morning, everyone was busy elsewhere, and Kyr was glad. No concerned faces, no caring questions, no one tormenting him with food or potions or salves. A quarter-moon had passed, but whenever anyone entered his cell a terrible tension still gripped his body, no matter how often he assured himself that he was safe. On top of that, everyone wanted something from him, whether they said so or not. Rajani and his Companions wanted him to be a gods-cursed hero, of all things! Medari wanted him to heal and be strong so he could feel less guilty about co-operating with Gauday.

Maybe Gauday's relentless demand for his submission had made him sensitive to the tug of others' desires. All he knew for sure was that it was a blessed relief to be alone.

Lying there half-asleep, he heard Gauday whispering again: *"You are mine. You are my boy. Come to me. You are mine. We belong together forever. Come to me. You are mine."* Kyr didn't know if what he was hearing was just memories or impressions left over from his time of torment. Somehow they seemed realer than that. Angry at this intrusion, Kyr thought, *I'm glad they threw Gauday in that dark hole! Ha! Even with a little light, he is probably quite scared. Let* him *be the one to suffer now!*

But then he sighed in dismay. *Ah, gods, do I hate him after all? I fought so hard not to. Zhovanya forgive me, it's hard not to wish him ill.*

Approaching footsteps made Kyr tense up, but he was glad for the distraction from his thoughts and memories.

"Time for some pain-killer." Medari handed Kyr a cup, and he drank the dose gratefully.

"Do you need anything else?"

"No, thanks." Yearning for the peace only solitude gave him, he hoped the healer would return to his other duties, but Medari took a seat on the stool.

"Sorry I haven't been here much, today. With the villagers and all their family members arriving from every direction, I've got my hands full these days. You won't believe how much this place has changed since Rajani took over."

"Oh?"

"He's sent Companions out to inform all the villages of the changes. People are coming from all over to look for kidnapped kin, and to lodge complaints against Gauday and his men. Village leaders are arriving to discuss the new laws and procedures."

"Mmm-hmmm."

"Naturally, some peddlers have arrived and there's a small market outside the walls, growing larger every day. It's quite busy: a tinker; a cobbler; farmers with their produce; eggs and chickens; weavers with cloth goods to sell; even a fortune teller." Medari paused. "Well, I can see you're not very interested in all this."

"Sorry. I'm still very tired."

"Alright, I'll check on you later." The healer rose and left, a worried frown on his face.

Kyr sighed, realizing how tired he truly was, tired of trying to survive in hell, tired of trying to keep his soul safe from the traps of hatred and fear, tired of this torment called life. *"Zhovanya, won't you take me Home now? I've done as You asked. You promised we would be together. Please let me come Home to You."*

The Goddess remained silent. Grim doubt arose, telling him that there would be no such blessing for him. *Perhaps She still wants me to suffer. Perhaps my penance will never end.*

# Chapter 17

# Anger and Hope

On a sunny, breezy morning a quarter-moon later, Rajani smiled as he crossed the courtyard, which was now busy with villagers trading news and gossip, and children chasing each other, yelling and laughing. In a roped off area at the center, a pair of Companions practiced hand-to-hand fighting, grunting and cursing good-naturedly. Excited half-grown boys watched them fight with wide eyes. The flag of Khailaz, a dancing golden Goddess on a deep blue field, fluttered over them all from the new flagpole near the front gates. Rajani's heart lifted. Perhaps it had all been worth it.

In the infirmary, he found Medari busy checking a Companion's leg wound, inflicted by one of the maddened Slaves. "This is healing well. You'll be fine. You can report for duty tomorrow morning." The Companion nodded and left.

"Good morning, healer. How is he today?" Rajani nodded toward Kyr's cell. Lowering his voice, he added, "He seemed upset and angry yesterday."

"He's still sleeping." Medari worked methodically, cleaning up his work table. "After what he's been through, it will take months for him to recover, if not longer."

"I'm sure you're right. I can't help worrying, though." They exchanged somber looks. "We must do everything we can to help him," Rajani said.

"Agreed."

"I've sent some men to hunt for your family, but no luck so far."

Medari's lips thinned and he looked down for a moment, then turned to the hearth. "Want some tea?"

"Thanks."

They sat sipping tea and talking quietly about the ongoing changes at the fort. Rajani finished his tea and set his cup down. "The village headmen are due today to discuss who the new governor should be. Politics, pah!"

Though he'd kept his eyes closed, Kyr had been listening, gritting his teeth to keep from bursting out with bitter comments. *Gods damn them! How can they go on like that, as if this place hasn't been the worst of hells for me? As if I hadn't been a few moments from losing my soul to Gauday's madness? Gods and demons, I want to KILL them!*

Shocked by his unfathomable fury, Kyr took a deep breath and made himself relax his clenched fists and rigid shoulders. *What am I thinking? Am I going mad after all?* Close to panic, he called out. *"Teacher, help me! Don't let me go mad now! Dekani? Dekani!"*

*"Alright, son, alright. Take it easy. I'm here."* Dekani waved his hand and they were instantly standing in the flowery meadow outside his cottage. *"Come with me."* Dekani beckoned Kyr not toward the cottage, but down the path that led into the forest. As they strolled along the path, the eternal serenity of the tall trees soothed Kyr's soul, as did his teacher's steady presence. A quiet trickling spoke of a creek somewhere nearby.

After a while, he was calm enough to speak. *"I'm so angry! I'm afraid I am going mad after all."*

Though Dekani appeared a bit shrunken and his hair was now completely gray, he spoke as firmly and kindly as ever. *"It's all right, Kyr. Now that you are safe, all the anger you didn't dare to feel before is coming up."*

*"I should just be angry at Gauday, but I'm angry at everyone, everything!"*

*"Have you asked yourself why?"* his teacher asked gently.

*"Gods and demons!"* Kyr swore, reluctant to look within. They continued walking in silence until they came upon a large patch of wild ilys. Kyr stopped and stared at the flowers, remembering his first experience with them, how unworthy he had felt in the face of their delicate, graceful beauty. Now, he felt even worse.

*"I feel poisoned, so different from them all—from Rajani, Medari, the villagers, the Companions, even the soldiers. They are so innocent, so blind!"* Again his fists and shoulders were tightly clenched. *"They make me so mad!"*

"*They have not have not suffered as you have. You resent that?*"

"*Gods damn it! YES!*" he shouted. A flock of small birds whirled up from a nearby bush and flew off, piping in alarm. Kyr stormed up the trail, and Dekani followed him. After a while, Kyr stopped and turned to face his teacher. "*Sorry.*"

"*Of course you are angry. You have every right. Come, let's sit over there.*" A carpet of dried leaves and twigs crunched under their feet, releasing a musty scent. Dekani led them over to seats on a large, bare log, silvery with age. "*Alright, I want you to focus on your breath. You are very good at it, after your ordeal. It's a skill you can use now, too.*"

Kyr glared at his feet, feeling the resentment his teacher had named rise up inside him like a bitter flame. "*Ah, gods! They have no idea what I've been through. I hate them for that!*"

"*Yes,*" said Dekani. "*Just notice this feeling, and watch your breath.*"

Kyr puffed out his lips and shook himself. "*Alright, I'll try.*" For a time, the only sound was the rasping song of hidden insects. Focusing on his breath, Kyr watched the flame of bitterness burning in his core. Slowly it died down to dull embers, revealing a black, painful lump in his heart. He jumped up as if he'd been stabbed.

"*It's not just them I hate. It's me! Gauday corrupted me, Dekani. He's ruined everything Naran and Jolanya did for me! LOOK!*" He yanked his tunic off, revealing lines of lurid scars snaking over his torso and arms. "*His marks are all over me, and worse, deep inside me. Every night—every cursed night!—I dream of what he did, and—Goddess forgive me!—I hate it and crave it, almost as badly as I craved the Rod. What's even worse, I catch myself imagining doing it to some innocent.... Ah, merciless gods!*" He sank back down on the log and buried his face in his hands.

"*You have made tremendous sacrifices, and your friends know that. They want to help you. They have asked how, but you have turned away from them. Remember what Zhovanya said? Do not turn away from love.*"

"*LOVE?*" Kyr leapt up from the log and began to pace, leaves and twigs crackling under his feet. "*Love hurts! I love Jolanya but she is forbidden to me. My heart aches for her all the time. Tenaiya loved her sister and brother. Now she cries because they are dead.*" He whirled to face Dekani. "*Gods curse it! Do you realize that Gauday loves me—in the only way he knows how, the way the Soul-Drinker trained us both?*"

"*That's not love!*"

Kyr ignored him, stomping back and forth, hitting his palm with his fist. *"I fought so hard to keep from hating him! But his 'love' has poisoned me, made pain and pleasure inseparable, made me hate for anyone to touch me again, or even talk to me. Everything hurts, everything my friends do seems so—so meddlesome. Now I—merciless gods!—I hate everyone!"*

*"No, you don't, son. You just need time to heal. I'll help you. Let me help you, please!"*

*"NO! I can't stand this! I went through the healing at the Sanctuary, only to end up here, like this. Enough!"* He held out his hands in a pleading gesture. *"I've done what Zhovanya asked. The Sanctuary is safe now. Why must I keep on living? Why?"*

*"Oh, son,"* Dekani whispered, his face full of anguish, tears slipping down his cheeks.

*"Gods, what did I say?"* Shocked at his imperturbable teacher's breakdown, Kyr knelt before Dekani. *"I've hurt you. I'm so sorry."*

With a melancholy smile, Dekani said, *"You see? You still know what love is."*

Kyr gave a startled laugh. *"I guess I do."* He sighed, his anger draining away. *"Well, I have you to thank for that. You won't let me forget, no matter what. You are a relentless taskmaster."*

They shared a rueful smile. Kyr got up and sat on the log beside Dekani. After a few moments, he murmured, *"Perhaps I can purge myself of Gauday's poison, somehow."*

*"Gauday's poison? Hmmm."* Dekani stared at Kyr with an abstracted gaze. Kyr felt an odd feathery touch, as if his teacher were looking all around and into him. Trusting Dekani, he kept still.

*"Ah! I see it now. You're partially bonded with Gauday. Some portion of what you're feeling is his, not yours. Undoubtedly, he's scared and furious; and deep in his soul, I'm sure he feels corrupted, despairing, like an outcast—just as you have been feeling."*

Now that Dekani had pointed it out, Kyr could sense the link between him and Gauday. *"Merciless gods! It's not over! I'm still not free of him!"* His skin crawled with disgust and fear. *"I can't stand this! Dekani, we've got to break this cursed bond. Can you do it now? Please!"*

*"I'm sorry, Kyr. I don't know if I can. I am not as strong as I was. All this has taken a lot out of me."* Dekani looked shaken and ashamed. *"Maybe by the time you get to Ravenvale, I'll have my strength back...."*

172

Kyr looked at him with great disappointment, then looked away. *"Ah, Goddess,"* he sighed, rubbing his aching forehead.

After an awkward silence, Dekani said, *"Until we find a way to break that link, you must try to sort out your true feelings from the echoes of his."*

*"I guess I must, but I'm so tired. I just want to go hide, somewhere I don't have to deal with anything or anyone."*

*"I know, son,"* Dekani said in a weary tone.

Kyr glanced at him and nodded. His teacher had fought Gauday almost as hard as he had. They were silent for a little while. Then Kyr asked, *"What must I do now?"*

*"This current ordeal is in some ways no different than what you went through with Gauday. It takes the same skills. Soften. Breathe. Forgive yourself. Forgive others."*

Kyr raised an ironic eyebrow. *"Is that all?"*

*"If you can endure Gauday's torments without losing yourself in hatred, I'm sure you can handle this. Most of all, you must not let yourself do what Gauday tried so hard to make you do—hate him and yourself."*

*"Guess you're right. No point in fighting so hard to keep out of that slime pit, and letting myself fall into it now, is there?"*

*"That's right. Now, son, let me do what I can for you."* Dekani moved to stand behind him and placed his hands above Kyr's shoulders. A gentle flow of blue kailitha bathed Kyr's heart and soul, soothing and calming. It was much weaker than the flood that Dekani usually sent.

Dekani lowered his hands, and Kyr turned to give him a grateful smile. Looking pale and spent, Dekani said, *"Now we must stop. You've been here a long time. If you are having trouble sorting out your true emotions from Gauday's, call me."* Dekani bowed and disappeared.

Back on his cot in the infirmary, Kyr felt relieved to know that a "large part of the anger and despair he'd been feeling was not his own, but Gauday's. And he felt more hopeful and at peace. *Dekani is still with me. And there's Rajani and Medari. They will help me break the link to Gauday. Goddess, forgive me for my doubt and despair. Zhovanya nara lo, Zhovanya nara lo, Zhovanya nara lo.* Soon he drifted into a restful sleep.

Kyr? I've brought your noon meal." It was Medari, balancing two trays of food.

Kyr woke slowly, and, for the first time without trembling in dread, without cobwebs of nightmares. He yawned and sat up against his pillows, wincing as his scabs pulled, then took the tray the healer handed to him.

"Thanks." He looked at the inevitable bean stew and picked up the fresh bread, instead. "Busy today?"

"Yes," Medari answered. "More and more folk from the villages are arriving, with the usual complement of scrapes and ailments."

"This place must have changed a lot." He shook his head. It still seemed ludicrous that this place of torment was now full of ordinary people going about everyday business, but it didn't anger him.

"It's quite amazing," agreed Medari. "You seem better today, am I right?"

"A quarter-moon of rest has helped, and your care." He spooned up some bean stew. Today, it had a spicy new flavor, and he began to eat with more enthusiasm.

"I'm sure you will need a lot more than that to recover, Kyr," Medari said somberly. "I was wondering if you might need to return to this Sanctuary you told me of. Seems like you need their help again."

Brusquely, he said, "No, I can't go there." *I couldn't bear to see Jolanya and not be able to be with her.*

"Why not? They helped you recover from years of the Soul-Drinker's torments. Surely they can help you with this too."

"I have my reasons. Leave it alone, Medari."

With a puzzled frown, the healer let the subject drop.

A few days later, Rajani came in, looking harried. He pulled up a stool by Kyr's cell and plopped down on it. "Gods, it's peaceful in here. I had to escape for a few moments, and you're my best excuse. Do you mind?"

"Escape what?"

"Details, disputes, decisions! You wouldn't believe all the wrangles people can get into. Gah! I'm a Warrior Mage, not a governor."

"More meetings?" Kyr remembered all the meetings at the cabin in the woods so many months and leagues ago. He frowned, recalling how innocent he had been back then, a cruel Slave of the Master, yet pure in a way: still living in darkness unsullied by the light of love. A dark innocent.

"Yes, endless meetings," Rajani laughed. "Well, never mind all that. How are you doing today?"

"Well, anything is better than...," Kyr snapped, then winced at his harsh tone.

"Gods, Kyr, I'm so sorry. Gauday is a vicious monster."

"You have no idea how vicious." He almost added, *And you took too damn long to get here!* He bit his lip, afraid to say anything. *What am I doing? Is this* my *anger or* Gauday's?

After an awkward pause, the Warrior Mage burst out, "What can I do for you, Kyr? If there's anything at all, I'll do it. If you need to talk about anything or.... Please, please tell me!"

For his friend's sake, Kyr took hold of himself and searched for something that might help. "Well, one thing that helped me get through all this was the Zhovanaya chant. Maybe you could sing it for me? My voice is still too wrecked."

"Uh, well, I'm not very good...." Rajani took a deep breath. "But I'll try." He sat up straighter and, after a moment, began to chant. "Zhovanya nara lo, Zhovanya nara lo, Zhovanya nara lo." As he sang, Rajani's face relaxed into a rare peacefulness. Kyr repeated the chant in his mind. Rage and tension drained from his body and mind, slowly replaced by gentle serenity.

*After a time, Zhovanya's Presence filled the small room. To Kyr, She appeared first as a vast figure of pure darkness sitting with the stillness of a great mountain, a stillness so deep that it could absorb all anguish, erase all nightmares. As She drew closer, she grew smaller, becoming a beautiful woman with luminous golden eyes, Her face radiant with kindness and grace. In his mind, he knelt before Her and raised both hands together before his heart, pleading.*

"Zhovanya, I have done as You asked, given all I can. I am used up, crippled, poisoned. Don't leave me here to spread the poison to others. Please, please take me home to Your Heart."

*She placed one hand, palm down, above his cupped hands. A green river of tenderness and love poured through Her hand and into his, flooding his being, soothing his heart and soul.*

175

"NEVER FORGET, YOU ARE MY BELOVED.
LIVE."

*He bowed his head in submission.* "I am Yours,
Zhovanya. As You command." *Tears filled his eyes as he
shut away his longing for the final refuge from suffering.*

"What's going on?" Rajani sounded concerned.

Kyr rubbed his eyes to hide his tears. "Never mind. I'll live." He kept
his rueful laugh to himself, and faked a yawn instead.

"You're sure you're alright?" Rajani looked at him doubtfully.

"Thanks, Rajani. Your chanting really helped, but I need to rest
now."

After the Warrior Mage left, Kyr sighed and settled into his
blankets. Though he felt reassured of Zhovanya's love, he also felt
unutterably weary, and couldn't keep from wondering: *What more does She
want of me?*

One evening, Rajani brought supper for the two of them, venison
stew and slices of fresh bread, still warm enough to melt the butter
smeared on them. The wonderful scent of the warm bread brought Kyr's
appetite to attention and he began to eat steadily.

Soon enough, their bowls were empty, and they were sipping honey-
sweetened tea.

Rajani asked, "How was it for you today?"

"Better."

"I have a surprise for you. We're preparing a room for you next door.
It will be ready soon."

"A room just for me?"

"Yes. Many people are helping to make it comfortable for you. I
hope you will like it." Rajani was clearly anxious that his surprise be
pleasing.

"Thanks. It will be nice to have some privacy." Kyr wasn't sure it
would be, but he didn't want to disappoint Rajani.

The Warrior Mage smiled, looking relieved. "It will be yours until
we head home."

"Home?"

"Ravenvale. It's where I grew up. Luciya, too."

Kyr snorted. "Zhovanya answers prayers in Her own way." It wasn't the home he had begged Her for, but perhaps it would be an answer to his prayer.

"What?"

"Uh, well." Kyr paused. *If I explain that I was praying for death, Rajani will be upset. How can I distract him? Ah.* "It's just that I know so little of what 'home' is. Tell me about this Ravenvale."

Rajani's eyes lit up. "It's a small valley between steep cliffs. The entrance is through a tunnel through the cliffs. Very defensible and safe. You can tell we're getting near by the sound of the waterfall that roars down the cliff to the east of the entrance. When we get through that and into the valley, you'll hear the ravens cawing. There's always a mob of them making a racket somewhere. They think they own the place."

"Ravens are those large black birds?"

"Right. We call the main house the Rookery because it's built around a huge old oak that the ravens call home. The house sits beside a lovely lake, and is made of gray stone. Over the generations, people kept adding rooms and levels, so it's a bit of a maze. Then we have various cottages scattered throughout the valley, but most aren't in great shape. We're putting a number of our people from the City to work repairing and rebuilding. There's rich farmland that's been left fallow for years. We're starting to farm it again. It's so beautiful, Kyr! Soon it will be like it was when I was a boy."

Kyr's eyes were closed, so Rajani reluctantly reined in his enthusiasm for the rebuilding of Ravenvale. "When you're well, we'll go there. I'll show you all my favorite places."

"Mmmph?" Kyr yawned hugely. "Sorry, Rajani."

"Never mind. I shouldn't be bothering you. Rest well."

After Rajani took their trays and left, Kyr settled down into his blankets. He lay awake for a little while, aching for a place of safety, rest, and healing. Tentatively, he began to hope it might be this long-unknown place called home.

# Part Six ~ Horror and Grace

*"Every scar has a story to tell,
a path to beauty and meaning."*

—Justine Musk

# Chapter 18

# Cleansing Fire

Kyr was hoping everyone would forget about him. The ceremony was about to begin but he was still in his new room, sitting on his new bed. He did appreciate the privacy of solid walls and a door instead of the bars of his cell in the infirmary, but the luxury of the room was unsettling.

For the past half-moon, while he was recovering some strength, strangers—Companions and villagers from this baffling new community at the fort—had cleaned and polished the room next door to the infirmary until every surface gleamed. And now it was his room, filled with gifts from many of these new people.

Along the left wall, there was a comfortable box-bed topped by a patchwork quilt, a multi-colored rag rug on the floor beside the bed, and a pinewood chest at its foot. Opposite the bed sat a table and two stools near the hearth, in the back right-hand corner of the room.

Most of the new clothing he'd been given remained in the chest. He could only tolerate wearing the loose, dark blue tunic and breeches of smooth linen that Rajani had provided. Anything else irritated his half-healed cuts and burns. He'd never understood what Gauday was up to, but his tormentor had inflicted the cuts and burns in a deliberate pattern, leaving him with small scars twining all over his torso, back, legs, and arms. Viewed objectively, it was even rather graceful. Perhaps Gauday was actually making him more beautiful. *Gods! What am I thinking?* Kyr shuddered in revulsion. *Curse you, Gauday! Stay out of my mind!*

To block out Gauday's insidious suggestions, Kyr focused on the gifts he'd been given: a cobalt-blue ceramic oil lamp; iron hearth tools; a tin-sheathed box for logs and kindling; muslin curtains on the window

181

by the door and the small, high window on the back wall. He shook his head. All he'd ever owned before was a few items of clothing.

The previous day, Rajani had ushered him into the room, and said, "This is all for you: gifts from the people of Khailaz."

"What am I to do with all this?" Kyr spread his hands in a helpless gesture. "This must be a mistake. I've never even met these people. Why are they…?"

"I know you don't agree, but people see you as a hero. They are eager to do something for you. You mustn't insult them by refusing their gifts."

He'd acquiesced, but still felt uneasy. *Why is everyone treating me so kindly? What do these strangers want of me?* Maybe he was being too suspicious, but after months of Gauday's sly manipulations and deceitful sympathy, it was difficult to trust anyone.

Now he was hiding out, hoping to avoid the purification ceremony. He didn't want to be exposed to reminders of his ordeal, or to celebrate Gauday's overthrow. He just felt sad about the entire sordid experience—sad for himself, for Medari, even for Gauday. He could not forget what he had seen with Zhovanya's eyes: Gauday's soul shriveling in agony over all he had done.

Kyr pulled his knees up and wrapped his arms around his shins. While others apparently saw him as a self-sacrificing hero, he felt like Gauday's scarred and wretched whore. He'd rarely been outside the infirmary in the past half-moon, and then only when few were about, early in the morning or late in the evening. The last thing he wanted to do was face the large crowd of strangers now gathered outside in the yard.

There was a quick rap on his door and Medari stepped inside, letting in sunshine, cool air, and the crowd's cheerful chatter. "You don't want to witness the purification?"

"No. I'm tired." Kyr's excuse sounded shopworn even to him.

"I think you need to come, Kyr. You most of all," Medari said gently. "Seeing Gauday's instruments of torture and degradation burned will help you realize more fully that you are free of that madman. And it might help to stop your nightmares. Will you come?"

"Gods, if it will stop the cursed nightmares…." He got up and shoved his feet into his new sandals, then hesitated. "Stay with me?"

"Of course."

They went out toward the large crowd standing around a large heap of objects in the middle of the courtyard. Kyr swallowed hard, afraid he was going to be sick. The spring sunshine revealed Gauday's instruments of torture and degradation: the four-poster bed with its straps and chains; the scrolls of evil spells; the sorcerous workbench and all its vile ingredients; the whips and flails; the burning rods; and the vicious, slender knives. Even the rare and luxurious silks and furs had been added to the pile.

People were eyeing the vile heap, with a rustle of questions and comments. A young male villager, one of the many new arrivals, pointed at something and asked with morbid fascination, "What was *that* for?" Kyr flushed in shame, knowing how it had been used on him. Nearby, a village matron exclaimed, "By all the lower gods, how sickening!"

Kyr slowed, but Medari urged him forward. The crowd caught sight of them. Pinned by hundreds of pairs of eyes, Kyr stopped dead.

"That's our Liberator!" he heard a voice cry.

"He killed the Soul-Drinker!" chimed in another.

"He saved Khailaz!"

"Gods bless him!"

Kyr's face was burning. He heard nothing of their admiration, only a susurrus of hissing whispers; saw only disgust in the staring eyes. He turned to flee to his room, but Medari grabbed his arm and whispered fiercely, "You have shown me your tremendous courage all these months. Now show *them*."

Medari's words sparked a blaze of defiance in Kyr's core. He straightened, shrugged off Medari's hand, and stared back at the crowd. *Gauday did his worst, and I survived! Go ahead and look!*

Unbeknownst to him, his gaze was as fierce and empyreal as that of the Firebird reborn from the flames. Many among the crowd bowed, while some stared open-mouthed. All of them sensed that they were in the presence of one who had gone beyond ordinary human experience into realms of unimaginable horror and grace.

Except for those on duty, nearly two hundred green-clad Companions fell to one knee in unison, clapping their right hands to their hearts in a gesture of deepest honor. Startled, Kyr glanced over his shoulder, but there was no one behind him. *What are they doing? They can't be kneeling to me, can they? Are they mocking me?* The flame of defiant pride guttered in a welter of confusion and shame. He looked down, wishing he had never left his room.

A breeze of sighs gusted through the crowd as his gaze left their faces. To be freed from Kyr's devastating gaze was a relief—and also a loss. At Rajani's gesture, the Companions rose.

"Come on, son," Medari said. "Let's take our places so the ceremony can begin. Soonest begun, soonest done." Kyr scraped up some courage and followed the healer through the crowd toward the inner circle surrounding the pile of Gauday's instruments. He kept his eyes on the ground, seeing booted or sandaled feet stepping back quickly. He missed the expressions of respect and deference on people's faces, and suspected they were drawing away from him out of disgust. Medari led him to the empty space by Rajani's side.

The Warrior Mage stepped forward, and raised his voice. "Today, we take one more step in our campaign to rid Khailaz of all means of torture and subjugation. From now on, we shall live safe and free from oppression!" He raised his hand and pointed his blackwood wand toward the center of the heap.

"SHAI'YA!"

At Rajani's commanding shout, Kyr jerked his head up. Before his eyes, pure white mage-fire blazed up in a fury of sizzling sparks, engulfing the pile in fierce flames. At this, the crowd erupted, hurling acrimonious cheers and virulent curses at the Soul-Drinker, his Slaves and particularly Gauday. Medari joined in, eyes blazing, fists raised above his head, venting months of suppressed fury at their captor.

As the fire raged higher, everyone shuffled back, away from the intense heat. But Kyr was lost in a trance of horrified fascination.

"Step back, Kyr. You'll get burned."

"Yes, he burned me," Kyr moaned. "Burned and cut and...."

"It's over now, Kyr," Rajani soothed. "See, everything is burning up. It will all be gone soon. Step back now." The Warrior Mage took him by the elbow and tugged him away from the fire. Kyr stumbled back a few steps, trembling, his eyes still locked on the pyre.

"Gods, maybe this wasn't such a good idea," Rajani muttered to himself. "Listen, Kyr," he said softly. "It's over. He can't hurt you anymore."

"Hurt me? Yes! He DID hurt me, over and over! He never stops." Rage urged him to take a flaming brand from the fire, throw it into

Gauday's prison cell, and listen to *him* scream and beg. No, no. *He* had been the one who screamed and begged as Gauday chanted, *"You are mine, mine! You always do whatever I wish. I am your Master now! Come to me. I am your Master. Do as I say. Come free me!"*

Blindly, he turned and began walking toward the dark hole where Gauday was now imprisoned.

Rajani caught his arm. "Where are you going?"

"What?" Kyr looked around in confusion. "I—I don't know."

"I'm sorry, Kyr. I didn't realize this would be so hard for you. It'll be over soon. I'll stay with you." Rajani set a comforting arm across Kyr's shoulders. The weight of Rajani's arm on his shoulders brought Kyr back to reality. However, as he had been before the Kailithana's deep healing work at the Sanctuary, Kyr was once again unable to bear any touch for more than a few moments, thanks to Gauday's tortures. He quickly shrugged off Rajani's arm. Rajani glanced at him briefly, and silently guided him back to his place in the widened circle.

Kyr caught sight of the fire again. In that moment, everything seemed to be moving with dreadful slowness. All sound faded into insignificance except the hissing, crackling roar of the brilliant white blaze. He watched in a trance of revulsion and relief as his bed of torment, black against the raging white flames, slowly crumbled, and burned to ash. Gauday's venoms went up in lurid sparks and vile smells. The whips and flails burned blood-red, writhing like serpents, until they too were gone. In the heat of Rajani's mage-fire, even the metal knives and rods twisted out of shape, melted, and finally dissipated in clouds of sulfurous smoke. After an eternity, the blaze died down, its white flames subsiding into the pale orange of ordinary fire.

Shuddering, Kyr tore his eyes away and fought to come back to himself. Dekani spoke in his mind. *It's over. It's over. That nightmare is over. Let it go.* This *is what's real now. This here now. Focus on what is around you now.*

Kyr took a couple of deep breaths and made himself meet Rajani's concerned gaze.

"It's over, Kyr," the Warrior Mage assured him." Can you believe that now?"

"Yes, I think so." He hoped it was true.

"Will you be all right? I'm sorry, but…" Rajani gestured toward the group of village elders awaiting his attention.

"Yes."

"Good. Enjoy the feast!" Rajani turned away.

Kyr closed his eyes and focused on his breath until he felt more in control, then looked around the courtyard, focusing on the details. Near the kitchens, sweating boys turned spits, roasting haunches of venison or pork over beds of coals. Women and girls hurried to set out bowls and baskets full of food on plank tables set up for the feast. Most of the yard was filled with Companions and villagers dancing to a triumphant tune played by fiddlers, drummers, and pipers.

The forest-green uniforms of the Companions made sober counterpoints among the riotous array of colors and costumes of the villagers, who had all turned out in their traditional finery. Women with olive skin, short dark hair, and slanted eyes wore plain leather vests and leggings, and elaborately engraved gold armbands. They were dancing with each other, bright teeth flashing in their dusky faces as they laughed. Long-haired men wearing black leggings and knee-length tunics in ruby, emerald, or gold, with wide leather belts and tall boots, shouted and leapt exuberantly, vying for the attention of dark-skinned women in white dresses bordered with colorful embroidery.

Striped turbans adorned the heads of women wearing black vests, with skirts in exotic patterns of yellow, green and orange swirling above their bare feet. Anklet-bells tinkled with each stomp and twirl. They danced with men in yellow tunics and loose blue trousers tucked into red boots, weaving intricate patterns together.

Children danced wildly or chased each other, screaming in excitement. Oldsters stood around the edges of the maelstrom, clapping and nodding in time with the music.

Overwhelmed, Kyr looked away.

On the other side of the fire stood the former soldiers and Slaves, guarded by Jakar and a dozen armed Companions. The ex-Slaves looked sullen or morose, but the soldiers seemed to be enjoying the spectacle, Craith among them. His face was a mirror of Kyr's heart, old terror warring with dawning relief. Kyr took a sudden breath. *Merciless gods, he's been through it himself. That's why he was so afraid of Gauday.*

Craith looked up from the fire and their eyes met. For a moment, they were alone together, the only two denizens of a private hell. Kyr longed to go to him, knowing that only he could understand what it had been like in that terrible room. But Craith turned red and looked away.

Jakar snapped orders and marched the prisoners back to their barracks. Kyr sighed and turned back to the fire. Little was left but glowing cinders. A sudden quiet fell as the musicians ceased playing, and people turned to face the main gate.

Twelve young men of all the different tribes marched through the gate into the yard, playing bells and drums in a solemn rhythm. Twelve young women in white dresses followed, carrying lit candles and baskets of incense. They paraded solemnly through the crowd. The adults took sticks of incense and lit them from the candles, then spread out to purify every nook and cranny of the fort with sweet, cleansing smoke.

They were all chanting "Zhovanya nara lo" as if it were a magical incantation. Kyr frowned. From their earlier shouts of acrimony, he knew that many had no idea what forgiveness was, or what it required. It would take more than sweet smoke to cleanse their minds and hearts of hatred and vengefulness. But it was a start, he supposed.

He remained where he was, staring into the embers, brooding on Gauday's life and his own, both twisted and corrupted by the same evil. *Day was driven mad by the Master's sorcery, and now he is a prisoner enduring further suffering. He is my Slave-brother. I must try to bring him Zhovanya's message of love and forgiveness. Him and my other Slave-brothers.* The very thought made him ache with exhaustion. He sighed. *If I can find the strength.*

Soon the crowd returned and gathered around the feast tables, babbling and crowing. Medari returned, sweaty from dancing, yet smelling of the sweet purifying incense.

"Come on, Kyr. Let's join the celebration. This is a great day!"

"Yes, well… I, uh…."

Medari took a closer look at Kyr. "You look exhausted. Go rest, son."

"Thanks, Medari." Kyr walked back to his room and closed the door, muting the music and noise of the crowd. He stood for a moment, shaking. Everything seemed bizarre and unfamiliar. He retreated to a bare corner and hunched up on the floor, wrapping his arms around his shins and burying his head on his knees. Images swarmed in his head liking stinging scorpions: the implements of his ordeal burning in the white-hot fire; Gauday's tormenting, pleasuring hands and mad, voracious eyes; Craith chained to that bed, screaming.

"Oh gods!' he groaned, sickened to realize that he'd become aroused. *The fort may be purified of Gauday's evil, but it's still in me. Goddess help me!*

187

Desperate, he returned to his lifeline, whispering, "Zhovanya nara lo, Zhovanya nara lo, Zhovanya nara lo."

After that day, Kyr kept to his room, feeling corrupted and ashamed. His exhaustion was bone-deep, and he spent most of the day resting, yet he rarely slept well. Even the fire of purification had not banished his nightmares. He couldn't meditate or pray. When he tried, vivid memories of the intense pain and pleasure of Gauday's tortures invaded his mind. Instead of Zhovanya's voice, he heard Gauday whispering spellchants or commands. Discouraged and angry, he struggled to separate Gauday's rage and despair from his own, but it was often impossible.

Despite the concern and care of his friends, life seemed flat and purposeless after the months-long battle against Gauday's determination to break his mind and possess his soul. Kyr puzzled resentfully over why the Goddess insisted he continue living. *Haven't I done what She asked? The Sanctuary is safe. She can't ask more from me, can She?* He shivered, knowing that She could, fearing that She might.

After another quarter-moon, he began to feel restless. Alone in his room, there was no escape from memories or whispers. Seeking distraction, he began to spend part of the day sitting on the porch of the infirmary, wrapped up in a blanket. Sometimes he wished for a dozen blankets, a hundred, anything that might make him feel shielded from trespass and injury.

He watched as the fort was transformed from an unkempt hellion into a proper lady: neat, clean, and cheerful. Under close supervision by Companions, the prisoners—soldiers and Slaves alike—were put to work, repairing sagging steps, porches, and shutters; whitewashing buildings; keeping the yard free of litter, and sprinkled morning, noon, and night to lay the dust. To Kyr, the fort's new personality seemed grotesque: a smiling mask on a rotting skull; ugly bones of reality hiding behind a pretty veil.

Even more baffling were the comings and goings of Companions and villagers, with their joking and arguing, and their mysterious busyness. The liveliness of the children was particularly perplexing. His only knowledge of family life came from Medari's stories. Fascinated and perturbed, he watched children playing, crying, being hugged or scolded by their parents. It was nothing like his boyhood in the Master's

Compound. Playing and crying had not been allowed. There had just been pain, obedience, and his only refuge, the ice.

The cheerful, bustling ordinariness that now reigned in the fort left him feeling like a ghost from a nightmare world, like a crippled monster wearing a pleasant mask. Obscene desires for the intensity of pleasure/pain Gauday had drummed deep into his flesh and bones plagued him in nightmares, and sprang upon him unexpectedly during the day, triggered by ordinary things: the scent of sweat, a child's playful scream, the sight of a man's hands. Such things would leave him shuddering with desire, terror, or disgust.

One morning, he noticed Craith supervising a crew of prisoners at work across the courtyard: white-washing a building, raking up debris, leveling out potholes. The tall redhead gave directions, joked with the Companions guarding the prisoners, chivvied the sluggards among his crew. His face was unshadowed and his laugh free and full. Kyr admired his strong, lean body and handsome face, remembering the love they had shared that one blessed, difficult night. Envy made his heart shrivel. *Craith's free of Gauday now, but I'll never be.* Images of what he would do to Craith's body in Gauday's special room invaded his mind, and shame replaced envy. *Goddess forgive me! I can't keep Day's poison out.* Kyr retreated to his room and knelt by his bed.

As Kyr bowed his head to pray for Zhovanya's help, his long, tangled hair brushed against his cheek. The touch reminded him of Gauday playing with his hair while crooning spellchants, caressing or tormenting all the while. Kyr shuddered with revulsion and yanked his hair back so hard that tears came to his eyes.

"Gods curse it!" he growled, leaping to his feet and stalking into the infirmary next door. No one was there. Kyr strode across to the cabinet where Medari kept his instruments and grabbed a sharp knife.

# Chapter 19

# The Hard Path

"Gods, Kyr! What have you done?"

Kyr jerked awake and nearly fell off his stool. "Oh! Oh. Medari. It's you." He righted himself and glanced at the floor. "Uh, sorry for the mess."

"Never mind that. Why did you do this to yourself?"

"It's *my* hair. I can do what I want with it."

Taken aback, Medari said hastily, "Well, yes, of course." He paused, and then carefully asked, "Would you mind if I, uh, evened it out a bit?"

"Um, well, alright. Sorry for snapping at you."

"Never mind." Medari was sure he deserved much worse for abetting Gauday all those months, but he kept that thought to himself. Instead, he located his scissors and trimmed Kyr's hair to just below his ears. It sprang into loose curls all over his head, giving him an angelic look at odds with his haunted eyes and gaunt, stubble-bearded face.

Medari held up a mirror. Kyr glanced at himself, and ran his hands through his hair. "That's better," he said, feeling lighter and calmer.

Medari set the mirror aside. "Do you want a shave?" Gauday had insisted that Kyr be clean-shaven.

Kyr rubbed his bristly face, and shook his head. He wanted to look nothing like the whore Gauday had made of him.

The next morning, Kyr emerged from his room and stood on the porch. It was an early Spring day of warm sunshine and cool, playful breezes, which tousled his short curls, tickling his ears. He brushed his hair back and glanced around, but no one seemed shocked by his short hair.

Little birds were twittering excitedly and darting back and forth with grass or twigs in their beaks. Children ran and shouted, as lively as the birds. Restless, Kyr went wandering around the fort, watching people going about daily tasks, chatting, laughing, and haggling with each other. He was relieved to notice that men wore their hair in all lengths and styles, as did the women.

"Momma! Momma!"

He came to an abrupt stop as a gangly boy and a little girl in pigtails raced heedlessly across his path. The two children flung themselves at a village woman and clung to her.

"Marja! We found you!" A man hurried to embrace them all in a close circle of tears and laughter.

"We missed you, Momma!"

"And I missed you so much!" The woman smiled at her children and hugged them to her, but there were tears in her eyes as she gazed over their heads at her man.

"You're safe now, dearest love," he said, gently wiping her tears away. "And we're together again. Let's go home." All still holding hands, they hurried away through the gate.

Kyr returned to the porch of the infirmary and huddled up in his blanket. *I'll never know who my mother and father were. They must've been a Slave and one of the breeders.* Sick fury filled him. *Gods curse Dauthaz! My soul was mired in evil from the very beginning! And, thanks to Gauday, it still is.* He wrapped his arms around his shins.

The man's tender words to his woman reminded Kyr of holding Jolanya in his arms, hearing what his heart most longed to hear. *"I love you, only you,"* she had whispered, just before he left the Sanctuary. Burying his head on his knees, he rocked slightly side to side in anguish. *Gods! Why do I keep thinking of her? Gauday has destroyed the man she loved. Besides, she's the Kailithana. Even if she could still love me, we cannot be together.* He once again tried to banish all thought of her, but his rebellious heart ached with longing. With clenched fists, he muttered, "Ah, cruel Goddess! How *could* You send me back into the arms of hate just as I found Jolanya's love?"

Frightened by his mutinous anger, he muttered, "Forgive me, Zhovanya, forgive me. I belong to You. I am Yours, I am Yours." Trying to regain some semblance of submission, he lost himself in the forgiveness chant, still his main defense against Gauday's nightmare.

"Want some lunch?"

Startled out of the fragile peace the chant had brought him, Kyr looked up. Medari was carrying a tray laden with slices of cold ham, cheese, and bread, and a jug of apple cider. Kyr nodded, though he resented this interruption. They went inside and took seats at the table in the infirmary's main room.

"You're still too thin. Eat up."

Kyr layered ham and cheese on a slab of bread and obediently took a bite. They ate in companionable silence. Kyr washed down a last bite with fresh, sweet cider, and glanced at Medari. "You should go on home to your family. Rajani is enough of a nursemaid."

"No, son, I want to see you strong first."

There was something evasive about the healer's tone. Puzzled, Kyr asked, "Isn't your family waiting for you? Worried about you?"

"Rajani's men haven't found them yet, but I'm sure they will." Medari waved a hand as if brushing away nagging insects.

*Oh, gods!* Kyr thought, his heart sinking as it dawned on him that no one had come to the fort searching for the healer.

Medari ignored him and went on brightly. "We'll go together when you leave for Ravenvale. Stonewell, my village, is on the way."

Baffled by Medari's blithe behavior, Kyr merely said, "As you wish."

"Now, Kyr, I've been meaning to speak to you. I've come to know you very well under the most difficult of circumstances. You are putting on a very good front, but you can't fool me." Though his words were stern, Medari's tone was gentle.

"What do you mean?" Kyr kept a neutral face but he was cringing inside.

"I know you are hiding a lot of pain. I understand why you might not want to speak of what you went through to others, but I can't help wondering why you haven't shared some of your current difficulties with me?"

Kyr looked down at his tightly clenched hands resting on the bare wooden table. He was silent for a while. *I know he wants to help, but what can he do?* He bit his lip, knowing the answer. He had learned it at the Sanctuary. Taking a deep breath, he plunged in.

"Gods, Medari. I just.... It's so hard to talk about. But you're right. If anyone can understand what Gauday did to me, it's you." He looked up at Medari, eyes full of anguish and shame. "I feel like such a monster, so corrupted. It was so intense, what he did to me. Pain and pleasure got mixed up. I dream of it, crave it." He stopped, fearing Medari's condemnation or disgust.

"It was severe, what he did to you. You can't expect to be free of it in just a month or two."

"I'm afraid of spreading his poison. Sometimes I want to take someone into that chamber...." Kyr saw the shock in Medari's eyes, and recoiled. Deeply mortified, he dropped his head into his hands. "Merciless gods," he whispered.

"I'm sorry, Kyr," Medari said, looking ashamed. "I guess I *don't* understand."

"Never mind." Kyr looked up from behind his polite mask. "Don't worry. I won't hurt anybody."

"I know. You are very strong, and kind."

Kyr kept his doubts about that to himself. "Thanks for your concern, Medari. Good night."

"But...." Medari's protest died on his lips. "Good night, Kyr," he said sadly.

In his room, Kyr sat on his bed, fighting shame and despair. He stared out the door, left open to admit the cooling night breeze. The full moon cast the shadow of the whipping post across the courtyard toward Gauday's prison. *I might as well be in there with him. I'm still trapped in his hell.*

He couldn't bear the thought of talking to anyone, after his disastrous attempt to talk with Medari. But he needed help. Stretching out, he closed his eyes. *"Dekani? Dekani? Can we talk?"*

Dekani met him at the cottage door and welcomed him in with wave of his hand. They settled into their chairs before the fire. *"What is it, Kyr?"*

*"I can block Gauday out most of the time, now, but I'm still finding this new life difficult. I don't understand what Zhovanya wants of me. I haven't even tried to carry out my Atonement. It seems impossible, and I'm just too tired of it all, or not brave enough."* He heaved a deep sigh. *"Gods and demons, I don't know why She insists I keep on living."*

*"You gave Her your submission. You don't want to take that back, do you?"*

Kyr was silent, remembering when he had begged the Goddess to accept his submission. *"No. But what do I do, Dekani? It's so hard, this path."*

"Let me think." Dekani stared into the fire for a few moments, then looked up. Kyr braced for some new, arduous task or discipline.

*"Of course, it would help to practice the skills you learned at the Sanctuary and here: breathing, meditation, Flowing Poses, the forgiveness chant, and prostrations. But I think you also need some reminders of your dedication to Zhovanya. Create an altar or chapel to Zhovanya, a place to meditate and chant. Perhaps you could create one where others could join you. You could introduce Her to others who have not known Her before."*

*"Gods, Dekani! Are you mad? I can't be a teacher. Gauday's poison is still in me."*

*"Only if you let go of all you learned during your ordeal: compassion; surrender; being present to what is. You have much hard-won wisdom you could share."*

Kyr shook his head. *"I can't, not yet anyway. I need more time to recover. You know how bad it was."*

*"Yes, son. I do."* Dekani's voice was gentle, sad, and compassionate. *"And I also know that it will help you recover if you keep your focus on what you learned and accomplished, not on what he did to you."*

*"That's easy to say. But I can't block the memories or nightmares...."*

*"No, they will plague you for a time. Just keep in mind that—difficult as they are to deal with—they are part of your healing, not a sign that you are poisoned or broken."*

*"That's good to hear. I hope it's true. As always, what you advise is not much easier than the problem I'm facing."* They exchanged rueful smiles, remembering Kyr's struggle to focus only on the present moment.

They sat in silence for a while. The fire now burned higher and radiated a gentle warmth that penetrated the depths of Kyr's tired heart. At last, he sighed and sat up straighter, squaring his shoulders. *"I guess I'm fated to live, so I must still fight for my soul. I can't let myself stay mired in Gauday's swamp. I will make myself an altar in my room. It will help me remember."* His heart felt lighter, thinking of rededicating himself to the Goddess.

Dekani beamed at him. *"That's right, Kyr. You have survived the worst. Now is not the time to give up. There's one more thing you need to do: ask your friends for help."*

*"I'm not sure what to ask for. The only thing that might help is to return to the Sanctuary. But I couldn't bear that, not with Jolanya there. Besides, Rajani wants to take me to Ravenvale, his home."*

*"What about Naran? I believe he would gladly come here or to Ravenvale to help you."*

*"Do you think he would?"* Instantly, Kyr tried to crush this small flower of hope, fearing to trust it. *"I'm not sure where he is or how to find him."* He rose, suddenly anxious to return to outer awareness. *"Thanks, Teacher. I can go on now."*

*"Remember to ask your friends for help."* Dekani bowed and was gone.

Kyr came back to outer reality, resolved to deal with this new ordeal called ordinary life, and to fight against Gauday's corruption. He looked around his room. It wasn't a Temple or even a chapel. How could he create his altar to Zhovanya? After much consideration, he moved his clothes chest from the foot of his bed to a spot under the small window on the back wall, next to the hearth. Then he set the rag rug in front of the chest. He knelt on the rug facing his rough altar.

Something didn't feel right. His back was tense. Looking over his shoulder, he realized that he felt too exposed with his back to the door. He turned his bed so the head of the bed was against the side wall, and the bed projected into the room, which made a protected alcove for his altar.

He went next door to the infirmary. Medari set aside his pestle and smiled hopefully. "How are you today?"

"Ah, better." He returned the healer's smile. "I'm making an altar to Zhovanya in my room. Do you have a candle and holder I could borrow?"

"Hmmm, let's see what I've got." Medari rummaged in a cabinet and brought forth a fat white candle. "I don't have a nice holder, but this might do for now." He pulled out a small pewter dish.

"Thanks, Medari. These will do fine."

"Glad to help." They smiled at each other, and Kyr felt the tension from their last difficult conversation ease.

In his room, Kyr set the dish and candle on the chest. Now it felt more like an altar. There was something soothing and hopeful in creating this small place of holiness for himself. He lit the candle, took his place before his small altar, and began to watch his breath, remembering the grace of being held in Zhovanya's heart.

"Merciless gods!" Memories of Gauday's torture and degradation were all he saw, all he was. He jumped up and backed away from the altar, vivid claws of agony slashing through his mind. Bumping into his bed, he abruptly plunked down on it, his heart racing. "Forgive me!" he groaned, horrified at having profaned Zhovanya's altar with his own corrupt presence.

*"That's right, my boy. You are* mine, *not hers. I am your Master. Come to me. Free me, and we will be together always."* Gauday's whisper was louder than ever.

*"SHUT UP! I am HERS, not yours. I will NEVER be yours. Leave me ALONE!"* Kyr's furious blast silenced Gauday.

Kyr returned to his place before the altar, and began to chant. "Zhovanya naralo, Zhovanya naralo, Zhovanya naralo, Zhovanya naralo." Slowly, he relaxed into the chant and let it fill him. After a time, Zhovanya's Presence enfolded him in purifying serenity.

# Chapter 20

# Bridges to Life

The next afternoon, Kyr wandered out to the barn, seeking to avoid uncomprehending eyes. He found a seat on a bale of hay at the back. Wrapped in warm earthy odors of straw, manure, and horse, he sat watching dust dancing in a stray beam of sunlight, keeping his mind on the chant and listening to the horses in their stalls munching, breathing, and swishing their tails at droning flies. Their undemanding presence and big, warm bodies spread a living calmness that soothed his soul. He drifted into a light sleep, soaking in the simple peacefulness of the barn.

Something cold and wet nudged his hand. Startled, Kyr opened his eyes. A dog was looking up at him, whining and wagging its tail. "Friend! I thought you were gone." His companion from his days chained in the yard wagged her tail faster and nudged his hand again. He patted her on the head and scratched behind her ears. The dog sighed happily and turned about so she could sit leaning against his leg. With his hand on her head, they sat together peaceably as the sunbeam drifted across the floor, never losing its complement of dancing particles.

At last, the ray of sun disappeared into oncoming darkness. Kyr stirred, feeling calm and rested but reluctant to leave this dusty, odiferous haven. He stretched, considering spending the night in the hayloft; but his stomach growled, reminding him it was dinnertime. "Come on, Friend, let's get some supper." He headed for the door.

Wondering if the dog would follow him, he looked back. Friend was hobbling after him on three legs. "What's wrong, girl? Let me see." He knelt and examined her leg, finding a ragged gash crusted with dried blood. "Merciless gods!" Furious that nothing innocent could go unharmed, he picked her up and headed for the infirmary.

"Kyr, wait." Medari's voice stopped Kyr at the door. "You can't bring that filthy cur in here."

"She's hurt!" Kyr could barely keep himself from yelling at Medari. "Please! You've got to help her."

"Why don't you put her in the barn for tonight and come have supper? I'll look at her in the morning when there's some light."

"NO!" Kyr shouted. "Help her NOW!" Glaring defiance, he brought the dog inside.

"Alright, Kyr, alright. Put her on the table." As the healer gathered rags, a bowl of water, and medicaments, he muttered, "I'll just have to cleanse the room after I treat her."

Kyr set Friend down carefully. "See, it's this leg. There's blood and she can't walk on it."

"Hold her head so she won't bite me. What's so important about this dog?"

Holding a lamp close, Medari examined Friend's leg, then washed the wound. Friend whimpered but stayed still, looking at Kyr with trusting eyes.

Still simmering, Kyr said, "Don't use that word—ever."

"What word?"

"Cur."

"The cut is not deep and it's not infected. She'll be fine. Hold onto her, now." Medari dabbed a brownish potion on Friend's cut.

She whimpered in protest, and Kyr demanded, "What's that? It's hurting her!"

"It stings at first, but it will help prevent flesh rot." The healer washed his hands, and looked at Kyr. "What is this all about, this dog, that word?"

"You know that's what Gauday and the other Slaves called me!" Kyr snapped. Seeing Medari's hurt look, he sighed. "Sorry. It just brings back bad memories." Calmer now that he knew Friend would be all right, he added, "This dog was my only friend those first months, when I was chained out. That's what I call her, Friend. She came at night after everyone had gone inside, and left before sunup, so you never noticed her. Slept with me every night—until the rains came." Both of them were silent for a moment, remembering that terrible night, how sick Kyr had been, and how lost.

"I'm sorry, Kyr. I had no idea what she meant to you."

"Sorry I got so mad." Silently, he promised himself to clamp down on his anger, never knowing how much was rightfully his and how much might be Gauday's influence.

"Alright, let's give her a good bath and an old blanket. She can sleep in your room." Medari fetched a low washtub, while Kyr hauled in buckets of water. It took three sudsings and rinses before the water ran clean, but Friend shivered through it all without resisting their ablutions. Medari reached for an old towel from a pile of rags in a basket. "Hold onto her while I…. Watch out!"

He jumped back as Friend leapt out of the low washtub. She gave herself a thorough shake, drenching Kyr and spraying cold water all over the floor, walls, and furniture. Medari burst out laughing. "Tried to warn you!"

"I'm sorry! I'll clean it all up. Don't punish her!"

"It's all right, Kyr. Don't worry. She's just being a dog." Medari was still chuckling. "You should've seen your face. You looked so surprised!" He laughed louder. "By all the little gods, she really soaked you."

Kyr smiled ruefully, looked down at his soggy self, and began to laugh, too, enjoying the long-forgotten joy of shared laughter.

"Why'd she do that?" He brushed uselessly at his clothes.

"Trying to dry herself, but she'll need a little help." Medari grabbed the ragged towel and started toward the dog, but she backed away, growling.

"Here." He tossed the towel to Kyr. "You better dry her off. I'll mop up."

A while later, order had been restored, and Friend was mostly dry. Her coat was now a silky auburn rather than a tangled, dull brown. The healer threw a last rag onto the pile of wet cloths. "Look at her! What a difference! She's quite the princess, now."

" Kyr grinned proudly. "She's pretty, isn't she?"

"I'm glad you brought her in."

Well, who's this?" Rajani asked, coming up to the porch of the infirmary. Kyr was leaning against the wall with his legs stretched out, Friend's head in his lap, watching the morning bustle. He glanced up at Rajani with a faint smile.

"This is Friend," Kyr said, ruffling her ears.

"May I join you?" At Kyr's nod, Rajani sat down next to Kyr. "Is Friend friendly? May I pet her?"

"I don't think she'll mind. Go ahead." Reaching across Kyr's legs, Rajani offered the dog his hand to sniff. When she gave it a tentative lick, he petted her for a few moments.

"She's quite pretty. Where did you find her?"

"She found me." He sighed, reluctant to explain. For the first time, he had simply been enjoying the day. But Rajani was looking at him curiously. "She kept me company at night when I was chained out to that." He gestured at the whipping post that still stood in the center of the yard. "Until the rains came." He shivered and pulled Friend onto his lap, needing the warmth and weight of her wiry body.

"Did that madman leave you out in the rain?"

"Yes."

"What happened?"

"What do you think happened? I had no protection, no escape from the rain, the mud, the cold. I got so sick, I nearly died." He blew out a breath. "Many times after that, I wished I had."

Friend was whining and struggling to get off his lap. Looking down, Kyr realized he was holding her too tightly. "Sorry, girl." He let her loose. She licked his face and settled down on the porch beside him. He rested an arm on her shoulders and glanced at Rajani. "Even Friend, here, had somewhere to go to get out of the rain. She wanted me to come with her...." He fell silent, his throat tight.

"Gods curse his...."

Kyr held up a hand. "Stop. He is my brother. I could so easily start hating him, but that's not what Zhovanya is teaching me. So I ask you not to tempt me with your anger at Gauday."

"Sorry." Rajani looked more baffled than apologetic. "Well, so.... He left you out all night in a storm? Gods, you must have felt helpless? Abandoned?"

Rajani's words were a knife, stabbing a festering wound. Through clenched teeth, he growled, "I don't want to talk about this."

"What did you learn at the Sanctuary? I am not your Aithané like Naran was, but I hope I am your friend. You can talk to me."

"Gods and demons! I suppose you're right. Give me a moment." Kyr made himself take several deliberate breaths until he had control of himself. "Alright. Yes, I did feel abandoned. By everyone, even Zhovanya." He hunched up and bowed his head to his knees, amazed how sharp the pain was, even after so many months and so many other torments. For a time, he remained silent. Rajani sat quietly on one side, Friend leaned against him on the other, breathing with him. Their presence eased his heart.

Sighing deeply, he raised his head. "Gods, Rajani. The one time I wasn't thinking about the past, and here you come with your damn questions."

"Sorry, Kyr. Guess it was Friend here who got me started. What I wanted to talk about was the future, not the past. It's a long journey to Ravenvale. You'll need to regain your strength. You need to start exercising, and you need to learn to ride."

"Ride? A horse? No, thanks!" Kyr said vehemently. "I'd rather walk."

"Oh? Why is that? It's a very long walk to Ravenvale."

"I was so glad to get off that horse when we got here, I almost didn't care what else they did to me."

"Don't worry, we'll take it slow. Just a short lesson, every other day or so. You won't get that sore again."

Kyr sighed. "Well, if you think it's necessary...."

"Once you get through the first few lessons, I'm sure you'll enjoy riding. Shall we get started?" Rajani jumped to his feet.

Kyr didn't move. He just wanted to enjoy being with Friend. He resented Rajani's intrusion on his first chance at some peace, felt angry at being constantly pushed and shoved and tormented by others' desires. "No. Not for a few days. I need to stay with Friend until her leg is better. She has a bad cut, but Medari treated it. He says she will be fine."

"Oh. Good. Alright, let me know when you're ready." Rajani got to his feet. "Duty calls. I'm glad Friend found you again."

"So am I."

Resting his head against the wall behind him, Kyr closed his eyes, puzzled by a sense of satisfaction. *Ah! I said "no." I'm not a helpless captive anymore, thank the Goddess!*

For the next quarter-moon, Kyr spent all his time with Friend. They napped together in the warm barn, and slept together at night. Her simple devotion was a balm for his wounded soul. Her leg healed quickly, and soon they were playing the game called "fetch." He learned it by watching children playing with their dogs. The past haunted him not at all while he played with Friend. With their daily romps, his strength began to build, his face to lose its ghostly paleness.

Early one morning, Rajani joined Medari on the porch of the infirmary. For a while, they watched Kyr playing with Friend.

"I was wondering what to do to get Kyr out of his room, get him more active. Looks like Friend got him started."

Medari smiled. "Yes, our ghost has returned to life. And a lowly dog is the miracle worker. Zhovanya's ways are strange."

"Indeed." Rajani's laugh held a bitter tone, but he ignored Medari's curious glance. He gazed out over the teeming courtyard, then stiffened. "What is he doing?"

Medari followed his gaze. Kyr and his dog were heading through the open gate of the fort. Rajani leaped off the porch and ran after the disappearing pair.

"What's the problem?" Medari muttered to himself. "Worse than a mother hen, the way he hovers over Kyr." He shrugged and went into his infirmary.

"Kyr, wait!" Rajani put on a burst of speed and caught up to Kyr. "Where are you going?"

Kyr stopped, frowning at this unnecessary question. The answer was obvious, but he answered it anyway. "Out."

"Out where?"

"Outside the fort. Into the woods."

"I'm not sure that's such a good idea."

Kyr's frown turned resentful, but he turned to go back to his room. Friend whined and looked longingly out the gate.

"Wait. That was not an edict of the cursed Soul Drinker. We're still discussing this."

"But you said...."

"I know. I was just starting to think about your idea, not making a decision. Tell me why you want to get out of the fort."

"The yard is too small and too noisy, with all these new people. We want to go for longer walks where it's quiet."

"Well, it's not entirely safe out there. I'll have a Companion or two keep an eye on you, from a distance."

"I don't want anyone watching me. I'm sick of it! Everyone always staring at me, or glancing at me, then looking away quickly. What, by all the hells, do they want, anyway? And I'm sick of being in this gods-cursed fort! I want to go out where I can breathe and not be reminded...."

"Ah." Rajani blew out a breath and dropped his shoulders. "I understand now. But I still want at least one Companion to go with you."

"No! I need to be *alone*. Friend will protect me, won't you, girl?" Friend looked up at him and panted happily.

"Alright, alright," Rajani laughed. "Go on, then."

Kyr eyed him, suspicious of this easy victory. Eager to get out into the forest, he merely said, "Thanks, Rajani."

The Warrior Mage hurried off to find Lorya. He'd have her keep an unobtrusive watch over Kyr.

Kyr and Friend threaded their way through the marketplace that had sprung up outside the gates of the fort. Peddlers set up their offerings on the tailgates of their carts, or spread their wares on blankets on the ground: motley piles and stacks of reed baskets; wooden buckets; wool blankets; baskets of golden grains, red apples, green vegetables, orange carrots; pewter mugs and plates; bolts of fabrics ranging from practical browns and grays to brilliant rainbow hues; and many things he couldn't name.

Women and men of all ages and varieties strolled along, eyeing the merchandise, carrying empty or partially filled baskets. Some stood gossiping with each other or arguing with the peddlers. While their voices sounded fierce—loud and fast—as they argued, their eyes flashed with amusement. Kyr concluded that it was more like a game than a fight. He wasn't sure what the point of the game was. But then he saw one argument end with a copper pot being exchanged for two silver coins. The two arguers shook hands in mutual satisfaction.

One large area was like an outdoor kitchen, with five or six sellers offering a variety of foods ready to eat. Aromas of grilling meat, bubbling stews, and pungent spices mingled with the odors of summer-dusty pines and sweat of humans and animals. Drooling, Friend started to head toward the fire where a man was roasting plump birds on spits.

Having no idea how to deal with this marketplace game, Kyr called, "No, girl! Come on." Friend hovered for a moment, then her tail drooped, and she followed him as he went on. In a quieter area, he stopped to catch his breath, bewildered by this hubbub of people and merchandise. Nearby, an older woman in a dress of multi-colored patches and an elaborate turban sat on a faded carpet. "Read your fortune, young sir?" she asked.

Puzzled, Kyr asked, "Fortune?"

"The star cards reveal all." She gestured, and suddenly small squares painted with a variety of images were spread out before her.

Drawn by curiosity and by the knowing look in her dark eyes, he took a seat on the carpet. With a sigh, Friend sat nearby, panting lightly. The woman took up the cards, shuffled them together, and handed them to him. "Divide the cards into two piles, young sir."

He obeyed. Then she picked cards alternately from each of the two piles, and laid them out in a circle. The cards showed different patterns of small white dots on a midnight blue background. Her calm serenity faded as the cards appeared, replaced with concern, then a kind of amazed horror. "Star-cursed!" she muttered, staring at the incomplete circle of cards. She pointed to the first card. "You were born under the star sign of the Fire-Bird—most auspicious, and most ominous."

Kyr was reminded of the time when Zhovanya had appeared to him as a wondrous Fire-Bird, and he had given Her his promise to become Her Vessel. He did not hear what the strange woman said next, as he was swept into the memory of that auspicious and ominous encounter.

*The Presence of the Goddess became more palpable—a swirl of numinous wildness, a subtle weight pressing him to his knees.*

*Vast wings enfolded him, and he was swept into divine reality. Everything was the same, yet enhanced to awe-inspiring proportions. Now he was standing on a broad ledge of an enormous mountain, under a satin sky of midnight blue. The solitary pine towered far above him, huge branches of deep green sweeping high and wide over a tall fountain surging up from a scintillating pool of diamond water.*

*A clarion cry rang through the firmament. Looking up,*

*he beheld a grace of fire soaring on wings of scarlet and gold. Fierce and serene, the Fire-Bird gazed down at him with the golden eyes of the Goddess. Her graceful form shimmered and shifted, flaring and billowing in all shades of flame and fire, trailing streams of gold and crimson, saffron and pale yellow across the deep blue heavens.*

*Spellbound, he turned to follow Her as she circled above the ledge. Warmth radiated from Her, driving away the night's chill, intensifying as She came closer, bathing him with scorching heat that did not burn, blazing light that did not blind.*

"BELOVED, IS IT YOUR WISH TO SERVE ME?"

*He spread his arms wide.* "With all my heart."

*Lightning flashed from Her eye, and the giant pine burst into glorious flame, more vibrant and alive than ever.*

"WILL YOU BE TEMPERED BY THE FIRES OF SUFFERING?"

*His heart quailed. More? he thought, but he said,* "I will."

*Thunder blasted the mountain, sending huge boulders crashing down, bounding past him so closely that the wind of their passage made him tremble.*

"WILL YOU BE HOLLOWED OF ALL YOUR FEAR AND CLINGING?"

*He smiled and gladly said,* "I will."

*The weight of the mountain crushed him into nothingness, yet he remained.*

"WILL YOU SURRENDER ALL, YET NEVER YIELD?"

*Still he said,* "I will."

"BELOVED, WILL YOU BE MY VESSEL?"

"O Holy One, it is my deepest desire."

"WHEN THE VESSEL IS HALLOWED, WE SHALL BE UNITED."

*Sun-bright, She flew toward him and he was swept up
in the brilliant fire of Her wings.*

Dazzled, Kyr opened his eyes and stared about, trying to get re-
oriented to the here and now. As the fortune-speaker placed the
final two cards in the circle she had created, her look of horrified concern
was replaced by one of astonished awe. She stared at the cards in silence
for many moments. Then she blinked, settled her shawl on her shoulders,
and met Kyr's curious gaze.

"Ah, young sir, you are indeed a Great Soul with a most significant
mission in this life! Yet your path is terribly difficult." Looking down at
two of the cards, she told him, "You have survived two hells already...."

Kyr snorted. *That's the gods-cursed truth!* Then he looked at the
woman in surprise. *How does she know that?*

The woman gave him a knowing smile. "I see I have your attention
now," she said, and pointed to a third card. "You face a further test—not
from your enemies, but from your friends."

Kyr groaned in dismay. "My friends? Goddess help me!"

The fortune-teller stared at the last three cards. After a few
moments, her countenance brightened. "Keep to your chosen path," she
advised kindly. "Keep faith with the Goddess, and you will someday
know great joy and fulfillment."

And she bowed from her waist with deep reverence. At this, Kyr
frowned and stirred restlessly. The woman went on, "Most cursed, most
blest of all! You and your Beloved shall renew the Sacred Balance! Oh,
young sir, I am most honored...."

"Enough of this nonsense!" Kyr jumped to his feet. "Come on,
Friend." He strode through the marketplace with Friend by his side,
grumbling to himself. *Great Soul? Hardly! Why do people keep making me
into some kind of damned hero? I just did what I had to do. And what is this
about a Sacred Balance? Crazy old woman!*

But an involuntary smile touched his lips, and he stopped right
where he was. Friend kept going, but quickly turned back and came to
stand looking up at him, wagging her tail slowly as if wondering what
was going on. Kyr ignored her, and stared off into the distance, musing.

*That old woman said I will be with my beloved again sometime!* He felt
like dancing right there in the midst of the marketplace. But then he felt

a chill, recalling that Zhovanya called him *Her* beloved. *Get yourself under control,* he told himself harshly. *That is all that the old woman's ramblings mean. Someday, when I have been scoured clean, the Goddess with allow me to be Her Vessel. I will never see Jolanya again. She is the Kailithana and is forbidden to me by her vows.*

He shivered and looked around. No one had noticed him staring off into nothingness, but Friend was looking up at him with wrinkled brow. "You're right, girl. Come on, let's get out of here." He took a deep breath, shrugged off his irritation, adding this latest puzzle to his hoard of mysteries, and headed for the edge of the marketplace.

He passed by a blonde woman sharpening knives for her customers on a small grindstone. Laid out on a black cloth on her table was a small selection of sharp, shiny knives. Kyr winced, knowing the pain they could inflict, and hurried toward the shadows of the forest.

It was a relief to follow a narrow path into the silent stillness of trees. They soon came to a small, gurgling creek, and Friend lapped eagerly while Kyr scooped up handfuls of the cold, clear water. It tasted of sunlight on stone. The path went along the creek, and they followed it as it grew larger and quieter. Tired, Kyr sat on a boulder by the water, watching sunlight glint off its smooth surface and listening to the soothing sounds of its flowing movement. Friend flopped down on the pine duff nearby and snoozed, occasionally twitching one ear at a circling fly.

As dusk turned the woods gloomy, Kyr started awake at a cracking sound. He looked around but saw nothing threatening. He stretched and rubbed his eyes. "Must've dozed off myself, eh, Friend?" She thumped her tail on the ground. "Come on, girl. Time to go back."

All Kyr knew of riding horseback was the torturous journey from the Sanctuary to the fort. He was not looking forward to his first riding lesson. He walked slowly toward the barn, with Friend at his side. Reminding himself to let the past go, he took some slow, full breaths of the fresh morning air, and noticed the quiet efficiency of Craith's crew of prisoners cleaning up the courtyard and sprinkling the dirt to keep the dust down. Aromas of toasting bread and frying bacon wafted from the kitchens, and people waiting in line to buy their breakfast murmured to each other. A few Companions, in their forest-green uniforms, kept watch at the front and back gates, and outside Rajani's quarters. More birds than ever chirped and squawked in the trees outside the fort's walls. The sassy blue ones called jays quarreled over scraps under the eating tables and benches near the kitchens.

Nodding to the Companions guarding the back gates, Kyr went through to the barn. Rajani was waiting for him just inside the wide door. "Heya, Kyr! Come, I have someone for you to meet." Kyr trailed reluctantly after the energetic Warrior Mage, imagining a riding instructor being someone like his cruel Slave Trainer.

"Here she is." Rajani stopped at one of the stalls. "Kyr, this is Lady. She is yours. Lady, this is Kyr." The horse's ears pricked forward. She stretched her large black head toward Kyr, and regarded him with dark liquid eyes. Kyr stepped back a bit, frowning. *Gods and demons! It's the same horse!*

"Don't worry. She is a fine lady, gentle and kind. Hold out your hand so she can get a sniff of you."

"She's so big!" Kyr protested lamely. But he could hardly blame the mare for his suffering on the ride to the fort.

"Just think of her as a large version of Friend here. She won't hurt you."

Slowly, Kyr extended his hand. She sniffed his hand delicately. "Her nose is so soft," Kyr said in surprise.

"Good. Now, hold your hand out flat, palm up." Rajani set a small apple on his hand. "To make friends with her, offer her this." Kyr's hand was trembling, and Rajani added, "Try to keep calm, Kyr. Horses sense how we are feeling and can pick up our nervousness or fear from us."

Kyr took some slow breaths until his hand was steady, and then extended his offering to Lady. She took it politely, barely grazing his palm with her soft lips, and happily crunched it up.

"Gods, she has such big teeth," Kyr whispered.

Finished with her treat, Lady regarded Kyr with her dark, liquescent eyes, and then sniffed him over. He kept still, though his heart was pounding. She gently rested her large head on his chest. Sudden tears rose to his eyes, and he wrapped his arms around her neck.

A man said softly, "Ah, she likes you. You will do well together."

Kyr blinked his tears away and looked around. Rajani said, "You've met Kuron. He will be your riding teacher."

Kyr bowed to Kuron. Kuron smiled and returned his bow. "She's a fine horse."

While Friend and Lady sniffed noses, Kyr turned to Rajani. "Do you mean you are giving her to me?"

"Yes, Kyr, she is yours. She is a steady, quiet mare and will be easy for you to ride and get along with."

"But I know nothing of caring for a horse!"

"Kuron will also teach you how to take care of your horse, and everything else you need to know. He comes from a tribe of horsemen, well-known for their skill and their love of horses. And now I will leave you in his talented hands. Sadly, I have a meeting to get to."

Kyr laughed at Rajani's doleful face. "Thank you, Rajani."

"Rajani is right," said Kuron. "She is a good horse for a beginner. We will meet here every other morning after breakfast. You have much to learn."

Kyr soon came to treasure these morning lessons, a time to set aside all his concerns and focus on the simple, earthy practicalities of caring for and riding a horse. Kuron was an excellent teacher, patient yet firm. Kyr enjoyed learning a new skill, and gaining some physical strength and competence.

Lady's gentle disposition and big, warm animal body were soothing and calming. Kyr loved to see her shining blackness after he had groomed her, despite his aching arms. He and Friend would sometimes come just to spend time with Lady in her stall, or watch her in the pasture munching grass and occasionally racing about just for the joy of it.

## Chapter 21

# Turning Point

Early one morning a few days later, Rajani spied Kyr and Friend heading for the woods, where they had been spending many afternoons exploring and napping, according to Lorya's reports. He hurried to catch up with them.

"Mind if I join you? I need to get away from all the dratted politics for a while!"

Kyr smiled. "Too many meetings?"

Rajani laughed in agreement and fell into step beside Kyr. Behind his back, he made a gesture to wave Lorya off for the day.

The two men tramped along the trail in companionable silence. The air was cool and fresh, smelling of pine and damp earth. Friend ambled along with them, sniffing the glorious complexity of scents that the dew-touched forest offered.

After a while, Rajani broke the silence. "You ready to start building up your strength?"

"Guess so."

"I'm not as busy as I was at first, so I can help. Let's meet on the mornings you don't have a riding lesson. We'll start with the same exercise regimen we did back at the cabin."

"Gods, Rajani. I knew so little of life back then." It seemed an age ago that he had lived at the secluded cabin with Tenaiya, Luciya, and Seranu, just beginning to learn that life held more than obedience and pain.

"Remember the first time I took you into the forest and showed you the trees and flowers?"

Kyr had a sudden, vivid image of the wild ilys in their delicate purity. "Ah, gods, Rajani, I could barely look at those flowers—the 'ilys,'

you called them. And now I'm back to where I started. No, much worse."
He cringed inwardly, feeling Gauday's poisons churning through his
veins: rage, violence, vile desires.

"Worse off than when we rescued you from that damned Watcher,
from the cursed Soul Drinker? How can that be?"

Suddenly, a tidal wave of fury and pain swept aside Kyr's iron
control. He whirled to face Rajani, shouting, "GODS CURSE IT! You
have no IDEA what Gauday did to me! He opened ALL those old
wounds, dug them deeper than EVER!"

Friend raced to his side, hackles raised, growling low in her throat,
glaring at Rajani. Afraid of what she might do, Kyr turned and ran into
the forest, calling, "Come on, girl! Come on!" Still growling, Friend
backed away, then turned and loped after Kyr. Stomping rage into the
earth, he ran until he had a stitch in his side. Coming upon a flat-topped
boulder by the path, he collapsed onto it, panting and shaking with
unreasonable rage. Friend plowed to a stop and stood tensely, watching
him with furrowed brow.

"Are you all right?" Rajani had caught up with them.

"GODS AND DEMONS!" Kyr jumped up, glaring at Rajani. "I'll
NEVER be all right! Not after what he DID to me!" Friend snarled and
lunged at Rajani, teeth bared.

"NO!" Kyr leaped after her just as the Warrior Mage kicked at the
dog to fend her off. Kyr took the kick in his ribs, but grabbed Friend.
"NO, girl, no! Stop it! Rajani, get away from us!" Grunting in pain, he
held onto the snarling dog until Rajani had backed up a good distance.

Seeing that the enemy had retreated, Friend whined and licked Kyr's
face, unsure if she had done something wrong. "Good girl, good girl," he
soothed, his own rage expended in the struggle with her. He sat up and
let her loose. She shook her ears, and settled down beside him. Never
before had anyone tried to protect him from harm. Comforted by her
loyalty, he stroked her back and sighed, chagrined at his furious outburst.
He looked around for Rajani, and spotted him standing beside a tall
cedar across the clearing.

"I think it's safe now. You can come back."

The Warrior Mage approached cautiously and knelt down a short
distance from the two of them. "That was a pretty hard kick you took.
Did I break anything?"

"I don't think so." Kyr explored his side gingerly. "I'll have a good-size bruise, though." Ruefully, he added, "How am I going to explain this to Medari?"

"Looks like you have a real guardian there. You might have to keep her leashed, if she's going to attack people."

"It's my fault for yelling. She's fine. I'll just have to leash my temper." He suppressed a groan as he got to his feet. "Let's go back." They started back toward the fort.

"Can you tell me what's making you so angry?"

"What's the point of talking about it? It's too damned late, anyway."

"Too late?"

So many feelings welled up in Kyr's heart that for a few moments, all he could do was stare at Rajani. Anger, pain, despair, and an absurd desire to laugh competed with each other; but even more strangely, tears won. "You just don't understand." He wiped his eyes with his sleeve.

"I want to," Rajani said gently. "Explain it to me."

In his tear-softened heart, he found a longing for someone to understand what he had been through. He sighed and sank down on the soft pine duff. Friend flopped down next to him, panting. Rajani sat opposite them. Sunlight filtered through the layered branches, gentle and warm, drying the dew, evoking the scent of dusty pine from the forest floor.

"You said it was worse, what Gauday did."

"It *was* worse."

"Why?"

"Gods, I don't know." Kyr was silent for a few moments. "The Master—I mean the Soul-Drinker—didn't care about me, one way or another. He just used me, like he did everyone else. He didn't hate *me*; he hated *everything*. The difference is…." Kyr paused. "Oh, that's it. Gauday *does* care. He hates *me* in particular, and he *wants* me, wants to possess me, to own my mind, body, and soul." He shuddered, recalling the vicious intimacy Gauday had forced upon him.

"I see the difference, but why does it make it so much worse?"

"Think of it, Rajani. When you fight a battle, do you hate your enemy personally?"

"Usually, I just want to defeat him, to stop him from hurting someone I am protecting, or to protect myself."

215

"Do you want to make him suffer as much as possible? Do you want to defile him, make him hate himself, make him worship you? Do you want to break his spirit, enslave his soul?"

"Gods, no!"

"Well, that's what Gauday wanted. The trouble is, he partly succeeded. I have to fight his poison every moment."

"What do you mean?"

"I feel what he feels: his rage, despair, hatred, lust, terror. He invades my dreams; and even during the day, I can still hear him whispering spellchants, trying to get to me. Sometimes it's hard to tell the difference between him and me."

"Gods above and below! Why haven't you told me this sooner?"

"I don't know." Kyr was silent for a few moments, reflecting. "I guess I haven't fully realized I am not his slave and whore any more. Or that there is any help for me. It's been so long...."

"Ah, Kyr...."

"No, don't apologize again." He held up a hand, fighting down a surge of rage, unsure if it was his or Gauday's. Then he went on. "This new situation at the fort—all these ordinary people bustling around—it seems like a strange dream. The fort is all prettied up, but it's like paint on a corpse to me. I keep waiting for the old barren bones to show through, for this charade to end, for Gauday to reappear and drag me back in there." He wrapped his arms around his aching ribs and fell silent.

Rajani frowned in thought, then said, "Listen, Kyr. I think I can help you with this. Meet me in your room at moonrise."

As dusk filled the courtyard and darkened his small window, Kyr sat cross-legged on his bed, leaning against the wall. Friend's head rested on his thigh, and she twitched as if chasing rats in her dreams. He stared at the flames in his hearth, trying to keep awake despite his tiredness, waiting for Rajani. He repeated the forgiveness chant to himself, but kept losing hold of it and nodding off.

At Friend's sudden bark, he jerked out of a doze. Someone was tapping on his door.

"Kyr, it's Rajani."

"Come in." He took hold of Friend's new leather collar. "It's all right, girl."

216

Rajani entered, carrying a green satchel covered with golden symbols. "Good evening, Kyr. If you're willing, I can set up some protection from Gauday in here. You might sleep better, at least."

"Gods, I'd be very grateful. What do I have to do?"

"First, grant me permission to shield your room."

"Yes, please do."

At Rajani's gesture, Kyr went to stand at the center of the room. Friend jumped off the bed and came to sit by his feet. He smiled at her. "Guess she's a part of this, too."

Rajani gave the dog a thoughtful look, then shrugged. "Can't see any harm in it." He pulled four candles from his satchel and set one in each corner of the room: red, blue, gold, and green. Then he took out a large, iridescent shell, crumbled a mixture of dried herbs and flowers into it, and murmured, "Shai'ya." The dried herbs began to smolder, giving off sweet-scented smoke.

He moved around the room, wafting smoke to every corner, saying "By the Goddess and all the beneficent gods, may this space be sanctified and protected." Then he circled Kyr and Friend, wafting the smoke around both of them. "By the Goddess and all the beneficent gods, may this man be blessed and safeguarded." His eyes twinkled as he added, "And his Friend, too."

Rajani set the shell on the hearth, the herb mix still smoldering, and settled on the hearthrug, facing into the room, his satchel on his left. Kyr sat on his right. Casting a suspicious look at the Warrior Mage, Friend wedged herself between the two men. They smiled at each other, and Kyr rested a reassuring hand on Friend's back.

"Now we ask for Zhovanya's guidance and protection." Rajani began to chant, "Zhovanya dagantalo, Zhovanya ganaralo."

"Zhovanya dagantalo. Zhovanya ganaralo." At first, Kyr stumbled over the unfamiliar words, but soon he began to relax into the new chant. "Zhovanya dagantalo. Zhovanya ganaralo." Their voices melded in quiet harmony. After a time, a deep peacefulness pervaded the room.

Then the Warrior Mage took his blackwood wand out of the satchel and rose. He pointed it at each candle in turn, and said, "Shai'ya!" Friend yipped in surprise as uncanny flames sprang to life, their colors matching the candles.

Rajani crossed the room to stand before the red candle with its red flame. Raising his arms high, he spoke in a deep, resonant voice. "I call upon the brilliance and potency of Fire to bless and protect this room from any malign influence, demonic or human, etheric or material, spiritual or mundane."

Standing before the blue flame, he let his arms drift down. "I call upon the grace and power of Water to bless and protect this room from any malign influence, demonic or human, etheric or material, spiritual or mundane."

Before the golden flame, he spread his arms wide. "I call upon the clarity and truth of Air to bless and protect this room from any malign influence, demonic or human, etheric or material, spiritual or mundane."

Before the green flame, he formed a circle with his arms. "I call upon the steadfastness and durability of Earth to bless and protect this room from any malign influence, demonic or human, etheric or material, spiritual or mundane."

Returning to the center of the room, he pointed his wand toward the four corners of the room, the window and, finally, the door. "Vaa'a lan ti!" he commanded.

The spectral flames of the candles flared up and united into a brief blast of brilliant white light that filled the room, soaked into the walls, floor, and ceiling, and went out with a sharp snap.

There was a sudden shock of silence. Kyr rubbed his ears, fearing he'd gone deaf. Friend shook her head vigorously, flopping her ears back and forth.

Rajani laughed. "I think it worked."

Kyr stood still, listening. There was an inner silence. No malign whispers, no alien rumbles of rage, fear, or despair. "Dear Goddess!" Shaking with relief, he staggered to the bed and sat down. "I had no idea it was that bad, until you stopped it just now. He's been at me this whole time, whispering and whispering."

"No wonder you've been slow to recover, having to fight him every moment."

"You'd think I'd be celebrating. Truth is, I'm exhausted." He slumped back against the wall.

"Me, too. That's the way, sometimes, when a battle ends." The Warrior Mage looked pale and tired.

"Thanks, Rajani. I know this kind of thing drains you. But it's a great blessing for me. Perhaps I can repay you someday."

"No need. It's the least I can do." A bitter taint in Rajani's tone made Kyr look at him sharply, but the Warrior Mage only said, "Well, I'm for bed. Sleep well."

Kyr smiled. "I think I might, for a change. Thanks to you."

Protected from Gauday's incessant whispers and suggestions, he did sleep deeply and well. The next morning, he stayed in his shielded room, enjoying the inner silence, starting to find himself again. Friend was still sleeping peacefully, curled up on his bed. In the blessed quiet, he dared to try to meditate. Sitting cross-legged before the hearth, he took some deep slow breaths, chanted softly for a while, then sought the deep silence.

"Merciless gods!" His body shuddered with remembered torment. Sick shame overcame him, recalling how he had screamed in pain, how he had begged for release, how he had cowered in fear. He buried his face in his hands, wishing he could hide in a dark hole forever.

Dekani's face appeared in his mind. *"You have nothing to be ashamed of, Kyr."* He waved a hand, and they were now in the familiar cottage. *"Let's get comfortable."* They settled into their chairs before the fire that always burned there. It seemed small today, and gave off little warmth.

Kyr looked at his teacher bleakly. *"I don't know if I can bear it, Dekani."*

*"Bear what?"* his teacher asked gently.

*"This life. I feel like a ghost, an angry ghost. No one, not even Medari or Rajani, can understand what Gauday did to me, or what I had to do to survive. And I still can't meditate, even with Rajani's shield. The memories are so vivid, so intense."*

*"You just need to give it some time, Kyr. Especially now with Rajani's shield in place, you should begin to recover."*

*"It's not just the memories."* Kyr hung his head, ashamed to reveal his worst secret. *"I still crave the ecstasy he drove me to. I keep imagining doing what he did to some innocent. Gods and demons! I'm just Gauday's used-up whore."*

*"That's not who you are, Kyr. You know that. You're the man who kept himself free of hatred, madness, despair, and vengefulness in the worst of circumstances. You're the man who sacrificed himself to protect Zhovanya's precious Sanctuary, and the people you love."*

*"Curse it all! I wish I'd never gone there! I'd still have had the ice, but She took that away from me, and sent me here."* Bitter tears threatened and he scrubbed them away angrily.

*"The ice would have been no defense. If you hadn't gone to the Sanctuary, you never would have survived what Gauday did to you. Without knowing what you were fighting for, you would have easily succumbed to what was so familiar to you. He'd be your Master now."*

Kyr sagged back into the chair's embrace. *"I suppose you're right. But still, I don't see any point now. What more can She want of me?"*

*"You can trust Her, Kyr. There's a reason for everything that's happened."*

*"What reason?"*

Dekani looked away. *"Ah, well, I am not sure we can know Her purposes."* His tone seemed evasive, but then he met Kyr's eyes and said confidently, *"She will guide you toward healing again."*

*"Perhaps She will."* He smiled a little. *"She gave me you, didn't She?"*

*"I want you to know how proud I am of you. All through this ordeal, you showed a depth of courage and a strength of soul that amazes me."*

*"Gods, not you too! Everyone treats me like some kind of hero, but...."*

*"You did better than any ten of them would have done in the same situation. Do not let shame destroy you after all you did to survive this hell without surrendering to hatred, fear, or rage."*

*"You wouldn't let me surrender, much as I sometimes hated you for that."*

*"Ah, well...."* Dekani choked up for a moment. *"I hope you will forgive me."*

*"Of course. Wouldn't have made it without you. Thank...."*

*"No thanks needed."* At his teacher's gruff tone, Kyr glanced at him in surprise, but Dekani smiled apologetically, and went on, *"Remember, son. Zhovanya forgives us all, and we must forgive ourselves, too."*

*"Why is that the hardest part, forgiving ourselves?"*

With a sheepish look, Dekani said, *"If you're like me, it's pure arrogance—assuming we must meet a higher standard than anyone else."* Kyr laughed in rueful recognition.

*"Alright, son. You were trying to meditate. Let's get back to that. It's important for you to reclaim your peace of mind. Chant with me now. Zhovanya nara lo, Zhovanya nara lo."*

Kyr joined in. With his teacher's steady support, the familiar chant calmed his mind and heart. His shame ebbed, and his torturous memories died away. The chant carried him deep into meditation. He did not notice when Dekani disappeared.

> *Kyr rested, floating on a dark lake of stillness and silence. Then a new wave arose, a bright wave of relief and gratitude for freedom from torment and degradation; for friends and Friend; for rest and peace.* "Thank You, Zhovanya, thank You."
>
> *A black swan with golden eyes floated on the dark lake under a black dome scattered with silver stars.*
>
> "YOU DID NOT TURN AWAY FROM LOVE. YOU HAVE DONE WELL, BELOVED."
>
> "Ah, Zhovanya! I have done as You asked. May we be united now? May I come home to You?"
>
> "THE VESSEL MUST BE SCOURED BY TRUTH, HOLLOWED OF ALL CLINGING, PURIFIED BY LOVE."
>
> "There is more I must endure?"
>
> "IF YOU CHOOSE TO BE MY VESSEL."
>
> *Kyr bowed his head. What is it She wants from me? How can I endure further testing? What if I cannot? Do I want to serve Her? He searched his heart, plumbed his soul. In his depths, he found an incandescent flame of love and gratitude to the One Who had blessed him with forgiveness and healing, rescuing his winged soul from the mire of evil and ignorance, remorse and self-loathing in which he had been trapped by the vicious sorcery of the Soul Drinker.*
>
> *Smiling, he raised his head.* "I am Yours, Zhovanya."
>
> "BELOVED, I AWAIT YOU."
>
> *The black swan unfolded vast wings and soared into the firmament, circling him once, wrapping him in a cloak of velvet darkness.*

Sometime later, he awoke from a deep, healing sleep, feeling apprehensive and joyous at once: joy for the blessing of Her Presence;

fear for what She would require of him next. He arose, added wood to the fire, and sat before his hearth to contemplate this precious encounter with his Goddess. "You are my strength, my solace," he whispered. "I must rededicate myself to You."

Over the next half-moon, with the protection of his shielded room, he began to practice meditation and chanting every morning and evening. Peace seeped into his abraded soul, and he felt Zhovanya's Presence more deeply. On the evening of the Apex of Spring, when Day and Night are equal, he and Friend went for their evening stroll in the forest. *Zhovanya nara lo, Zhovanya nara lo*, Kyr chanted silently, keeping Gauday's seductive, repellant whispering at bay.

The clean scent of newly sprouting pine needles filled the balmy air. Birds flitted among the trees, and the nearby creek rushed and burbled along in excitement, full of snow-melt and its own secret purpose. Kyr smiled at the caress of a soft, warm breeze on his cheek, and watched Friend sniffing after fascinating scents only she could detect. He had rarely known such peace and contentment. Unwilling for it to end, he wandered farther and farther into the forest, with Friend ranging from side to side as they went.

The path began to rise, and he knew he was entering unknown territory; but he went on, enjoying the challenge of the steep hill, the light sweat on his brow, the returning strength of his body. As the light began to fade, the twilight chorus of birdsong embroidered the air with a layered tapestry of sound. As he and Friend climbed, the pines grew farther apart, and then were replaced by low brush.

Soon thereafter, they reached the top of the hill, a bare knoll of stone and grit, lichens, and low-growing plants hugging themselves close to the scant soil. Friend sprawled on a patch of this springy groundcover, panting happily. Kyr turned in a slow circle, marveling at the wide view spreading below him. Beyond the dark-green sea of forest, rolling plains caught the light of the westering Sun, glowing with golden warmth. From this vantage point, there was no sign of human habitation. He was completely alone. He stretched his arms wide, welcoming a newborn sense of spaciousness and freedom. He threw his head back, laughing, and then shouted in delight.

"Kyyyyyrrrrr!" The wild cry of his soul-kin united with his joyous shout, as an eagle soared above him, so close he could hear the wind rustling through its feathers. His heart expanded with unreasoning joy, and his soul soared with the eagle into a sky flaming orange-pink and scarlet.

As the sky shaded toward ember-red and dusky purple, the eagle soared onward, dwindling to a dark speck, and was lost to sight. A glowing light behind him caused Kyr to turn toward the East, and he stared in awe as a huge, golden Moon rose above the darkening forest. A hush of magnificence and wonder held all in stillness as the setting Sun perfectly balanced the rising Moon. In this sacred moment outside time, the Divine Two gazed at each other across the world in longing.

Kyr sank to his knees in reverence between Them. "Zhovanya, Jeyal," he whispered, "Thank You for this blessing!" Tears sprang to his eyes as he remembered the golden mosaics of the Two in the sacred chamber at the Sanctuary, and his wondrous, sacred time with his beloved Jolanya. He felt his longing for her blend with the ancient longing of Zhovanya and Jeyal, of Sun and Moon, always searching after each other, rarely united.

Tears trickled down his face as he watched the Sun hide Her face in deepening colors of lavender, blue, purple, and black, and watched the Moon float higher, becoming smaller. Jeyal's light turned from gold to silver-white. In the soft gray dusk, Kyr bowed down, his grief and love for Jolanya welling up at last, after all the months he had kept it hidden away so that he could endure Gauday's barrage of torment and degradation. Now, alone, far from any human eyes, he could allow his sorrow to flood forth.

After uncounted time, he reached a quiet harbor where only his love for her remained. He rose and sat in quiet emptiness, neither joyous nor sorrowful. Gazing at Jeyal's serene face, Kyr was filled with a sense of renewed purpose. There was something he had to do for Zhovanya, for the Two, but he had no idea what it was. He knelt there, head bowed, praying, "Show me what I must do."

A whisper touched his mind. *"YOU WILL KNOW. CONTINUE."*

He sighed in acquiescence, knowing that he must continue on the hard path, without knowing where it would lead, what sacrifices might be required, nor even how to carry out his chosen Atonement.

Night's chill and Friend's cold nose on his cheek brought him back to the mundane reality of a chilly night, hunger, and a long path back through a dark forest to the fort. He got to his feet, rubbed his arms, and started to head back. But he could not see the path. Worse, he had no idea where it was. He stumbled around the hilltop, searching for the trail. There were many openings into the forest but none looked familiar. Friend's anxious whining echoed his growing fear. He knelt and petted her. "Come on, girl. Show me the way back." But Friend only licked his face uneasily.

# Part Seven ~ Fateful Decisions

*"One Tibetan monk... who had spent more than 18 years
in a Chinese prison labor camp... told me that
on a few occasions he really faced some danger.
So I asked him, 'What danger? What kind of danger?'
thinking he would tell me of Chinese torture and prison. He replied,
'Many times I was in danger of losing compassion for the Chinese.'"*

—The Dalai Lama

## Chapter 22

# A New Path

The forest, friendly by day, had taken on a gloomy, menacing feel. Raised in the Master's Labyrinth, Kyr knew little of the wild. Panic reared its fearsome head and glared at him. *Gods, I don't know what to do. I'm so far from the fort, no one would hear me if I yelled for help.*

"Are you lost?" A soft, unfamiliar voice spoke from the edge of the trees. Kyr jerked around and spotted a dark shape standing at the edge of the clearing. He crossed the hilltop warily. "Who are you? How did you find me?" As he got closer, he saw with relief that the person was a small, ordinary-looking woman.

"I'm Lorya. I, ah, just followed the path. It was a lovely evening for a walk. Sorry, I shouldn't have...." Her voice trailed off.

"I'm glad you did. We would've had a cold and hungry night if you hadn't found us." He wondered how long she had been watching him.

As he walked down the path to the fort with Lorya, Kyr noticed himself relaxing in her presence, feeling safer than he ordinarily did. Then he realized why: no woman had ever hurt or demeaned him. But he felt shy with Lorya, having had little chance to speak to an ordinary woman his own age. "Uh, thanks for showing us the way back. My name's Kyr, and this is Friend." He reached down to ruffle Friend's ears.

"Unusual name for a dog, but a good one." Lorya stopped walking and offered the back of her hand to Friend. After a good sniff, Friend gave her a little lick and wagged her tail.

"Well, for a long time, this dog was my only friend here." Kyr didn't want to talk about his dreadful story. "Uh, what brought you to the fort?"

Lorya was silent for so long that Kyr thought she hadn't heard his question. Then she said, "I came along with Rajani and the

Companions." It seemed to Kyr that she didn't want to talk about herself any more than he did.

Her soft voice hardly disturbed the silence of the darkening forest. "It was so beautiful with the Sun setting and the Moon rising."

Kyr's face went hot. "Gods, how long were you standing there?"

"I'm sorry. I didn't know what to do. I thought you might need help, but then I didn't want to intrude on your grief, so I ended up just standing there like a fool."

"Ah. Well, uh…. You won't tell anyone, will you?" Kyr couldn't keep a pleading note out of his voice.

"Of course not."

The path narrowed. He watched her shapely body gliding ahead of him, and found himself remembering Jolanya, remembering the sacred beauty of making love with her; imagining what it might be like to make love with Lorya, how intense the pleasure would be if he did what Gauday had shown him. Kyr stopped in his tracks. *Gods curse him! He's poisoned me. I'll never be able to be close with anyone again.* Kyr trailed after Lorya, keeping his eyes on the path. Close by his side, Friend whined and nosed his hand, but her concern was no comfort.

Soon they reached the outskirts of the fort that was fast becoming a village. Torches cast flickering light on the people packing up their wares in the marketplace or standing in line at the busy food booths. Cheerful chatter and the delicious odors of roasting meat filled the air.

"Well, here we are. Good night, sir."

"Thank you for rescuing us." His old stiffness had returned, a necessary protection to keep others safe from him.

"Glad to help." Her smile brought out her hidden beauty. She turned away and quickly disappeared into the crowd. Kyr sighed and patted Friend, feeling lonelier than ever.

After supper, he and Friend settled down in his shielded room. Deliberately, he turned his mind to his wondrous experience with Zhovanya and Jeyal, the magical moment when the Sun and Moon were in communion, and his renewed sense of purpose and dedication.

There was something he should be doing, something for Zhovanya. He puzzled over this while he got into bed. Lying there half-asleep, with Friend curled up by his side, he remembered Dekani's suggestion. He sat straight up. "That's it!"

Friend yipped and looked at him with a worried frown. He stroked her absently. She shook her ears and lowered her head to her paws. He lay back down, thinking, *Yes! To make a chapel for Zhovanya here, where my Slave-brothers and others could pray and chant, and learn of Her forgiveness. It would be a way to carry out my Atonement, at last.* A sense of relief and peace filled his dreams.

The next morning, he jumped out of bed, washed, and dressed. He paced back and forth, waiting for Rajani to arrive with breakfast, which they usually ate together in Kyr's room. Over warm biscuits and hot tea, he explained his plan to the Warrior Mage.

"Ah, good idea, Kyr. Many people are looking for a way to connect with the Goddess. This would be a big help, and we do have an empty room that might do. It's in a quiet corner, away from the gate and the market." They finished up their tea and went to inspect the room.

Dusty cobwebs drifted in the corners of the barren room and grit crunched underfoot, but Kyr's eyes lit up. "This will work. It's big enough. I'll clean it up."

"When did you learn how to clean?" Rajani asked, knowing that the drudges had done all that in the Soul-Drinker's lair.

"Gauday made me learn."

"Ah, gods. I, uh…." Rajani stifled another useless apology. "Well, we have plenty of prisoners to put to work. You don't need to do this."

"No, thanks. This is my work, my offering."

"As you wish." Rajani's voice held a new tone of respect. "Do you want me to shield the room?"

"That would be a blessing. Thank you."

A t first light, Kyr began scrubbing the empty, dusty room from top to bottom. Friend got bored, waiting on the porch for him, and wandered off on her own errands. He found he enjoyed this simple work. Making the room clean calmed something inside him. When it was done, he set the bucket, broom, rags, and mop outside on the porch. Standing in the center of the immaculate room, he looked around, trying to imagine what he could do with it. *It doesn't need much,* he realized. *A low chest or table for an altar, some sitting pillows. Maybe Rajani will know where I can get them. I'll ask him at the noon meal.*

On his afternoon walk with Friend along the path by the creek, he gathered a few things that spoke to him of Zhovanya's grace and beauty:

a dark, heart-shaped stone with glinting points of light like stars; a silvery piece of driftwood shaped and smoothed by water into a graceful flowing form; shining golden pebbles with eye-like markings.

Returning, he went into the infirmary. Medari was tending to a gangly boy with a broken arm, while his harried-looking mother, thin and angular, hovered nearby. "Oh, Jori, how many times I told you to be careful! I hope you have learned your lesson."

"Yes, Ma," Jori said in an exasperated tone.

"Listen to your mother, young man," Medari said sternly, but there was a twinkle in his eye. "There, now, you'll have to keep that splint and sling on for about a month and a half, if you want your arm to set straight. And I'll want to check on it every few days."

"That long?" moaned the boy.

"Don't give the healer any of your guff. Now come along." The mother marched Jori out, muttering about reckless boys who give no thought to what they are doing or how much trouble they cause their mothers.

Medari smiled after them. "Well, boys will make mistakes. That's how they learn."

Kyr frowned. He couldn't imagine being let off so lightly. Mistakes had been severely punished in the Soul-Drinker's hell. Even the slightest rebellious thought brought a sorcerous lash of pain from the omniscient Master.

"How can I help you, Kyr?"

Kyr shook off dark memories. "You know I'm setting up a chapel for Zhovanya. I would like to have a candle lantern for the altar. Do you have an extra?"

"Ah. Glad to help."

Lantern in hand, Kyr went straight to the chapel. As soon as he entered, Gauday's incessant whispering ceased. Kyr smiled in relief. In addition to shielding the room, Rajani had already brought in a low wooden chest. Kyr placed it in the center of the back wall, under the small window. On it, he set the things he had gathered: the candle lantern, the driftwood, and the stones from the forest. Thanks to Rajani, there was firewood in the hearth, and a flint striker on the mantel. Kyr lit the candle lantern and sat before the altar. The golden light gleamed on the water-smoothed stones, and highlighted the curve of the driftwood.

Focusing on his breath, he began to meditate. In the spaciousness of the clean, empty room, he felt as if he could breathe freely and fully for the first time. Here there was nothing to remind him of his ordeal. Here there was only simplicity and peace, protected by Rajani's shield.

Watching his breath ebb and flow, ebb and flow, Kyr's shame and tension lessened with each out-breath. Slowly, his mind quieted until there was only this moment, this inhale, this exhale. After a time, he felt as empty and spacious as the room. Zhovanya's Presence arose as a lightness in his soul, and he knew again that he was forgiven. Without thought, he began to sing the chant that had been his lifeline: "Zhovanya nara lo, Zhovanya nara lo, Zhovanya nara lo." Soon, he was lost in the chant that had saved his life, his very soul. His voice soared as he entered communion with Her.

In the infirmary, Medari stopped in the midst of filling small flasks with a potion for fever from a large jug. He listened for a moment, then smiled. He corked the last bottle, wiped his hands on a rag, and left to join Kyr. Slipping inside the new chapel, the healer quietly sat down a few paces behind Kyr and softly joined in the chant.

In the courtyard near the chapel, one person and then another, and another, turned toward the sound of the chanting, looking puzzled. Most shook their heads and returned to their own pursuits, but a few were drawn to the chapel by some power they felt but did not know how to name. Three women and two men gathered on the porch of the chapel. Having seen Medari enter, they too went in and sat down to listen, and after a while they joined in the chant. One by one, others who were drawn by the power of the chant trickled into the new chapel.

A long while later, Kyr returned to silence, and was startled to hear the chant continuing. Looking over his shoulder, he discovered a dozen people, Companions and villagers, sitting behind him. They slowly came to silence too, and opened their eyes. They smiled at him, and one woman, glowing with joy, whispered, "Thank you, thank you!"

Still feeling that lightness in his soul, Kyr smiled back. It all seemed quite natural. They sat together, no one willing to break the reverent silence. But after a time Her Presence diminished, and people began to shift a little. The joyous woman asked, "This is how we are to worship the Goddess?"

Unsettled by her question, Kyr looked down at his suddenly tight fists, feeling her desire for guidance, feeling unbearably unworthy of giving it. But the expectant hush was too demanding and he felt impelled to answer. "This chant is all I know to do. I am sure there are other ways, but I don't know them." Suddenly, Kyr knew he was lying, and added, "Well, except to be kind to one another, and to—to soften." Kyr looked down again, eyes dark with remembered pain.

Wanting to avoid more such questions, he rose and asked, "Does anyone know how we could get some sitting pillows, and perhaps a rug?" With a soft rustle of clothing, everyone else rose also.

A tall, thin village man with hunched shoulders replied, "If I can find some cloth and batting, I can stitch up some pillows. I'm a tailor but I didn't bring much material with me." Several women chimed in with offers of old dresses to use as material for the pillows, and old rags to fill them. Relieved that his distraction had worked so well, Kyr watched in bemusement as a group of eager volunteers hurried off to fulfill his requests.

Medari stepped forward, took him by the arm, and steered him toward the door. "Let's go find something to eat. It's noon." Kyr gratefully took this opportunity to escape the worshipful eyes of the remainder of the group, all still standing nearby, watching him. *Gods! What do they want of me?*

After eating with Medari, he hunted up Friend, and they went for a ramble in the woods. Kyr returned with a small bouquet of wildflowers for the altar. Someone had apparently seen him returning with the flowers, for, to his amazement, there was a graceful vase on the altar with water in it. After settling the flowers into their vase, he knelt there, feeling puzzled but grateful.

*How strange that people are so eager to help me. No*, he thought humbly, *it's Zhovanya they want to honor.* But still, he felt that lightness in his soul, a sense of possibility. *Maybe there's something for me to do, after all. So many know nothing of Her. Zhovanya*, he prayed, *guide me. Show me what you want me to do.* He received no clear answer, so he did what he most needed to do: dedicated himself to meditation, chanting, and prayer every morning and evening.

Three days later, the chapel was filled with people joining him in his morning devotions. Kyr was delighted that so many had embraced his offering, and were turning their hearts toward Zhovanya. After everyone left, he stood looking around the chapel in amazement. As word had spread of "the Liberator's request," many hands had eagerly fulfilled it. The chapel's wooden floor was shining with polish and strewn with colorful, patchwork pillows. Fresh flowers and candles for the altar appeared, as needed. He was glad that the chapel hadn't lost its original sense of spaciousness and simplicity, but had only deepened in quietness and peace, thanks in part to Rajani's shielding.

The humble serenity he had so painfully learned was returning, and his anger and despair were dwindling. Yet whenever he was not in the chapel or his shielded room, he had to constantly block Gauday's vile whispering. He sighed sadly, thinking of Gauday chained in the dark hole, lost in his hell of depravity, hatred, and madness. Kyr knelt before the altar. *Zhovanya, by Your mercy, may he be healed. If there is any way I can help him, show me.*

The next day, Kyr and Friend returned to the porch outside his room, after their morning walk. Friend flopped down, panting happily. Kyr sat next to her, idly ruffling the fur on her back, staring toward Gauday's prison. *Goddess forgive me, I've barely even thought about my Atonement lately; haven't even tried talking to Gauday or my other Slave brothers about Your mercy. But just the thought of seeing Gauday makes me shake! How can I face him?* Memories of Gauday's cruelty swarmed through his mind, and he buried his head in his hands.

A cold nose nudged his elbow and he looked into Friend's dark, liquid eyes. Gasping, he wrapped his arms around her warm, solid body. Patiently, she stayed steady, breathing with him as the torturous memories slowly ebbed. At last, he sighed and sat back, and she licked his cheek. Smiling a little at the sensation of her warm, rough tongue, he stroked her back. "Thanks, Friend."

Leaning back against the wall, he pulled her to his side, keeping one arm around her. She settled against him with a gusty sigh. Feeling calmer, he sorted through a myriad of conflicting feelings, but came home at last to the central fact of his existence: Zhovanya's forgiveness. Very quietly, he began to chant. "Zhovanya nara lo, Zhovanya nara lo, Zhovanya nara lo."

After a time, the chant brought him to serenity, and he prayed silently. *Goddess, what do we do with this lost soul? I don't think Gauday will*

233

*ever open his heart to You, but if there is any way to free him from his hatred and misery, please show me.* He sensed Zhovanya's approving Presence, but She gave him no answers.

Kyr sighed. *I guess the only way to know is to try. I'll have to go see him.* But sick dread filled him, and he couldn't force himself to move.

# Chapter 23

# Facing His Demons

After tossing and turning most of the night, Kyr jerked awake, his heart hammering in his chest. *Merciless gods! I have to face Gauday today.* Overwhelmed by dread, he called out, *"Teacher! Help me!"*

For long moments there was no response, and Kyr's heart raced toward panic. Then, Dekani appeared. *"I'm sorry, son. I was asleep."*

*"Are you all right, Dekani? You look, um, blurry or...."*

The Healer Mage frowned briefly and came more into focus. He waved away Kyr's concern. *"It's nothing. I'm still a bit worn out, that's all. What's the trouble?"*

*"I have to go see Gauday, try to speak with him about Zhovanya's blessings, maybe get him to open his heart to Her. But all I can think about is what he did to me."*

*"Ah. Alright, let me see what I can do."* Dekani closed his eyes and went into a deep stillness. Then he held his hands above Kyr's heart, and Kyr felt kailitha flowing into him like warm honey, soothing and calming. Dekani began to hum a low tone, and the flow changed, becoming cool and white, bringing Kyr steadiness and a sense of rootedness. His memories of torment paled, and Kyr sighed with relief. *"Goddess bless you, Dekani."*

He bowed to his Teacher with gratitude and respect. When he rose, Dekani was gone. *He looks so faded, like he's getting old*, Kyr thought. *I'd better not call on him unless I really need his help.*

At breakfast with Rajani, Kyr sat staring at his bowl of porridge, unable to eat a bite.

"Does your porridge have a bug in it?"

"What?" Startled, Kyr jerked his eyes up to look at Rajani. "No, no bug. Uh...."

"What's wrong, Kyr?"

Straightening his spine, Kyr called up the cool, white steadiness that Dekani had given him. "I have to try to reach Gauday, share Zhovanya's forgiveness and love with him. I want to speak to him. Today. Now."

"You want to try to help that vicious madman, after what he did to you?"

"Yes." Kyr met the Warrior Mage's glare squarely.

Rajani started to object, but then puffed out a breath. "Alright, I'll set it up for later this morning. There are some arrangements I must make first."

"What arrangements?"

"Never mind about that now. You'll see."

While Rajani made his mysterious arrangements, Kyr took Friend for their morning walk. As usual, Friend sniffed the "morning news" on bushes and trees, and left some of her own. As Kyr walked through the woods, he prayed for courage and equanimity, and for Zhovanya's guidance in reaching Gauday's soul.

Upon his return, a grim-faced Rajani awaited him outside the prison house. "Alright, Kyr. We've chained Gauday to the wall so he can't get at you. You can talk to him, but you must leave the cell door open and stay out of his reach. I'll be at the top of the stairs. If there is any sign of trouble, all you have to do is call out. He still has the power to inflict pain when he goes red-eyed, so if I hear even the tiniest sound of distress from you, I'll kill him. I won't allow him to hurt you ever again, and he knows that."

Kyr bowed to the fierce Warrior Mage. "I appreciate your concern and protection."

"Are you sure you want to do this?"

"No." Kyr took a deep breath. "But I must." Rajani nodded and led the way inside. He took up a position by the top of the stairs, alongside Kuron.

Carrying a candle lantern, Kyr descended those stairs toward the darkness below. The horror of his months as Gauday's hostage swam up and engulfed him. He began to shake, and stopped halfway down. Taking a deep breath, he focused on the cool, white strength of the kailitha he'd received from Dekani, and continued. In the dark hole, he sat down just inside the open door. He could see almost nothing at first, but he heard straw rustling and chains clanking.

"I brought you some light." Kyr set the lantern on the floor. While Gauday stared greedily at the candle, Kyr examined Gauday in morbid fascination. His elegant, disdainful tormenter was now a dirty, unkempt, wild-eyed prisoner—chained, gagged, and helpless. A dark beast rose in Kyr's heart, demanding Gauday's pain and blood, but he repeated the forgiveness chant silently until he felt more at peace.

He tried to imagine what was in Gauday's mind, then said, "You might be wondering how it is that all your tortures—so carefully designed to break me—failed."

Gauday jerked his eyes away from the candle's light and glared at Kyr. Their eyes met. It was as if a huge brass gong had been hit by a steel sword. Silent reverberations stunned them into immobility.

To Kyr, Gauday seemed a cruel demon one moment, a pitiable wretch the next. Gauday glared and muttered incomprehensible curses through his gag. Yet it was he who looked away first, breaking their strange state of suspension.

Kyr breathed a silent sigh of relief, then said gently, "You could not break me because the Goddess Zhovanya has blessed me. It was only by Her forgiveness and grace that I could endure what you did, without falling into the traps you laid, the traps of hatred and despair." As best he could, Kyr spoke of Zhovanya and Her Sanctuary, of healing and kindness and forgiveness. "She showed me that we are all Her children...."

Gauday growled and shook his head.

"Oh, I know," Kyr said. "You think we are the Soul-Drinker's children. But you are wrong. He was just a depraved little man with unholy power that no one should have. Zhovanya is the *Goddess*, vast as the cosmos, mother of all life." Gauday glared at him, contempt showing in every contour of his body.

Discouraged but unwilling to give up, Kyr plunged ahead. "With the help of the people at Her Sanctuary, I learned that She loves us all, no matter what we have done. She forgives us all, including me—and you. This is what I hope you will understand. You too can be forgiven and receive Her love and blessings."

Leaning forward, he looked at Gauday intently. "You can know yourself to be forgiven, if you allow yourself to surrender your pain to

Her. It is a hard path, very hard. But the way you have chosen—the easy path of hatred and vengeance—leads only to despair."

Gauday frowned, as if considering Kyr's words.

"I hope you have understood a little of this. If you sincerely repent and wish to seek atonement, I will speak for you, try to get you admitted to the Sanctuary."

Gauday nodded and pointed to his gagged mouth.

Caution warring with sudden hope, Kyr asked, "You want to speak to me?" Gauday nodded.

The thought of hearing Gauday's sinister, patronizing voice made him feel sick. He looked down for a moment, seeking courage. *I have to give him the chance to ask for help.* He turned and called up the stairs to Rajani. "Come take his gag off, please."

A frowning Rajani came down the stairs and confronted Kyr. "You're sure this is what you want? He won't enspell you?"

"He couldn't before, even with all his potions and tortures. I'm sure he can't now." Kyr spoke with more confidence than he felt.

Rajani stepped inside, and removed Gauday's gag. Gauday grabbed his water jug and gulped some water, but remained silent and still as a panther waiting for its prey. Rajani stepped out of the hole, but stood guard just outside the door.

"Well, my boy, can't we have a little privacy?" Gauday's voice, though hoarse with disuse, was as condescending as ever. It made Kyr shiver, but he turned and gestured to Rajani to back off. The Warrior Mage complied, but only went halfway up the stairs.

Seeing Rajani's implacable look, Kyr turned back to Gauday and said, "That's the best I can do."

With a disdainful smile, Gauday said, "Why, my dear Cur, I see you have recovered nicely from our little experiment. How did my lovely patterns come out? Do take off your shirt and let me see." He smiled with malicious delight as Kyr recoiled.

"If that's all you have to say...." Kyr rose and started to leave. But then, ignoring his revulsion and dread, he tried one last time. "Open your heart to Zhovanya. She will help you, if you truly ask."

Gauday was not listening. "You think you can escape me?" he gloated. "I have taught you too well, my boy. My mark will always be on you, deep inside. You are just like me now. You'll see." He leaned forward, staring at Kyr, his eyes turning red, and hissed, "Glarugh sa lo!"

The scars on Kyr's body flared up, pulsing with a sickening mixture of pain, pleasure, and lust. Stunned, Kyr's knees started to buckle, and he grabbed the door frame to hold himself up.

Gauday lunged against his chains, snarling, "How dare you come spouting your disgusting lies to me?" His voice rose to a rasping shout. "*I am your Master, not some bitch-whore of a dead goddess! You are MINE, MINE!*"

Brushing past Kyr, Rajani plunged into the cell, and slapped Gauday's gag into his mouth. Then he yanked his sword from its scabbard, placing the point on Gauday's neck. Gauday stared at him defiantly, but didn't move, or even breathe.

"NO! RAJANI! STOP! Kyr yelled. "He didn't hurt me. Don't kill him! Please!"

The Warrior Mage turned his head and looked at Kyr, eyes blazing. But his voice was controlled and neutral as he asked again, "Are you sure?"

"Yes. There has to be a better way. I just need time to—to sort this all out."

"Alright. For you, this one time. If this madman even so much as raises his voice at you again, he's dead." He looked back at Gauday with cold contempt. "You understand?" Gauday nodded carefully, and the Warrior Mage removed his sword from Gauday's neck, but continued speaking to his prisoner in a low, icy voice.

Kyr escaped upstairs, shaken and sick. Kuron took a look at Kyr. "You're pale as a wraith!" He took a flask out of his jacket pocket. "Here, sir. You'll be needing a good draught of this."

"Thanks." Kyr coughed at the harshness of the liquor, and handed the flask back. "Well," he sighed, his heart heavy with disappointment. "He hasn't changed a bit."

"If you don't mind my asking," Kuron ventured, "what were you trying to do, conversing with that mad sorcerer?"

"It's just something I had to do. Sorry, I have to go now." With Gauday's rage still beating at him from within, Kyr was desperate to get away He stumbled outside, feeling nauseated and shaky.

*Gods, why did I do that? What did I expect, some damn miracle? Of course he hasn't changed. How could he? All he's getting is more of the same kind of treatment he's had all his life. I'm an idiot! Just gave him another opening to get at me. I should have known better.*

239

Feeling worse by the moment, he headed for the forest. By the time he reached the gate, Friend, always alert to his movements, had joined him. She frisked around his stumbling feet, happy to be heading for the woods. "Stop it, girl!" At his abrupt tone, her ears and tail drooped and she trailed after him, wrinkling her forehead.

On reaching the shelter of the trees, he was overcome with nausea. He staggered away from the trail and fell to his knees, retching. Friend whined in concern and tried to lick his face, but he shoved her away. She slunk away and lay down nearby, her head on her front paws, looking miserable.

Kyr continued to heave up what seemed like his last three or four meals. When the spasms at last subsided, he crawled away from the mess and leaned against a cedar, shivering as if he were freezing. All the old horrors had been re-awakened by Gauday's verbal attack. "Oh gods, oh gods," he whispered. Then he groaned, as a terrifying thought hit him. *What if he's right? What if—Goddess help me!—what if his mark is too deep? What if I am like him now?*

"*Glarugh sa lo!*" Gauday's whispered command resonated in Kyr's mind, and inflamed the scars on his body, setting them pulsing again. "*Yes, boy, my mark is on your soul and your body. You are mine, you see? We are alike. We belong together. Come, free me!*"

"No, no, no!" Kyr moaned. Revolted and terrified by this new manifestation of Gauday's sorcery, he jumped up and fled unthinkingly. Friend gave a startled yip and followed him. Kyr ran a long way, but his scars kept pounding, arousing him with memories of Gauday's depraved torments.

Crashing through bushes, he slipped and fell down a slight slope, gasping as he landed full-length in the creek. The icy-cold water shocked him back to his senses, and halted the pulsing of his scars. "Gods, no!" Kyr whispered. "How can he be doing this to me now? I should never have gone near him!"

Friend stood on the bank, whining in concern. Kyr climbed back up to her and started walking in the direction of the fort, but then he realized that he wasn't ready to face his friends' inevitable questions. Wandering along the creek, he found a spacious, sunny dell with a large cedar at its heart, an ancient remnant of a long-lost forest. He stretched out on the wide circle of cedar duff, soaking in the sun's noon heat. For a time, sheer exhaustion allowed him to drowse without thought.

He woke to tree shadows blocking the sunlight. Shivering in his still-damp clothes, he moved to sit in the sunshine again, leaning against the wide trunk of the ancient cedar. Friend curled up next to him. He stroked her silky fur and tried to think clearly.

*Zhovanya says I must live, but how can I, with Gauday's poison in me? This pulsing of my scars, those depraved memories and desires filling my mind—this new sorcery could drive me mad. I could hurt someone! Gods above and below, I've got to get free of his madness.* He cried out silently, "Dekani? Zhovanya? Help me!"

But only silence answered, though it was a blessedly empty silence with no hint of Gauday's whispers. *Where is Zhovanya? Dekani? Why aren't they answering me?* Exhausted and forlorn, Kyr hunched up, resting his arms on his knees and his head on his arms. This anguish of aloneness was deeper even than the night the rains came. Yet it felt different—somehow significant, and necessary.

Friend whined softly. He sat up and wrapped his arm around her. "That's right, girl. You're here with me, aren't you?" She licked his chin and relaxed against him. Calmed by Friend's warm, solid simplicity, he rested, watching stately sunbeams glide slowly through the trees.

The touch of the warm sun felt like a caress on his cheeks and arms, as it baked his clothes dry. Remembering the healing power of the Great Tree at the Heart of the Forest, he settled into the embrace of the shaggy-barked cedar. Subtle and silent, a sense of connection with trees and earth, air and sun pervaded his soul.

In that moment of stillness, he came to a new understanding. *My life is my own, not Gauday's, or Dekani's, or even Zhovanya's, though I have chosen to serve Her. No one can really understand what I suffered in that private hell Gauday invented, nor what I learned of the torments his soul is suffering. No one can take the burden of recovering from Gauday's torments off my shoulders, no matter how much they care. It is* my *task to take on, or to walk away from.*

With sudden clarity, he saw that, at one level, each of us *is* ultimately alone in this life; that there are things that cannot be shared or understood by another—and that no one is to blame. Some things are ours alone to deal with.

He heaved a deep sigh, with a feeling of settling into harness, as he had seen draft horses do when getting ready to pull their load. *It's up to me. I must find a way to go on, myself. I can't let Gauday shape me into a monster in his own image by giving in to my own fear and woundedness. I've got to fight him and his sorcery! And I have already made my choice,* he reminded himself. *I chose the hard path a long time ago, though I had no idea what it meant or where it would lead me.* He snorted. *Merciless gods! If I had known, I never would have had the courage to choose this path!*

Then an image arose in his mind: the Triumph of Love, the sculpture he had carved as a gift to the Sanctuary. For the first time, he saw his life as something he had to shape on his own, just as he was the only one, when sculpting, who could decide what chisel stroke to make next. A wrong choice could ruin the whole sculpture; but if he held back and did nothing, the sculpture would remain locked in the stone forever.

Remembering the fear and excitement of making that fateful decision—taking that stroke, seeing that each stroke led the way to the next—Kyr was amazed to realize that he actually *was* shaping his own life, by making his own choices. He was proud that he had chosen the hard path, to go to the Sanctuary and to persist through the difficult transformation he had undergone there. Upon that ledge on the mountain behind the Sanctuary, he had chosen to serve Zhovanya.

Though it had led to so much suffering, he even felt a certain pride in his choice to leave the Sanctuary and turn himself over to Gauday. And he was proud that he had endured it all and achieved what he had set out to do: protect the Sanctuary and all its residents. With a slight smile, he sat up straighter and lifted his chin. Faintly, he sensed Dekani smiling, too.

Breathing in the cedar-scented air, soaking in Friend's loyal affection, Kyr focused his attention on the warmth of the sun, the light breeze making the cedar boughs sway silently, the chuckling of the nearby creek. Occasional chirping told of small birds high in the trees above, and served to emphasize the stillness and abiding peace of the ancient cedar.

And through that stillness came an ethereal caress, a memory of an embrace, of Jolanya whispering, *"I love you."* He crossed his legs to sit in meditation pose, filled with a new determination to honor the Kailithana and all she had done for him. *This is my choice: I will let her work shape me, hers and Naran's and Zhovanya's, not Gauday's. Somehow I must become again the man Jolanya loved.* With this decision, he felt as if he were growing roots down deep as the cedar's, and becoming as tall and steady as the cedar itself. Kyr began to sing the Zhovanaya chant, while silently praying for healing and redemption for himself and his tormenter.

"There he is!" Rajani exclaimed, hearing Kyr's chant echoing through the trees, somewhere off to the side of the path. The Warrior Mage followed the sound of his voice and soon found him sitting under a cedar, eyes closed, still chanting. Rajani stood still for a few moments, taking deep breaths, shedding his worry and hurry to find Kyr, who continued chanting peacefully.

Friend came over and gave Rajani a thorough sniffing. He greeted her with gentle pats. Then the faithful dog looked hopefully up the trail toward the fort. When Rajani sat down near Kyr and joined in the chant, she gave a huffy sigh and sat nearby, her ears twitching to the sounds of evening creeping through the forest: birds' sleepy cheeping; twigs and branches rustling in the gentle breeze; unseen creatures venturing to the creek for a drink.

After a time, Kyr and Rajani let the chant die away. A deep peace pervaded the glade, now shadowed by the tall cedars. Kyr sighed and stretched, feeling empty and clear, yet more solid in himself. He glanced at Rajani, who was still in meditation. *Ah, my guardian, always rushing to my rescue,* he thought fondly, wondering why his friend was always so concerned for him. *I guess that is what friends do for each other,* he thought, smiling to himself over one of his favorite mysteries of this life beyond the Soul-Drinker's lair.

Rajani opened his eyes. "I was sure that you would be having a hard time, after that scene with Gauday. But your voice sounds so strong and sure! I'm amazed!"

"Well, it was rough there for a while." In keeping with his new determination to find his own way, Kyr didn't explain what he had been going through. "Gauday's poisonous words made me ill, but I'm all right now."

"I don't know what miracle has happened here," Rajani said, raising an inquiring eyebrow, which Kyr ignored. Rajani shrugged. "Well, it's good to see you so clear and solid." Then he rose and offered Kyr a hand. "Let's go back. I think there's fresh venison tonight."

At the mention of food, Kyr's stomach growled loudly. Laughing, he took Rajani's proffered hand and rose. "Gods, I *am* hungry!" Friend jumped up eagerly and led the way back to the fort.

Walking with his two friends, canine and human, Kyr felt a faint glow of pride, knowing that there had been no miracle from outside—that he had recovered from Gauday's sorcerous attack with no help from anyone, not even Zhovanya. Yet he had a feeling that to fully recover from Gauday's torments, he would need to ask for help, even so. He longed for Naran's wisdom and unrelenting compassion, and wondered if he could ask for his Aithané's help outside the Sanctuary. *Dekani is right. Part of shaping my own life is asking for help when I need it.*

But his satisfaction was tinged with sadness that he had been unable to reach Gauday. And hidden in his heart was his grief and longing for Jolanya. Buried even deeper was a wordless belief that this grief was part of his ongoing penance for the terrible suffering he had inflicted on his victims as a Slave of the Soul-Drinker.

# Chapter 24

# Struggle for Justice

The next evening, Rajani and Kyr were in Kyr's shielded room, eating supper at the small table near the hearth. Friend slept peacefully nearby, tired out from their long ramble in the woods. When they finished, Kyr set the stew bowls down on the floor. Friend snorted awake, scrambled up, and eagerly slurped the bowls clean. Rajani chuckled and tilted his stool back so he could lean against the wall behind him.

"How is the shield holding up? Keeping Gauday out of your mind?"

"It's working well."

"Good. You seem to have recovered from your encounter with Gauday?"

"Yes, but I am worried about Gauday and the other Slaves...."

"What? Still?" Rajani straightened, and his stool thumped forward, startling a yip out of Friend. "After your last interview with that madman? Gods, Kyr, why? *I* hate that crazy monster for what he did to you. Why don't *you?*"

Kyr steeled himself and met the Warrior Mage's irate glare. "Please, Rajani, try to understand. If I had let myself hate him, I would be as lost as he is. He would have dragged me down into his pit of hatred and self-loathing. Don't you see? Zhovanya taught me that my only defense was love and forgiveness."

"But you don't have to use that defense now. You're free!"

Kyr shook his head. "Letting myself hate him now would make a mockery of what I fought so hard for, all these months here."

"Gods and demons, Kyr," Rajani slumped a little and blew out a breath. "I don't know how you can be so forgiving. Didn't you ever hate him?"

245

"Yes," he sighed. "After that night in the rain, when I lost faith. But that road only led deeper into hell. I nearly lost myself in hatred and despair, nearly drowned in Gauday's madness."

"What saved you?"

"Ah, well…. I prayed for help. And my prayer was answered."

"By the Goddess?"

"Mmmm," was all he said, still bound by his promise not to reveal Dekani's presence. "I want to see Gauday again soon, and my other Slave-brothers. I have to try to bring them Zhovanya's grace."

"There's no point. We're planning to execute them soon."

"WHAT? NO!" Kyr jumped up and glared at the Warrior Mage. Startled awake, Friend looked around for the threat, growling in her throat. "Rajani, you mustn't! They are all victims of the Soul Drinker as much as anyone else. As small boys, we were *all* tortured into becoming his mindlessly loyal and obedient Slaves!"

"*I* know that! But most people don't. They demand justice for all that Gauday and his henchmen did here: stealing, kidnapping, rape, murder. They want to see them all dead. And so do I!"

Friend came over to Kyr's side, whining at the tension between the two men. "It's all right, girl. It's all right," Kyr crooned to her, taking a moment to pet her and to calm himself down. Then he asked, "What is this 'justice' you speak of? It sounds like revenge."

"Well, I suppose it's a more controlled version of revenge than mob violence. But the Circle is trying to establish a system of laws that will result in peace, order, and fairness to replace the random cruelty of the Soul Drinker's tyranny. To do that, we first have to show that those who harm others will be punished. Starting with Gauday."

"*I* harmed others, many of them." Kyr leaned forward and stared at Rajani intently. "Doesn't everyone deserve a chance at healing and redemption like I was given at the Sanctuary—that *you* gave me by bringing me there?"

The Warrior Mage shifted uncomfortably. "You deserved that chance for liberating us from the Soul Drinker. And you *wanted* to do penance for your sins. Does Gauday? Do any of your so-called Slave brothers?"

"How *can* they?" Kyr demanded. "They have never had the slightest chance to learn about the reality of love and forgiveness. Goddess forgive me, I sometimes wish Gauday would suffer as I did!" He shook his head, perplexed and upset. "But I cannot forget what I saw with Zhovanya's eyes."

"Zhovanya's eyes?" asked Rajani.

"When I was desperate," Kyr answered in a soft voice, "I prayed for help. The Goddess bade me see Gauday's soul through Her eyes, and I did. His soul is in agony over what he has become, what he has done, though he does not realize this. He blames his suffering on others, especially on me." Kyr looked away silently, dealing with an uprush of painful memories.

After a few moments, he looked back at his friend. "What good would inflicting more pain on him do for anyone? Will it ease our suffering? Right some kind of balance?" He looked at Rajani intently. "Hatred, revenge, punishment—that's the easy path, the one that led Gauday into his own hell of cruelty and madness. Naran taught me that." He took a deep breath, steeling himself for Rajani's reaction. "We must give him the same opportunity I had to seek forgiveness and atonement."

"What? You mean, let him go to the Sanctuary?" Rajani glared at him in outrage. "He'd destroy that place with his spell-casting in no time. No, that's out of the question," the Warrior Mage said, in a tone that brooked no opposition. "Besides, you know he wouldn't honestly seek expiation. He's beyond saving, Kyr."

"Zhovanya forgave *me*," Kyr said firmly, "and he is my brother, lost in the Master's madness as I was. If I deserved the chance to redeem my soul, so does he. They should all have the chance I had. Gauday and the others should all be taken to the Sanctuary."

"NO!" Rajani slammed his fist down on the table, and Friend jumped up in alarm, growling. Kyr went to her, calmed her down, and urged her out the door. Meanwhile, Rajani took a few breaths to calm himself down.

"Sorry, Kyr. But Gauday would bring immense suffering to all those at the Sanctuary, with his devious cruelty and sorcerous powers. As for your other 'Slave brothers,' as you call them, there are far too many for the Sanctuary to deal with. And we can't leave them running loose, causing havoc. No, we have to execute them, put them out of their misery. Perhaps they will learn of Zhovanya's forgiveness after they go to Her."

"Killing Gauday and his men won't undo the damage they've caused. People know that, so what do they *really* want?"

"Gods, Kyr, you are still such an innocent. They want Gauday and his men to suffer as they have."

"Gauday *has* suffered. He *is* suffering. I can feel it at this moment. All of us Slaves have suffered more than most of you can imagine. *Why* can't you understand that?"

"Think of the tremendous suffering the Soul Drinker and his Watchers, Gatherers, and Slaves inflicted on all of Khailaz for six generations. *That's* what people care about."

They glared at each other. The Warrior Mage showed no signs of softening.

Kyr's heart sank. He could never carry out his Atonement if Rajani put his Slave brothers to death. He tried one more time. "Please, Rajani, think about it. What will really help the people heal? Vengeance or forgiveness?"

"I'll think about it. We'll talk tomorrow." Rajani stalked out, still frowning.

Confronting the powerful Warrior Mage had taken all Kyr's fortitude and energy. Bone-weary, he curled up on his bed and stared at the fire until his eyes sagged shut. Deep in the night, he wakened to a brush of velvet wings.

*"WHAT THEY WANT IS TO BE HEARD. LET THEM TELL THEIR STORIES. AND YOU TELL YOURS. LET EVERYONE TESTIFY."*

The next morning, Kyr found Rajani in his office. What had been Gauday's gloomy parlor was now a place of brisk efficiency. The dining table was Rajani's desk, littered with scrolls, quills, a bottle of ink, and three bright oil lamps. Shadows lurked only in the corners of Kyr's memory.

Seated at the table, Rajani was conferring with a village elder, his dark head close to the gray one, bent over a parchment. A row of chairs lined the wall next to the door. A woman in a colorful patchwork gown and an elaborate turban sat in the first chair, tapping her foot impatiently. Kyr took a seat next to her.

"Will that do?" asked Rajani.

"Aye, m'lord." The elder scrawled his signature on the parchment. Rajani signed it, sanded it to dry the ink, and handed it to the older man, who carried it off, looking satisfied. Rajani made a few notes in a logbook and looked up.

"Ah, Kyr, come, come."

"But I'm next," protested the woman.

Rajani came to his feet. "I'm sorry, madam. The noon meal is about to be served in the courtyard. Please enjoy our hospitality and return this afternoon."

"Well, you've kept me waiting so long, I *am* hungry." She laughed as if she had made a joke, but still seemed annoyed. "I'll be first in line after lunch."

"Thank you for your patience." Rajani ushered the woman out, and spoke to the Companion on duty outside. "No interruptions unless it's an emergency."

They settled into the two comfortable chairs by the hearth, and Rajani asked, "What's on your mind?"

Ignoring the sick clenching in his stomach, Kyr forced back memories of crouching chained and naked by that same hearth, took a deep breath, and began. "I've been thinking.... One thing I learned at the Sanctuary is that telling the story of what happened to you is part of healing and letting go. So I think what people need, including me, is a way to tell their stories in front of everyone, including those who harmed them. Maybe this would be healing for everyone."

"By all the little gods! You *have* been thinking, haven't you? So you're saying to let everyone testify to the harm Gauday or his men did to them?"

"Yes, that's the word, testify. I think people would feel more satisfied if they got to speak. And they might not want to get revenge so much. With Zhovanya's help, maybe people could even find a way to forgive."

"But that could take months. We can't spend the time for Testimony about each Slave." Rajani thought for a few moments. "Alright, here's what we can do. Gauday will be the representative of all his men. After all, he was their commander. And, Kyr, you've got to be realistic. We can't just forgive them and let them go. Best we could do is keep them all in prison forever. And that would be a lot of trouble and expense."

"Rajani, we can't just kill them all. We'd be no better than Gauday. Not all of them did terrible things; and those who did not should at least be allowed to live, maybe even earn their freedom somehow. It's not fair to treat them all alike."

"Ah, gods, Kyr! You're just making this more complicated! But...." Rajani sighed and slumped back in his chair a little. "I see that I'm too anxious to be done with this. And you're right. To truly establish fairness, we need to investigate each case, and decide what to do with each man. I'll call for a circle of wise-women to decide these cases while the people testify about Gauday. Will that satisfy you?"

"Yes! Thank you, Rajani!" Kyr smiled, filled with gladness that he had made a step toward fulfilling his Atonement.

"However," the Warrior Mage said, "Gauday will be executed. I'm sorry, Kyr, that's the best I can do."

He met Rajani's eyes and said softly, "If *I* can forgive him, others may be able to." Kyr's gaze was eloquent of much suffering and hard-won compassion.

The Warrior Mage looked down. "Gods, Kyr. I don't know how you can.... Never mind. Just don't hope for too much." Rajani grabbed a sheet of parchment, dipped his quill-pen in the ink bottle, and began to write. "Alright. I'm drafting a proclamation of the Days of Testimony to begin in a half-moon. This will not be easily arranged. We have to give notice to all the surrounding villages so all who wish to testify can get here. This will extend our stay here by a month or more."

Kyr said decisively, "It's worth the wait."

"It may be," Rajani said thoughtfully. "These Days of Testimony might be what the Circle has been searching for, as a way toward healing the wounds the Soul-Drinker inflicted. Thanks, Kyr. You are wiser than I. And once again, Khailaz is in your debt."

Kyr tried to shrug off this praise, but a shy smile illuminated his face.

Later, in his room, he sagged onto his bed. He was exhausted, yet exhilarated. He'd stood his ground, and the confrontation had been fruitful. He'd carried Zhovanya's message to Rajani, and together they'd come up with a new kind of justice. Now there was a chance for his Slave brothers and even Gauday, though it was probably not a very big chance. He'd done his best.

A quarter-moon later, Medari, Rajani, and Kyr were in Kyr's shielded room, having supper together. Kyr was relaxed and peaceful, enjoying the company of his friends. Friend was curled up on Kyr's bed, already asleep.

"The new governor is due to arrive tomorrow," Rajani reported. "Thank all the gods! I've had my fill of local politics."

"I guess that means you are almost done here?" Medari inquired.

"Well, we still have the Days of Testimony to get through. Then we'll be leaving." Rajani picked up the teapot and filled their mugs with a steaming brew of calming herbs.

Thinking of having to testify against Gauday, Kyr shivered. *Gods, I am dreading that!* His scars started pulsing faintly. He looked down to hide his sudden tension, as he fought to quell the lurid memories the pulsing stirred up, and to refocus on the present moment.

Meanwhile, Rajani was saying, "By the way, Medari, we can escort you to Stonewell village. It's on our way to Ravenvale."

"Good," Medari said. "I was hoping for that. I'd like Kyr to meet my family." Rajani raised an eyebrow, but said nothing.

Kyr shared Rajani's concern. Why hadn't anyone from Medari's family come to the fort? But he smiled and said, "I'm looking forward to that, Medari. I almost feel I know them, after all the tales you shared with me."

"Well, time for my nightly rounds." The Warrior Mage rose and headed toward the door.

"Rajani, wait."

The Warrior Mage turned back toward Kyr. "Yes?"

"I was wondering if you could send someone to find Naran?"

"Of course," Rajani said gently. "I'm fairly sure he's still at the Sanctuary. I know he will want to do whatever he can for you. I'll have him meet us here or at Ravenvale, depending on how long it takes to find him."

"Thanks, Rajani," Kyr said. "Good night."

As Rajani left, Kyr noticed Medari's frown. "What's wrong, Medari?"

"Who is this Naran? I'm right here. Can't I be of any help? I've been through it all with you. I know what you have suffered."

"True, Medari. It's just that Naran is the one who helped me at the Sanctuary, helped me face all that I went through as a Slave. He has a special skill for this kind of help." Kyr winced inside at what he had to say next, knowing it might further alienate the two of them. "I do understand your desire for vengeance against Gauday. But I don't share it. At least, not on most days." He spread his hands. "That makes it difficult to go into these things with you."

"I see," the healer said doubtfully.

"Please, Medari, understand that I do appreciate all you did to help me here, and hope to count you as my friend for life."

Medari sighed. "I think I understand." He stood up and fetched two mugs, pulled a flask out of his jacket, and poured some of its contents into each mug. With a smile, he handed Kyr a mug, raised his, and said, "Friends for life!" They sat quietly, sipping sweetberry wine. After a short while, Kyr could hardly keep his eyes open. Medari took their empty mugs and said goodnight.

Kyr shoved Friend over and crawled into bed. She made a slight sound of protest, but quickly settled down to her dreaming. He lay quiet, thinking about the day and all he had been through. The wonderful sense of clarity and serenity of the afternoon was obscured by the haziness of the liquor, his weariness, and his worry about the upcoming ordeal of testifying. Doubt crept into his tired heart. *Naran might not come, and I don't know if even he can help me. But there's no one else who might be able to help cleanse me of Gauday's venom.* In a sudden anguish of hope, he thought, *Oh, Goddess, I wish he were here now! Getting through the Days of Testimony would be so much easier if he were.*

Just the thought of Naran's deep kindness and strength steadied him, and reminded him of the compassion and forgiveness he had received at the Sanctuary. *I promised to pass these blessings on. I must try again to pass them on somehow.* "Oh!" he gasped, sitting up suddenly, struck by a new thought. Friend grumbled her objections. Kyr petted her absently, thinking, *If Naran gets here, I can ask him to help Gauday. Maybe together we can break through his madness. But, what about the cursed smoke from the Crown? It's still in Gauday. Can we get past that? Could Rajani cleanse Gauday of the smoke-beast? Would he? I guess not, not with his attitude.*

Kyr scrubbed his scalp in frustration. *Merciless gods, this Atonement of mine seems impossible! Every road seems blocked.* He sagged down onto the bed again, his mind whirling. Finally, he concluded, *All I can do is ask Rajani, and Naran, if he gets here.* He started to relax. *Wait. No point in asking Rajani and Naran to help Gauday, if he rejects the hard path. I'll have to give Gauday his choice first. Gods, that means I have to see him again. Well, I survived last time.* Old fears tried to raise their heads, but Kyr deliberately focused his mind on the present moment. Listening to the familiar, comforting sounds of Medari tidying up next door in the infirmary and of Friend's steady breathing, he eventually fell asleep.

The next day, Kyr arranged with Rajani to visit Gauday again, with the same safeguards as before. When all was ready, Kyr opened the trap door, took a lit candle lantern, and descended the stairs to the black hole, praying it was the last time he would ever have to enter this dark place. As before, Rajani waited at the top of the stairs.

Kyr entered the cell, set the candle lamp on the floor, and sat down facing Gauday, who was once again chained and gagged. The prisoner glowered sullenly from his straw pallet. Kyr began repeating the forgiveness chant to himself, continuing until his heart softened and he could sense Gauday's soul-deep pain. Then he looked at Gauday, eyes soft with compassion.

"My brother, I'm here to let you know your choices. You know that the Warrior Mage and the villagers all want you dead, and plan to execute you after the Days of Testimony. That is one choice: the easy path of despair, hatred, and death.

"However, there is another path, the hard path that I have chosen. It is a path of healing, repentance, and forgiveness. If you can show me that you truly seek to repent for your crimes, to be cleansed of the Master's filthy poison, and to face the pain that burdens your soul, as I did at the Sanctuary, I will do whatever I can to see that you can take this hard path." Kyr leaned forward, and spoke with urgent kindness.

"I want you to know what choosing this hard path means. You will have to come to understand how evil the Soul-Drinker was, and what terrible things we did as his Slaves. We inflicted horrific suffering not only on the sacrifices, but also on their families and loved ones. You will learn the terrible pain of losing a loved one, and even worse, knowing that your loved one is suffering terribly as a sacrifice."

Gauday stared at Kyr as if he were speaking gibberish, and laughed behind his gag until he started choking on it, then had to take deep breaths through his nose for a few moments.

Kyr waited him out, then went on. "Worse, you will have to face how much pain and torment you suffered as a young boy being tortured and twisted into becoming a Slave, and as an obedient Slave of our vicious Master." Gauday shook his head in fierce denial. "Yes," Kyr said gently but firmly. "We all have suffered horrendously at the hands of our so-called Master." Gauday looked away. Kyr sighed unhappily, but continued, determined to finish what he had started.

"In addition, you will have to learn a whole new way of living, things we never knew as Slaves: kindness, friendship, forgiveness, compassion, and love. If you are lucky, you will come to know our Goddess, Zhovanya, and Her love and forgiveness for us all. I can't really explain these to you. You will have to experience them for yourself."

Gauday was ignoring him. Kyr understood too well why. Most of what he had said was beyond Gauday's small, dark world and incomprehensible to him. But Kyr still hoped that his Slave-brother might turn toward a gleam of light from the greater world where hope, love, and kindness were possible.

"My brother, this is all I can tell you: this hard path and its rewards are innumerable, and impossible to explain to one who has never known anything but the Soul-Drinker's hell. However, I assure you," Kyr said with passionate intensity, "it is worth *any* price. I hope my words touch your heart, even though you may not understand anything I have said."

Gauday growled through his gag and shook his head, but Kyr ignored him. "I am giving you the choice, as I was given, between the easy path of death, or the hard path of cleansing, healing, and forgiveness. I will give you some time to think about this." Closing his eyes, he settled down into meditation, calling on Zhovanya to guide this lost soul, silently chanting, "*Zhovanya, ganaralo ya zhanto.*"

At first, Gauday's restless movements on his straw pallet and the clanking of his chains were distracting, but Kyr persisted, and slowly sank into a deep meditation. He felt Zhovanya's Presence fill the small, dark hole with peace and love, as with a warm, golden light. His heart expanded with gladness and hope.

"GAAAAGGGHH!" Gauday's howl shattered the peace and silence, even muffled as it was by his gag. Kyr gasped, and his eyes flew open. His tormentor was writhing in his chains and howling as if being tortured.

Rajani raced down the stairs and entered the cell with sword drawn. "NO!" Kyr leapt up to stand between the Warrior Mage and the prisoner. "It's him, not me, Rajani. I don't know what is wrong with him." Kyr found that his hands were shaking, and clasped them behind his back.

Rajani peered over Kyr's shoulder at Gauday, who was subsiding into moans and shivers. "What did you do to him?"

"Nothing. I told him he had a choice between death and the hard path. Then I went into meditation, and called on Zhovanya to guide him. I felt Her Presence fill this hole, and then he started howling and writhing as if in pain."

"Humph." Rajani snorted. "Well, I guess he couldn't abide Her Presence. Not surprising."

"Take off his gag, please. I have to find out what is going on with him."

"Alright. But I will wait out here. He's too dangerous, especially to you." Rajani removed the gag, and stepped outside the door.

"No, no, no," Gauday whimpered, looking around the cell wildly, then sagging with relief. "It's gone." Then he turned on Kyr with a roar. "TRAITOR! YOU KILLED OUR MASTER! I HATE YOU AND YOUR CURSED BITCH-GODDESS! I'LL NEVER FOLLOW YOUR BLASTED HARD PATH! NEVER! KILL ME NOW!" He lunged at Kyr, but his chains jerked him to a halt. Kyr jumped to his feet and backed out of the hole.

"Alright, Kyr." Rajani put a hand on his shoulder. "He's made his choice. Enough now. Go on upstairs."

Kyr trudged up the stairs, heavy-hearted yet oddly relieved. Rajani was right. Gauday had made his choice. There was nothing more Kyr could do.

# Chapter 25

# Days of Testimony

It had taken a half-moon. Villager after villager had stood on the Attestants' newly built platform, which was raised about ten hand-spans above the ground and situated at the far end of the courtyard, opposite the main gates. The Attestants gazed down at Gauday, who was chained to a strong post set in front of the platform, and gagged.

The Warrior-Mage himself stood guard over Gauday, ready to suppress any effort to inflict pain with his red-eyed sorcery. Having had this power reflected back on him once by Rajani's magic, Gauday had so far made no such attempts. As the Warrior Mage and the new governor had made clear at the start, this was to be an orderly procedure.

Facing the platform, the crowd of Attestants and other villagers were seated on row upon row of rough wooden benches that extended halfway to the gates of the fort. Companions, armed only with batons, stood along the sides of the crowd to keep order, and had to intervene several times to keep a distraught man or woman from rushing forward to attack Gauday.

The Attestants spoke of theft, abduction, rape, and murder, all perpetrated by Gauday and his band of Slaves, and abetted by some of the soldiers. With tears, shouts, and shaken fists, the villagers spoke of lives taken or ruined, families and livelihoods destroyed, children stolen, property vandalized, hearts broken.

As each day began, Gauday had sat erect in his chains, stiff and arrogant, flashing angry, disdainful looks at the speakers. Now and then, he glared scornfully at the group of prisoners, obviously despising them as traitors to himself. But as the day wore on, he slumped against the whipping post and stared sullenly at the ground, doing his best to ignore the whole proceeding.

Pale and grim, Kyr had sat silently at the back of the crowd, forcing himself to listen to it all. Sometimes the testimony made him physically ill. Sometimes tears streamed down his face. Sometimes he could barely restrain himself from attacking Gauday. Only the presence of the Warrior Mage and the Companions kept him and many others at bay.

Each night, he had crawled into his bed, exhausted by the emotions that stormed through him: grief and outrage; sickening fear caused by the mere sight of his torturer; dark dreams of revenge. Knowing Gauday as he did, Kyr knew how best to make his tormentor suffer: darkness and humiliation would be his primary instruments of torture. Over and over, Kyr banished these dreams of vengeance, clinging to the forgiveness chant, struggling to keep to the hard path.

In addition to the Testimony against Gauday, there had been the judgment of the other prisoners. Guarded by half a dozen fully armed Companions, the ex-Slaves and the soldiers, Craith among them, had sat on the ground behind and to one side of the villagers, but close enough to hear what the Attestants said. As the Days of Testimony went on, each prisoner was taken to be judged and sentenced by the Council of Wisewomen, one from each village. They sat on stools in a semi-circle near the main gates, each wearing the colorful, traditional garb of their homes. Carefully, they listened to the villagers who came to testify about a particular Slave or soldier, as well as to each prisoner, before consulting together to make their judgments.

Once judged, most men were taken outside the fort to be tattooed with a mark on the hand indicating the length of his sentence and the village to which he would be sent to work out his time. Others, deemed too dangerous or unredeemable, were branded on the forehead, their howls of pain piercing the air, then sent under heavy guard to the barracks to await transport to the desert prison where they would spend their lives.

Now it was the night before Kyr was to testify. He sat on his bed staring out the door, which he had left open in the hope of cooling breezes after a warm day, a hint of the Summer to come. Friend was sprawled in the doorway, snoring gently. Kyr envied her untroubled sleep. His own mind was churning with questions and doubts, his stomach roiling with apprehension and fear. *Can I keep control and speak from forgiveness and compassion? Or will I go mad, ranting at Gauday for all he did to me?* His scars flared to life at the mere thought of the torments he had suffered. Quickly, he turned his mind away, and the sickening pulsations of his scars died down.

*Well, only a few of these villagers, these ordinary good people, lost control and tried to attack Gauday, and they had suffered almost as much as....* He sighed deeply with a new realization. *No, I can't say that. How can I compare my torment to someone losing a loved one? I cannot know their pain, nor they mine. All we can know is that we all still do suffer from what Gauday did to us.* The weight of all that suffering bore down on him. He slid down and curled up on his bed, lying on his side, facing the door.

He stared out at the moonlit yard, where Gauday, guarded by three Companions, remained chained to the whipping post, curled up on the ground with one ragged blanket, just as Kyr had been. *Serves him right!* Vindictive satisfaction flared up, but so did his scars. Immediately, Kyr returned to the forgiveness chant, silently repeating it until he could release hatred once again; and soon, his scars stopped their poisonous pulsing.

He turned his thoughts to the Days of Testimony, wondering whether the villagers were finding their way toward forgiveness, as he hoped they would. *It's strange, but being together, hearing the others' stories, makes it easier somehow to bear my own pain. Maybe they feel the same.* His heart assuaged by this new sense of kinship with the other Attestants, he began to relax. As the tide of sleep arose, he prayed, *"Guide me tomorrow. Let me speak as You would have me speak."*

In the morning, Kyr woke, amazed that he had slept at all. Today was the last day of Testimony, and he and Medari were to be the last to speak. He rose, washed, and dressed in the new clothes Rajani had provided: a loose white shirt and dark blue breeches. There was also a matching jacket, stockings, and tall, dark-brown boots. It was similar to a Companion's uniform. Kyr looked at the soldierly accoutrements, and left them where they were, thinking, *I am not that kind of fighter.* He slipped his feet into his old, comfortable sandals and went into the main room.

Tension made it impossible for him to do more than drink a few sips of tea. His porridge congealed in its bowl, untouched, as he sat staring blindly out the open door, lost in memories of torment, wondering if it would ever end. Each day was difficult, but the nights were torturous. The painful, arousing nightmares had returned ever since his first visit with Gauday, and the darkly sensual throbbing of his scars demanded release.

Medari's soft voice startled him. "How are you faring?"

Kyr drew his gaze back from memory and looked at Medari. "Gods, Medari, I am not looking forward to this. I don't know what to say."

"Just tell the truth. Tell them all what he did to you." Medari's voice had an undertone of vengefulness that made Kyr draw back.

"It's not that simple for me, Medari," Kyr said, disappointed.

With a puzzled glance, Medari rose. "Well, time to go."

"Merciless gods!" Kyr froze, dread flaring up, verging on panic. But then he closed his eyes, and silently called on Zhovanya for guidance. *Zhovanya, ganarali, Zhovanya, ganarali, Zhovanya, ganarali.* Then he followed Medari out the door, keeping his mind on this chant. They walked together toward the Testimonial Platform. The crowd was larger than ever, and noisy with chatter. However, when people spotted the two of them, there was a sudden silence, followed by a surge of whispered comments. Kyr nearly turned around, then, hating the way people were covertly staring at him. *What do they want? They are like vultures hovering over a carcass!*

Kyr and Medari made their way toward the platform in a hush of whispers. Kyr spotted Rajani halfway across the compound, talking with the new governor. As they approached the whipping post, he and Medari stopped to stare at Gauday, chained and gagged as usual, and guarded by two Companions.

Gauday, darting glances of hatred in every direction, didn't notice them at first. When he did, he shook his chains at Kyr, eyes turning red with rage, and Kyr's head began to ache. But before the sorcerous, gut-wrenching pain that Gauday could inflict set in, a Companion slapped the prisoner in the face. Gauday glared up at his assailant, but the red was gone from his eyes, and the incipient pain in Kyr's head vanished. Kyr wiped the sweat from his brow.

Rajani hurried over and spoke to Gauday with cold menace. "You try that again, and I'll kill you." Gauday snorted derisively, as if to say, *"Go ahead!"*

Medari and Kyr glanced at each other and moved on, climbing the steps up to the platform. Kyr looked around at the sea of upturned faces, remembering the sense of kinship he had felt with his fellow sufferers, these human beings like himself. But today, he felt cold and distant. Their eyes seemed to claw at him with their curious stares. He and Medari took their seats, and Rajani, as usual, began the last Day of Testimony by saying a prayer to Zhovanya for justice, then calling on the first Attestant.

All Kyr could focus on was what he might say when it was his turn. His own rage bade him erupt in furious condemnations as many another had done, but he knew that would only be more of what Gauday had spewed into the world. He dragged his mind off that track and returned to his silent repetition of the forgiveness chant. Slowly, it had its effect and he began to calm down.

The day dragged by, as one after another, people testified to the hurts they had suffered. Kyr hated being up in front of the crowd, the focus of so many curious eyes. *Gods, I want this over with! Perhaps I will just show them my scars and be done with it. They will speak for me. I won't have to say a word.* Relieved by the thought of this simple solution, Kyr drifted into a light doze, induced by an exhausting week and the warm Spring sunshine.

"You'll be next." Medari nudged Kyr awake, then rose and stepped to the rostrum. Tersely, he described his abduction, his family held hostage to ensure his compliance. "Even worse, Gauday forced me to break my sacred Healer's Oath to heal and do no harm. This vicious madman insisted that I keep Kyr alive to suffer endless tortures. And for what? Only to feed his insatiable appetite for revenge and power, just like his vicious Master." Medari's restrained fury was chilling to see, especially from a gentle healer. Kyr listened grimly, trying to keep his breathing even, to keep the chant in his heart, but his heart was pounding so hard that he shook with its every beat.

Medari took a deep breath and leaned forward, staring intently at the crowd. "What he did to all of us, especially to Kyr, was despicable and inhumane. We should destroy this vicious, craven sorcerer, just as Kyr destroyed the Soul-Drinker. Then we will be truly free of the long nightmare!" The crowd erupted in a tumult of ferocious cheers.

Kyr sat frozen in his chair. *Listen to them. They are out for blood. They won't want to hear what I have to say.* Near panic, he called out silently, *"Dekani, Zhovanya, help me!"*

261

Deep within, his teacher's face appeared, radiating love and faith. *"Remember what She said? You are Her Beloved. She is with you. Listen within. Do you not feel Her Presence?"* Kyr closed his eyes and opened his mind. Paying attention now, he did sense Her Presence, a glowing, golden warmth surrounding and filling him. Dekani smiled. *"You see? Go now and speak for Her."* Kyr took a deep breath, letting Dekani's love and Her Presence steady him. Zhovanya came very near and he was lifted into a state of gentle exaltation.

Meanwhile, Medari raised his hands to quiet the crowd. "There is one more Attestant. Let him speak." A breathless, quiet descended, and all eyes turned toward the last man, sitting stone-still at the back of the platform.

As Medari headed down the stairs of the platform, Kyr remained unmoving, deep in rapport with Zhovanya. The crowd—normally somewhat restless, with people coming and going, whispering to their neighbors, or sobbing quietly—became absolutely still and silent, awaiting with a kind of morbid awe the testimony of the Liberator, the one who had freed them from the Soul-Drinker, and Gauday's most tormented victim.

*Zhovanya nara lo, Zhovanya nara lo, Zhovanya nara lo.* The chant gave Kyr the strength and serenity to go forward. He went to the edge of the platform, ignoring the podium. He stood looking at Gauday, kneeling in chains below, for a time. Then he slowly removed his shirt, revealing the lines of still livid scars snaking over his torso and arms in elegant twining curves. A gale of gasps rushed through the crowd.

"This you did to me," Kyr said slowly, speaking directly to Gauday. "This and much more." Pausing, Kyr bowed his head, seeking what was essential to say, praying again for Zhovanya's guidance. Looking again at his tormenter, he continued, "You did your best to humiliate me and break my spirit. You tried to enslave me as a mind-bound tool to use for the oppression and torment of others, a fate far worse than death to me." Many in the crowd gasped in horror, while Gauday snickered behind his gag, but Kyr ignored them all, and continued.

"You did not count on our rightful Goddess, Zhovanya. Only Her gifts of counsel allowed me to avoid the traps of despair, hatred, and self-loathing that you set for me." Kyr smiled a little and put his shirt back on. "You are my brother, still lost in the Master's madness, and I am sorry for you. Again, I offer you Her blessings. Please listen and try to understand. As She did for me, Zhovanya will restore your soul with forgiveness and love when you allow yourself to feel the pain of your victims, and your own."

Time seemed suspended as everyone looked at Kyr in astonishment. To him, it seemed as if everyone was frozen except himself. Looking down, he saw that some villagers were looking at him with awe, others with confusion or anger.

The stunned silence was torn by a muffled scream of fury. Gauday hurled himself toward the platform. His chains jerked him to a sudden halt and he fell onto the hard-packed dirt of the courtyard. His guards grappled with him as he writhed in a frenzy of contempt and hatred.

Watching sadly, Kyr waited until Gauday had been subdued and was again crouching by the post, glaring up at him. He continued speaking directly to his tormentor. "You nearly did succeed, you know." As Gauday growled incomprehensibly through his gag, Kyr shivered with old terror, and returned to his silent repetition of the forgiveness chant. The crowd too remained silent, staring in fascination at Kyr.

When he felt Zhovanya's Presence again, Kyr opened his eyes. There were a number of gasps at his warm, golden gaze. Even Rajani looked startled. Kyr wondered what was wrong with him that they should stare so. But he set that aside and went on speaking to Gauday.

"Do you know what those Goddess-given gifts were?" Kyr asked Gauday gently. "No, I know you don't. Well, first, She gave me a word. 'Soften,' She said to me as I left the Sanctuary, and that word became my shield. When I forgot her word of counsel, I stiffened against what you were doing to me. That only made it worse, and it led me downwards toward the black pit your soul lives in."

Kyr sat down on the edge of the platform, wanting to be closer to Gauday. The crowd shifted a little but remained mesmerized, while Rajani stepped closer so that he was almost between Kyr and Gauday. Kyr took no notice.

"Later, when I was about to give in to your entrapments, She gave me another gift." Kyr paused and looked more deeply into Gauday's furious eyes, seeing the terror and agony buried there. "She let me see into your soul, and still does." His former tormenter shook his head in furious denial.

263

"Do you remember when you lost control and beat me with your fists?" Kyr noticed vindictiveness creeping into his heart, and paused, returning in his mind to the chant once again. After a few moments, he had regained his serenity, and continued. "Do you remember what it was I said to you that triggered your outburst?"

Gauday gargled against his gag and tried to cover his ears with his hands. But the guards grabbed his arms and forced them down. Kyr almost took pity on Gauday, then. He didn't know if it was true compassion or subtle vengefulness that made him continue. "I said, 'It makes me sad to see your soul in so much pain.' Remember?" Gauday writhed, vainly trying to escape. Relentlessly, Kyr went on. "She showed me how your soul suffers untold agonies from what you have done, from what the Soul-Drinker has made of you."

Jumping down off the platform, Kyr moved to kneel in front of his tormenter. Rajani placed his hand on his sword, while the guards kept firm hold of Gauday's arms.

Looking into Gauday's desperate, crazed eyes, Kyr said softly, "It will be all right. You are going to the Light soon. No more darkness for you. Don't be afraid. Zhovanya's mercy is infinite. Her forgiveness will wash your soul clean."

Gauday stared at him, his eyes bewildered and frightened, but then his habitual rage replaced fear, and his eyes started to glow red. Rajani's sword rang as he drew it, but Kyr's warm, golden gaze stopped him. In awe, the Warrior Mage stepped back and sheathed his sword. Kyr turned his lambent gaze on his tormenter, and its warmth touched Gauday's scarred and twisted heart. Sudden tears filled Gauday's eyes and trickled down his cheeks.

Kyr nodded and rose, satisfied that he had done his best to reach Gauday, glad that he apparently had done so. "Don't be afraid. Zhovanya loves you and will forgive you." As he turned away, Gauday wiped his eyes roughly with his ragged blanket, and growled to himself behind his gag.

Kyr returned to his usual seat at the back of the crowd, next to Medari. "What are you doing?" the healer demanded loudly. "Is that all you're going to say? You told them almost nothing of what that monster did to you. I can't believe this!" Others in the crowd muttered their agreement.

264

Kyr gazed at Medari and the others with eyes still golden and full of compassion. "I'm sorry, my friend. Zhovanya has shown me that the path of vengeance is an endless nightmare. For my own soul's sake, I will not take that path."

There was an awed silence. After a few moments, a rustle of whispers spread through the crowd, as those further back asked those near enough to hear, "What did Kyr say to that monster at the last?" Many shook their heads in awe or consternation as they heard what Kyr had said. Others stared at him, astonished or angered by his compassion.

Another question was asked by many. "Who is Zhovanya?" Those who knew answered this question, and the answer spread, generating ripples of amazement through the crowd.

"The Goddess? Our old Goddess has returned?" asked a dark-haired woman, with a dawning smile of hope.

"Didn't the Soul-Drinker destroy Her?" wondered a recently arrived merchant, still in his dusty leathers.

"The Goddess is alive?" a little flame-haired girl with two long braids asked her mother.

"Yes! The Goddess is alive!" joyously answered a nearby green-clad female Companion.

Meanwhile, Kyr sat with his head bowed, feeling Zhovanya's Presence drain away, leaving him empty and weary. He wondered if he had been kind or cruel. *Perhaps it would be easier for Gauday to remain in ignorance. After all, his soul will still go home to Her in any case.* He sighed, glad it was over, and fairly sure he had done his best to speak as Zhovanya had desired. A feeling of relief and satisfaction came over him, and he raised his head.

His eye was caught by a man's green-eyed gaze. Craith was staring at him with awe and reverence. *Gods, Craith, don't look at me like that. I'm the same man you loved that one night. This was Zhovanya's work.*

Their eyes met. Kyr felt almost drowned by the desperate need in Craith's eyes, the need for understanding and forgiveness, such as Kyr himself had needed so badly, and had received at the Sanctuary. Craith knelt, placing his fist over his heart and bowing his head in deep respect, as did five other prisoners.

Kyr frowned and looked away. But he found many in the crowd staring at him: some with awe and respect; some with puzzlement or curiosity; some with baffled anger. Up on the platform, Rajani began to speak to the crowd in a carrying voice, and everyone's attention shifted to the Warrior Mage. Kyr, shaken and worn out, took this chance to escape all the judging, demanding eyes, and headed back to his room.

# Part Eight ~ Fierce Blessings

*"As I walked out the door toward the gate*
*that would lead to my freedom, I knew*
*if I didn't leave my bitterness and hatred behind,*
*I'd still be in prison."*

—Nelson Mandela

# Chapter 26

# Rope of Light

Exhausted and relieved, Kyr slept late the next morning, undisturbed by lurid nightmares or throbbing scars. After washing and dressing, he went into the infirmary. Medari looked up from setting out a lunch of bread, cheese, and apples. "Well, I'll bet you're glad the Testimony is over. I certainly am! We'll put Gauday out of his misery and be going home in just a few days."

Kyr merely nodded, thinking, *Out of his misery? Yes*, Gauday *will be, won't he?*

"Let's see how you are doing this morning, son." Medari took one of Kyr's wrists and felt his pulses. "Hmmm. Sit down, while I make some strengthening tea. We could both some after that ordeal." Kyr sat on a stool by the table, and watched Medari bustling around, tossing this herb and that root and a handful of dried flowers into a teapot, then ladling in hot water from the always simmering kettle on the hearth-fire.

"This needs to steep a bit." Medari set the teapot and two mugs on the table, and took a seat. He fiddled with his mug, twisting it back and forth, then looked up. "Uh, Kyr, well, I want to apologize…. You know, I don't understand how you can be so forgiving of Gauday. But…. Well, I am sorry that I can't follow your example." Medari's face turned red, and he looked down. "Zhovanya must have taught you much. I hope you'll forgive my ignorance?" The healer looked up, with hesitant hope in his eyes.

Glad that Medari was no longer angry with him, Kyr said, "Of course. And I hope that someday you will come to understand Zhovanya's love for all Her children." With a smile, he added, "Even you."

"So do I." Medari's answering smile didn't erase the doubtful sadness in his eyes. He poured tea for them both.

After lunch, Kyr made it as far as the porch outside his room. Exhausted by the Days of Testimony and his nightmares, he sat and slumped back against the wall. Friend jumped onto the porch, wagging her tail madly. "Yes, girl, it's over, finally. I'm glad to see you, too." She'd been banished to the barn during the Testimony. He gave her a hug, and she licked his face with slobbery enthusiasm. "Alright, girl, alright!" he chuckled. "Settle down." He wiped his face on his sleeve, and patted the floor next to him. She curled up contentedly beside him. Resting his hand on her warm, silky back, he soon drifted into a doze.

"Um, sir?" a voice asked sometime later.

*Gods, now what?* He rubbed his eyes, trying to wake up. "Oh, it's you. What is it, Kuron?"

"I'm sorry to bother you, sir, but.... Uh, the prisoners.... Well, a few of them.... They want to speak with you."

"They do? Why?" Kyr sat up in surprise, and Friend raised her head.

"They want to know about Zhovanya, sir. I thought you would want to...."

*What I want is to sleep for a day or two more*, Kyr thought. But then he sighed, realizing that he had a promise to keep, a promise he had made to Jolanya and Naran to pass on the blessings he had received at the Sanctuary. *If I can't reach Gauday, perhaps I can pass on Zhovanya's blessings to these prisoners.* "Alright," he said, standing up and squaring his shoulders. "Bring them to the chapel. I'll be there shortly."

In the chapel, Kyr found a half-dozen prisoners kneeling just inside the door, Craith among them. The prisoners were under guard by three annoyed-looking Companions. Noticing the prisoners' tension, Kyr turned to the sergeant. "Please wait outside."

"Yes, sir." The trio of Companions went outside onto the porch, closing the door behind them.

At Kyr's nod, the prisoners stood up.

"Come, let's sit by the altar." When they were settled, Kyr took a moment to light the candle and compose himself. Then he looked around the half-circle of nervous but hopeful faces. They were all soldiers, except—he was glad to see—one former Slave. Craith introduced the men to Kyr. Jorem, the former Slave, was a tall, swarthy man from the western desert. Kinar and Zurano were stocky brothers from the far North, light-skinned, with eyes the pale aqua of glacial ice and hair the color of snow. Brol was a beefy dark-skinned bald man with defiant green eyes. Jarki was a slight man of sand-colored hair, skin, and eyes, who seemed to fade into the background.

Kyr smiled. "I'm glad you are here. How can I help you?"

Craith took the lead, his voice soft and hesitant. "Sir, what you said yesterday.... Well, it was so different. It was like I'd been living in a dark dungeon and you threw open the doors to a whole new world of light." The other prisoners nodded at this, while Craith went on. "Especially when you spoke about Zhovanya, and how She helped you endure...." He choked to a stop, blushing furiously. "Ah, gods and demons! I should have killed him! I let him keep you in there for a month, and never even tried to stop him. I am so sorry." He dropped his head into his hands.

Kyr stared at him. *By all the gods! He's actually apologizing to me!* With an unfamiliar sense of gratification, he said gently, "Zhovanya forgives you, as do I."

Craith looked up with a tentative smile, and rushed on. "Uh, I know we have no right, after how we treated you, but... would you tell us about this this Goddess you speak of, this Zhovanya? She must be a real Goddess. *You* are the proof, if you can forgive Gauday."

Touched and disconcerted, Kyr bowed his head, wondering what he could possibly say to meet the desperate need he saw in these men. He repeated the chant to himself a few times, and prayed for Zhovanya to guide his words, then looked up and met each man's gaze.

"Zhovanya is the Light," he began, "and yet She knows the darkness. She is holy, and yet She accepts us with our worst sins. She is everything that is. When we turn toward Her, She welcomes us, no matter what we have done." Kyr saw the disbelief and confusion in most of the men's faces, and tried another approach.

"You know what I did as the Soul-Drinker's Slave: torture, rape, and murder. My only understanding of life was to please the Master." Now the men were nodding in recognition. Feeling encouraged, Kyr continued. "But after I spent time with Rajani and other kind friends, I came to understand the terrible harm and evil that I had done as a Slave. I nearly went mad with remorse." The prisoners stirred uneasily, shoulders hunched up with guilt. Softly, Kyr said, "Yes, it is difficult to think of the crimes we have committed, the people we have hurt."

Kyr hoped they would understand what he was about to say. "At Zhovanya's Sanctuary, I was taken in and offered help and healing despite—no—*because* of my crimes." He sighed, remembering the painful process of facing and revealing his crimes to Naran. "It was difficult, but with a lot of help from the guides there, I faced my own crimes and was deeply blessed by Zhovanya's forgiveness and love." An anguish of longing silenced him for a few moments, a longing to be there again in Her Temple, in Her Heart.

The men were watching him with anxious or wary eyes, so he took a breath and went on. "And now I am working to forgive myself."

The men looked puzzled. Craith protested, "You have no need!"

Kyr shook his head. "I have chosen to atone for my crimes, if it takes the rest of my life. What happened here is part of my Atonement. And so I have done my best to accept it, to soften, and to forgive." He couldn't keep from adding, "Though many times during my captivity here, I would have given almost anything to escape or die." Several men sighed and nodded, their faces softening. Kyr realized that sharing his pain had touched their darkened hearts more than anything else had.

"I'm so sorry...," Craith said in a choked voice.

Kyr held up his had to forestall further apologies. "I forgive you, Craith, and all of you." With a rueful smile, he added, "I can even forgive Gauday—most days."

"But how *can* you be so forgiving?" protested Craith. "Gauday tormented you terribly!"

"Despite the terrible things I did as a Slave, Zhovanya forgave me and took me into Her Heart. I have promised to pass on this blessing, no matter how difficult it may be." Kyr bowed his head, a painful lump in his throat. His heart was in turmoil with memories, some terrible, some sacred. He took several deep breaths. Then he looked up and said with quiet passion, "Zhovanya loves *all* Her children, even you, even me. She *will* welcome you if you choose the hard path." The men in the circle were looking lost and forlorn, as if unable to imagine such a kind fate for themselves.

"Of course, you can choose the easy path of despair, blame, rage, or hatred, but that only leads into darkness—even madness, as Gauday's example shows. Or you can choose the hard path, as I did. I assure you, it will be worth more than you can imagine. It's like Craith said: coming out of a small, poisonous dungeon into a wide, bright world where kindness, light, and love are possible." Kyr knew he spoke the truth, yet tears filled his eyes. *Zhovanya, please! Cleanse me of Gauday's poison. Help me return to your bright world!*

Meanwhile, Craith leaned forward, his fingers gripping his knees. "Listen to him! You saw. Kyr is the proof! You know he can teach us, help us leave the dungeon that the cursed Soul-Drinker dragged us into as young boys. Don't you remember your family? Your mother? Didn't you know something better before the Gatherers grabbed you? I did." Craith went on to share a few memories of his childhood. The other men listened and nodded, except for Jorem, the former Slave, who looked puzzled and sad.

While Craith spoke, Kyr surreptitiously wiped his eyes, and tried to calm down. His own emotions were clouding his mind, and he knew he needed help. *Dear Goddess, show me how to proceed. How do I help these men?* A breath of cool clarity touched his mind, and the next step became clear. Craith had finished his story and there was a pensive silence in the room.

"Thank you, Craith, for reminding us that life holds much more than the Soul-Drinker allowed us to know." Kyr gave Craith a grateful smile. "Now, men, if you choose this hard path, here's what we will do: we will meet regularly to talk of our crimes, our pain, our remorse, our blessings. You will come to our meditations in this chapel every morning and evening. You will learn the forgiveness chant and repeat it to yourself throughout the day. You will begin to be kind and helpful to others, and to soften and step back when you want to rage at or hurt someone, or yourself." Remembering the first time he had spoken with Naran at the Sanctuary, he added, "You must also agree to three rules: No secrets. No lies. No violence to others or yourself."

Brol and Jarki crossed their arms over their chests, and the others looked dismayed. "Gods and demons," breathed Jorem, "you don't ask much, do you?"

"Yes," Kyr said. "It is harder by far than anything you have ever done, but I will help you as much as I can. And I know Zhovanya will too."

Like a soft cloud of light, Zhovanya's Presence became tangible in the room, bringing a deep quietness.

For a little while, Kyr sat with bowed head, allowing the men time to sense Her Presence if they could, and to think about their choice.

Then he slowly looked around the circle. "Who will choose this hard path? Remember, no matter what you have done, you can be blessed by Zhovanya's forgiveness and love."

Desperate as a man at the bottom of an empty well, Craith grasped the rope of light Kyr had tossed down. "I choose the hard path." He smiled with relief.

Jorem looked at his hands as if they were covered in blood. Then he looked up and nodded emphatically. "Yes, I, too."

The twins, Kinar and Zurano, glanced at each other and spoke in unison. "We also."

Kyr looked at Brol and Jarki, but they sat in silence with their arms crossed. "I am sad to see you turn away from this path. You are sure you cannot join us?" They would not meet his eyes.

"Please don't let the Master's evil rule your lives any longer. Join us." They shook their heads, refusing the hard path for the third time.

"Alright, let me know if you change your minds." Kyr sighed and gestured for them to leave. They made their way out of the chapel, and back to their familiar prison.

As the door closed, Kyr looked at the four remaining men, fellow penitents on the hard path, and unexpected joy filled his heart. His eyes alight, he said, "Welcome, brothers! It will be difficult, but I promise that your souls will be so glad!" They smiled with him, looking reassured.

"Alright, let's begin." Kyr taught them the chant and its meaning. Then he began the chant. "Zhovanya nara lo, Zhovanya nara lo, Zhovanya nara lo." Hesitant and shy, first Craith and then Jorem, Zurano, and Kinar joined in. Woven into their chanting, the chapel was filled with silent exultation, as if the Goddess Herself were singing.

That evening, when Kyr brought the four penitents to the chapel, many of the villagers present angrily objected to allowing the prisoners to join the meditation. Kyr said firmly, "These men have chosen the path of atonement and redemption that Zhovanya offers, *even* to former Slaves, such as *myself*." At this reminder, most of the objectors sat down, looking sheepish.

A handful still stood, ready to argue with Kyr, but he straightened to his full height. "If these men cannot come here to meditate, neither can I." The last of the objectors sat down then, unwilling to drive the Liberator out of his own chapel, though a few still looked mutinous.

"Let's remember the meaning of our chant." Kyr said. "Zhovanya nara lo. Zhovanya forgives us *all*." He sat down before the altar, and began. Soon the chapel was filled with the resonant sound of the chant arising from all those present. Seeing the four prisoners taking part in the devotions, Kyr's heart lifted with the thought that perhaps all he had suffered truly was for a worthy purpose. By bringing people into Her Presence here in this small chapel, perhaps he was becoming Her Vessel, as the Goddess had asked him to be on the mountain ledge at the Sanctuary.

The next day, after morning devotions at the chapel, Kyr returned to the porch outside his room and found Friend there. He sat beside her and hugged her close, soaking in her loyalty and love, until she wriggled in protest. When he released her, she bounded off to join a pack of dogs barking at a departing caravan of villagers with their horse-drawn carts, heading home now that Gauday's fate had been decided. Trailing behind the dust of the wagons, a half-dozen chained prisoners walked, guarded by two mounted Companions.

Alarmed, Kyr jumped up and looked around the yard. Rajani was not in evidence, but Kuron was nearby, bent over by his dapple-gray gelding, cleaning its hoof. Kyr hurried over to him. "Kuron, where's Rajani?"

Kuron set the horse's hoof down and straightened up, an odd expression on his face, as if he were seeing a marvelous stranger. "The commander went back to his office, sir."

Kyr thanked him and left, puzzled by Kuron's formal, almost reverent tone. Approaching Gauday's former quarters, now Rajani's office, Kyr's legs grew heavy, and he slowed to a stop, sick with old terror. He took a deep breath, dragged his mind back to the present, and went in.

He found Rajani immersed in a conversation with the new governor, a dark-skinned woman wearing a long, white caftan and layers of gold necklaces. Medari had told him that her name was Ayesha. Not wanting to interrupt, and pulled by morbid curiosity, Kyr slipped past them and into the hallway beyond.

Passing by the bedroom where he had spent so many miserable nights with Gauday, he continued down the hall to the door that led to the small red-lit room, the scene of his worst torments. His scars began throbbing as he stood before that door. Finally, he reached out a trembling hand and opened it.

The light was a dim yellow from a small window, now uncovered, not the lurid red he remembered. Nothing lurked in the corners but stacks of wooden boxes and burlap bags. He stepped inside, closed the door, and burst into laughter. "Oh, gods!" he spluttered. "Look what they've done! They've turned it into a *storeroom*! It's so—oh, gods!—so ordinary, so dull!" He sank down onto one of the larger boxes, still chortling. But his laughter died away as he realized that Gauday's chapel of horror and misery still existed—in his nightmares. "Merciless gods," he murmured, "will I ever escape this place?" Whispers filled his mind. *"You're mine, boy, mine forever. Come to me. Release me. Take me away from here."*

"Curse it!" These whispers were not mere memories. He'd let his guard down and Gauday had invaded his mind again. Shaking his head at his carelessness, he began chanting quietly. "Zhovanya nara lo, Zhovanya nara lo." Refusing to pay any attention to his tormentor's insidious whispering, he continued singing until he had banished Gauday's whispers and reached some serenity. Then he let the chant die away, and looked around, making himself see what was real now: a half-empty storeroom holding nothing but boxes and sacks. With this weapon of truth to counter the encroaching past, he left, closing that door firmly behind him.

He found Rajani at his desk, buried in parchments and scrolls. "Sorry to interrupt your work, but I have a question."

"Ah, Kyr, good! I need an excuse to get out of here. I'm suffocating in ink and dust. Let's go." Rajani emerged from his nest and they went outdoors. "What do you want to know?" Rajani asked as they began to stroll along the boardwalk.

"I saw a caravan leaving with six prisoners. Where are they taking them? What's happening to Gauday's men?"

"Oh, sorry, Kyr. I didn't want to bother you. You had enough to deal with during the Days of Testimony." Rajani went on, "The Wise-women's Council decided that each village will take a few prisoners as indentured labor to help rebuild what they destroyed. New barns, rebuilt homes, and good crops will hardly compensate for the lives that were taken or shattered, but it's better than nothing."

"You aren't sending murderers into the villages, are you?"

"No, no. The vicious ones, mostly Slaves, will be sent to a prison in the desert." Rajani's forbidding tone told Kyr that those men would never leave that prison.

"Ah." Kyr thought sadly, *They'll never have a chance to redeem their souls.* But it was out of his hands and, with a sigh, he consigned them to the mercy of the Goddess. "How will the others be treated?"

"The villagers agreed to treat the prisoners properly. They'll be given adequate food, clothes, shelter, and rest, and they won't be beaten as long as they work hard and behave well. They can even earn their freedom, after they have served for twelve years. But if a prisoner causes trouble, he'll be turned over to us, and we'll decide what to do with him then. If he commits an actual crime, he will be subject to the laws of the village. Alright, Kyr?"

"Yes, that's good. What about the prisoners who have chosen the hard path, my penitents?"

"Don't worry," Rajani smiled. "They're coming with us to Ravenvale."

"Good. Thanks, Rajani." By now, they'd reached the main gates of the fort.

Rajani looked longingly at the trail into the forest, but stopped by the gate. "Well, I'd better get back to work. I'm trying to finish up everything so we can leave after Gauday's execution. By all the gods, I swear there are more details to tend to than stars in the sky!" He headed back to his office.

Kyr returned to the porch by his room, thinking about Gauday's men being sent out to the villages. *They're still slaves, but it will be better than anything they've known before: honest work, fair treatment. Rajani is doing well at building his system of justice.* He sat down and leaned back against the wall. *Ah, Goddess! I'll be glad to leave this whitewashed hellhole.*

Two days before Gauday's execution, the fort was crowded with people come to witness Gauday's demise. Kyr was making his way through the noisy, colorful throng to the chapel for morning meditation. He was saddened by the general atmosphere of vengeful jubilation.

The chapel was half-full. Kyr was glad to see all four penitents there. As those present joined him in the chanting, Zhovanya's Presence grew strong. Attracted by their singing, visitors trickled into the chapel. Some

277

stood for a few moments, looked around in curiosity, or frowned in bafflement, and left. Others smiled and found places to sit, and joined in the chanting.

During the silent meditation period, grief filled Kyr's heart—grief for Gauday and all those whose lives had been perverted by the Master's evil. He feared that the cycle of hatred and vengeance was continuing, for there were many who had not been drawn to Zhovanya's grace, who had come to the fort merely to celebrate Gauday's execution. *"What can I do, Zhovanya?"* he prayed silently. *"How can this cycle be ended?"* All that came to him was to try again to speak of Her blessing of forgiveness and mercy.

At the end of the meditation, as people began to stir, Kyr rose. "I would like to say something. Will you stay a moment?" He was surprised when everyone kept their seats and waited respectfully for him to go on.

"You know the Zhovanaya chant means 'Zhovanya forgives us all,' do you not?" Many nodded, and Kyr continued. "I want to say that Her forgiveness includes *everyone*, even Gauday." He took a steadying breath, and added, "Even the Soul-Drinker."

People glanced at each other, puzzled and disturbed. Kyr saw their confusion, but was impelled to speak the truth that he had so painfully won. "Zhovanya sees the truth hidden in each soul, knows the pain that drives some to depravity, evil, or madness. She taught me to see with Her Eyes, and I saw into Gauday's soul. What I saw is beyond any suffering you or I can imagine. For all he has done, Gauday's soul writhes in utter torment, unable to rest for even a moment."

Kyr gazed at the stunned audience, wondering if they could understand his next request. "I ask you to join me in praying for Gauday's soul to return to Zhovanya, to be washed clean by Her forgiveness. And for all the former Slaves and soldiers to find redemption and healing, as I did."

While many gazed at him reverently, others were frowning and muttering to their neighbors.

"Those who do not wish to remain may leave now." Kyr's voice had a slight edge of steel in it. A dozen new-comers stomped out, looking stormy. The rest awaited his next words. Kyr was happy to see that Rajani was among them.

"Zhovanya taught me to soften my heart, to forgive, to see beyond my own pain, beyond the behavior of those who hurt me, to *their* pain and its source." Everyone was watching him intently, the four penitents most of all. "I could not have done this without Zhovanya's help." Many looked relieved that they could not expect such compassion from themselves. But then Kyr added, "If you ask, She will help you see as She does." And at this, many looked away, discomforted.

With gentle zeal, Kyr pleaded, "All of us have been hurt by the Soul-Drinker or by Gauday. If we follow the easy path of blame and revenge, we will end up in an endless nightmare of hatred and anger, punishment and retaliation. Please, join me in following Zhovanya's way of forgiveness. And I ask you to try to bring Her mercy to the prisoners sent to your village: forgive them and help them forgive themselves." He smiled. "And don't forget to forgive yourselves for any short-comings of your own."

His words fell as a blow to many a prideful, angry, or grieving heart. A half-dozen more left the chapel, and Kyr sadly watched them depart. Knowing nothing else to do, he began the chant again. Some joined him because their hearts recognized his wisdom. Some joined him out of respect and admiration, without a deep understanding of the truth of his words. Others did so merely wanting to be seen to be pious. Yet as they chanted, Kyr and others sent silent prayers for their former oppressors, and Zhovanya's Presence became palpable, bringing peace to all those who had remained.

After a time, Her Presence eased and Kyr let the chant die away. After a moment of silence, Rajani stood and gave Kyr a deep bow of respect before returning to his duties. At that, everyone rose. A number of people followed Rajani out. Kyr was surprised when others came forward to thank him. Some offered embraces. He couldn't help tensing against anticipated pain or encroachment, but he made himself endure these well-meant hugs. As soon as he could, he headed for his room, trying to shake off his tension and return to Zhovanya's peace.

*Well, I've done what I could to speak of Zhovanya's mercy. It's out of my hands now, thank all the gods!* He trudged up the steps to find Friend sitting on the porch, awaiting him. He knelt and wrapped his arms around her, burying his face in the silky fur of her neck. "You are more forgiving than a lot of the people here, aren't you, girl?" He snorted at an odd thought. "I guess we're just Zhovanya's loyal dogs, you and I."

279

# Chapter 27

# Hand of Compassion

Late the next morning, he stumbled sleepily into the infirmary, and found Medari sitting alone, head bowed. On the table before him sat a bottle of amber liquor and a glass, half-full of the same.

Kyr grabbed a stool and sat beside the healer. "Gods, Medari, what is it?" The healer looked up, his eyes red-rimmed and glassy. He picked up his glass and drained it. Grabbing another glass from the shelf just behind him, he filled it and shoved it toward Kyr. "Here, you'll need this."

"Just tell me."

Medari shrugged and refilled his own glass. Twisting it around and around, the healer stared blindly at Kyr. In a dull, flat voice, he said, "Someone just arrived from my village. She brought news. They're dead. That whoreson killed them all, six months ago!"

A dreadful chill prickled Kyr's skin. "Your—family?"

Medari nodded and gulped down half the liquor in his glass.

"You mean, all this time, he trapped us with a lie?" Moving like a wooden puppet, Kyr drained his own glass. "And I've just been praying for his filthy soul!" The amber fire burned down his throat and ignited red rage. He jumped to his feet and hurled the empty glass at the wall and it exploded in a hundred pieces.

At this, Medari's daze shattered, and he broke down sobbing. Seeing this, Kyr forced his own rage down, and turned to his ally and friend. He could find no words remotely adequate to address this malevolent betrayal. All he could do was keep vigil with Medari as he sobbed in great, choking, body-shaking gasps.

It was one of the hardest things he had done, keeping back his own rage and grief, in order to stand witness to a friend's. Kyr longed to steal a sword, and hack Gauday to pieces. *Merciless gods! If I did that, I'd be as bad as he is.* He shook his head like a bear at bay, so torn he felt as if he were flying apart. *I know Dekani is tired out. But I need help!* He focused his mind and called, *"Dekani, Dekani!"*

A moment later, Dekani appeared in Kyr's mind, and quickly absorbed the news about Medari's family. *"I know this is a terrible betrayal, son. Of course, you are furious. But as always, the only true help is in remembering Zhovanya's love and forgiveness for us all. Don't let this throw you off your path. Here now, I'll do what I can."* He raised his hands and sent a soothing flow of deep blue through Kyr's mind and heart. With this help, Kyr managed to stay by Medari's side, fighting the red tide of vengeful rage, and returning his mind to the forgiveness chant whenever his mind lapsed into vindictive fantasies.

At last, Medari subsided into a deathly silence. After a few moments, he shambled into his own room, taking the bottle with him.

Alone, Kyr grabbed Medari's half-full glass and drained it. His mind ran over and over what Gauday had done to them both. *Now I understand those who left the chapel when I spoke of forgiveness. Gods and demons! How I hate Gauday for this!*

A strange rattling sound made Kyr look down. His hands were shaking, and knocking the empty glass against the table. With an effort of will, he set the glass aside, and took a deep breath. *What are we going to do? What can I do to help Medari?* He found no answers, but he had to do *something*. He jumped up and went to find Rajani.

"That heartless monster!" Rajani slammed his fists onto the table, knocking over a stack of papers and sending quill pens flying. "Gods curse his soul!" He took a breath and unclenched his fists. "How is Medari taking this?"

"What do you think? He's drinking himself into a stupor," Kyr snapped, then added more softly, "But he did cry for a while, at least." Kyr choked back a sob of his own. "Gods, Rajani, I couldn't think of a thing to say to him."

"No, of course not. What can one say in the face of such vicious treachery?"

"There must be something we can do for him!"

Rajani thought for a few moments. "Well, the execution is tomorrow. We could offer Medari the chance to perform it."

282

"No! He'd be betraying his Healer's Oath. That would only add to Medari's burdens." His own rage arose, cold and clear as ice. "But *I* could do it."

Startled by Kyr's lethal tone, Rajani said carefully, "At the Sanctuary, you said you wanted no more blood on your hands, remember?"

"I've got to do SOMETHING!" Kyr erupted, his rage suddenly burning hot.

"I understand. But as you said yourself just yesterday morning, we mustn't walk the path of hatred and vengeance. It will only lead us back into hell."

Kyr stared at Rajani, stunned to have his own words coming back at him. Then his shoulders sagged. "Gods, was it only yesterday morning?" It seemed an aeon ago that he had been praying for Gauday's tormented soul. He groped unsteadily for a chair. Rajani guided him to one of the shabby, overstuffed chairs by the hearth, and took the other chair. Kyr slumped back in the chair, feeling ancient with tragedy.

"You're right, Rajani. Or I am," he said tiredly. "I can't kill him out of rage and vengeance, can I? It would go against everything I have learned, make me just like him." He buried his face in his hands. "Merciless gods! This nightmare never ends!"

"No, Kyr. It's almost over," Rajani was almost begging Kyr to believe him. "We'll put an end to him tomorrow, and then we'll go home."

"Home...," Kyr whispered, with such baffled longing that tears sprang to Rajani's eyes.

"You'll see. Life will be better there." Rajani sighed at the inadequacy of his words, hoping they were true. The prophecy did predict that Kyr had one more hell to face, but Rajani had no idea what it would be.

Kyr straightened and looked at Rajani silently for few moments. "Better? I hope so, but it's hard to imagine." His voice held fathoms of weariness and grief. "Well, I've got get back to Medari."

Trudging back toward the infirmary, Kyr glanced toward Gauday's prison. His fury lurked, demanding vengeance; but it was now partially eclipsed by a great sadness at the cruel tragedy that had entangled so many souls in such pain and suffering. His only comfort—and it was a thin one—was recalling the first time he had seen Zhovanya. She had been dancing in the Temple at the Sanctuary, embracing joy and sorrow, cruelty and beauty, love and hatred. "Zhovanya nara lo," he whispered. "I am Yours. Show me what I must do."

What came to him then was a memory of Jolanya at the end of the Kailithara, asking him to pass on the gifts of healing and compassion which he had received, and his promise to do so. And so he asked himself, *What would Jolanya have me do? Ah, gods. She would not want me to let my rage control me. I must let it go.* It seemed almost impossible, but he resolved to try.

Medari's door was closed and there was no sign or sound of him. Kyr stood in the main room, wondering if he should intrude on the healer's grief. Taking a breath, he went quietly to Medari's door and carefully opened it a crack. Medari was curled up on his cot, clutching the empty bottle, in a deep, sodden sleep. Kyr gently closed the door, filled the tea kettle and hung it on the hearth-hook over the bed of hot coals. He settled onto a stool by the table.

"For you, Jolanya," he whispered, closing his eyes. And he began watching his breath—still flowing in, flowing out—despite it all. Tears came, and he watched them fall, one by one. Rage flickered and flared, demanding action. He noticed it, and let it go, keeping his focus on his breath. When he reached a place of some quietness, he began repeating the chant silently. Slowly, everything else faded away.

In this place of peace, he witnessed his grief, anger, and discouragement with gentle compassion. And he asked again, *"Zhovanya, show me what You want me to do."* Then all was silence.

And into this silence came Her Presence, enfolding him in a profound stillness. And into this stillness came Her silent questions. *"WILL YOU BE THE HAND OF COMPASSION? WILL YOU FREE HIS SOUL?"*

For a time, Kyr remained deep in Her stillness. Then the sound of the kettle boiling brought him gently back to ordinary awareness. Rising, he made a pot of tea, using the calming herbs that Medari often had used in teas for him. His movements flowed from the stillness, his thoughts from Her silence. *Yes, it must be me. No one else knows Gauday's soul as I do. Only I can act with compassion. Only I can free his soul from the cycle of hatred and vengeance.*

He set out a mug and waited. In a while, Medari stumbled forth and went out to the latrine. On his return, Kyr steered him to sit at the table and poured him some tea, putting a hot mug between the healer's cold hands. Medari, looking as if he had aged twenty years in one day, gripped the mug and slowly sipped the soporific tisane, staring blearily at nothing. "Thanks for the tea," he mumbled. "I need to sleep."

"I will end it," Kyr said with quiet certainty.

"Good." The healer drained his mug, and shuffled back to his room, cumbrous with grief and exhaustion.

Kyr sat a while yet, then rose and sought out Rajani once again. He found him outside, supervising the building of a scaffolding. "No, no," the commander snapped. "The trap door must open instantly so his neck will break. I don't want some damn spectacle tomorrow. Just a quick kill." The workmen bowed and returned to their labors.

"Rajani," Kyr said.

The Warrior Mage turned, and a look of surprise came over his face. "What happened, Kyr? You seem different, so calm and steady."

"I asked Zhovanya what She would have me do." He closed his eyes for a moment, recalling Her fierce compassion. "I must do it."

"Do what?" Rajani asked in a mystified tone.

"Perform the execution." No rage, no grief marred the stillness of Kyr's bearing. "May I borrow your short sword?"

"But Kyr, hanging is the best way." Rajani gestured toward the scaffolding rising up in the center of the courtyard. "It's quick, clean, and no one's hands need be tainted with that monster's blood."

"I must do it personally."

Rajani frowned. "I thought we agreed that acting from hatred and vengeance is not the way."

"True. It must be done with compassion in order for his soul to be freed from hatred." He smiled grimly at a sudden realization. "And, as you have named me, I am the Liberator." Kyr's gaze was as dispassionate as an eagle's. His words rang with ineffable truth.

The Warrior Mage stared at Kyr in awe. "By all that's sacred, Zhovanya doesn't ask much from you, does She?"

A soft smile touched Kyr's lips. "I am Hers."

"You know how to make a quick kill?"

"I had a lot of practice as a Slave."

Rajani's face went red. "Ah, of course...." He turned back to the workers. "There's been a change of plans. Tear this down." With much consternated muttering, the workers began undoing what they had just done, eyeing Kyr curiously.

The evening before the execution, Kyr sat tensely on the edge of his bed in his room, while Friend slept curled up on the rag rug before the hearth. He couldn't eat, and he knew he wouldn't sleep. His Goddess-given serenity had abandoned him, and his mind was awhirl with anxious dread. Underneath that lay his ferocious anger at Gauday for wantonly killing Medari's family.

"Ah, Zhovanya," he muttered. "Why must Medari suffer this grievous loss? He is a good man, a healer!" But there was no answer, and Kyr couldn't keep his bitter thoughts at bay. *Perhaps She does not care! Perhaps She sees our suffering as merely part of Her Dance.* An even darker thought intruded. *Why does this torment never end? Perhaps She wants me to suffer forever?*

He sighed and scratched his new beard. *I can understand that. I have much to atone for. But why Medari, why all these innocents whom Gauday has hurt so much? I don't understand that at all! How can She allow all this pain?* A bolt of rage broke through his control and he jumped to his feet. *Gods and demons, I hate him! I'll kill him slowly, make him suffer! Now!* He started for the door, but Friend jumped up and barked, forehead wrinkled in concern. Startled out of his trance of fury, Kyr turned back and knelt to hug her. With a deep sigh, he murmured, "You're right, girl. This is not the way."

He released her and moved to kneel before his small altar. *Goddess, forgive me! I am Yours. I know Your ways are not for me to understand. I will do as You have asked. But please, please help me release my anger. I cannot free Gauday's soul when I am filled with hatred.*

Again, there was no response. The world felt empty of divinity. Knowing nothing else to do, Kyr resolved to spend the night in meditation and prayer in the chapel. He pulled a blanket off his bed and rolled it up. Kneeling, he touched foreheads with Friend for a moment and she licked his face. "Sorry, Friend. You must stay here tonight without me." Her dark eyes seemed deep with loving awareness, and she made no protest as he shut her in his room.

In the chapel, he sat on a pillow before the altar, wrapping the blanket around his shoulders, as much for comfort as for warmth. Lighting the candle, he set himself to meditate. But rage, grief, and horror welled up so strongly that he could only beg, "Zhovanya, guide me! Zhovanya ganarali, Zhovanya ganarali, Zhovanya ganarali."

After a time, exhaustion and despair overcame him, and he curled up under his blanket, sure he was incapable of carrying out the execution with the necessary compassion. Staring at the steadily burning candle, he whispered, "I'm sorry, I can't do it, Zhovanya. I can't, not after he butchered Medari's family so needlessly, and lied about it to keep us trapped in his madness. Goddess forgive me, I hate him!"

Kyr relaxed then, giving up the wearisome struggle against his rage and hatred. He let himself imagine slowly torturing Gauday to death, as he had learned so well to do for the Soul-Drinker; imagined Gauday's pleas and shrieks; saw his eyes slowly going empty as he died. Then he felt the emptiness in his own soul at what he had done, if only in his own imagination. Oddly, this allowed him to slip into a peaceful doze. And then, like a whispered benediction, Her gift of counsel came back to him. *"SOFTEN."*

Surrendering even further, he sat up and resumed his meditation, breathing through his heart, allowing himself to soften, allowing his anguish to flood through him. His grief and rage erupted in a wordless wail, a lament for all the suffering he had known and caused, for Medari and all the villagers, for Gauday and all the prisoners. With all the suffering in the world, he feared his lamentation would last forever. But soon enough, the flood of pain drained away, leaving him silent and empty.

In the deep void of silence, Kyr saw that he was once again insisting on his own will, insisting that things should be different, should be the way he wanted them to be. He remembered that when Gauday's tortures were driving him to despair, his salvation had been to let go of all ideas of who he was or what he need endure. He remembered his promise to bear a lifetime of pain, if that was Zhovanya's Will. With a deep sigh, he let go again of his stubborn resistance.

Like a river of blessings bursting through a dam, Her Presence poured upon him, returning Her serene stillness to his soul. Seeing again with Her eyes, he knew that even Gauday's treachery was part of the unfathomable Tapestry of Life that She was weaving with Her sacred Dance of defilement and holiness, suffering and bliss. And he knew that he could carry out his next step in the Dance.

At first light, Kyr returned to his room, moving in an inner oasis of stillness. With a reproachful look, Friend let him know what she thought of him locking her in his room alone. "I know. I'm sorry, girl," he said, hugging and petting her. Reassured by his quietness, she calmed down. "Go on, girl. Go on over to the kitchen and find your breakfast." She wagged her tail and bounded off.

He knocked gently on Medari's door but there was no response. Bowing his head, he prayed for heart's ease for his grieving friend. Then he washed and dressed in his oldest clothes, the gray ones Gauday had given him after the rains came, now ragged and stained.

After a solitary breakfast, Kyr started toward the chapel for the usual morning meditation, but stopped on the porch in dismay. The courtyard was a slow swirl of color and movement, full of people who had gathered to celebrate the demise of a cruel tyrant. They had come from all over, wearing their traditional finery (as they had for the Cleansing): red, green, or blue tunics; white dresses bordered with colorful embroidery; striped turbans; wide skirts in patterns of orange, yellow, and green; red boots; and gold armbands flashing in the new summer sun.

Yet it was more subdued than the Cleansing gathering. No children were present, and there was an ominous tension in the air. People greeted old friends with quiet hugs, or spoke nervously with their neighbors. A few sobbed on a friend's shoulder. Others stood alone, glowering at the center of the courtyard, where a new, tall post had been set into the ground.

Kyr steeled himself, and, staying on the boardwalk that ran along three sides of the courtyard to avoid the crowd, walked quietly to the chapel. No one in the crowd noticed him, a silent man dressed in shabby gray clothes.

The chapel was empty, but he knelt before the altar and began. "Zhovanya nara lo, Zhovanya nara lo, Zhovanya nara lo." Soon Rajani, the penitents, and others of Zhovanya's most faithful devotees filled the chapel and joined the chant. Their steady chanting wove a tranquil thread above the subdued chatter of the gathering in the courtyard. Zhovanya, grave and impartial in Her fierce compassion, danced unseen but clearly sensed by most of those in the chapel. When the chant ended, there was a solemn hush as everyone remained absorbed in Her Presence.

But then the noise from the crowd outside grew into a loud growl. A woman shrieked, "There he is! There's the beast that killed my baby!" A man thundered, "You monster! You stole my boy!" Booted feet marched, and Jakar bawled, "Make way! Make way!"

In the chapel, Rajani said quietly, "They are bringing Gauday out now. Are you ready?" Kyr, steeped in Zhovanya's silence, merely nodded.

At first, few among the crowd outside noticed when Rajani and Kyr emerged from the chapel, followed by the two dozen followers of Zhovanya who had joined them there. But a ripple of silence spread out through the entire crowd as the group of devotees walked toward the center of the courtyard.

There Gauday now stood, gagged and bound tightly to the new post, guarded by two large Companions, Kurano and Jakar, in their dark-green Companion uniforms. Gauday's expression was at once angry, defiant, and contemptuous, but Kyr could see the fear behind his defiance.

The somber Warrior Mage took his position on a small dais near the post. His stern, commanding presence hushed the crowd, and then he spoke. "We are here to witness an execution. This is a solemn occasion, for it is a dreadful thing to take a life, even for just cause. Please remain quiet." Then he stepped down, pulled his short sword from its sheath, and handed it to Kyr. At this, many in the crowd gasped.

Kyr took the sword from Rajani. The leather-wrapped hilt in his hand and the lethal reality of the sword shocked through him like cold lightning. His breath stopped, and he closed his eyes. Then he saw Zhovanya dancing as She had when he first saw Her in the chapel at the Sanctuary: birthing, celebrating, suffering, laughing, dying. Her fierce, loving smile was just for him, and he felt Her Arms around him.

Austere and serene—Goddess-touched—Kyr stepped forward, sword in hand, and spoke to Gauday. "Zhovanya has bidden me to send you to Her this day. Her grace and forgiveness are infinite. Do not be afraid."

As he placed the sword under his tormenter's sternum and angled it toward his heart, he locked eyes with Gauday. At first, Gauday glared at him with hatred and scorn. But then, as Gauday felt the cold steel of the sword touch his chest, fear filled his pale blue eyes. Through their partial bond, Kyr sensed the turmoil of terror, rage, and madness that filled Gauday's mind, but it did not breach his Goddess-given serenity.

Softly, he said, "I do this not out of vengeance but out of compassion, hoping to free your soul from the brutal cycle of fear, hatred, and revenge." Despite his words, he could feel a taint of vengeance creeping into his heart. For his own sake as well as Gauday's, he closed his eyes and prayed silently for guidance. *"Zhovanya, ganarali, Zhovanya, ganarali, Zhovanya, ganarali."*

A delicate touch on his own eyes revealed a deeper truth. Behind Gauday's fear and anger, there was deep relief, as if a great burden was about to be lifted from his soul. And then Kyr saw Gauday in a whole new light.

The great tapestry of life-threads that Zhovanya had shown him filled his mind, Gauday's thread paralleling his own. Kyr saw that Gauday's life was part of the sacred, relentless Dance of light and dark, life and death, evil and love. Just as he had shaped his sculpture of Love with sharp chisel strokes, each person sculpted every other person in his or her life. Though Gauday's chisel strokes were crueler than most, Kyr still found in his heart love for this man who had sacrificed so much to test him, refine him, and sculpt him into becoming the Vessel that Zhovanya needed him to be.

Meeting Gauday's furious, terrified gaze, Kyr said to him, "You have been a harsh teacher—and I thank you." In that perilous, sacred moment, all of Gauday's madness, rage, and fear dropped away. He returned Kyr's gaze calmly, soul to soul, and gave him the slightest of nods.

Kyr knew then that his tormenter was ready. "May you know Her forgiveness." With a quick, strong upward thrust, he made the killing stroke, keeping his eyes on Gauday's. Kyr saw Gauday's shock and pain—but just at the end, as his life ebbed from his body, a brief flicker of surprised joy. For a timeless moment, they were both bathed in the golden radiance of Zhovanya's Presence, as She welcomed Her lost child Home.

There was a pendant silence, as if the entire crowd had drawn an in-breath and no one had yet breathed out. Kyr stood there with Gauday's heart-blood washing over his hands and arms, until the light was gone from Gauday's eyes. Then he slowly drew the sword out of the body, and said quietly, "He is free."

# Chapter 28

# Aftershocks

Gauday's face was peaceful in death as it had never been in life. Kyr stood and stared at the body. The sword dangled from his lax hand, dripping blood onto the ground. The peace and serenity that had filled him before the execution drained away with Gauday's life blood. *"Ah, Goddess!"* he wailed silently. *"Why do You take him and not me?"* Bitter tears sparkled, tracing a clean path through the splatters of gore on his face.

Where there had been a link with his tormentor and Slave brother, now there was emptiness. Into that emptiness came a cloud of darkness. A foul odor invaded his nose, mouth, and throat. He started coughing, and backed away a few steps. Rajani handed him a flask and he filled his mouth with the harsh liquor, swished it around, and swallowed it. The vile taste receded, and he took some deep breaths, feeling shaky and disturbed.

Few in the crowd knew what to make of the gentle words he had spoken aloud to Gauday, nor of his slow tears. Many were awed by what they took as tears of grief and compassion for the madman who had tormented him for so many months. Even though most of them had come expecting to cheer and celebrate the death of a vicious predator, no one wanted to be the first to break the silence that followed Kyr's words.

Almost no one.

*"Free?"* Medari cried, his voice shaking with rage and anguish. Usually neat and composed, he was disheveled and wild-eyed with grief. "You have freed that monster from his corrupt life—which is far better than he deserved—but *we* will never be free from the harm he did to us!" Medari's furious words echoed Kyr's own bitter thoughts and sent an ominous chill clear down to his bones.

"YAAAH!" Many voices screamed their agreement with Medari. A stone flew through the air, hitting the corpse with a thick thud that unleashed the beast of vengeance. A handful of men began scouring the courtyard for stones. The devotees shook their heads in dismay, and Craith shouted, "NO! This is not Zhovanya's way!" But the angry men began hurling the stones at the corpse. Kyr flinched at each sickening thud, downcast that so many had not heeded his demonstration of forgiveness and compassion.

"STOP!" Rajani roared, and gestured to the Companions. They immediately moved into the crowd, confiscating stones, subduing the few men who resisted. Aghast at what his words had unleashed, Medari backed away, turned, and hastened back to his room. Kyr thought vaguely of following him, but his limbs were so heavy he couldn't move.

The Warrior Mage took hold of his blackwood wand hidden inside his jacket, and muttered "Shai li!" Suddenly, he seemed to grow larger and brighter, drawing every eye. He spoke in a voice of calm authority. "We will not have anarchy and viciousness here. Khailaz will be ruled by law, not mobs or tyrants. Your rage at this despicable torturer is understandable and just. But he has paid the full price for his crimes. That is the end of it."

Rajani paused, shining even brighter, and threw out his arms, now speaking in a hearty tone. "Let us celebrate our new order of freedom and fairness!" As he had arranged ahead of time, a collection of fiddlers, flutists, and drummers were set up on a porch across the compound. At his nod, they broke into a lilting tune of hope and jubilation. The crowd applauded, and turned away to the feast that lay waiting by the kitchen, ignoring Gauday's corpse and his dazed and bloody executioner.

The Warrior Mage turned to Jakar. "Get the body down and bring it to the infirmary right away. We don't need to leave it here as a reminder or target for further misbehavior." Then he stepped to Kyr's side, gently took the bloody sword out of his hand, and gave it to Kurano. "Clean this off and put it away safely until I can do a cleansing ritual with it."

Kyr's knees started to buckle, but Rajani put an arm around his shoulders and guided him to the well. Lorya awaited them with soap, rags, and a bucket of water. Kyr sat on the edge of the well, still weeping slow, silent tears as they washed off the blood of his Slave brother, who no longer was lost but gone home to Zhovanya.

For Kyr, Zhovanya's blessing of serenity had been lost in a chaotic sea of resentment, envy, and grief. Ever since that vile taste had filled his mouth, memories of all that he had suffered since leaving the Sanctuary had been tumbling through his mind, ripping open the half-healed wounds in his soul, tearing down his long-held defenses against the degradation and pain that Gauday had inflicted on him.

In Kyr's room, the Warrior Mage helped the youth strip off his blood-spattered clothing, and wiped off a few last streaks of gore. Kyr was cold and trembling with shock. Rajani grabbed Kyr's warm winter cloak off its hook behind the door.

"Here, put this on."

Kyr wrapped his cloak around his shoulders, and sat on his bed, hunched up under his cloak, staring blindly at nothing.

Rajani pulled a stool over and sat by the bedside. "It's over now, finally over."

"For him."

Rajani winced at Kyr's harsh, despairing tone. Gingerly, he asked, "Are you having regrets about...?"

"Not about killing Gauday. It was what Zhovanya asked me to do."

"Then what *is* upsetting you?" Rajani asked, perplexed.

Kyr didn't answer for a while. The Warrior Mage waited with outward patience, but his thoughts were in a whirl. *What's wrong with him? He should at least feel relieved that his tormentor is gone, shouldn't he? I know he has one more hell to go through, according to the damnable Prophecy, but by all the little gods, this can't be it already! Zhovanya, hear me! He needs some time to recover, and enjoy life, or he'll never be able to fulfill the rest of the Prophecy.*

Then Kyr looked at Rajani with eyes gone dark and bitter. "I have done all She has asked. And there is nothing here for me, except trying to find a way to live with what *he* did to me." He clenched his fists and demanded, "Why does She take *him* home—and not me?"

"But, Kyr," Rajani protested, "life will be better now, don't you see? You are free of Gauday, and we are about to get out of here and head home to Ravenvale. What makes you say this now?"

"I don't know." Kyr couldn't bring himself to speak of the surprised joy he'd seen in Gauday's eyes, or his sour envy of that joy. "It's just that I'm so cursed tired."

293

"No wonder, after what you just did," Rajani said gently.

Medari came in from the infirmary, carrying a mug of steaming tea. "This will help you rest. I made it good and strong."

"Thanks, Medari." He sat up and took the mug, glad for the warmth of the tea and the sleep it would bring him.

Pulling the other stool to Kyr's bedside, Medari sat down, moving stiffly, as if he feared he might shatter. However, he was no longer disheveled but neat, composed, and under rigid self-control. "I want to apologize for my outburst out there. I didn't mean to trigger that kind of outrageous behavior."

"Not your fault," Rajani said, and Kyr nodded in agreement.

"Yes, it was," Medari said. "And I regret undermining what you were doing, Kyr. The Goddess was truly with you. You showed both Her forgiveness and Her justice." The healer sighed. "You must be very disappointed in me."

Lost in his own regrets, Kyr could barely recall what he had said or done before executing Gauday. *Gods, was that me out there? No,* he realized, *it was Zhovanya acting through me. And now where is She?* His brief laugh was harsh and mirthless.

Seeing Medari's hurt look, Kyr said, "Sorry, that wasn't about you." He took a breath and sought for the strength to be kind. "Don't worry about what you said, Medari. I understand how you feel, and," he added bleakly, "I agree with you. We may never be free of the harm Gauday did to us."

Rajani frowned at this melancholy assessment, but Medari sighed and relaxed a little. "Thanks, Kyr. Now, is there anything you need?"

Kyr scratched the scar around his neck. "Got anything to stop this itching?"

"Has it always itched or did it just start?"

"It just started, right after I sent Gauday home."

Medari nodded and disappeared into his infirmary. Rajani helped Kyr into bed. Kyr was shivering despite the summer heat and the warm tea. Rajani spread Kyr's cloak on top of the quilt.

Medari returned with a salve that he gently spread on the scar around Kyr's neck. "Alright, that should help. We'll let you sleep now," Medari said, and led Rajani into the infirmary.

Kyr pulled the covers higher, and lay there, brooding. The itching reminded him of how he'd acquired the scar on his neck, and all that followed from that. It was the scar where the Collar had burned him. When Rajani destroyed the Soul-Drinker's Rod with magical fire, he had unknowingly also destroyed the other two sorcerous implements of the Soul-Drinker's power, the Collar and the Crown. Kyr had been wearing the Collar, and it burned when the Rod did. Unfortunately, the evil smoke-ghost from the Collar had invaded Kyr, causing his terrible craving.

Months ago, when he was first chained out to the whipping post, Kyr had seen a similar scar around Gauday's head. Kyr had realized then that Gauday was wearing the Crown when it too burned, and that the smoke-beast from the Crown had invaded Gauday. That remnant of the sorcery embedded in the Crown by the Soul-Drinker had given Gauday his sorcerous power of inflicting pain with his red-eyed glare, but it had also driven him deeper into the Soul-Drinker's madness and evil.

It had been the very act of freeing Kyr from the Collar's smoke-beast which had taken the life of the Tree Warden, Svahar, the great Healer Mage. Kyr sighed, as he again felt the weight of his remorse over Svahar's death. *Well, at least, I freed Gauday of the smoke from the Crown before he died. I could see his eyes clear at the last. Perhaps I did carry out Zhovanya's request. Perhaps his soul is free. Dear Goddess, may I know such a blessing some day!*

The itching had ceased, and the soporific tea was having its effect. Unutterably weary and bereft, Kyr slept.

Next door in the infirmary, Rajani and Medari sat at the table, with mugs of tea near to hand and half-empty lunch plates pushed aside.

"I'm worried about Kyr," the Warrior Mage said. "He had seemed at peace recently. He even did the execution with amazing mercy and grace. Now, all of a sudden, he is wishing he was dead."

"Well," Medari shrugged, "he probably just needs to rest. What he did was grueling, to say the least."

"I don't know." Rajani shook his head in frustration. "Just feels like something strange is going on."

A thumping on the stairs and a knock on the door interrupted their discussion. Two prisoners under the direction of Jakar entered, carrying Gauday's shrouded corpse.

"Set him in the barred cell," Medari directed. As the men maneuvered the body around the table, the wrapping fell away from Gauday's head.

"Stop!" Rajani stood and came around the table to examine the dead man's face. "What's this?" Gauday's long hair and bangs had fallen back, revealing a red scar circling his head. "That's odd. This scar looks like the one Kyr has around his neck."

One of the prisoners, a thin, gray-haired Slave, gave a nasty laugh. "Got it when the Crown burned. Saw it myself back in the Master's lair. Served 'im right, arrogant whoreson! Thought he could steal the Crown and replace our Master. Ha! Look where it got 'im—and us with 'im." He shook his head in disgust.

"Alright, get on with it," Jakar growled. The prisoners set the body in the barred cell, and Jakar herded them out of the infirmary.

Medari locked the cell and pocketed the key. "That should keep anyone from molesting the body. What do you plan to do with it?"

"I hadn't thought that far." Rajani sat back down on his stool by the table, and rubbed his forehead wearily. "Best thing is probably to bury him in an unmarked grave, let him be forgotten quickly. I'll deal with that tomorrow. For now, I'll post a guard at your door, just to be sure."

"I'm glad of that. Thanks." Medari was silent for a moment, listening. "From the sound of it, I'd guess the festivities outside are dying down. Gods, what an exhausting day."

"Indeed. Well, I'd better go make an appearance, and get a sense of how the winds are blowing with this crowd. I hope they got some idea of what Kyr was doing, and of our new regime of order and fairness. Let me know if Kyr wakes." As Rajani walked across the yard toward the crowd around the feast tables, something was nagging at him, but he was too tired and distracted to think about it.

Late that night, Kyr awoke in darkness. His envious bitterness came back with frightening ferocity. He rose and dressed, careful not to awaken Friend, who had joined him unnoticed sometime earlier. Leaving her curled up on the bed, he silently slipped outside and went into the chapel. Kneeling before the altar, he started the forgiveness chant; but after a few repetitions, his voice broke and he could not continue. Bowing down, forehead to the floor, he whispered, "I have done everything You asked. You took Day home. Don't leave me here." But She remained silent and withdrawn.

Kyr stretched out prone on the floor, burying his face in the crook of one arm. His heart was hard and dry. All he could think of was his life of agony, his impossible love for Jolanya—and the brief gleam of surprised joy in Gauday's eyes. *Gods, why did I ever submit to Zhovanya? I cannot even end this misery by my own hand, as long as She insists that I live.* For a moment, he considered disobeying Her; but then he shuddered. Betraying his submission to Zhovanya would make his life a bleak and meaningless horror. Neither obedience nor defiance offered any escape, but obedience at least was familiar and gave his suffering some significance.

He sighed, remembering another reason against taking his own life: he would end Dekani's existence, too. *Well, maybe he can help me, as he has so many times.* "*Dekani? Dekani? Please, I need your guidance.*"

It seemed a long time before Dekani appeared, and when he did, he had the appearance of a white-haired old man, leaning on a staff. "*I'm here, son.*"

"*Gods and demons, Dekani! What happened? What's wrong with you?*"

Dekani laughed a little. "*Well, it appears that even I grow old. Don't worry. I'm all right. But the same cannot be said about you. Come, let's go sit by the fire.*" And they were in Dekani's familiar cottage in their old comfortable chairs.

"*Sorry I haven't called you much lately, Teacher. Seemed like you needed to rest.*"

"*You have been doing remarkably well without me.*" Dekani's eyes crinkled with his kind smile. "*What is it you need help with?*"

Here in this inner sanctuary, life didn't seem quite so intolerable. "*I sent Gauday home to Zhovanya today.*" With a heavy sigh, Kyr sank further into his chair. "*I am so envious of him.*"

"*Do not imagine that he is in bliss,*" Dekani said. "*His soul must face up to the pain he has caused, before he will know Zhovanya's forgiveness. But you have earned Her blessings, many times over.*"

"*I cannot feel Zhovanya's grace right now. I can hardly remember it.*"

"*I know. It's difficult to remember at times like these.*" Dekani's voice was deep with sadness and wisdom. "*All we can do is to remember that we have known Her grace in the past, and trust that it is there, even when we are blocking it with our despair.*"

*"Ah, Goddess!"* Kyr breathed, leaning forward, putting his elbows on his knees and burying his face in his hands. In a muffled voice, he said, *"Gauday is dead. The fort has been cleansed of his evil, but it's still here, in my dreams, in me."* He looked up, full of self-loathing. *"He's ruined everything! Everything I learned and became at the Sanctuary, he's twisted and poisoned. These nightmares, the pulsing of my scars.... I can't stand it, Dekani!"*

*"Trust Her, son. And trust yourself. You have so much strength and sweetness in your soul, you can fight Gauday's evil, just as you freed yourself from the Soul-Drinker's. Here, this will help."* He held his hands just above Kyr's heart, sending a reddish-gold flow of love and faith that warmed Kyr clear through. He relaxed into the cushions of his chair, and his fears and doubts subsided.

Dekani lowered his hands into his lap and sat back.

*"Thank you, Teacher. I don't know how I would survive without you, nor how I can repay you."*

*"All I ask is that you be sure you get to Ravenvale with Rajani, and stay there until...well, for at least a year. It's very important. Promise me?"*

Kyr gazed back at his beloved teacher, wondering what made this so important to Dekani. But since he planned to go to Ravenvale anyway, he said, *"Yes, I promise."*

Dekani smiled, looking relieved. *"Feeling better now, son?"*

*"Yes, Teacher. Thank you again for everything."*

Dekani bowed and was gone. Only the fire burning in the small hearth made any sound, hissing and crackling. Then all was blackness.

Kyr woke, cold and stiff on the floor of the chapel. He pulled himself up and knelt before the altar. *Zhovanya,* he prayed, *help me release my bitterness and envy.* Ever since he had killed Gauday, the world had seemed a place of senseless treachery and suffering, and it still did, despite Dekani's kindness and help. Without his forbidden beloved, Jolanya, life seemed to stretch out before him—an endless barren plain.

In the courtyard, Craith was enjoying listening to the joyous chorus of birdsong that greeted the rising sun. The prisoners were expunging all traces of the execution, and cleaning up after the feast. Having earned the trust of his guards, Craith had been delegated to supervise the crew, while the Companions on guard stayed warm in the kitchen, drinking tea and occasionally checking on the prisoners. Leaning against a porch post, the redhead watched his crew working steadily. He had selected this particular crew from among those prisoners who found the sensible and fair regime Rajani imposed on them preferable to Gauday's erratic cruelty. They worked willingly, glad that Gauday was dead, joking among themselves, and Craith had little to do.

A harsh, broken thread of sound disturbed the dawn's peace. Turning his head, he sought the source of the dissonance. *Ah. It's coming from the chapel. Someone—a man—grieving.* Craith shrugged. *None of my business. He turned back to survey his crew.*

But he couldn't put the man's distress out of his mind. As he listened, he found himself remembering a night months ago. While out checking on his lackadaisical sentries, he had heard Kyr's sobs of despair coming from the dark hole of his prison. *Ah, gods! That's who's in the chapel.* Disturbed, he couldn't reconcile the serenity and compassion of the man who had executed Gauday with the sounds of wretchedness coming from the chapel. But he recalled one of the rules he had chosen to live by: to be kind. *If anyone deserves some kindness, it's Kyr. But would he want it from me?*

He debated a moment more, then stepped over to Jorem. "I'll be in the chapel. You keep everyone working, will you?" Jorem eyed him curiously but merely nodded. The four penitents had quickly developed a closeness and trust through their shared commitment to following the hard path.

Opening the door of the chapel quietly, Craith peered inside. Kyr was prostrate before the altar, shoulders wrenched by harsh sobs. Craith's heart began to pound in trepidation at the thought of trying to approach Kyr, let alone offer him comfort. *Goddess, if You hear me, help me know what to do.*

Taking a breath, he entered the chapel and went to kneel beside the man he revered as his soul's savior. Kyr's despair was an echo of Craith's own during the half-moon he had been the one kept in Gauday's torture chamber. In a soft, hesitant voice, he asked, "Sir, what's wrong? How can I help you?"

Lost in anguish, Kyr failed to notice Craith's presence. All he was aware of was his despair at the prospect of a life without Jolanya, and dealing with the painful mutilation that Gauday had wreaked upon his body and mind.

Craith hesitated, recalling how he had contributed to Kyr's torment, torn between wanting to be kind, and fearing Kyr's justified anger. *I've chosen the hard path*, he reminded himself. *This is how I begin.*

*Zhovanya, guide me*, Craith prayed humbly, doubting he deserved any answer. But then his mind went back to before he had been taken to become a soldier in the Master's army, to memories he usually kept carefully buried. He remembered his mother cradling him in her arms, soothing him over some long-forgotten boyhood tragedy. Without further hesitation, he took Kyr into his arms and held him against his chest, rocking him gently. "Shhh, shhh, shhh," he soothed, as his mother had done so long ago.

Kyr stiffened, and started to push away from Craith. But Dekani appeared in his mind, saying gently, *"Stop, Kyr. Let Craith comfort you. I know it is hard to trust anyone, but you must learn again to receive what kindness others offer."*

Dekani's words unleashed in Kyr a long-denied need for human solace, drowning his shame and fear. *Craith's been through it. He's been in that hell. He understands, better than anyone else. And he was so kind that night we made love.* With a deep shudder, he sagged into Craith's embrace. The big man tightened his grasp, easily taking Kyr's full weight. "Shhhh, shhhh, shhhh." As Kyr relaxed, Craith's solid, warm body became again a haven from sorrow and suffering. Kyr rested there, his harsh sobs softening into slow tears, and then into a quiet emptiness.

Kyr drifted into an exhausted sleep. Craith smiled with protective tenderness. Humming a simple melody his mother had sung to him before the Soul-Drinker's Gatherers had snatched him from her arms, he continued to rock Kyr gently.

Yet, even there in the chapel, in the embrace of kindness, Kyr could not escape the nightmares that haunted him. *"You're mine, mine, my boy, my slave,"* Gauday crooned. *He was trapped in Gauday's cruel arms. Yet the relentless hands were touching, hurting, pleasuring.* "No, no, no," he moaned, *fighting to get away*—and awakened to find himself still cradled in Craith's arms.

Nightmare images of his friend at the mercy of Gauday's depraved cruelty filled Kyr's mind, and his scars began to throb with pain-pleasure-lust. He gazed at Craith with hungry, seductive eyes. There was an answering flash of desire in Craith's green eyes, but then he flushed and looked away. Kyr hastily disentangled himself and moved back, sitting hunched up with his arms around his knees, sick with self-disgust. The foul taste was strong in his mouth again. *Merciless gods, Gauday's evil ruins even this small blessing of kindness.*

"Will you be, um, all right now, sir?" Craith asked diffidently.

Kyr rubbed his face. "I'll manage." As Craith started to rise, Kyr put a hand on the redhead's arm. "Thank you for your kindness." He gave Craith a grateful smile, hiding his chagrin and lingering desire.

"Whatever I can do for you, I'm glad to." Craith bowed and left.

As Craith returned to his duties, his brief moment of desire and shame was overshadowed by a swell of humble awe and gratitude that he had been called upon to comfort the valorous man called the Liberator. Standing in the middle of the courtyard, he raised his eyes to the golden-rose light gracing the dawn sky. *Goddess, let me serve our Liberator in any way You desire. I ask for nothing more in this life.*

Spotting Craith, Jorem leaned his rake against the porch railing and approached his friend. "Heya, Craith, you were gone quite a while. What's going on?"

Still in his prayerful reverie, Craith reluctantly returned his gaze to earth and looked at his friend. "All I can tell you is that we must try to find a way to be of service to the Liberator."

Jorem eyed him doubtfully. "We are prisoners. We have no say in our fate." But Craith did not respond, returning to his contemplation of the dawn's glory, a sign to him that Zhovanya had heard his plea.

A lone in the chapel, Kyr turned to face the altar and sat a while longer, aching for the peace and clarity he had known at the Sanctuary. *Gods, I can't tolerate kindness or closeness without Gauday's poison seeping in, ruining everything. I mustn't spread his poison. Can't let myself touch anyone, if this is what will happen.* The contrast between how he had been after the Kailithara with Jolanya, and how he was now was so painful, he nearly cried out again. *I don't know if I can keep my promise, Jolanya. Forgive me if I cannot become again the man you helped me become. I will try, but Gauday's mark cuts deep.*

Zhovanya's command that he continue to live seemed unbearable. Yet he found a small flame warming his heart, kindled by Craith's kindness. Being held with tenderness was a rare and precious experience, and this time with Craith had reminded him that there was more to life

301

than suffering and cruelty. Perhaps there were reasons to go on living, after all. He sighed and bowed his head. "As You will, Zhovanya. I am Yours."

As he said this, he was struck with a realization: that the god or demon that had used his hands to choke the Soul-Drinker to death must have been the Goddess Herself. And surely it was She Who had been speaking through him when he gave his Testimony, and when he had spoken to Gauday that morning. Humbled and awed, he knelt and bowed his head to the floor, and repeated, "I am Yours." A warmth of love enfolded him, and his despair receded.

# Chapter 29

# Freedom and Submission

Kyr glanced around his room for the last time. It had been a refuge from the cruel vagaries of his life, especially once Rajani had shielded it. When Gauday died, the shield dissolved. Since then, Kyr's nightmares had intensified so much that this room no longer felt like a haven.

On his bed sat a satchel containing his few belongings: clothing; the driftwood and stones from his private altar; a small pillow from the chapel; the quilt from his bed. He was wearing the new clothes Rajani had given him: a cream-colored linen tunic with tan leather riding pants, matching long jacket, and tall brown boots. There was also a leather hat with a wide brim, to keep off sun and rain. The heavy clothing irritated Kyr's still-sore scars, but was necessary for this long journey on horseback.

"Are you ready?" The Warrior Mage poked his head in Kyr's open door.

"Yes, let's get out of here." He picked up his satchel.

"That's all you're taking?" Rajani asked as they stepped down to the courtyard.

"There's not much I want to remember about this place."

"No, I suppose not. Well, we'll be out of here in just a few moments." Rajani hurried off for a last consultation with Ayesha, the new governor of Juradiché, as the fort, now a village, had been named. It was now the seat of the new government of the Southern Pines area, the place where law and justice would be spoken and carried out.

Kyr's black mare, Lady, was saddled and waiting. He scratched behind her ears, then rested his head on her neck. "You're my Dark Lady now. You'll take me away from this hellhole, won't you?" She nodded and blew, as if agreeing. He mounted up, eager to be gone.

The courtyard was brimming with villagers and their horse-drawn wagons, drovers and their ox carts, assorted walkers and riders. Kyr spotted Rajani shaking hands with Ayesha. She laughed heartily, making her golden necklaces sparkle. Rajani bowed to her and mounted up. Astride Akbara, his bright sorrel stallion, in his black leathers with his shining black hair tied back sleekly, the Warrior Mage cut a commanding figure.

He motioned to Kyr to join him in the lead, and they started forward, closely followed by the commander's personal guard: six Companions selected for their trustworthiness and battle skills. Laray, Kuron, and Jakar were among them. Next to black-clad, raven-haired Rajani, Kyr felt like a pale tan shadow astride his dark mare.

The people remaining behind were lined up on either side of the gates, waving and cheering. The Warrior Mage nudged Kyr's leg with his booted foot. "They are honoring you. Give them something, a smile or wave or bow." With a startled glance, Kyr complied, waving at the crowd, but his jaw was clenched and he could not muster a smile.

As they went through the gates into the forest, Kyr nearly turned back, unreasoning fear telling him that Gauday's cruel grasp could not so easily be broken, that he had no place in the world beyond Gauday's hell. Again his scars flared up, and he was assaulted by memories of duress and torment. He hunched his shoulders and his grip on the reins tightened, causing Lady to stop.

Rajani looked back at him. "Heya, Kyr, what's wrong?"

"Just, uh, memories." He clucked to Lady and they went onward through the early morning gloom of the forest. Kyr glanced backwards, but the trees had already hidden the fort from view. For a moment, he couldn't believe it, but then he told himself firmly, *It's behind me. I am free of that place forever!*

Squaring his shoulders, he faced forward, determined to enjoy his release from Gauday's hell. Using all the self-control he had so painfully developed, he kept his attention in the present moment. As they crested a ridge and headed down the trail, putting hills between them and the fort, Kyr breathed a deep sigh of relief.

The tall pines straggled further and further apart; and then, they broke through the trees. Open grassland spread out before them, the wind-blown grasses rippling and gleaming on either side of the dirt track they were following. He looked out to the far horizon. *No chains, no walls, no doors! O Goddess, I'm free! Thank You!* His whole being expanded with this gift of spaciousness. Sensing his excitement, Lady danced under him and tossed her head. Kyr laughed. "By all the gods, Rajani, it's good to be out of that hellhole, at last!"

"At last!" Rajani shouted. The six Companions cheered, and their horses joined in, frisking and snorting. They all seemed as glad as Kyr to be out on the wide plains. "Come on!" Rajani kicked Akbar into a trot, and they left the caravan behind, creaking and jangling along at its slow pace, guarded by the rest of the Companions.

A short while later, Kyr called out, "Stop!"

The Warrior Mage raised a hand to call a halt, but cast him a questioning glance.

Kyr pointed back the way they had come. A small figure was hurtling toward them. "Look, it's Friend!"

Rajani smiled. "You named her well."

She soon bounded up, barking her gladness to have found her pack-mate. They started off again at the slow pace of the caravan. Pink tongue lolling, Friend loped happily at Lady's side.

Wide blue skies and warm golden sunshine competed for glory with green fields emblazoned with wild red poppies. Drunk with relief and freedom, Kyr was glad to be on the move, not caring where they were going so long as it was *away*. With a yell of pure joy, he urged Lady into a gallop and raced off down the trail. Rajani smiled, and let him go, signaling the Companions to do the same.

When Lady tired, Kyr stopped to wait for the column to catch up, eyes hungrily drinking in the spacious splendor around him. *I'd be glad to travel like this forever and never arrive anywhere.* Alone in the wide world, he could finally breathe fully. Air had never tasted sweeter, the touch of the sun's warmth had never been more welcome. Hope, long buried, began to unfurl and poke its head above the darkness in which it had been entombed.

Kyr threw his head back and raised his arms to the sky. "Ah, Goddess, thank you for this day! Whatever comes, I am grateful for this moment." A faint cry reached his ears and he searched the skies, spying at the zenith a dark shape gliding in a lazy spiral. Yearning to fly free, as he had long ago as a boy in his inner haven under the ice, he whispered,

"Just this once, Zhovanya." A feather-touch of Her Presence sent Kyr's soul soaring in communion with the great eagle, his soul-kin, his talisman of faith.

Unconcerned, Lady chomped up the green grasses at the verge of the road. Friend soon arrived, panting heavily, and flopped down in the grass near Lady's nose. The mare snorted in annoyance, bringing Kyr back from empyrean heights. He stroked Lady's neck, enjoying her silken-warm strength. Friend thumped her tail on the ground, but didn't get up.

Kyr dismounted and knelt to pet her. "Ah, Friend, sorry! We ran off without you, didn't we? And now you're worn out. You'd better stay in Medari's wagon from now on. Come on, let's get you some water." Leading Lady by her reins, he started walking back toward the caravan, with Friend trotting alongside.

Soon, they reached the dusty, noisy caravan. The wagons and carts creaked along, dangling pans, lanterns, and tools, which clanked with each step of the plodding oxen or huffing draft horses. Meanwhile, people shouted over the noise, complaining or laughing; children ran about, shrieking; and infants squalled. Luckily, Medari's canvas-topped wagon was near the front of the line.

"Heya, Medari!" Kyr liked the new greeting, which had spread among those at the fort from one of the tribes that had come there.

The healer gave Kyr a startled look. "Gods, you look so—different!"

Kyr laughed, his brown eyes sparkling. "Getting out of that hell-hole does wonders for a man!" He attempted to comb his wind-tossed golden-red curls with his fingers. "May I ask you a favor? Friend keeps chasing after Lady and me. She's getting worn out. Can you keep her in your wagon?"

"She's welcome here with me," Medari said. "You'll have to tie her up, though. She'll just run after you again if you don't."

"Thanks. I will."

Kyr tied Lady to the back of the slow-moving wagon, and opened the half-gate. He and Friend jumped into the canvas-topped wagon. He closed the gate, took a drink from the waterskin, and poured some water into Friend's bowl. A short search turned up a piece of rope, with which he tied his faithful dog to a strut of the wagon. "You stay here with Medari, girl." With a reproachful look, she curled up on a folded burlap bag. Giving her a last pat, he climbed out of the front of the wagon and sat on the bench beside the healer.

Kyr wanted to share his new-found joy, but the healer's somber face forbade that. So he merely said, "It's good to get away from that cursed fort."

"That it is," Medari said with false cheer. "Go on with you, now. Enjoy your freedom. Friend and I will be fine here."

Aware of the healer's grief but unwilling to lose hold of his own rare joy, Kyr put an arm around his shoulders and gave him a quick hug. "Thanks, Medari."

He rode forward to catch up with Rajani, his delight in moving freely under the vast blueness of the sky surging up again. The Warrior Mage glanced over at him and smiled. "Come on, Kyr, let's race to the top of the hill up ahead!"

"Yaaa!" Kyr kneed Lady into a gallop. Rajani laughed and urged his horse forward. Off they rode, whooping and shouting, for the moment carefree as innocent boys. Taken by surprise, Rajani's guard thundered after them.

As they traveled through the glorious late-Spring days, Kyr kept his mind focused on the present, determined to enjoy his hard-earned freedom. Whenever a concern arose, he banished it with the thought, *Naran will help me when we get to Ravenvale.* Every day, he rode at the forefront, often racing ahead alone for the joy and peace of being on his own in the wild beauty of the world. The aroma of sun-warmed grasses became the scent of freedom for him. His soul, long deprived, greedily treasured up every color of flower, every curve of hill or stream, every note of laughter or song, every caress of wind or sun, as they made their way toward this place Rajani called home.

On the fifth day, he had ridden far ahead, when he saw an unusual sight on these wide plains: an oak tree crouching near the top of a small hill. Kuron had told him that a tree on this plain probably meant water nearby. Thirsty and hot, he turned Lady toward the tree. A short canter brought them into its shade.

He dismounted, tied Lady in the shade, and sat with his back against the oak. For a few moments, he rested there, feeling a deep kinship with that lone, tenacious, wind-twisted tree. He was reminded of his time with the Great Tree called the Heart of the Forest, and how the Tree and its Warden, Svahar, and Tenaiya with her herbs and gentleness, had healed him of the terrible craving for the Rod's pleasure. *Gods, I miss them both. They were so kind! Perhaps this tree is a child of the Heart of the Forest. I wish it could heal me the way Svahar and the Great Tree did: just pull Gauday's poison out of me the way they pulled out the craving.* He sighed, wondering gloomily how he would ever recover from Gauday's torments without their aid.

Thirst nudged him to quit brooding. He listened for the sound of water. Hearing only the creaking of the tree's breeze-tossed branches, he set off to explore the hill.

At its crown, he found an outcropping of granite boulders, which formed a rough circle. At its center was a bowl of crystalline water, rippling and sparkling in the sun as water bubbled up from a tiny spring. At this, his thirst redoubled, reminding him of the times when he had been tormented by thirst during his captivity. He had learned then to never take for granted the preciousness of water. He knelt near the tiny pond. "Dear Goddess, thank You for this gift." Reverently, he filled his hands with the cold, exquisite, life-giving liquid, and drank.

Satisfied, he took a seat on a flat-topped boulder and looked around, enjoying the spaciousness of sky and grass-clad earth that spread out in all directions. But then, reawakened memories of his months of torment at Gauday's hands arose and would not be banished. Anguish stabbed his core, so sharply he could barely breathe. He bent forward, wrapping his arms around his middle, and gasped, "Ah, Goddess! Why?"

For an answer, all he heard was water rippling, oak branches rustling, hidden insects chirping. With a sigh, he surrendered again his demand for understanding, and bowed his head to his knees. He let himself go quiet: no thought, no desires, only breathing. His withered soul soaked in the silence, purity, and sustenance of this sacred place. In the silence, a vision came to him of his soul-kin, the Eagle, arising from the muck of Gauday's madness, being cleansed by the crystalline water, and beginning to unfurl its wings. His anguish ebbed and he thought, *Perhaps I will recover from this, too.* Here, days away from the fort, it was beginning to seem possible.

The sound of creaking wagons reached his ears. He filled his waterskin, returned to Lady, poured water into his pannikin, and gave her a drink. Then they set off to rejoin the caravan.

Every evening after supper, he joined Craith and the other penitents for chanting and meditation. They would find quiet spots away from the bustling camp, by a stream or in a copse of trees. Kyr placed a stone at the center of their circle. It was his favorite stone from the altar at the fort. One half was light gray, the other charcoal-colored. A white line of quartz zig-zagged across the face of the stone, separating the light from the dark.

Others might add a flower, stone, or other treasure to their improvised altar. They always began by quietly singing the forgiveness chant. After a time, they returned to the silence of meditation. Kyr was pleased when villagers and Companions began to join them.

At night, however, he battled nightmares, which had grown worse since he executed Gauday, as had the pulsing of his scars. In addition, he had a small, nagging cough, and the foul taste in his mouth came and went. Nothing Medari had given him had helped eliminate the taste nor lessen the cough, but as it wasn't getting worse, Kyr ignored it, too.

One night, after a quarter moon of steady travel, Kyr sat next to Rajani by the campfire, listening as his friend spoke about the beauties of Ravenvale, where their journey would end, and of his plans for restoring the community there. Kyr could barely imagine such a place, nor that he could belong there. His scarred heart dared not even dream of love or joy, but he found himself hoping that, at last, he would find the safety, rest, and peace he longed for in Ravenvale.

Later on, he lay in his bedroll on a mattress of flattened prairie grass, staring up at the star-flecked darkness. Insects were creaking and buzzing in the peaceful night, and a cool breeze was making the tall grasses rustle. He was reluctant to sleep, knowing that nightmares waited to torment him. *Gods, I'm so tired of not sleeping well. Maybe Dekani can banish these cursed dreams for one night.* He called his teacher, and in the next moment he was sitting in the cottage by the fire, facing Dekani.

*"What is it, son?"*

*"These nightmares are still plaguing me. I'm worn out from lack of sleep. I'm hoping you could banish them for one night, at least?"*

*"Hmmm. Well, let me see...."* Dekani leaned forward, looking into Kyr's eyes, now a muddy dark brown. He frowned. *"What's this? There are tiny worms of color in your eyes. Tell me exactly what happened just as you sent Gauday Home."*

Kyr took a moment to steady himself, then described what happened in as neutral a manner as he could manage. *"I watched his eyes. I saw his pain and fear, but then he looked surprised, and glad. I felt the bond between us break, leaving an emptiness in me. Then a bad smell and taste filled my nose and mouth and I started coughing."*

*"And you have had more trouble with your scars and the nightmares since then?"*

*"Yes. What are you getting at?"*

Dekani sighed and sat back in his chair. *"I have bad news, Kyr. The evil smoke that Gauday took in when the Crown burned...."*

*"Merciless gods! It's in me now."* Kyr's skin was crawling. *"Oh, gods, Dekani! Get it out of me!"*

*"I'm so sorry, son. I still don't have my strength back."* At the panicked look in Kyr's eyes, he held up his hand. *"Wait, son. Let me finish."* Kyr took a deep breath and blew it out, and Dekani continued. *"When you get to Ravenvale, you must ask Rajani to do a cleansing ritual for you. With his help, we can purge you of this last remnant of the Soul-Drinker's sorcery."*

*"I hope I can last until then."* Kyr failed to keep the despair and bitterness out of his tone.

*"I will block some of the nightmares so you can get better rest."* Dekani sounded so sad and remorseful that Kyr did his best to disguise his disappointment and fear. He smiled and said, *"That will be a big help, Dekani. Thanks."*

*"Good night, son."* Dekani and the cottage disappeared.

Kyr became aware again of the peaceful prairie night, now poisoned for him by the sickening awareness of the Soul-Drinker's sorcerous smoke lurking in his own mind. "Goddess, why this too?" he whispered. He ached to know why the Goddess demanded so much. "Why?" he whispered. Then a gentle tide of somnolence spread through him, Dekani's gift, and he fell asleep with his question on his lips.

He was in a vast Temple. Brilliant stars and galaxies swirled overhead. This ceiling was upheld by glowing columns of golden light. The floor was an infinite dark ocean, rippling and glimmering with blue-green fire. Deep peace pervaded his soul. *"Home, at last!"* he whispered. *"Ah, Zhovanya, thank You!"*

For a time, he rested there; but then the Temple began to dim, and he felt himself returning to his difficult life. *"No!"* he cried. *"Zhovanya, don't send me back!"* But the Temple continued to fade. In soul-deep distress, he begged, *"Dear Goddess, at least tell me why!"*

The Temple brightened, and Zhovanya appeared, Her head touching the stars, Her feet, the ocean. She shone brighter than all the stars. She was so vast that Kyr felt as small as an ant. Yet Her voice was warm and intimate.

*"YOU WHO ARE TO BE HALLOWED*
*BY MY PRESENCE*
*MUST BE HOLLOWED*
*OF ALL YOUR FEAR AND CLINGING.*

*YOU WHO ARE TO BE FILLED*
*BY MY PRESENCE*
*MUST BE TEMPERED*
*BY THE FIRES OF SUFFERING.*

*YOU WHO ARE TO BE THE VESSEL*
*FOR MY PRESENCE*
*MUST BE INURED*
*TO ECSTASY AND AGONY,*
*TO HOLINESS AND DEFILEMENT*
*IF YOU ARE TO ENDURE*
*THE FILLING AND EMPTYING.*

*YOU WHO ARE MY CHOSEN SHALL BE*
*CURSED AND BLESSED,*
*ABANDONED AND FULFILLED*
*BY MY PRESENCE AND MY ABSENCE.*

*IF THE VESSEL HOLDS AND DOES NOT SHATTER,*
*IF THE CHOSEN SURRENDERS ALL YET NEVER YIELDS,*
*THE SACRED BALANCE SHALL BE RENEWED,*
*AND PASSION, PEACE, AND LOVE*
*WILL FILL YOUR DAYS."*

Kyr woke, shivering with a strange mixture of dread and hope: dread of what more Zhovanya would require of him, and hope at the thought of Her final promise. *Passion, peace, and love? Sounds impossible, but—may it be so!* He sighed. *I still don't know what that means, to be Her Vessel. Nor whether I can endure any more of this "hallowing" She requires.* Yet the peace of that sacred Temple filled his heart and soul, and he rested quietly, watching the stars' slow journey through the dark vault of the sky.

# Glossary

**Pronouns**

Lo — us all, me, you, us, them (exact meaning depends on intention of speaker)
Li — I, me
Lai — we

**Chants**

"Zhovanya nara li" — Goddess forgive me.
"Zhovanya nara lo" — The Goddess forgives us all/ Goddess, forgive us/them.
"Zhovanya dagantalo" — Goddess protect us.
Zhovanya ganaralo" — Goddess guide us.
"Ganarali ya zhanto abaharo" — Guide me to this lost spirit.
"Zhovanya, ganarali vida!" — Goddess, guide me home!
"Jeyal, volara donorulai" — Jeyal, we offer You our hearts.
"Jeyal sumaralai" — Jeyal, we call You.

**Phrases**

"Final Grace" — Death, granted by healers to those in intolerable pain who cannot be cured or helped in any way.

**Magical Commands**

"Ji Tal!" — "Stop!"
"Kaa'a-tay!" — "Open!"
"Kaa'a ta lak!" — "Break!
"Kiiiyaaa, KA!" — Command to direct (or redirect) an arrow, or blow, or spell to its target
"Shai!" — "(Let there be) Light!"
"Shai li!" — "(May) I shine!"
"Shai'ya!" — "Burn!"
"Ta'a Kor!" — "Sword!"
"Vaa'a lan!" — "Unite!"

"Vaa'a lan ti! — "Be whole!"
"Waa-Rah!" — Command to raise the wind
"Waa-Rah Tavor!" — Command to raise a whirlwind

**Words re: Naran**
Aithané (AI-thahn-ay) — Listener, Confessor
Phanaithos (Fa-NAI-thos) — Speaker, Divulger
Phanaithara (Fa-NAI-tha-ra) — Divulgence, Confession, Journey to Forgiveness and Self-Forgiveness

**Words re: Jolanya**
Kailitha (Kai-LI-tha) — Divine healing energy
Kailithana (Kai-li-THAHN-a) — The high priestess who channels the kailitha to heal those most damaged, e.g., by torture or rape.
Kailithara (Kai-li-THAR-a) — The healing journey led by the Kailithana
Kailithos (Kai-LI-thos) — One who is going through the Kailthara.
Kailithama (Kai-li-THAM-a) — Sacred chamber in which the Kailithara takes place.

# Author's Afterword

Kyr's story is intense and moving. Reading it may have opened up some feelings and areas inviting exploration. To help in deepening your experience of *Fierce Blessings* and how it may have affected you, here are some questions for contemplation and/or discussion, as well as resources if further support is needed.

The healing journey often is a spiral, with ups and downs, progress and backsliding. When we persist, we may find ourselves facing the same challenges or difficulties over again. But with each turn of the spiral, we can bring with us the new awareness and understanding we gained through facing the challenge previously. Over time, we may see that the spiral has been moving us toward our deeper, higher selves all along.

> ➤ Have you found yourself facing the same difficulty or challenge over again? In relationships? In therapy? In work situations?
> ➤ When you look back, do you see whether or not your journey through life follows this spiral pattern?
> ➤ Have you faced returning challenges with greater awareness and deeper understanding? Have you been able to handle the challenge in a more mature way?

Kyr's challenges: In Book One, *Dark Innocence,* Kyr recovered from severe abuse and grew to become a kind, creative, and loving man. In Book Two, *Fierce Blessings*, he again faces torment and abuse, a turn on the spiral. His challenge is to hold on to what he learned and the person he became at the Sanctuary. To do this, he must find a way to avoid hatred and despair, and to forgive Gauday in order to protect his own soul. Ultimately, with the help of Dekani and Zhovanya, he manages to retain his compassion and forgive his tormentor. As he sets Gauday's soul free of the Soul-Drinker's sorcery and madness, he is even able to see Gauday as his fierce teacher.

315

With each difficulty, we can blame or forgive. We can hold each difficulty in our lives as unfair and cruel, and see ourselves as victims. Or we can see each challenge, no matter how painful, as a stepping stone toward our deeper selves, and see each person in our lives, no matter how hurtful, as our fierce teacher. We learn that forgiveness is something we do for ourselves, to free our own souls from hatred, vengeance, and bitterness.

## Questions for Contemplation or Discussion

➢ Does Kyr's story inspire you to be more forgiving and compassionate, even toward those who may have harmed you? Or do some transgressions seem unforgivable to you?

➢ How have you viewed the difficulties you have faced? As stepping stones, or as obstacles?

➢ Can you see those who have harmed you as your fierce teachers?

# A Story That Heals:
# An Interview with a Survivor

The first book of this trilogy, *Dark Innocence*, has been helpful to some readers, inspiring them to return to or continue on the "hard path" of healing, recovery, and transformation.

Here is an excerpt from an interview with Tetja Barbee, who graciously allowed me to interview her about her experience of reading the book.

> "By living vicariously through the characters...I could safely start to heal old wounds, and question things about my own beliefs. And it all happened through the story's presentation of terrible suffering, acceptance, and growth.... I cried and laughed a lot, and consciously decided that if these characters can face such horrendous pain and evil, and come out to a place of lightness and beauty and love, so can I.
>
> "As a result, I have been able to forgive someone with whom I was very angry for a long time.... I have committed myself to deepen my recovery process. And I'm enjoying the effects of personal realizations about my own path in life....
>
> "Rahima, I want to thank you for having such a keen sense of a person's suffering. and the hurdles one can face while dealing with it...and for helping me jump the first hurdle!"

*Published on my blog, 04/02/13.*
*For full interview, go to:* http://www.starseersprophecy.com/tetja/

# Resources

If this story has stirred up strong feelings or difficult memories for you, please seek the support of a counselor or group. For referrals, contact the local chapter of professional organizations, such as:

> ➤ AAMFT – American Association of Marriage & Family Therapists: www.aamft.org
> ➤ AHP – Association for Humanistic Psychology: www.ahpweb.org
> ➤ APA – American Psychological Association: Referral Service: http://locator.apa.org/

# Acknowledgments

I am very grateful to Book Developer extraordinaire Naomi Rose, my editor and publisher (Rose Press, www.rosepress.com), for her unfailing faith in and support for this story and author. Her great sweetness, patience, and wisdom, combined with her editorial skills and ear for nuance and connection, are rare and invaluable.

I want to acknowledge the importance of several of my teachers and their approaches to inner work: Strephon Kaplan Williams, Jungian-Senoi Dreamwork; Gisela Schubach De Dominico, Sandtray Worldplay; Natalie Rogers, Person-Centered Expressive Arts Therapy; and Chris Zydel, Painting from the Wild Heart. From them, I learned to listen to, trust, and safely express whatever is arising from within, dark or bright, ugly or beautiful, horrifying or inspiring. From my experience with these approaches, I learned to listen to the messages of the darkness as well as of the light. This trilogy is a direct result.

Much appreciation to Chris A. and Chris Z. for their friendship and support, and for their thoughtful comments on *Fierce Blessings.*

Most of all, I am forever grateful to my beloved husband for his infinite support for my unfolding, for his patience and delight with his mad-artist wife, and for reading various drafts, catching typos, and pointing out incongruities in the manuscript with his logical engineer/physicist mind.

And always, I bow to that mysterious Source from which this story flowed into my awareness, through my heart, and onto the page.

# About the Author

Rahima Warren is an intuitive artist, eclectic mystic, and a third-generation native of California. She resides with her husband in Northern California, where she periodically chases squirrels off the wild bird feeders, and deer away from her roses. Her life-long love of fantasy fiction is her parents' fault: they left sci-fi & fantasy magazines with fascinating cover art lying around the house, which she began to read as soon as she could.

For 20 years, she was a licensed psychotherapist, but retired in 2006 to focus on her intuitive painting, creative writing, and spiritual studies. Delving into the deep mysteries within, she has retrieved many gems of wisdom and healing. Through a surprising and unexpected alchemy, these inner gems coalesced with her love of imaginative fiction into an enthralling and sensuous adventure of the soul in her trilogy, *The Star-Seer's Prophecy*.

Drawing from her experience with her clients, and from her own inner journey, she writes with a depth of wisdom, compassion, and emotional and spiritual authenticity about the challenges of this fierce blessing, life as an "earthly being."[1]

*Dark Innocence*, Book One of the *Star-Seer's Prophecy*, was published by Rose Press in 2012, and is available in print and all e-book formats. This book, *Fierce Blessings*, is Book Two. Rahima is currently editing Book Three: *Perilous Bliss*.

---

[1] "*Human (like homo, 'person')* comes from the Latin for earth *(humus)*...(and meant) 'people' in the sense of earthly beings (in contrast with the immortal gods)." From *Dictionary of Word Origins* by John Ayto.

# About Rose Press

*Books & Other Fragrant Offerings*
*to Bring You Home to Yourself*
www.rosepress.com

In our time of reading for information, Rose Press seeks to offer you books and other fragrant offerings that will live in your heart like an eternal time capsule, releasing their healing medicine as you need it.

"Fragrance" is not usually associated with books. Books, we tend to think, in our speeded-up age, are about ideas, entertainment, steps for helping us to be more new and improved.

And yet there have been books that are mirrors to the soul—or marvels of excavation, revealing the vast treasures hidden within. There have been books, the journey of whose reading swept readers up into their remarkable world, leaving them at the end with the passage of that journey in their bones, and the fragrance of that atmosphere still hovering invisibly near. There have been books so deeply entered into by their authors that turning the pages of these books transmitted to their readers more than a whiff of the understandings and evocations embodied in the book: they helped to form the readers' very being.

This is the vision of Rose Press books: that in taking them into yourself, you discover what is truly in you, and it opens your heart like petals opening to the light. That said, getting to the more subtle fragrance—the distillation of more earthbound, sometimes sludgy experience—is often what book writers dream of and work in the trenches to do. Behind the most exquisite fragrance left with a reader by a book is the author's composted experience (all the years and memories and ideas and possibilities dreamed of and lived through, written and refined) that produced such perfume. So what is left on the page is the offering: the "fragrance," one might say. All the dregs have been churned up and left to sink to the bottom, leaving only the gift of the book.

This, then, is what the reader gets to experience: a hint of the churning process, but ultimately, the fragrance.

When 10,000 rose petals are gathered in the dark of early morning, placed into retorts filled with solvent, and heated over time until their oil rises as a liquid distillation, then you have just 16 ounces of that most prized (and expensive) of aromatics, rose essence (rose absolute). In the same way, Rose Press Books are the distillation of their authors' essence, distilled over time and many revisions to bring you into contact with the gift of something fragrant and indescribably beautiful within yourself.

Writing these books entails a journey, and reading these books is also a journey. And you, afterwards, will be the carrier of that journey in the world: burnished, more yourself than before, and smelling—even after everything—like a rose.

# The Star-Seer's Prophecy

## Book Three:
# Perilous Bliss

The Star-Seer's Prophecy *continues to unfold in the final volume of the trilogy,* Perilous Bliss *(Book Three). Will Kyr finally become the Vessel of the Goddess Zhovanya? Or will he shatter from the intense hallowing She requires in order for this world-saving transformation to take place?*

As *Perilous Bliss* begins, Kyr is plunged into the third hell of the Star-Seer's Prophecy. In unearthing long-hidden secrets, he realizes what his circle of allies has long known: that he is indeed star-cursed.

The *first hell* (in Book One) was the betrayal of his innocence by the Soul-Drinker—a horrible, degrading life, certainly, yet one shared by all the slaves and therefore not directed towards him in particular. And Kyr *was* a dark innocent. The all-pervading abuse was the only thing he knew, then. He had nothing to provide a contrast—no inkling of love, friendship, goodness, compassion, hope.

The *second hell*, however (in Book Two), *was* personal—as Kyr's rival, the former slave Gauday, sought to humiliate and wound him in a targeted, sadistic way. This hell was even more unbearable than the last because, this time, Kyr *had* experienced love, compassion, and goodness first-hand. Yet he kept his commitment to atone, and stayed on the hard path of compassion and forgiveness.

And now, in the *third hell* (Book Three), Kyr undergoes a most intimate and harrowing betrayal by the very people he has relied on and trusted the most. Alienated from his friends, himself, and, worst of all, his beloved Goddess, he is thrown into a storm of rage and despair. Utterly devastated, he abandons his vow to help others, and flees from everyone and everything he has known. In a mysterious tower, he finds the solitude that is all he can bear.

But the time has come, at last: the stars are moving into the pattern foreseen long ago by the Star-Seer. Can Kyr find a way to return to the hard path in time to fulfill his promise to Zhovanya? Can he endure this last hell, and become—as Zhovanya promised—the full, illuminated partner of his beloved Jolanya?

———————

After coming all the way through *Dark Innocence* and *Fierce Blessings*, how could you *not* read *Perilous Bliss*, the third volume of this trilogy?

Don't miss the dramatic conclusion! Find out why Kyr is the only one who can fulfill the Prophecy, and renew the land, its people, and the Sacred Balance of Khailaz—and whether he will do so.

To be put on the notification list for the publication of Book Three, *Perilous Bliss* (due out in 2016), contact the author at rahima.warren@gmail.com.

CPSIA information can be obtained at www.ICGtesting.com
Printed in the USA
BVOW05s1653130515

400255BV00002B/104/P